The Fun Times Brigade

PRAISE FOR *The Fun Times Brigade*

"Lindsay Zier-Vogel's *The Fun Times Brigade* is a breathtaking and brilliant novel that so accurately captures the indie music scene, new motherhood, and the deeply complicated path of becoming a mother. Zier-Vogel gives words to many thoughts I was never able to express as a new mom, and her story will stay with you for a very long time." —Dani Kind, actor, *Workin' Moms*

"*The Fun Times Brigade* is a precise evocation of the love, isolation, and identity crisis of early motherhood, beautifully colliding in this novel with ambition, creative drive, and the bumpy road to finding ourselves. Tender, honest, and human in the best ways."
—Heidi Reimer, author of *The Mother Act*

"Lindsay Zier-Vogel writes with lightness about love and loss and loyalty. *The Fun Times Brigade* truly sings."
—Carrie Snyder, author of *Francie's Got a Gun*

"With pitch-perfect descriptions of the love and panic of new motherhood alongside fresh and authentic stories of music and musicians, Zier-Vogel balances hope and sadness in a truly unique and beautiful story. I could not put this one down."
—Jennifer Whiteford, author of *Make Me a Mixtape*

PRAISE FOR *Letters to Amelia*

"An understated literary work with a historical underpinning, *Letters to Amelia* celebrates singular desires and pays homage to intimacy in the face of social scrutiny." —*Foreword Reviews*

"A multi-dimensional account of the life of a woman who remains not only a feminist icon but a figure of undefined mystique. I'm sure Amelia herself would be pleased." —*The Miramichi Reader*

"Zier-Vogel's writing transcends the boundaries of time while remaining firmly rooted in the Canadian cultural landscape." —*Room Magazine*

"Zier-Vogel's imagined lovers' correspondence connects the real Earhart not only to a broken-hearted library tech but also to us and our landscape, bringing to life this singular woman's brave, soaring spirit." —*Toronto Star*

"A wonderfully readable book, and the only reason you'll want to put it down is so that you can pick up your phone to do your own Amelia Earhart research." —*Quill & Quire*

Books by Lindsay Zier-Vogel

Fiction
Letters to Amelia (2021)

Books for Children
Dear Street (2023)

a novel

THE FUN TIMES BRIGADE

LINDSAY ZIER-VOGEL

Book*hug Press
Toronto 2025

FIRST EDITION
© 2025 by Lindsay Zier-Vogel

"Ripple" words by Robert Hunter, music by Jerry Garcia © 1971 (Renewed) Ice Nine Publishing Co., Inc. (ASCAP). All Right Reserved. Used with permission of Alfred Music.

ALL RIGHTS RESERVED

No part of this publication may be reproduced or transmitted in any form or by any means, electronic or mechanical, including photocopying, recording, or any information storage or retrieval system, without permission in writing from the publisher.

The Fun Times Brigade is a work of fiction. Where real-life figures appear, the situations and incidents are entirely fictional and not intended to depict actual events or persons.

Library and Archives Canada Cataloguing in Publication
Title: The fun times brigade / Lindsay Zier-Vogel.
Names: Zier-Vogel, Lindsay, author.
Identifiers: Canadiana (print) 20240524330 | Canadiana (ebook) 2024052649X
  ISBN 9781771669412 (softcover)
  ISBN 9781771669429 (EPUB)
Subjects: LCGFT: Novels.
Classification: LCC PS8649.I47 F86 2025 | DDC C813/.6—dc23

The production of this book was made possible through the generous assistance of the Canada Council for the Arts and the Ontario Arts Council. Book*hug Press also acknowledges the support of the Government of Canada through the Canada Book Fund and the Government of Ontario through the Ontario Book Publishing Tax Credit and the Ontario Book Fund.

Book*hug Press acknowledges that the land on which we operate is the traditional territory of many nations, including the Mississaugas of the Credit, the Anishnabeg, the Chippewa, the Haudenosaunee, and the Wendat peoples. We recognize the enduring presence of many diverse First Nations, Inuit, and Métis peoples, and are grateful for the opportunity to meet and work on this territory.

For my mom

Let there be songs to fill the air.
Grateful Dead

PART ONE

1

SPRING IS A BLUR THIS YEAR—AMY SEES PURPLE crocuses from Alice's bedroom window during those hazy first few days, but her nipples hurt too much to register what they are. The air smells different, though, when Max opens the window—it has lost its metallic edge and is looser, greener.

One morning after a particularly awful night, the tree outside their bedroom window has tiny green leaves that have never known wind or punishing rain. And she sees forsythia during a shuffle up the street, but then her organs feel like they're going to fall out of her body, so she turns around and shuffles home.

Until this year, Amy was always on tour in April and May, so she's used to a patchwork of spring—cherry blossoms in Vancouver, snow flurries in Regina, tulips in Ottawa, blizzards in Fredericton. But this spring, she sees all the flowers bloom—the snowdrops, the crocuses, the daffodils that rise up with bright yellow trumpets, their wide-open faces almost too brave to bear. The allium grows as the tulip petals fall, their towering stalks higher than the fence, their onion-like buds ready to burst for days. When they do, they are like fireworks caught and held, and perfectly purple. Amy cuts them and brings them inside—spherical explosions on the dining-room table that she can see from her breastfeeding corner on the couch. She needs to remember that there is more to the world than Netflix-fuelled cluster-feeding, and the strange half-awake, half-asleep state of her life.

Alice is four weeks old, her head rounder and less cone-shaped than it was when she was first born, her eyes that deep newborn blue that everyone says will change. She kicks away invisible ninjas and conducts orchestras with her tiny hands. She fights sleep and loves milk and hates baths. Her fingernails are daggers even after Amy bites them, swallowing those tiny half moons instead of spitting them out.

Like lightning, Amy has become someone's mom, and it's still a shock that she and Alice are separate, though they are and they aren't. When Alice falls asleep on Amy, their heartbeats pressed against each other's, they are back to being a single entity, but Alice has her own lungs, her own voice, her own will that she asserts in the middle of the night.

It's pitch black and Alice won't stop screaming. It's gas probably, or the whole mixing up day and night thing that's been going on for way longer than Amy ever thought possible. Amy bounces up and down, holding Alice's swaddled body against her chest, wondering if her stitches have fully dissolved. She's so tired—cobbling together an hour, two hours of sleep in a row. She doesn't know what time it is—she made Max hide the clocks in the bedroom. Her body knows it's only been an hour since she was up last, and she doesn't need bright red numbers taunting her at 3:00 a.m., 4:00 a.m., 5:00 a.m.

Amy bounces and sways. *Maybe singing will lull Alice back into not-screaming*, she thinks. She's spent most of her adult life singing kids' songs—touring, recording, performing on TV, but her mind is blank. She has no songs, nothing.

Eventually, she sings the only thing that comes to her—the Sleep Country Canada jingle. She sings it on a loop, again and again while Alice screams. They bounce, Amy sings, and eventually the pitch of Alice's crying isn't quite as dire. She whimpers. Her eyes close. She's almost asleep and Amy whisper-sings the jingle again. Alice is sleeping, her tiny red face scrunched up against Amy's shoulder.

Amy lowers herself carefully into the glider—a beautiful, fancy glider that looked so much nicer than all the other old-lady gliders in the store—but it is so uncomfortable. She regrets buying it, but she didn't know about stitches then, about separated abs, about how awful it would be to not sleep for four weeks and counting—

Amy sits, too upright to sleep, Alice a tight muslin chrysalis on her chest, and the songs come flooding back. "Baby Beluga" and "Itsy Bitsy Spider." *Out came the sun and dried up all the rain.* She wills herself to remember them for when Alice wakes up.

"What did you do today?" Max asks Amy when he gets home from work. He reaches for Alice.

The answer is nothing. The day was a hamster wheel of nursing and diaper changes and swapping out damp breast pads and trying to get Alice to sleep. Hours bled into each other as Amy and Alice swayed and bounced and paced and Amy kept trying to get up the energy to leave the house.

Today was one of Max's research days—he's a math professor, and does the impenetrable kind of math, though he wouldn't call

The Fun Times Brigade

it that. Pure math he'd call it—geometric topology. "Like, maps?" Amy asked on one of their early dates. But it wasn't maps—he studied topological quantum field theory, invariants of manifolds, homotopical algebra, and moduli spaces, Amy learned, not that she knows what any of those words mean—and today, he got to sit in his silent office and follow a thought, any thought, to its end. No one needed to be fed, or burped, or convinced to nap. Amy envies him for his research days, but she's envious of his teaching days, too, when he gets to stand in front of a classroom of students, and go for lunch with colleagues, and drink coffee with his PhD candidates. A whole day of interacting with people who love what he loves; a whole day of being out of the house.

Amy can't remember the last time she left the house. Tomorrow, she promises herself. Tomorrow, she will leave the house. She walks upstairs, while Max murmurs to Alice about his meeting with the dean. It's a relief to not be the only adult in the house, but her arms are hollow without Alice in them.

When she wakes up the next morning, Amy remembers her promise, and during Alice's morning nap, she pulls out the wrap they got as a shower gift. It's a long, grey piece of fabric and it seems impossible that it'll hold a baby. But she wants to become one of the moms she'd see when she was pregnant, walking into the coffee shop and ordering cappuccinos with babies strapped to them. She opens up her laptop and finds a YouTube video and follows along, wrapping the fabric around her belly, and over her shoulders. She makes an X in the front, an X in the back, but it's not right. She tries again and again, and she's tangled in fabric when Alice wakes up, yowling and hungry. Amy pulls at the knots and yanks the grey fabric over her head, then sits back in her corner of the couch and nurses Alice, cursing the mom who made it look so easy in the YouTube video.

"We have to leave the house," Amy tells Alice, but Alice screams when Amy tries to put her in her stroller, and Amy can't handle trying the wrap again, so they stay inside, and Amy cries as quietly as she can while Alice falls back to sleep on her. *Tomorrow*, she tells herself, as she starts the second season of *Schitt's Creek*. She'll leave the house tomorrow.

After Max leaves for work the following morning, Amy wraps the fabric around and over, around and over, a criss-cross at the front, a criss-cross at the back. She doesn't let herself hesitate. Alice starts crying when Amy shoves one leg, then the other, through the diagonal fabric, but she does it. Almost. It's too loose. She puts Alice back down on the couch and starts again.

"One more time," she says as Alice kicks and cries.

And this time, it works. Alice's little legs are in, bum lower than her knees. Amy can rest her lips on the top of her head. She bounces to get Alice to stop crying. "See? Look at us!"

Amy takes a picture in front of the mirror and sends it to her best friend, Julie. *I think we did it!*

It's almost nine and the sun is warm on her face. Squirrels dash across the sidewalk, and a FedEx guy carries boxes to a neighbour's front door, and a toddler walks past her drunkenly pushing a wagon. The mom smiles at Amy and Amy smiles back. She presses her lips to Alice's head and beams—she's finally one of them, a capital-*M* Mom.

She turns onto Bloor with Alice tight against her chest, but the traffic is loud and there are so many cars, and six dogs with a dog walker, and a man on a bike who shouldn't be on the sidewalk, his basket clinking with empties. The coffee shop is still a block away, but it's too much. Too loud and too busy and Alice hasn't gotten her vaccines yet and Amy keeps imagining a car jumping the curb and slamming into them, pinning them against the window glass of the nail salon. She turns around and rushes back up the street, trying to breathe.

Amy opens the gate to the backyard. It's quiet back here. Alice is safe. There are violets blooming on the lawn. Their neighbour's lilac has just burst into bloom. Amy sits on the patio chair and tries not to feel like a failure.

She sends Julie a selfie with the lilacs in the background. *Tried to make it to the coffee shop, but ended up here*, she writes.

Gorg, you two! Julie writes back. *Enjoy that sun!*

The tulips and daffodils are long gone, but the peony bush Max planted from his grandmother's backyard a few years ago is growing taller. Amy closes her eyes and reminds herself that the goal was to get outside and here she is, outside. She looks at the photo of her and Alice again. She did it. They did it. She can get coffee another day.

Amy opens the notes app on her phone and types: *Potential spring song.*

Leaf green

A line of sparrows (guest flute? Clarinet??)

Violets as polka dots

Ants and peonies

She tries humming something, then realizes it's the tune of "Puddle Jumping."

Sunhats and sunscreen (title?)

Strawberries and

Amy stares at the screen trying to think of another *s*-word.

A snail named Simon?

Alice wiggles in the wrap and starts whimpering, so Amy stands and starts to sway. She glances at the list on her phone and tries to will it into a song. She hasn't written anything new since she got pregnant with Alice. She hasn't touched her guitar, or even her ukulele, in months. For the first time in over a decade, she doesn't have a Fun Times Brigade show coming up, or a recording session, or songs to write for a new album. Instead, it's just Alice, every day.

"This baby will be the greatest song you'll ever write," someone wrote in a card at her baby shower. It seemed beautiful when Amy was still pregnant, but now it feels stupid. Alice isn't a song, she's a baby. A crying, pooping, burping, nursing, crying baby.

Alice starts ratcheting up and Amy starts bouncing more vigorously, wondering if the neighbours can hear. "Shh, shh, shh," she says, bouncing Alice up and down and patting her back.

"Blue met Yellow and they gave a high-five. They did a little dance and they did a little jive," Amy sings. "The Crayon Song" is the Fun Times Brigade's biggest hit.

Alice keeps screaming.

"Crayons, crayons. Dancing, twirling, skating, swirling, all the colours are unfurling."

Alice shrieks against her chest.

"Yellow met Red and they gave a high-five. They did a little dance and they did a little jive." Alice starts gulping and Amy keeps bouncing, keeps singing.

Eventually, Alice's eyes begin to close again. "And just like that Yellow and Red looked around and said . . . Orange."

The Crayon Song strikes again! Amy texts Fran. *Just got Alice from full scream to asleep before Purple!*

Amy waits to see the little bubbles of Fran writing back, but nothing. She sways with Alice and wonders if Alice will let her sit down.

She copies the text and sends it to Max and Julie.

Way to go, superstar mama, Julie writes back right away.

Nice one, Max writes back and Amy tries not to think about the hours before Max gets home unfurling impossibly in front of her.

I've got chicken marinating. I'll grill kebabs when I'm home, Max has written. Still nothing from Fran.

Amy opens the notes app again. She used to be able to sit down and churn out lyrics, whipping out a song in an hour, sometimes less, but now she's stuck bouncing and swaying in her backyard, unable to even walk down to Bloor to get herself a coffee. She doesn't know who she is without a guitar in her hands. She doesn't know who she is without an audience waiting for an encore.

Alice wakes up and starts to fuss again. Amy untangles her from the fabric wrap and unclips her bra, trying to get Alice to latch.

Alice is enough, Amy tells herself, turning her phone off. She doesn't need music right now. She has everything she needs right here.

2

AMY STOOD UNDER A TENT, ON A MAKESHIFT stage, with a few dozen children standing on the scrubby grass. She could hear Sarah Harmer singing on the mainstage and forced a smile. She was twenty-seven years old and singing "Baby Beluga" while two kids fought over a melting popsicle. Playing the kids' stage was her way of getting in front of the selection committee, she reminded herself. She'd have a better chance of playing one of Royal City Folk Fest's bigger stages next year—probably not the mainstage, but at least the Sun Stage, or maybe even the Lake Stage.

She sang the second verse twice, but no one seemed to notice.

"All right, one final song." She played "Skinnamarink," her standard closer, and wondered if she could still make the last part of the mainstage set.

She missed Sarah Harmer and was sitting at the meal tent, eating a scoop of lukewarm lentils on undercooked brown rice, when Fran and Jim came up to her. She recognized them immediately.

The Fun Times Brigade

They had been folk musicians back in the seventies and were a pretty big deal, at least in Canada. Fran still wore long, flowy skirts, but Jim had retired his fringed vests and had shorter hair and a trimmed beard. They introduced themselves as if they weren't Canadian music legends Fran & Jim.

"You were wonderful," they said, in unison, or almost unison.

"Pardon?" Amy said, confused about what they were talking about.

"On the Rainbow Stage," Jim said.

"Oh," Amy said, shocked that they had been there.

"You played our son's neighbour's birthday party," Fran said. Her hair was tied back in a long braid. "Albert hasn't stopped talking about it!"

Amy vaguely remembered Albert, whose music-themed party had been at a newly renovated town house in the Annex and the kids had played along with guitars made out of shoeboxes with elastics.

"Thank you," Amy stammered. "Wow."

"We were thinking," Jim started, "we should jam."

"Jam?"

"You know, play some music together in the kids' tent."

"Oh, okay," Amy said.

"Wonderful!" Fran said. Her smile was so radiant that Amy felt warm in its presence.

They met that afternoon, roughed out a set list, and played without mics or a sound guy. They sang the standards—"If I Had a Hammer," and "Blowin' in the Wind," and "Puff the Magic Dragon"—and kids danced in the tent while parents swayed on the sides.

It had been so long since Amy had played with other people, she had forgotten the magnetic power of feeding off the energy of others.

"That was so good!" Fran said afterward, her face flushed. "We should do this back in the city!"

"Yeah, sure!" Amy said, flattered that these folk legends wanted to play with her again.

The next week, Amy went over to Fran and Jim's. Mid-August clung to her skin in a thin layer of sweat and grime, and her guitar case was sweaty on her back. She had bitten one of her pinky nails to the quick and had to keep herself from biting the other one off, too. It was just a meeting, she tried to remind herself, and if nothing came of it, she had plenty of birthday parties lined up for the fall. Before she could even ring the doorbell, Fran opened the door.

"Amy!" Fran pulled her into a tight hug like they were old friends. She smelled like ginger. "Come in!"

There were piles of books everywhere, and mugs on every surface. It smelled like stale coffee and old coats, and there was a pile of unopened mail next to a JUNO award. Amy left her guitar case in the front hall and followed Fran to the kitchen. There were daisies in a Mason jar on the kitchen table. "I've got soup on," Fran said. It was twenty-five degrees too hot for soup, but Amy nodded.

"I didn't ever really learn how to cook," Fran said, apologetically, ladling soup into a bowl. "We were on the road until I was, what, Jim, thirty-two, thirty-three?"

"Something like that," he said, coming up from the basement. He didn't hug Amy and didn't extend his hand, and Amy wasn't sure if she should read into it or not.

"Jim's the real cook around here," Fran said.

"Sometimes," he said, his blue eyes so intense Amy had to look away.

Fran handed her a bowl. Amy waited for her to fill more bowls for her and Jim, but she just handed Amy a spoon.

The Fun Times Brigade

"Are you a vegetarian?" Fran asked her.

Amy was afraid the wrong answer would be no. They were bona fide hippies after all, but she couldn't lie. "I'm not," she said.

"Oh, thank god!" Jim said.

"Everyone back in the day was a vegetarian, and looking back, I think we were all hungry all the time," Fran said.

"And high," Jim added.

"True," Fran said.

"Next time I'll make burgers," Jim said.

Amy couldn't believe she was sitting at Jim and Fran's kitchen table eating unsalted sweet potato soup, with the promise of hamburgers *next time*. They started telling her about Yorkville. "When it was a hippie paradise, not full of Bentleys and valet parking," Jim said. They'd gotten their big break at the Mariposa Folk Festival, where they met Bruce Cockburn, who insisted they sing backup for him. "And then Bruce introduced us to Valdy, who introduced us to his manager, and we got our first record deal," Jim said.

Amy knew this—they had played with Valdy at Massey Hall, and opened for Gordon Lightfoot on a cross-Canada tour, and sang with Joni Mitchell at a famous Yorkville folk club.

"In the mid-eighties, our asshat manager said our sound was stale and we were let go from the label," Jim said. "We thought we were done, but we miss performing."

"You know that feeling when you're onstage and the audience is there, right with you and you're all about to go somewhere together?" Fran asked Amy, pulling three beers from the fridge. "That feeling. That first note, that first chord. I miss that."

Amy nodded. She knew what Fran meant, except that Fran's feeling came from standing on a stage in front of thousands of people, where Amy's came from an audience of fifteen.

"We've found buyers for our bookstore," Jim said, "and we want to get back onstage."

Fran handed each of them a beer. "Ben wanted to be here, but we thought it would be nicer if we could all just see what it feels like."

"Sorry, who's Ben?" Amy asked.

"Our new manager," Jim said, pouring his beer into a glass. "Ben Campbell. He says there's no big Canadian kids' group, not really, and thinks we could be it."

A kids' group? Amy didn't know what they were talking about. They were Fran & Jim. They were a folk band, not a kids' band, and being a folk musician was everything Amy had ever wanted. In university, she'd carried her guitar on her back to every class, and went to every open mic in the city. She was once called "Toronto's answer to Dar Williams" in a music zine. They spelled her name wrong, but she Mod-Podged the quote to her guitar case anyway. For years, she hoped someone would discover her at Free Times Café, or at the tiny coffee shop in the market that always smelled like burned beans. She had only started playing for kids by accident—as a favour for a librarian friend that multiplied into birthday parties, and school visits. She still played "real" shows at night, even though the "real" shows paid her in beer and the kids' shows paid her rent.

"We need a third to make this work," Fran continued.

"And that's where you come in," Jim said.

Amy felt her neck warm. They wanted *her*?

"We told Ben about playing with you at Royal City," Fran said.

It *had* been fun playing with them, even if it was for kids, and maybe this was a way to finally get her foot in the door.

"But if we're going to do this, we're going to do this without a big label. Without any label," Jim said, his voice resolute. "We'll have Ben, but that's it."

"We got royally fucked over," Fran explained. It was shocking to hear her swear, and Amy didn't get it—why wouldn't you want a label backing you? Being signed to a label was the gold standard. It was all she'd ever wanted.

"They'll take your money right out from under you," Jim insisted. "And before you know it, they're giving you an ultimatum—make a synth-pop record or you're out."

Amy would definitely make a synth-pop record if someone paid her to do it. "How will it work then?" she asked.

"Ben knows everyone in the industry," Fran said. "We'll just hire everything out. A recording studio, a sound engineer, a distributor once we've got the albums made, a publicist."

"We can choose who we want. Handpick them," Jim said.

"Okay," Amy said slowly, not quite ready to think about managers and engineers and distributors. She picked at the label of her beer, trying to steady herself.

"Why don't we just play for a bit?" Fran asked.

Amy nodded, relieved. "Sure."

They went down to the basement, where guitars, banjos, and mandolins hung on the wall, a pedal steel angled in the corner. They all tuned their guitars and Fran started playing and Jim started playing and Amy's fingers took over and she was playing, too. They played old folk standards, and eventually Fran and Jim's song "Fly Like a Butterfly." Amy couldn't believe she was in Fran and Jim's basement playing their most famous song. They sounded solid, their voices dovetailing together, and it felt like they'd been playing with each other for months, not minutes. And then Jim got them all another beer and they kept playing.

"So, are you going to do it?" Max asked later that night. She had let herself into his place and crawled into bed beside him.

"Yes," Amy said, without hesitating, her chest still thrumming.

3

AMY BACKS OUT OF THE DRIVEWAY SLOWLY AND Alice screams, red-faced and enraged in her car seat. Amy tries using her voice to calm Alice down, reaching awkwardly behind her, trying to stroke Alice's head with her right hand. But Alice screams so hard, she starts choking, and Amy pulls over without using her turn signal. Cars honk and a taxi driver calls her a cunt.

Fuck fuck fuck fuck. She almost hits a cyclist opening her door. "I'm sorry. I'm sorry!" Amy yells to his middle finger.

She rushes to open Alice's door. She's not choking anymore, but her face is red, tears wet on her cheeks, her tiny hands in fierce fists. "I'm sorry. I love you. You're safe. You're okay," Amy says, kissing Alice's tear-streaked cheeks, but she keeps screaming and screaming.

Amy is afraid that if she unstraps her, she'll never get her back in.

"We're almost there," Amy lies. "We're close, baby girl. Deep breath. You're okay."

But she's not okay and now Amy is not okay. Alice won't settle, and Amy gives up and gets back in the front seat and drives, crying. "We're almost there," Amy calls to Alice, and wishes she had asked Max to stay home and drive them, so she could be in the back seat.

Of course Alice stops screaming when Amy finally parks the car, though her face is still red and blotchy.

In the elevator, a woman leans over the car seat and touches Alice's cheek. "What an adorable little one. Such a precious time. Enjoy every minute of it," the lady says before getting off at the fifth floor.

Precious? Is that what the last half hour was? Amy can't make her face smile in response.

Ariana, the midwife who delivered Alice, is on call today. Amy knew there was a possibility of not seeing her for her final six-week appointment, but when she carries Alice into the examining room, she feels abandoned. She wants the person she literally trusted with her life, with Alice's life, to be here, to tell her that it's all going to be okay, that it's going to get better, or easier, something.

Instead, it's Susannah who sits on a swivelling chair and doesn't even fully turn toward Amy while she goes through the postpartum depression checklist and makes sure Amy knows that breastfeeding isn't a form of birth control. Amy makes a joke about never having sex again, but Susannah keeps going through her list and it makes Amy miss Ariana even more.

Susannah looks at Amy's vagina while the student midwife waltzes around the small room with Alice.

"The sutures have all dissolved. It looks fine," Susannah says.

Fine? What does fine mean? Amy needs superlatives. She needs affirmations. She wants Susannah to tell her that it's perfect, that it's back to normal.

Alice starts fussing and Susannah says, "She sounds hungry." Amy fed her right before they left, but if anyone knows the sound of a hungry baby, it's a midwife. Amy's nervous about Susannah critiquing Alice's latch, but she doesn't look up from her desk, where she's signing the discharge papers.

"My son's a huge fan," Susannah says, handing Amy an envelope to give to Alice's pediatrician.

"Pardon?" Alice keeps popping on and off and Amy knows she's gulping in air.

"Your show is the only TV I let him watch," Susannah says.

"Oh! Thank you." No one has ever mentioned the Brigade here. Amy assumed no one knew.

"I got him tickets to your Roy Thomson Hall show for his fourth birthday, and he lost his mind with joy," she says. "We love 'The Crayon Song.'"

"Blue met Yellow and they gave a high-five," Amy half sings.

"They did a little dance and they did a little jive," Susannah finishes and laughs. "What a lucky little girl you are to have such a talented mama." She pats Alice's head.

Tears prick at the back of Amy's eyes and she remembers standing backstage with Fran and Jim at Roy Thomson, Jim squeezing their hands, saying, "Let's do this, fuckers!"—he always insisted that if he swore before getting onstage, he wouldn't slip up in front of the kids. She remembers stepping out into the heat of the lights, the crowd cheering—that world is a thousand miles away. Amy ducks her head, pretending to check on Alice's latch.

"I'll leave your notes here," Susannah says. "Take your time. No rush."

And that is that. Their last midwife appointment. There will be no one monitoring Alice anymore, checking her weight or her reflexes, pressing on her stomach, or giving Amy tips about different nursing positions. There will be no one to ask her how she's doing, even if she always says, "Fine."

The Fun Times Brigade

Amy tells Max not to make a big deal about Mother's Day. "Alice is only six weeks old, I'm barely a mom," she jokes, but she is lying. She is *only* a mom. Mom has eclipsed everything else she has ever been.

She nurses Alice in the early hours of Sunday morning, then goes back to sleep while Max plays with Alice downstairs. It feels like a cliché—letting Mom sleep in on Mother's Day, but Amy needs the sleep so desperately, she gives in.

When she wakes up, Alice is back down, and Max is talking to his mom over FaceTime. "Hi Sheila," Amy says, and waves to the screen.

Amy was hoping Max would've made her breakfast, but the kitchen is too clean for Max to have made anything, so she pours herself a bowl of cereal. After he hangs up, Max hands Amy a cup of coffee and an envelope. She waits for him to pull out a bag or a box, but he doesn't. Amy reads the card and blinks back tears. He thinks she's crying at what he's written.

"You really *are* a great mom," he says, kissing the side of her head.

"Thanks."

"You okay?"

Amy nods.

"You're not okay."

"I'm *fine*."

"You didn't mean it when you said not to make a big deal. I knew I should've done something. Shit."

"It's fine."

"No, it's not. You're crying."

"It's the postpartum hormones."

"Damn it. I *knew* I should've done something," he says.

Amy wants to crawl back into bed and sleep for the rest of the day. She wants this day to be over already, but Alice is going to be up soon and will need to be nursed.

"I'm just going to run out," Max says when Alice is up.
"Come on, Max. I don't want a pity present."
"But I have an idea!"
"Please don't."

Amy goes back to bed after feeding Alice. Max takes her out so the house will be quiet, but Amy's too disappointed to sleep. Why did she say it was not a big deal? Why did she sabotage herself? And how could Max not see that of course it was a big day no matter what she had said? Instead of sleeping, Amy stands in the shower, and tells herself it's fine. *Today is going to be fine. It's just a day, anyway.*

Down in the kitchen, Max has strapped Alice into her bouncy chair and she kicks her little feet, while Max stands over a frying pan. "Ta-da!" he says, waving his arm to the vase filled with peonies, a fancy bottle of Prosecco, and a bag from the cheese shop.

"All raw cheeses! The ones you missed while you were pregnant!" he says. "And double-smoked bacon." He makes Amy a runny omelet, with bacon on the side, and Prosecco and the stinkiest cheese.

She gives in to the gift, to the morning, to feeling celebrated. She takes a picture of the plate, with flowers in the corner and adds #*FirstMothersDay*.

They drive over to Amy's mom's, and Alice falls asleep in the back seat.

"And how's my little boogitybub?" Mom asks, leaning over the car seat.

"Mom, she's sleeping!" Amy insists.

Max carries the car seat inside, and Alice keeps sleeping. Bill hugs Amy hello and tells her she looks wonderful, which is a lie, but one Amy gladly accepts. Her mom and Bill met when

The Fun Times Brigade

Amy was in Grade 11 and got married just after she finished her first year of university. He can be a bit boring, but he's also warm and is a steadying anchor to her mom's unpredictability.

Amy leaves Alice sleeping in her car seat in the front hall and joins everyone in the living room.

"I remember my first Mother's Day," Mom says from the couch. "You were, what, three and a half months old. Your dad didn't remember. Didn't get me a damn thing. No brunch, no card, no flowers, nothing."

Max starts to confess, but Amy cuts him off. She can't be like her mom, and she doesn't want Max to be like her dad. "We had a lovely morning," Amy says, and tells her mom and Bill about the raw cheese and the bacon and the champagne.

"I still don't get why you had to avoid all that stuff anyway," Mom says. "We didn't when we were pregnant."

Amy holds her tongue. She spent forty weeks defending her choice not to eat cold cuts, she's not going to go back there now.

"And all of this breast is best? I mean, you were fed Pablum and you're fine. You were too, probably, right Max?"

"I'd have to ask my mom," he says. "Ames is doing an amazing job, though. Alice is gaining weight like a champ. She barely even dropped any of her birth weight."

"You look tired," Mom says to Amy.

"I am," she says. "Alice has been up every two hours for the last few nights."

"I remember those days," her mom says.

It was decades ago, Amy wants to say. You don't remember. And besides, you always brag about me sleeping through the night. But she doesn't say that, either. "You're always welcome to come over and take her for a walk so I can nap," she says instead.

"Oh, I've done enough pram walks to last me a lifetime," Mom says.

Amy breathes in through her nose and reminds herself that her mom's always been this way. "I already know fractions," she'd say when Amy would ask her for help with her homework. "Now it's your turn."

Bill brings out a plate of mini quiches and asks Max about work. Max tells him about the paper he's working on with his collaborator in France, the intro to calculus class he's teaching, and the grad course he's prepping for the fall. Amy just sits there—no one asks her about work. As soon as she had Alice, it was like she didn't have a job anymore. She eats three mini quiches in a row.

Alice whimpers in her sleep, and Amy can feel the letdown begin to tingle—the crackling of lightning but softer, prickling down from her collarbone.

"How's your father?" Mom asks Amy.

"Fine," Amy says. "Good." The last time she talked to him he'd set up an RESP for Alice, and she still hasn't sent a thank-you card. He moved to Calgary a few years ago, and Amy visited him when she was on tour, but he's not great at talking on the phone, and whenever Amy thinks of calling him, it's the middle of the night, or way too early with the time difference.

Alice wakes up, and Mom insists on holding her before Amy feeds her.

"She's hungry," Amy insists.

"She's fine," Mom says. "Come here, little one. I've made a new piece I want to show you." She carries Alice over to the fireplace. "This is Athena, the virgin goddess of wisdom, though god knows virginity and wisdom are not actually linked." There are feathers sewn to the canvas along the edge of Athena's dress, and the owl has papier-mâché-ed eyes. It's terrifying.

Amy excuses herself, and sits on the toilet-seat lid, staring at her reflection in the mirror over the sink. One of Mom's papier-mâché clowns leers over her shoulder. After her dad moved out, the house filled with grey and white blobs, newspapers that had come to life while Amy was at school, swelling and bulging in strange, unreadable ways. The eighteen-foot papier-mâché dragon Mom made for a Lunar New Year festival hung in the living room for years, a series of crows that were part of a pilot for a kids' show that never made it to production were caught mid-cackle behind the dining room table until Amy left for university.

She pulls out her phone. There's a *Happy Mother's Day* text from Julie and another from her friend Emily, but nothing from Fran.

Everything okay? she types to Fran, but then deletes. *Happy Mother's Day!* she writes and adds the tulip emoji.

In the living room, Amy hands her mom her Mother's Day gift and takes Alice back. Mom opens the gift bag while Amy gets Alice to latch.

"A scarf!"

Of course it's a scarf. It's Amy's go-to gift for her mom.

"It's beautiful," she exclaims, running her hands along the spring-green fabric.

Alice pops off and Amy has to turn her back on the room—Mom admiring her scarf, Max telling Bill about the new engineering dean—to get her to relatch.

Amy doesn't spend enough time burping Alice, and the car ride home is excruciating. Alice screams and Amy climbs into the back seat at a red light. She wails and Amy starts crying, too. "You're okay. You're okay," she murmurs while Alice rages, and she's not sure if she's talking to Alice or herself.

4

FRAN AND JIM AND AMY HAD RECORDED SIXTEEN songs, but they still hadn't decided on a name. Jim wanted "Jim, Franny & Amy." Amy thought it also sounded too much like their folk band, "Fran & Jim" with her tacked on, but didn't have to say anything because Fran refused to be called "Franny" and Ben said it was derivative. "Too Sharon, Lois & Bram."

They tried out the Playground Revival, the Dancing Hearts, Kangaroo Zoo, the Silly Butterflies, and Kazoo Attack, but nothing was quite right.

"What about the Fun Times Brigade?" Fran said as Ben was wrapping up a meeting about their first potential tour.

And from the moment Fran said it out loud, they all knew it was the one. They were the Fun Times Brigade, and Ben got them marching-band costumes for their first photo shoot.

The Fun Times Brigade

"Not a bad show this afternoon," Jim said, handing Amy a whisky at the back of the tour bus after their first tour stop. Amy didn't really drink whisky, but she accepted the drink as Parry Sound disappeared behind them. It seemed unfathomable that they were already touring, but they had done a series of successful shows in Toronto, and run-outs to Kingston, Guelph, and Waterloo, and now had thousands of CDs sitting in a warehouse in Mississauga, and they were touring it. Touring the shit out of it, as Jim liked to say. Amy didn't know how they would ever fill all these venues, but Ben kept showing the ticket-sales reports on his laptop, and in the span of a few months, Amy had gone from being a struggling singer-songwriter playing birthday parties to pay her rent to playing auditoriums with musical legends.

"You need to up the tempo on 'She'll Be Coming 'Round the Mountain,'" Ben said over his beer, his right knee jiggling. "And you need to slow down the pace in the middle of the set. The energy gets too wild, and it's too hard to bring them all back down for 'You Are My Sunshine.'"

"I still think it was a solid show," Fran said and sipped her glass of chardonnay. She made a face and got an ice cube from the tiny bar fridge.

Most of Amy's musician friends were crashing on acquaintances' couches and playing empty dive bars in the middle of nowhere, and it was strange to be travelling in this fancy bus. Before the tour, Amy had googled images of tour buses to know what she was getting into. Was it like the party buses people rented for proms or weddings? And where would they sleep? The bus had a little sitting area in the front, behind the driver, and another at the back of the bus, cordoned off by sliding doors. The sleeping area had two bunks on each side, top and bottom, with curtains for privacy. Amy took the top bunk, on top of Fran's lower bunk, and she tried not to worry about rolling off in the middle of the night.

Their driver's name was Marcus and after introducing himself, and giving them a tour of the bus, he told them the code word—*flowers*. If anyone said *flowers*, it meant they had to take a shit, and he'd find the next rest stop.

"Why can't we use the washroom?" Amy whispered to Fran at the back of the bus.

"He'd have to clean the tank by hand," she explained.

"Oh my god," Amy said, horrified. "Got it."

Flowers, she repeated to herself, though there was no way she was going to forget it.

In Sudbury, Jim taught Amy how to ask for more monitor in a sound check, and in Sault Ste. Marie, Fran taught her how to put on stage makeup so she wouldn't get washed out by the stage lights.

"I think we should add 'Baby Beluga' to the set list," Ben said between Thunder Bay and Winnipeg.

Jim rolled his eyes.

"We can do our own version of it, a bit more folky, with some finger-picking and three-part harmonies," Fran suggested.

But Jim hated doing covers, especially Raffi or SLB covers—that's what he called Sharon, Lois & Bram.

"How's this?" he asked, pulling out a piece of paper and drafting a new set list without "Baby Beluga." Amy glanced at Jim's messy handwriting and made out the classics—"Itsy Bitsy Spider" and "Baa Baa Black Sheep," and Fran and Jim's "Fly Like A Butterfly" at the end so all the grandparents would go wild.

"Sure," Amy said, knowing that Jim would switch it up mid-show anyway.

"Works for me," Fran said.

Ben's cellphone rang and he ducked into the bunk area of the bus to take the call.

"You're shouting into the mic," Jim told Amy after Ben slid the divider closed.

She felt embarrassment prickle at the backs of her eyes, but was grateful Jim hadn't said anything in front of Ben. She knew she was singing too loudly—her throat had started hurting in Sudbury—but she had no idea how else to draw the kids in and keep them with her. She was used to performing for a handful of people who were more interested in ordering another beer than listening to a song about her most recent breakup, that or a living room full of kids touching her guitar or wrestling with a sibling at her feet. She wasn't used to auditoriums with hundreds of seats, plus balconies.

"You've got to spread your energy to every corner of the space," Fran suggested.

Spreading her energy around sounded woo-woo, but after finishing a show in Winnipeg with a raw throat, she was afraid she was going to lose her voice completely, and that would be the end of her career with Jim and Fran, so she tried it out.

She stood onstage in Brandon, Manitoba, and imagined her energy like a purple beam spreading throughout the audience. It felt weird, and she almost missed her cue to start "Old MacDonald Had a Farm." She wasn't sure it worked, but she tried it again in Regina, and again in Swift Current, and Saskatoon, and by the time they played Medicine Hat, her throat hurt less and Jim had stopped telling her she was yelling.

5

MAX INSISTS THAT AMY GO OUT ON HER OWN while Alice naps.

"I'm good," Amy says. Beyond a shower, or sleeping in on the weekends, she hasn't been away from Alice since she was born.

"You keep saying you need some alone time," he says. "Here's your window. Just go get a coffee."

Amy instinctively grabs the diaper bag but catches herself and digs around the front hall closet for a purse. Wallet, keys, the biography of Stevie Nicks she started when she was pregnant and hasn't read a word of since. She wants to say goodbye to Alice, but she doesn't want to wake her, so she stares at the monitor.

"She's fine. We'll be fine," Max insists. "Go, have a break. You deserve it." He kisses her and Amy stumbles down the sidewalk. She makes sure her phone's ringer is on. She can be home in two minutes if she needs to be.

The Fun Times Brigade

She gets a latte and sits on a stool in the window and opens her book. She stares at the page, then checks her phone. Nothing. She reads a few pages and checks her phone again.

Look at me, out on the town, Amy texts Fran and sends a photo of her latte and the coffee shop window.

Looks amazing! My view is less inspiring, Fran writes back right away and sends a picture of a hospital waiting room.

How's Jim doing? Amy texts Fran.

His skin was bothering him, so his doc asked us to come in, she writes back. *I just wish I could focus on something. I just had to rip out six rows of the sweater I started.*

Bah, Amy writes back. *That sucks.*

I think I hear the nurse. Got to go.

Love you! Love to Jim, Amy writes back. She sips her coffee and rereads the page she has open.

Is Alice up, she texts Max.

Yup, he texts back.

She ok? She hungry?

She's fine.

Send me a picture. Amy holds her phone, waiting for a photo.

I thought you wanted to be alone.

I do.

Alice is fine. We're fine.

Just send me a picture. I want to see her.

You always say you want alone time but now you want me to send pictures of Alice?

Yes.

Yes to what?

Yes to all of that.

He doesn't write anything and Amy looks through photos of Alice on her phone and wonders how Max doesn't understand this.

Amy was twenty-six when she met Max, singing at kids' birthday parties and open mics. He was twenty-eight and three years into his PhD. They were both friends of friends at a house party and when everyone else went outside for a smoke, they ended up in the kitchen looking for more beer. He was tall, his hair in floppy dark curls that made him look a bit like a Muppet. He was wearing a faded Wu-Tang shirt, and the minute she saw him she knew she was going to kiss him. She did kiss him that night after their friends had left, dizzy, frantic moths flying above their heads at the porch light, and then they stumbled to his place because it was closer than hers.

They spent the first few months fooling around after Amy would host open mics and get paid in free beer. It was before they had cellphones, so she'd show up at Max's apartment and hope he was still trying to work through some strange math assignment, or he'd leave a message on her answering machine about which bar he'd be at with his PhD friends. No matter how drunk they were, he always made sure she came first, at least twice and she'd sleep over, or he'd sleep over and they'd have sex one more time in the morning, then they'd go their separate ways until the next weekend, or the weekend after that.

And then one weekend, groggy and slightly hungover, he asked if Amy wanted to go for brunch.

"Like, a date?" she asked.

"Do you want it to be a date?"

She didn't know and she couldn't quite figure out what they'd talk about for the hour and a half it would take to eat brunch. It ended up being longer than that because they had to stand in line first, but they didn't stop talking—about his parents, about hers, about school and music and where they grew up—both in Toronto, though Amy was in the west end and he was in the north end of the city. And then they went back to her place so she could change her clothes and brush her teeth properly, and they had sex again, but this time it was different. It felt like potential relationship sex. It was the first time Amy hadn't been at least buzzed and it was still good. Maybe even better.

So they did post-sex brunch dates for a while until Amy asked if Max wanted to come to her roommate's birthday party.

"Like, a date?" he asked and Amy punched him in the arm.

Those early days feel so long ago now. These days, she misses Max while he's at work, wishing he were around to see Alice trying to roll over, or bang on pots with a spoon, but as soon as he texts that he's on his way home, she's annoyed that he's been away all day, talking to adults, being himself. By the time he walks through the door, she puts Alice in his arms and says, "She needs a new diaper." Or "I have no idea what's for dinner." And then she goes up to their room or sits in the backyard by herself with a gin and tonic.

But then she'll see his back in the middle of the night, the door to his office open a crack, the blanket slipped off, his back, broad and freckled, on her way from the bathroom and she misses him, she misses them. She'll debate tiptoeing into his office, lying with him on the couch with his arm around her, but then Alice'll mewl and she'll hurry back to the bedroom, where she'll tell herself, rocking Alice's bassinet, that at least one of them needs to be sleeping.

We're doing tummy time, Max finally texts, with a photo of Alice on her mat.

Amy starts crying suddenly, like a nosebleed, and leaves her half-drunk latte, stumbling out of the coffee shop, grateful for her sunglasses. It's so bizarre to think that that poppy seed, that apple, that watermelon, growing in Amy, was her, the Alice that is lying on her mat. That her growing fingernails and lungs made Amy so sick for so many months. It's impossible to remember how sick she was. It's impossible to remember even being pregnant now.

Lindsay Zier-Vogel

Amy stands on the sidewalk and stares at the photo through tears, incredulous.
I'm on my way back, she texts Max. *See you in 5.*

6

AFTER THE SUCCESS OF THEIR FIRST ALBUM, FRAN and Jim and Amy wrote original songs for their second album, *The Rainbow March*. Amy had never written for kids before but found it far easier than trying to turn a breakup into a song that didn't sound like a cliché. They wrote "Battle of the Snowsuit," about a sentient snowsuit that refused to be put on by a kid who wanted to go outside and play, and "The Rainbow March," about a bunch of colours having a parade. Ben was convinced the title track was going to be their big hit, but it was "The Crayon Song" that blew up.

They started selling out venues, and before they'd even finished the West Coast leg of their tour, Ben got merch made and booked them an East Coast tour, flying them straight to Halifax. They were out east when Ben saw a crowd of people down on the waterfront asking for Fran's, Jim's, and Amy's autographs. Jim was on a mission to find the best burger in Canada, and

The Fun Times Brigade

they were sitting on a patio after their Halifax show, finishing up dinner, when a bunch of parents and kids recognized them.

"No more drinking in public," Ben said that night on the bus.

"What do you mean 'drinking in public'?" Jim asked.

"Drinking," Ben repeated, "in public."

"You're kidding," Jim said.

"Optics," Ben said, his voice resolute. "You're not a folk band anymore. You're a kids' band, and we can't have the media pick up any photos of any of you drinking. Or smoking," he added.

"I don't smoke," Amy said, feeling like she was the target of his addendum.

"No hotel bars, or taking the tour bus to the liquor store," Ben said. "I don't even want to see a liquor store bag anywhere near any of you."

"This is horseshit!" Jim said. Fran insisted it'd be fine, and Amy was somewhere in between. She was twenty-eight and being told she couldn't go out with her friends for a drink. Ben conceded that a glass of wine with dinner was okay if they were out, but only one, and never a bottle for the table, and they had to be careful in small towns where everyone would recognize them.

"I'm working on a deal with Crayola," Ben said from his bunk on the bus. "We can't have anything jeopardize that."

When they got to Fredericton, Ben made Amy go through her Facebook and delete any photos where she was in a bikini, or holding a drink, or even at a party. "It's an image thing," he insisted. Amy thought he was being paranoid, but she did it anyway.

It was fine at first. When she got home after the tour, she made sure not to post any photos of her with a drink, but she started feeling skittish at parties, afraid someone would tag her in a photo where she was holding a beer in the background, or Ben would see a photo of her with any kind of glass and assume it was booze.

"You're not doing anything wrong," Max insisted.

And Amy knew she wasn't, but she was the youngest member of the Brigade. She didn't have an established music career to fall back on, and she didn't want to be responsible for the downfall of the band.

But drinking in hotel rooms got old fast, and on their next tour, with Ben back in Toronto, Jim and Amy started going out again. Fran wouldn't have anything to do with it, but in Vancouver, Jim and Amy went out for sushi and requested a private room so they could drink too much sake. In Calgary, they ate steak frites and drank Argentinian Malbecs in a dark corner of an old steak house Jim loved. "There's no way there'll be kids there," he promised Fran.

Max proposed when Amy got home from the second leg of their *Rainbow March* tour with his grandmother's sapphire ring. Ben had already booked shows the following summer, though, so the only weekend they could get married was the following Labour Day weekend. Amy was away for most of the spring and summer, so Max organized the flowers and the officiant and took deposits down to the restaurant and found a place to host their rehearsal dinner. He and his sister made the chuppah and Amy and Max made seating arrangements over the phone when she was at a hotel in Edmonton. She managed to be home for the tasting at the restaurant but was out east when they had to finalize cake decisions, so Julie went with Max and they decided on a lemon tier, a chocolate tier, and a carrot-cake tier to cover all of their bases.

Amy was afraid the ceremony would feel like a performance, but standing up there, under the chuppah, it felt like it was only her and Max and the officiant she had only ever met over Skype. Max wrote an equation for them that made all his math friends

The Fun Times Brigade

laugh. Amy had agonized over her vows all summer and ended up telling the story of coming home from the first Brigade tour, when she knew Max was her home. She barely managed to say it all without crying. They traded rings and kissed and Max stepped on the glass and they were married.

They had a weekend away for their honeymoon, and when they got back, Ben called Amy and Fran and Jim into his office to tell them that he'd sold "The Crayon Song" to Crayola.

Amy had money, actual money, for the first time, and decided it was time to buy a house. Her performing schedule drove their real estate agent nuts, but she and Max eventually found a detached house in the west end and the first thing Amy hung were the posters from the Brigade's first tour. At the housewarming, Amy told everyone that it was the house that crayons bought.

7

ONE MORNING AT THE END OF JUNE, ALICE FALLS asleep on Amy after she finishes nursing. Amy's water bottle is on the coffee table, just out of reach. She tries to shift closer, but Alice squirms, so Amy gives up and starts scrolling through Instagram. She's liking a photo of Max's nephews playing basketball when Jim and Fran's son, Arlo, calls. She answers quietly, and he tells her they're throwing Jim a barbeque on Saturday. "For his sixty-sixth!"

Jim's birthday! How could she have forgotten?

Fran and Amy threw him a surprise every year—balloons falling from the stage ceiling while they sang "Happy Birthday" with the audience in Comox, a catered picnic another year in Charlottetown, tickets to see Daniel Lanois another year. She loved conspiring with Fran, all of the whispering and planning and organizing when Jim was picking up coffees or loading the bus.

"Is it a surprise?" Amy asks Arlo.

The Fun Times Brigade

"No, no, not this year," he says. "Mum thought it would be one too many things."

"Totally," Amy says. Of course there's no surprise this year. "How's he doing?"

"He's good. I mean, tired, but apparently that's normal."

Amy feels guilty for forgetting Jim's birthday, for turning into that mom who can't see beyond her baby. She misses him. She misses Fran. She misses the three of them together and has to remind herself that they'll get back to playing together when Jim's treatment wraps up and Alice doesn't need her 24-7.

Arlo tells her to come by any time after four thirty "No gifts, though. Dad insists."

The night before Jim's barbeque, Alice doesn't sleep well, and in the morning, Amy can't find any clothes to wear. When she finally finds a dress that fits, she realizes she can't breastfeed in it.

"You look amazing," Max says, kissing her neck.

"But I can't feed Alice," Amy says, trying to unzip it.

"What about," Max says, rifling through her closet, "this one?" He pulls out a striped wrap dress.

"I don't know," Amy says. It's a bit short, but she can breastfeed in it, so she hangs it up in the bathroom.

Amy doesn't usually have plans and doesn't see much of anyone these days, and she's nervous that Alice is going to go down for her nap late, or sleep late, or spit up all over her outfit once they get there. She packs and repacks the diaper bag, until Max insists they have everything they need.

Alice doesn't sleep late, but when Amy goes upstairs to change her, there's nothing to wipe up the poop.

"Max!" she yells from the top of the stairs, even though he's out for a run. "Max!"

Amy's frustration eclipses her anxiety as she sticks Alice in the bathtub.

"There are wipes downstairs," Max says when he gets home. "There's a full Costco box."

"Downstairs," Amy says. "I was upstairs. Two flights away from the wipes. What am I supposed to do, carry a poopy baby into the basement to get wipes?"

"Sorry," he says shrugging.

"Why is it up to me? If you finish the wipes, bring more up," she says.

They don't talk as they get ready for the party, and Max buckles Alice into her car seat and carries her out the door. Amy knows she's overreacting, but she turns up the radio so they don't have to talk on the drive over. They still aren't talking when Max parks up the street from Fran and Jim's. Part of her wants to make up before they go into the party, but Max doesn't say anything and she leaves him to get the diaper bag and carries Alice in her car seat around to the back gate.

"Ames! Alice!" Fran greets them, the silver bracelets on her wrist jangling together like a song. She's wearing her signature summer skirt—long and flowy in a deep indigo.

Amy is flooded with relief when she sees her. "I've missed you," she says into Fran's neck as she hugs her.

"I've missed *you*!" she says. "And would you look at this chubby little bunny."

Alice kicks while Amy unclips her from her car seat. She passes Alice over to Fran.

"You are a fierce little munch, aren't you?" she says while Alice yanks on her hair. "What a grip!"

"Before I forget," Amy says, handing Fran a bottle of vitamins. "There've been studies that say patients with higher levels of vitamin D might have better outcomes."

The Fun Times Brigade

"You're so thoughtful," she says, squeezing Amy's hand. "I'll add this to his regimen."

"Amy," Ben says. Amy hasn't seen him since he dropped off a gift right after Alice was born.

"How are you? How are things?" Amy asks, watching Fran dance Alice over to Arlo's kid, Levi.

"Good," Ben says. "We're on a new Apple playlist that is bringing in some huge streaming numbers."

Amy wants to ask if there are any other kids' musicians putting out albums, vying to take their place, but she doesn't want to seem insecure. He asks if she got her SOCAN cheque. Amy nods, grateful for both the money and the quarterly reminder that she is a musician.

"The live album is being mixed right now," Ben says, "and we're still set for a spring launch."

"Great," she says, though promoting a Brigade album is completely unfathomable at the moment.

"And you?" Ben asks. "You good?"

Amy nods noncommittally. When she was pregnant, she dreamed of summer picnics and trips to the Island, and patio drinks with the stroller, and backyard barbeques—everything she'd missed over the last twelve years when she was soundchecking on blazing hot stages, or stuck on a tour bus, driving from music festival to music festival. Except Max is teaching two summer courses and, it turns out, babies aren't supposed to wear sunscreen until they're six months old. Alice is only two and a half months, which means Amy spends her days trying to cover up Alice's pudgy, sleeping calves and wrist rolls, and she's always fussing over sun hats and muslin blankets. She's become a mom who fusses over sun hats and blankets.

"I've been writing," Amy blurts out, even though she hasn't been, not since she wrote the spring ideas on her phone.

"See—you were scared you wouldn't be able to be creative, but look at you," Ben says.

Her throat burns with shame, but she makes herself smile.

Ben's girlfriend, Cathryn, hugs Amy hello, and she's grateful for the interruption.

"How's she sleeping?" Cathryn asks.

Amy hates that everyone asks about sleep, as if any baby sleeps. She shrugs. "Oh, you know," she says, and leaves it at that.

Fran hugs Max, and Amy wants him to put his arm around her, but he accepts a beer from Arlo's wife, Sina, and walks over to Levi, who is throwing a little plastic figure with a parachute off the stairs over and over again.

Jim sits with Arlo on lawn chairs, and Amy doesn't realize how much she's missed him until she sees his face break into a huge smile. She knows it's chemo, not radiation that makes your hair fall out, but it's still a relief to see his salt-and-pepper beard and caterpillar eyebrows that always need to be tamed before every shoot.

"Happy birthday!" Amy says and leans over to hug him. He's a bit thinner than she remembers, though not eating side-of-the-road Tim Hortons all summer will do that to anyone.

"And hello to you, little Alice," Jim says, reaching his arms out and taking her from Fran. "Look at these long fingers. Haven't we been saying we need someone on keys?"

Seeing Alice in Jim's arms makes Amy teary. With her dad in Calgary, and Max's dad in Florida, Jim is the closest thing Alice has to a grandpa. She pulls out her phone and takes a picture of the two of them.

He bounces her on his knee and sings an improvised version of "Harvest Moon."

Fran takes her from Jim. "I need all my baby snuggle time," she says tickling Alice's cheeks with her nose. "I mean look at these cheeks. I just want to eat them."

The Fun Times Brigade

Amy hands Jim the gift bag.

"No gifts!" he says, and shoots Arlo a look.

"I told her!" Arlo says.

Jim and Levi team up and pull the handfuls of tissue paper out of the bag. Levi wears the tissue paper on his head, and Jim pulls out the ukulele. Amy got the lyrics of one of Jim's favourite songs etched on the back. He runs his fingers along the text. "Would you look at that," he says.

"What does it say, Jimbo?" Sina asks.

"It's the Grateful Dead," he says, reading the quote.

There's a collective pause.

"'Ripple,'" Arlo says.

"This is amazing, Ames."

"Lanois wasn't playing a gig this summer, so this'll have to do," Amy deflects.

"I love it," he says. He tunes the ukulele and starts singing "Ripple." Fran joins in and then Amy. Sina picks Levi up and sways next to Arlo. They join in after the chorus. It's been so long since Amy's sung for anyone other than Alice, something in her cracks open and she has to gulp in a deep breath of air to keep from crying.

"La-la-la. La-la. La-la-lah-lah-lah." Even Max joins in for the ending.

"Would you look at that," Jim says about Alice's wide-eyed stare. "She loves it."

"That's what happens when you have a musician for a mama," Fran says.

Amy wants Jim to play something else. She wants to sing together again, sing for the rest of the night, but she's afraid if she tries to speak, she'll sob.

"And Ames has been writing," Ben tells everyone.

"Amazing!"

"Good for you!"

Amy avoids looking at Max. "Just playing around with a few ideas," she says.

Jim hands Amy the ukulele. "Play one for us!"

"Oh, they're not ready. Not yet," she insists.

"I can't wait to hear them," Fran says.

Amy takes Alice and sniffs her bum. "She's wet," Amy says, even though she's not. She carries Alice inside, and after she's changed her, she's relieved the conversation's moved on to the owners of Fran and Jim's old bookstore.

Fran insists on holding Alice when the burgers are ready so Max and Amy can eat.

"These are delicious, Arlo," she says, even though the quinoa's burned and crumbles away from the black beans.

"I wanted burger-burgers, but not even the birthday boy gets what he wants with these two around," Jim says, nodding to Arlo and Sina.

"We're trying to get him on a high-protein, plant-based diet," Sina says.

"Soy-free, though," Arlo adds.

Alice starts to lose it when Amy's midway through her second burger.

"Can you take her?" she asks Max, annoyed she even has to ask. He bounces her up and down, but she keeps wailing. Amy stuffs the rest of her burger in her mouth. "This might be our cue."

"You can always put her down here," Fran offers. "I think there's a Pack 'n Play somewhere."

"Thanks, but we need to get her home," Amy says, wishing she were the kind of mom who could just put her baby to sleep wherever. She hugs Jim and Arlo goodbye, and Sina doesn't let her carry her plate inside. Amy gives Levi a high-five, and he asks why Alice cries all the time.

"Just when she's tired," she says and feels so defensive it's embarrassing. He's four. What does he know?

The Fun Times Brigade

Amy hugs Jim goodbye one more time as Max straps a now-screaming Alice into her car seat. "Happy birthday," she says into his shoulder.

"I love the uke," he says. "It's really something, Ames."

Fran hugs Amy tight, and Amy wants to tell her about being frustrated with Max. She wants Fran to tell her that it's going to be okay, that it's normal. To let it go. She wants to tell Fran she hasn't written a single thing. She wants to tell her that she feels like she's back in TV land now—the 4:00 a.m. wake-ups, the hurry-up-and-wait, never having time to talk to her friends, and always having to smile while everyone tells her how grateful she should be.

"There's nothing more perfect than those early days with a little one," the woman at the fruit market told her the other day.

You're so lucky to be home with her, some girl she knew in high school posted on Facebook.

"Soak in every blessed moment," an elderly woman said while Amy was trying to get the stroller into the coffee shop. And she smiles and smiles until her face might break, clenching her jaw to keep herself from screaming.

"Thanks for coming," Fran says. "It means the world to Jim. To me, too."

"Of course!" Amy says. "As if I'd be anywhere else."

Fran hugs Amy again. "Love you," she says into her shoulder and Amy wants to tell Max to take Alice home and for her and Fran and Jim to go into their basement and jam. She just wants to jam and disappear into music until she feels like herself again.

"You bring that little girl of yours by any time, okay?" Fran says, giving her one more squeeze.

Amy nods and doesn't let on how impossible it would be to get there around Alice's nap schedule.

8

RIGHT BEFORE THEY WENT ON TOUR FOR THEIR fifth album, Ben called Fran, Jim, and Amy into his office.

"CBC's interested in a TV show," he said.

"A TV show?" Amy asked, excited. After spending every summer on the road, she was feeling antsy to do something new, something different.

"The money's good," Ben promised. "Really good."

"But the boob tube?" Jim asked. "Aren't kids sedentary enough?"

"It would mean kids would be watching you instead of some mutant turtle karate show, or whatever other garbage is on," Ben said.

"We can make it what we want it to be," Fran said.

Amy nodded, excited.

"It's an opportunity to shape the kids' TV landscape," Ben said.

"We want to really connect with children," Fran said in their first meeting with the network execs. "If we're going to be invited into their living rooms, we want it to matter. Children are sponges. They're complex beings, open to everything. They're not a discriminating audience, and so it's our responsibility to provide them with good art."

The network execs only cared about ratings, but the production company was receptive to Fran's philosophy, and Pam, the showrunner, was also into creating connections with kids.

"I know you're used to playing to huge audiences, but onscreen, you need to play for one child, in their living room," she said on their first table read. "The writers are going to make sure the energy ebbs and flows—a high-energy song, and then a quieter song."

In each episode, the Brigade went to a different place—a forest, where they sang "The Green Grass Grew All Around," and a meadow where they had a picnic and sang "The Butterfly Song." They went to the zoo, and to a farm, and to a swimming pool. They got to shoot at the museum after hours, and at an empty school they filled with desks. For one episode, they went to the children's hospital and performed on the cardiology ward.

Fran was a natural and the producers didn't care even if she went off script, and despite his years of smoking pot, Jim had a steel-trap memory, so every retake was because Amy was standing looking like a deer in the headlights, panicking about her lines. She remembered lyrics no problem, but for some reason lines made her whole body freeze. It was funny at first, but by the fifth episode, it was an issue. Jim sent her links to mnemonic devices. Fran bought her bottles of ginkgo biloba, and suggested she try singing her lines, but nothing worked.

"Try an acting coach," Pam suggested, and sent Amy the name of someone she knew. Amy memorized Shakespeare soliloquies, and poems by Mary Oliver. She even tried writing her own lines for the show, but nothing worked. Finally, Jim suggested Amy lead the kids in singalongs—that she was good at—and the writers started giving her knock-knock jokes—the only thing she could reliably remember.

Each show opened with Fran introducing an instrument, then Jim played an old folk tune for a semicircle of kids with shakers and spoons and tambourines, and Amy told a knock-knock joke. She hated that that was her schtick, but she had no choice.

After the first season, Pam left to work on a puppet show and the network brought in Ann-Marie. She was a drill sergeant and only cared about ratings.

Amy tried to talk to Ben about it, but he said his hands were tied. "We have no say," he said. "Besides, Ann-Marie brings good numbers. She's going to do great things for the show."

"Bigger! More energy!" Ann-Marie yelled on set, insisting on take after take. Amy heard the clap of that slate in her dreams, the yelling for quiet. Each episode took a week to shoot, and there were twenty-four episodes in every season. At least with performing live, the energy of the crowd fed her, but when they were shooting, it was just a director asking them to sing a song again, and again. And again. So much forced happiness for the burly guys behind the cameras. The cheeriness was cranked to eleven and Amy resented it.

Max was back from his post-doc in Berkeley and racing the tenure clock at Waterloo, and Amy never saw him. She never saw her friends, either, except for Fran and Jim, but it was different on set. They were always on, always working. She was supposed to be happy—she was successful, she was making money, good money, as a musician, and she had a hit TV show—except the pace was relentless. They'd shoot Monday to Friday, and then

The Fun Times Brigade

play matinees on Saturday and Sunday, and they'd go on the road a few days after wrapping each season—Ben never wanted to miss the summer festival circuit. He said that if they did, they'd lose their audience and then there would be no point in having a TV show.

The royalties from the opening song were worth it, Amy reminded herself at every 5:00 a.m. call time, and during the hours she spent in hair and makeup. She just had to get through the day, the week, the season, she told herself while the floor director yelled for quiet.

"Everyone in position."

"Cameras rolling, sound speed."

"Scene twenty-one, B camera. Take six."

9

"ALL RIGHT, BABY GIRL. IT'S TIME FOR YOU TO take a bottle," Amy tells Alice the day she turns three months. "Mama needs to get back to work eventually." They don't have any shows booked until their live album comes out next spring, but she wants to be able to say yes if Ben books them for something sooner.

Max takes Alice downstairs, and Amy sets up the pump Julie recommended—tubes and plugs, and suction cups. It hurts at first. Her nipple pulls and stretches until it fills the huge cylindrical attachment. It's awful, but the pain subsides as the milk starts trickling into the removable container. It's grotesque—the motor's perverted moan and her nipple, purplish and pulsing, but if it means Amy can perform again, then she's going to pump.

She starts doing it three times a day, as if pumping more is going to make her be able to perform sooner, but then her milk production is out of control and her boobs are swollen and sore and Alice chokes every time she tries to nurse. Amy's afraid she's going to get mastitis, so she starts doing it twice a day, then just once.

When the bags of pale yellow breast milk edge out the Tupperwares of spaghetti sauce and the ice cream in the freezer, already taking over the spot they used to keep gin, Amy tries giving Alice a bottle, but Alice won't take it. She refuses the ones they got at their baby shower, and the slow-flow ones Amy orders online, and the fast-flow ones Max buys on the way home from work. Max makes a spreadsheet and they try long, narrow nipples and faceted nipples and anti-colic nipples. They try the kinds that Julie's kids used, then the kinds that Max's nephews both took. Max polls his colleagues and gets another round of suggestions that Alice refuses, and then he FaceTimes Amy from Walmart and tries to see if he can match a bottle nipple to the shape of her nipple. Alice hates that one the most.

"She won't take a bottle," Amy sobs to Julie over the phone, "and I'm never going to be able to work again."

"Sometimes frozen milk has some weird enzyme thing, and it tastes weird to babies."

"Really?"

"Try pumping and getting Max to give her a bottle fresh and then see."

They try, but Alice still refuses. Even if Amy sits on the porch so Alice can't smell her, she refuses. They try heated milk, cold milk, freezer milk, still-warm-from-Amy's-body milk. They retry every bottle, every different flow, every nipple, but Alice rejects all of them. The Tupperware drawer is a wasteland of rejected bottles.

Alice is going to be in kindergarten before Amy will be onstage again.

"That's not true," Julie insists. "She'll be eating solids soon enough, and then breastfeeding will be just supplementary. The balance will tip."

Amy wants to believe her.

Amy kicks the pump under the bed and puts all the bottles in a labelled garbage bag in the basement.

"There's got to be something," Max says. "We can figure it out."

"Max, this isn't some theorem that needs to be proven," Amy said, needing him to give up.

"How's the bottle-feeding going?" everyone asks—Julie, the barista, Amy's mom, Max's mom when she calls from Florida.

"It's not," Amy admits, and tries not to panic about being the only person who can feed Alice for the foreseeable future.

10

BETWEEN THE RELENTLESS SHOOTING SCHEDULE, and being on the road every summer, Amy realized that once you missed a milestone birthday, or a wedding, or another baby shower, friendships were hard to resuscitate. People said they understood, but they didn't, not really, and eventually invitations to drinks and cottage getaways and dinner parties petered out.

She didn't care about cottage invites when she was playing big festivals with amazing lineups, she tried to convince herself. Except the Brigade played in the middle of the day, when most musicians were just pulling into the festival parking lot, and they had to get straight onto the bus the minute they were done.

"Who needs to see a Hawksley Workman set when we could be working on our next album?" Jim said cheerily, climbing into the back of the bus after a show in Edmonton.

But Amy wanted to see him play. And k.d. lang, and Basia Bulat, and Amelia Curran. She climbed into the back of the bus and stared out the window while Jim played around with his guitar.

The Fun Times Brigade

"What about this for an intro?" he asked, finger-picking.

"I love it!" Fran said, coming through the curtain with a cup of tea, and Jim and Fran worked out a chorus for a new song about a groundhog who liked cheese while Amy watched a yellow canola field blur past the window.

She loved them, Fran and Jim, and was grateful that out of all of the musicians, they had picked her to be in their band. The Brigade had become bigger than she'd ever imagined—they sang national anthems at hockey games, and threw first pitches at baseball games, and met the prime minister. She was living the dream, but they'd been on the road for seven years, and had shot three seasons of the show and Amy was getting tired of singing about potties and snow pants every day. And it was getting to be hard being around a couple all the time. Fran insisted she wasn't a third wheel and included Amy in all of their plans—hikes in Canmore on a rare day off, dinner at a seafood place in Halifax they remembered from a booksellers' conference years earlier, Jim's never-ending obsession with finding the best burger in the country, visits to old friends of theirs who'd bought a hobby farm on Salt Spring Island. But Amy was at least twenty years younger than everyone, and there were only so many nostalgic Mariposa Folk Festival stories she could handle. She wanted to be around people her age, so she started making excuses—feigning exhaustion, and telling Jim and Fran that she was going to order room service—but then she'd go out to a restaurant she'd read about online, or tag along with the sound crew for poutine before the tour bus left for the next city. They weren't friend-friends, but at least they were closer to her age.

"Why don't you write an EP, not for kids?" Emily suggested when Amy called her from the road.

Lindsay Zier-Vogel

When she first joined the Brigade, Amy expected that she would play "real" shows at night—shows for adults, in bars. It was possible, scheduling-wise—Brigade shows were always in the afternoons, so her evenings were free. But when she got home from their first tour and played a gig at the coffee shop where she used to play, it was so anticlimactic she couldn't bear to do another.

But maybe Emily was right. Maybe writing an adult album was exactly what she needed. Songs used to pour out of her when she was working at the coffee shop all those years ago. She couldn't keep up with the lyrics and melodies that would arrive unbidden while she was trying to make a foam heart on someone's cappuccino, but as she sat in her bunk on the way to Quebec, while Fran and Jim jammed in the back of the bus, Amy stared at the blank sheet. All she had written about for years were crayons and raccoons and jumping in puddles. She didn't know how to write about love anymore. She didn't know how to write about heartbreak. She pulled out her guitar and played around with a few chords, but no words came. Nothing. She put the guitar away and went to the back of the bus, where she poured her and Jim a whisky and listened to him and Fran take turns telling her the story of their first time playing Massey Hall.

11

AMY IS NURSING ALICE IN THE CORNER OF THE couch when she gets a text from Max. *Happy pi approximation day!*

He sends a photo of a table of at least ten kinds of pie.

Key lime or apple? he writes. *Naheed brought peach, and there's rumours there's a Boston cream pie en route.*

When Amy first met Max, she knew about pi Day on March 14—3.14—but at Waterloo, they celebrate pi three times—March 14, and today, July 22, because 22/7 is a fraction that approximates pi, and then again on the 314th day of the year, after mid-terms. On each of the three days, the department serves pie at the main math building, and everyone ends up at Grad House for beers.

Apple please! she writes back, and realizes how hungry she is. Breastfeeding makes her ravenous. Amy gets Alice down for a nap, and flips laundry from the washing machine to the dryer, and folds a basket of tiny baby clothes, and then another, load after load.

After Max gets home, Amy stands in the shower and lets the water drip into her ears and blot everything out. She had bought fancy shampoo online that smells like rosemary and mint, and she stands under the hot water breathing it in until the heat fades. She loves standing under the too-hot water, letting it fill her ears, though her hair falls out in alarming clumps, and she has to clear the drain, the clot of postnatal hair like a still, wet mouse in her palm.

Never in her life has Amy spent so much time scrubbing her scalp with shampoo or rinsing out conditioner. She is permanently in a shampoo ad, except for her swollen, leaky breasts, and her soft, pouchy belly. She wants to embrace this softness, this roundness, her areolas darker than they'd ever been, though she can't remember what colour they'd been before, and her nipples larger, longer, maybe? She can't remember her old breasts, but she knows they weren't these ones. These ones aren't hers. She doesn't want to look at them. She doesn't want Max to look at them, though she doesn't hesitate whipping one out to nurse Alice on a park bench, or at the coffee shop, or wherever.

She combs conditioner through her hair and worries about Jim—is he eating? How's his skin? Is he in pain? Is he scared? She can't bear to think about him, or Fran, scared. Amy's never seen either of them scared—sad, mad, happy, everything else, yes, but never scared. Fran says Jim isn't up for visitors, so Amy sends them links to radiation-friendly smoothie recipes and pictures of Alice, and photos from their last summer tour.

Her hair is still wet when she joins Max on the couch. He's got a piece of peach pie on the coffee table. Alice is sleeping and Amy has a few hours before she'll be up again to nurse.

"I need to get some work done with Hugo," Max says, handing Amy a fork.

Hugo is a topologist who lives just outside of Paris, and they've been working on papers together since Max got his job at Waterloo.

"Okay," Amy says slowly, picking at a piece of crust.

Max doesn't say anything.

"Wait, you're not planning on going to Europe right now, are you?"

"Well, no, not just me," he says. "I was thinking we could all go."

"What? Max! Seriously?"

"It could be fun," he says.

"The time difference, for one, would be a nightmare, and god, Alice cries all night. We'd be kicked out of any hotel we stay in."

"They love kids there."

"Maybe in Spain, or Italy. Not in France."

"Hugo said it would be fine."

"Oh, I'm glad he'll be putting Alice to bed every night. Sounds great. Honestly, there's no way, Max. I can't even believe you'd think it was a possibility."

"Naheed and Rachel took Alim to Seoul when he took his sabbatical."

"A, she's a trailing spouse, so she can just follow him around, and b, Alim was at least three when they went. It's different with a baby, Max."

He doesn't say anything.

"I'm not flying across the ocean so you can hang out with Hugo while I'm trapped in a hotel room with a crying baby."

"We could get a flat for a month. I was thinking it could be a nice vacation."

"Vacation? Jesus, Max! No, and besides, Jim is still in treatment. I can't just leave the country." All of the calm from her shower is gone.

"Okay, okay, I thought it could be fun."

"It would *not* be fun, at least not for me. And isn't the whole point of the internet so that you don't have to travel to work?"

"It's different in person," he says. "Whatever, it's fine. I'll see if he can come here."

Amy leaves her pie unfinished and crawls into bed. She's a version of tired she wouldn't have believed a few years ago. A deep, bone-weary tired. She's tired of being tired. She's tired of complaining about it, but it's like weather—omnipresent, immersive. It's like rain that falls for three weeks, and then four weeks and then forever. How could she not talk about it? How could this ever become normal? But here she is.

She's started to lose words. Simple words, important words, names of people and things and ideas. She forgot the Brigade's tour manager's name one afternoon and had to look it up in her email, even though she spent years on the road with Cora. Worst of all, the tired edges out any hope of writing a new song or thinking beyond Alice's next nap. She can barely think about tomorrow, and here's Max assuming they could pack up and go to Europe just like that.

Everyone says babies are hard on marriages, and she's starting to wonder if they should've done more work before getting pregnant, if they should've waited. Would that mean they'd be more on the same page now? She pulls a pillow overtop her head. But if they had waited, they wouldn't have Alice, and the thought of not having her is unbearable.

PART TWO

12

WHILE AMY WAS SHOOTING THE FOURTH SEASON of the Brigade TV show, Emily invited her to an afterparty at her musician boyfriend's house. Daniel played with BIKES—the band's full name was the Dovercourt Bicycle Collective, but everyone called them BIKES. Their first album was instrumental, the kind of album that all the hipster boys swooned over and critics didn't know what to do with, and were afraid of seeming like they didn't know what they were talking about, so they gave it good reviews. For their second album, *Free Wheel*, the founding members rented the same cottage where they recorded their first album and lived together for two months, writing and recording. Peaches joined them for one track, and one of the songs was picked up by Sun Life Financial and, just like that, they were a big deal. After that, they kept adding members and BIKES became the in-club of Toronto musicians.

Amy knew she shouldn't go to the party—her call time was 5:00 a.m., but Max was marking and she hadn't seen Emily in months and was desperate to spend some time with anyone outside the production crew.

When the cab pulled up to the lead singer's house, there was a knot of people smoking on the porch, and another clump in the driveway smoking weed. Inside, all of the guys were in skinny jeans with slouchy toques, and all of the girls there looked like Emily—lithe, with French-braided crowns and vintage dresses. Amy felt old, and she was, comparatively. At thirty-six, she had fifteen years on these kids, and she felt ridiculous in her jeans and striped top.

"I'll find us drinks," Emily said.

In the living room, a JUNO award sat on the mantle next to a bong.

"Here," Emily said, handing Amy a plastic cup full of beer. "How's it going? How's Max?"

"I thought his PhD defence was stressful," Amy told Emily, sipping her beer, "and then the post-doc applications, but it turns out this tenure thing is next level."

"Shit," Emily said.

"Yeah. I keep telling him that no one's been rejected for tenure in like, thirty years, but it doesn't help. Between him stressing out about publishing another paper before his tenure committee meets, and my shooting schedule, we don't really see a lot of each other," Amy said.

"You should take a weekend off and go somewhere."

"Ha," she said. "I don't even remember what having a weekend off is like."

Someone blasted Godspeed You! Black Emperor from the living room, and Emily finished her beer. "Want to wander?" she asked.

They eventually found Daniel on the back deck. He pulled Emily in for a kiss, and Amy stood, awkwardly looking at the flowerpot full of cigarette butts. The lead singer from Great Lake Swimmers was sitting on a patio chair with a woman who looked familiar.

"Dan, this is Amy. Ames, this is Daniel," Emily said.

Amy went to shake his hand, but he pulled her in for a hug, then kissed both of her cheeks.

"So good to meet you," he said. "You're the kids' musician, right?"

Amy smiled and wished for one night she didn't have to be the kids' musician.

"Yeah," she said. "I've heard a lot about you."

"All good things, I hope!"

Emily smiled and slipped her arm around his waist. "How was the show?" she asked.

"Fucking killer. So good. You have to come to our next one. Amelia, you, too."

"It's Amy," she said, but he was waving over the lead singer of BIKES.

Jason looked exactly like he did in all of the press photos—handsome in that clean-cut-generic-white-guy sort of way. He had a rockabilly haircut, all clean lines and a severe part, so much different than the shaggy mops that most of the other guys had.

"This is my girl, Emily," Daniel said.

Emily winced at the possessive and introduced Amy.

Jason had wide eyes and a huge smile, and Amy recognized that post-show adrenaline.

Jason and Daniel talked about the set, about some session drummer named Phil, about their upcoming Montreal show. Amy wanted to ask Emily about her new dance piece, about the cellist she was thinking of hiring if she got a Canada Council grant, but the guys were too loud. Eventually, Amy got bored

The Fun Times Brigade

of listening to them talk shop, so she excused herself under the pretense of getting more beer. What she really needed was water.

The kitchen was crowded and there was a thick blanket of pot smoke filling the room. The clock on the microwave said midnight and her 5:00 a.m. call was getting closer and closer. It was going to be a very long shoot day unless she got some sleep.

"Beer?" a woman with a bleached blond bob and a *Reading Rainbow* crop top asked, handing Amy a red Solo cup.

"Oh, thanks, but I'm okay," Amy said.

"No, you're clearly not. Your hands are empty, and I've got two," she said.

"Okay," Amy said and took the cup from her. "Thanks."

"I'm Samantha," she said.

"Amy."

"Nice to meet you," Samantha said, holding out her beer. They clinked plastic cups. "So do you know anyone here?"

"My friend is dating—well, not dating, I don't know, seeing?—the BIKES drummer."

"Daniel." Samantha nodded.

"Yeah. I came with her. And you?"

"Yeah, I know a few people here," she said.

"Wait," Amy said, feeling like a complete idiot. "You're the bassist. For BIKES."

She nodded.

"I'm so sorry. Of course I recognize you."

"Oh, don't apologize. There's like a thousand people onstage at any given show."

"I know, but—"

"So, what do you do, Amy? Or, what's the question we're supposed to ask that's not capitalist and career-focused? What do you do that brings you joy?"

"Ha," Amy said. "Joy, eh?"

"Right? Someone—a complete stranger—asked me earlier tonight what fulfills me and I was like, what, are you my fucking therapist? But really, what do you do?"

Amy almost lied. She almost said she was an accountant, but Samantha was so open and friendly. "I'm a kids' performer."

"Performer, like juggling and riding a unicycle?"

Amy laughed. "I wish. I play"—she paused—"guitar, ukulele, you know, kazoos. I'm great on the kazoo."

"You're on that show! The Fun-something. My sister's kid loves that show."

"The Fun Times Brigade," Amy said, equal parts flattered Samantha knew of the Brigade, and mortified, especially in this room filled with real musicians.

"And you're married?" Samantha glanced down at Amy's ring.

She nodded and thought about Max sitting in his office with Method Man blaring in his headphones.

"Here I was, thinking I could just hit on you, but you're fucking married."

Amy felt her neck starting to flush, delighted that the BIKES' bassist wanted to hit on her.

"Well, if I can't take you home, we might as well play some music, right? Come," she said, pulling Amy out of the kitchen.

"I don't know," she said, but followed Samantha upstairs.

The first room wasn't a bedroom, but an empty room with instruments and a bunch of amps. A guy in a toque had a guitar plugged in, and someone else was playing keys. Samantha walked in and pulled a guitar off the wall and handed it to Amy. The guys didn't stop playing. Samantha took a bass. Amy couldn't remember the last time she'd jammed with strangers. She was drunk enough that it overrode her hesitancy, and the music was loud enough that she could barely hear herself.

"Yeah, girl!" Samantha yelled over the music.

Amy didn't even know what she was playing, but her fingers were on the frets, and it made some sort of drunken sense.

Eventually, she ducked out of the room briefly to text Emily that she was jamming with Samantha upstairs, and Emily texted back and said she was going to head out with Daniel.

You told me to remind you about your 5am call, she wrote.

It was two thirty. "I've got to go," Amy yelled into the room. Samantha looked up and Amy gestured to her watch, to the stairs.

Samantha put her bass down and came out in the hall. "You're going already?"

"I have to be on set at five."

"Oh god. Well, good luck to you." She handed Amy her phone. "Put in your number."

The next morning, while Amy was trying desperately not to fall asleep in the makeup chair, her head pounding despite the handful of Advil the hair person gave her, she got a message from Samantha.

That was so much fun last night, even if you are straight. You should play with us. We're doing a little tour to Montreal, but when we get back. I talked to Jason about it. He's totally into it.

Jason Evans wanted her to play with them?

Amy copied the text and sent it to Emily. *Is she asking me to play with BIKES?*

Yeah, she is. You going to do it?

Of course I am, Amy wrote back.

YOU'RE GOING TO BE IN BIKES!

Stop it. I'm going to go to one rehearsal.

13

AMY TRIED TO NAP IN HER TRAILER WHILE THE crew was doing takes of a school group making paper airplanes, but she was too excited to sleep. The BIKES rehearsal was that night, and she was counting down the minutes. After she got home from set, she tried on a dress, but was afraid she looked cute, so she put on the same jeans she'd worn to the BIKES party.

She took a selfie in the mirror and sent it to Emily.

You're overthinking it, Emily wrote back. *No one's going to care about what you wear. They just want to play with you.*

They just want to play with me, Amy told herself in the mirror. She looked at Samantha's Instagram—her bleached blond hair was effortlessly shaggy, and she had the most perfect denim jacket. Amy scrolled, trying to see if jeans and a grey T-shirt were going to be okay, and found a picture of Samantha with her arm around Tegan, or maybe Sara. Did she date one of them?

"You look very hipster chic," Max said when Amy went into his office to say goodbye.

"Stop it."

"You look good," he said.

"Lipstick or no lipstick?" she asked.

He shrugged. Amy texted Emily. *STOP OVERTHINKING IT*, she wrote back. But then sent a lipstick emoji.

"I can drive you over," Max said.

He was sitting at his desk with assignments spread out in front of him, his blue pen interrupting indecipherable pencil scrawls.

"I'm okay," Amy said. "I've already called a cab."

"You sure?"

The thought of him dropping her off made Amy feel like when her dad insisted on dropping her off at school dances, then she felt guilty. "You're in the middle of marking, I'm good."

"You could take the car."

"I'm okay," she said. She didn't want to look like some suburban mom showing up in a Volvo. "Cab's on its way."

Amy knocked on the front door, but when no one answered, she let herself in and stood awkwardly in the entryway with her guitar. There was a pile of shoes—Converse and combat boots and worn-out Stan Smiths.

The living room was full of people, and there was a case of beer on the floor near the kitchen. Amy recognized a few people from the band's web page—Jesse, the horn player who used to play with the Weakerthans; Robin, the trans guy who played keys on their last album; and Joseph, who played on the first two albums but then took a break. Everyone looked like they had just rolled out of bed, except for one of the singers, Sandra, who was standing in the corner smoking a joint with a guy Amy didn't recognize. She had on bright red lipstick and her bangs were immaculate. She wore a short silver dress with a Peter Pan collar, and Amy was relieved she hadn't worn the flowered dress she'd briefly considered.

Amy didn't see Samantha, but Julie Doiron was sitting on the couch, bent over her guitar. Julie fucking Doiron! She was an indie legend.

"Hi," Christophe said, extending his hand. He was the lead singer and was taller than Amy expected, wearing a slouchy grey toque and a flannel collared shirt. He had a waxed moustache with symmetrical curls.

Amy put her guitar down and shook his hand. "Thanks so much for having me," she said, wishing she didn't sound like she was at a business conference.

"Can you remind me of your name again?" he asked.

"Amy, sorry. I'm Amy."

"Amy," he said, trailing off.

"Amy Scholl."

He nodded, but she could tell he had no idea who she was.

"Samantha asked me to come," she said and wanted to crawl into a hole. Of course Christophe Williamson wouldn't know who she was.

"Oh, wait, you're the kids' musician! Jason mentioned something about you coming."

Amy nodded.

"I didn't recognize you without the pigtails."

She hadn't worn pigtails on the show since the first season.

"Guys! It's Fun Times Amy!"

She really didn't want to be Fun Times Amy, but everyone in the living room turned toward her, and someone shouted, "Welcome!"

"Amy!" Samantha came out of the kitchen. "I'm so glad you made it!" She hugged Amy and handed her a beer and Amy had never been so relieved to see someone she barely knew. "Everyone, this is Amy."

The Fun Times Brigade

"Oh yeah, from TV!" Nathan or Joseph, she couldn't remember, said from next to the amp. "My kids love your show."

She said thank you and took a sip of beer. It was lukewarm.

"Jennifer Castle might be coming, too," Samantha said, "but she's recording something with Chilly Gonzales, so she might not make it."

Jennifer Castle! Amy tried to keep her face composed.

"All right!" Jason shouted. "We're going to start in five. And Mary from *Exclaim!* magazine is here to film rehearsal. They're going to do a feature before our Toronto Island show."

Amy reflexively put down her beer. She could hear Ben's voice warning her that the show could be cancelled because of it, but fuck it. She was playing with BIKES tonight, and Ben had no jurisdiction over what she did here. She picked it back up, drank it fast, then helped herself to another.

"All right. We'll warm up with 'The Studio off Dundas Street,'" Christophe said. "You can play tambo," he said, handing Amy a tambourine. She had never heard anyone call it a "tambo" before.

Daniel counted them in and Amy's arms prickled with goosebumps. She wished her twenty-year-old self could see her now.

The song was on BIKES' last studio album, and the chorus was easy enough to pick up—"Leave Dundas behind, leave it all behind. I will meet you there, I will meet you there."

While Jason noodled around with his guitar part for "White Squirrel," Nathan, the trumpet player in the threadbare Orange Crush T-shirt handed everyone another beer. Amy knew she shouldn't have another—she was shooting the episode's knock-knock jokes in the morning and beer did her skin no favours on camera, but she took one anyway.

"I wrote something," Nathan said after Jason finished.

"Awesome. You know we're always open to new tunes," Jason said. "Let's hear it."

"It'll need guitar and bass, definitely drums, but you know, I'm open to whatever," he said.

"Let's hear it," Joseph said from the couch.

Nathan moved over to the keyboard and sang without playing first, and then introduced the piano mid-song, the keys building. He was asking someone to sit next to him, to go home with him, to let the night spill out like ink in milk. It was so beautiful it was almost unbearable.

"I like it," Jason said when the song was done.

Joseph nodded.

"Yeah, I love the chorus," Sandra said, and Julie Doiron agreed.

Christophe nodded thoughtfully. "I'm not sure it's the right fit," he said. "It's almost too dreamy, you know?"

"Okay, yeah, totally," Nathan said quickly. "Just playing around with stuff."

"Anyone else have anything?" Jason asked.

No one said anything, and Samantha handed Nathan a joint.

They played a few more songs from BIKES' most recent album, and then one instrumental song from their first album. It was long and felt a bit self-indulgent. There was no structure to it, no focus, it seemed to Amy, but then what did she know?

Just after midnight, Amy slipped upstairs to the washroom. It reminded her of living at the house near the market where her roommates would never clean, and the toilet stank of piss. She put the seat down, but hovered above the seat, not wanting to actually sit down.

Still rehearsing, she wrote to Max.

Still marking, he wrote back.

Julie Doiron is here!!!

???

Indie singer-songwriter from back in the day. Em was obsessed with her.

The Fun Times Brigade

Someone knocked on the door.

"Just a sec!"

Amy flushed the toilet and washed her hands. The only towel was a threadbare beach towel hanging on the back of the door. It was damp and smelled like mildew.

I feel like a fucking musician!! Amy wrote to Max, but then deleted. It sounded twee when she wrote it out. *Don't stay up*, she wrote instead. *I'll text when I'm in a cab.*

14

DURING ONE OF HER MIDDLE-OF-THE-NIGHT internet searches about bottle-feeding, Amy stumbles on an article about the importance of socializing babies. *It tends to happen naturally through play dates with your mom friends*, the article says. But other than Julie, Amy doesn't have any mom friends, and she definitely doesn't know anyone with a baby the same age as Alice. The article insists it *plays an important role in childhood development, building confidence and social skills.* "Fuck," she says under the hum of the white-noise machine. Max is sleeping in his office, and Alice grunts in her sleep in the bassinet beside the bed. *Starting at three to four months, babies need to start broadening their horizons and interacting with other infants*, Amy reads.

In the morning, Max insists they don't have to worry about socializing Alice yet. "She's still so little," he says.

"She's almost four months," Amy tells him.

The Fun Times Brigade

She sends Max the article, even though she knows he won't read it. Julie tells her to go to Baby Time at the library. Amy's hesitant at first, but it's close by and it's only forty-five minutes, and what else is she going to do on a Wednesday morning? She loads up the bottom of the stroller during Alice's first nap and finds her library card. If she chickens out, she can always get a few picture books for Alice and then it won't be a wasted trip.

Of course on the one day Amy wants to leave the house, Alice sleeps later than usual and then takes forever to nurse, and as soon as Amy's got the stroller down the porch stairs, Alice poops everywhere—an up-the-back, blow-out poop mommy bloggers write jokey posts about. But it isn't funny. It's gross and Alice kicks mid-change, and then both of Amy's hands are covered in poop. There's poop in Alice's hair, but there's no time to give her a bath, so Amy uses a wipe and tells herself it's just milk poop. It's fine.

She feels guilty, though, pushing Alice down the street with poop in her hair.

There's no room for strollers in the foyer of the library, so Amy wheels the stroller back outside. She's terrified someone will steal it, but the only other option is to turn around and go home and she's already come this far. She can't bail now.

Alice is still fussy, so Amy bounces her, and follows a mom with a tank top that says BOY MOM down the stairs. Amy adds her sandals to a huge pile of shoes, wishing she didn't have chipped nail polish from weeks ago. She's here for Alice, she reminds herself. She used to run these. It's going to be fine. And besides, it's not even an hour.

There are at least forty people—moms, and a few nannies—sitting cross-legged, babies crawling and nursing and chewing on pacifiers. Amy finds a small bit of carpet in the corner and spreads a muslin down in front of her like everyone else has done.

"He's in the ninety-seventh percentile for weight, ninety-second percentile for height," Amy hears one mom saying and tries not to balk—Alice is in the fifteenth percentile.

"Did you hear about the BabyCity Easy Walk stroller recall?" another mom asks. "Kids are choking on the bar thing."

Amy feels a rush of relief that they got the Yulla Kid stroller.

"I heard a kid died."

Amy smooths Alice's non-existent hair over her head and kisses her fontanelle.

"They want to start a class action or something."

Amy overhears BOY MOM talking about French immersion, and it takes her a moment to realize she's talking about school-school, not daycare. How is anyone thinking about kindergarten and school buses when their babies aren't even crawling yet? But two moms have already done walk-throughs of their local schools, and BOY MOM is planning on moving in the next year so she's in the right catchment area.

Amy's relieved when the librarian walks in. She is tall and elegant, with high cheekbones and short red hair. Amy is suddenly desperate to be her friend. She'll go up afterward and introduce herself. She'll totally know the Brigade if she's a children's librarian and Amy can offer to bring in some CDs or do a signing. But after the librarian does her Raising Readers spiel, she introduces Brenda, a short woman with blond hair who's been trying to connect her phone to the speakers, and leaves the room.

Brenda's voice is nasal and flat when she starts singing "The Wheels on the Bus." She rolls her fists over each other, but not in time with the music. She opens and closes her hand-doors off the beat. Amy tries to block her out by smiling at Alice and making her little fist tell the people to move on back. The librarian doesn't pause, but goes straight into "Baby Beluga," then "Skinnamarink," which is a closing song, never the third in a set.

When Brenda finally stops singing, she pulls out a book. "This is a story about a lion and a rabbit," she says. Amy sits Alice up higher on her lap, even though they're five babies deep and there's no way she'll ever be able to see the illustrations. Hell, Amy can't see the illustrations.

When she played shows with the Brigade, Amy saw the women in the audiences as only moms—she didn't give their worlds beyond their kids a single thought. But now she wishes they all had name tags, not with their names, but with what they did in the world before they listened to stories about lions and rabbits and lifted up babies to smell their bums. Amy pegs the woman next to her with the huge engagement ring as a lawyer. She imagines the woman in front of her is an artist—she looks thoughtful, and artsy with her messy, but still somehow chic bun. The woman next to her is a VP of something important, PR maybe. It's bizarre to think that these women used to spend their days thinking big thoughts, doing work that made companies a lot of money, work that mattered, or at least was valued by someone, and now they just sit around and listen to stupid generic stories read by a woman who doesn't pause long enough for the babies in the front row to see the illustrations, but everyone around her is taking it in like it they're in a board meeting and it's a PowerPoint presentation that their fiscal year depends on.

Alice starts whimpering, a whine that will turn into a full-scale wail if Amy doesn't do something fast. She scoops her up and bounces her, but Alice won't settle. She isn't supposed to nurse for at least another hour and a half, but Amy's too far away from the door to be able to duck out if Alice starts ratcheting up, so she pulls her shirt down and unclips her bra.

Brenda says the walking and crawling babies can come up and play freeze dance. They seem impossibly large and capable, these twelve-month-olds, and Brenda flicks through her phone until she says, "Ready? And go!"

It's the trumpet intro to the *Big Band* version of "The Crayon Song." Amy's cheeks flush and she ducks her head over Alice. But no one knows who she is. These babies are too young to watch the Brigade TV show, and she doesn't look anything like Brigade Amy with her maternity tank top and no makeup.

The tuba line thuds.

"Dancing, twirling, skating, swirling crayons." Brenda pauses the music just before the trombone slide, and the kids don't freeze. Of course they don't. They're way too young to understand freeze dance. She starts it back up again, singing nasally over Amy's, Fran's, and Jim's voices.

"Yellow met Red and they gave a high-five and they did a little dance and they did a little jive."

Amy wants to sing Fran's harmony. She wants to point out the trombone part at the bridge, and the dueling trumpet section that took way too many takes. Instead, she sings quietly into Alice's wispy hair, afraid if she catches anyone's eye, she won't be able to stop herself from telling them that she wrote this, that this is her singing, her playing the kazoo.

The librarian cuts the music off before the final chorus. *Wait!* Amy wants to yell out. Let the kids hear Jim's amazing guitar work at the end.

"And we'll see you next week," the librarian says, her hands clasped at her heart.

Amy unlatches Alice and does up her bra. Alice starts fussing, and Amy has to bounce her on her hip while she finds her sandals in the bottlenecked, shoe-strewn hall.

At the landing at the top of the stairs, a mom with a baby in a sling puts her hand on Amy's arm. She's got tight curly hair and bright pink lipstick. "Wait, are you—"

The Fun Times Brigade

Amy wants to yank her arm back. She wants to rush out the door. She doesn't want to be recognized, not looking like this, with bags under her eyes and the stretched-out maternity tank top she wore to bed last night.

"You are! You're"—Curly Hair waves her hand—"from the Fun Times Brigade! I thought it was you in there."

Amy nods and lifts Alice up on her hip. "Amy," she says, putting on a bright smile she hasn't used since the Brigade's last show.

"Amy! Right!"

"That's me," Amy says, trying to see if there's a way she can get out of this politely, but the woman is standing in front of the door. If she were Jim, she'd just walk away.

"Oh my god, this is amazing. This is so amazing! And we just sang your song in there! How cool is that? My oldest is the biggest fan! I mean, me too, but holy shit. Whoops, I shouldn't be swearing in front of your baby. Sorry, I'm so sorry."

"It's okay," Amy says.

"I read her birth announcement on Facebook. Alice, right?"

Amy nods and pats Alice's back, wishing she could leave.

"I watch your show with my oldest," Curly Hair says. "I think we've watched every single episode about three hundred times! God, that one on Centre Island is his favourite—when you're singing on the Ferris wheel? That's the best."

"Thanks," Amy murmurs.

"But you're not over," Curly Hair says. "The band's not done-done, right?"

"Oh, no. Just a little break until Alice is a bit older," Amy says. They had decided to keep Jim's diagnosis private. "We've got some stuff planned for the new year."

"Ooh, what? I've got to get tickets for Milo if you're doing a show in the city. He'll love it."

"We're still firming up dates," Amy says, shifting Alice to the other hip.

"Of course. Of course. And then the next generation can be fans, too," Curly Hair says, hiking her diaper bag up on her shoulder. "Right, Elliot? You get to see the Fun Times Brigade, too!"

"I'm so sorry, but I've really got to get going," Amy says.

"Oh my god, of course. Could we maybe have a picture before you go? Milo will freak."

Amy smiles brightly the way she knows Fran would, and pretends her tank top doesn't smell like sour milk. "Sure."

Curly Hair asks a man walking into the library to take a picture. After looking at it, she gets him to take another. "Can I hug you?" she asks Amy after she's approved the photo.

Amy forces a smile. "Sure."

They side hug awkwardly, their babies smushed between them and Amy rushes out the door, into the blazing heat. She straps Alice into her stroller—thank god it's still there—in record time and starts down the block. She pulls out her phone. It's only twelve. That was the longest hour of her life. She decides as she sprint-walks home that she's not going back to Baby Time. She'll go over to Julie's on the weekends so Alice can be around another baby—Leo's only fifteen months older. That'll have to do.

15

AFTER EVERY BIKES REHEARSAL, AMY JOINED THE band on a tour of dive bars where Sam or Sandra knew the bartenders. They'd finish one pitcher, then another, and Sam would hand out shots, and, even though there was no room, they'd move the tables and dance.

"Oh my god, I love this song!" Amy yelled to the ceiling of the Dirty Opossum when "Be My Baby" came on.

"What even is this?" Sam asked.

"The Ronettes!" Amy yelled. She had done a lip-synch to this song for her Grade 7 talent show and still knew the choreography.

"Are they're playing it ironically?" Sandra asked.

Amy passed out on the couch when she got home, and the room was spinning when she woke up.

"Jesus Christ," Max said the next morning, thumping down the stairs. "I was scared shitless when I woke up and you weren't home."

The Fun Times Brigade

"I was here," Amy mumbled into the couch cushion. Her mouth was so dry it was hard to make out words. She reached for her water glass, but knocked it over.

"Are you still drunk?" Max asked.

"Fuck. No. I mean yes." Amy got up to get a cloth to clean up the water.

In the kitchen, Max turned on the coffee grinder. It was a saw inside Amy's skull.

"I'm going to bed," she said.

"Don't you have a shoot today?"

"Not till later," she mumbled.

"Are you going to be home for dinner?" he asked.

"I think so. I don't know. Text me," she said, climbing the stairs, too hungover to think about eating.

He texted Amy from work that day and insisted she double-check that playing with BIKES wasn't in breach of her Brigade contract.

"It's fine," she said, showing him the stapled papers she'd signed years ago when he got home. "See?"

And so, at the next BIKES rehearsal, when Jason handed her a creased piece of paper—a contract, Amy realized after smoothing it out—she signed it. She had finally signed a contract with a record label, though technically, it was a contract with BIKES, who had a contract with a record label. There wasn't much on it—just that she would get paid for shows, but not rehearsals, and the album they were going to record would have a separate agreement.

Amy wondered, after she'd signed it, if she should've run it by Ben first, but he'd been such an asshole lately, tacking on meet-and-greets to every single show without so much as a heads up, and refusing to talk to production about the increasingly early shoots.

"My dream of signing with a label has finally come true," she said to Max when she got home. She poured champagne into the coupes they got in a flea market in France a few years ago when she tagged along on one of his research trips. "And now I'll get to play for real audiences!"

"Brigade audiences are real," Max said.

"You know what I mean."

"You don't have to be disparaging about them."

"I'm not. I'm just excited to play for adults."

Max shrugged and took the glass she handed him.

"Okay, imagine that all you ever wanted to do was teach university math classes," Amy started.

"That *is* what I want to do."

"Right, so then imagine that you still got to teach math, except you were teaching kindergarten."

"It's not really apples to apples," he said.

"Yeah, it is. I've always wanted to play music-music, not kids' music, except I got my break playing kids' music and now I finally have a chance to play music-music and I don't need you shitting on that."

"I'm not shitting on it," he said. "I just don't want you to sell short all the stuff you've done with the Brigade."

"Can we just celebrate?" she asked, raising her glass. The bubbles sparkled on the surface.

The champagne made her head feel light, and she got Max to take a picture of her raising her glass. *To exciting new projects*, she wrote as the caption, then added #*BIKES*. Ben was going to be furious that she was holding a glass of champagne, but whatever, it was her personal Instagram, and she wasn't just a Brigade musician anymore.

Ben didn't say anything about the photo, and seemed amused by Amy joining BIKES.

"Good for you," he said on set, and then asked if they were looking for management.

Amy shook her head. "They're more..." she waved her hand. They were like Jim was about labels, but with any kind of authority or management. They used the Weakerthans manager to look over contracts, but for the most part, Jason and Christophe insisted on doing things their way. They said they had enough experience from all their years in the music industry.

At first, Ben didn't mind Amy ducking out of a few late shoots, but then he started getting annoyed by the circles under her eyes and her exhaustion from juggling late-night BIKES rehearsals with 5:00 a.m. call times.

"Come on, Ames," he said in her trailer one afternoon when she was trying to take a nap over the lunch break. "You're letting us all down here."

"I *always* forget my lines," Amy insisted. "You know that. Everyone knows that. It's why I do the knock-knock joke thing."

"You just don't have enough energy. You're flat."

"Okay, okay. Just let me sleep now and I'll be fine this afternoon."

"And don't be late tomorrow."

"I won't!"

Amy didn't tell him that she was going to play BIKES' Island show but let him know about the Montreal tour she was missing because they had a Brigade show in Hamilton the same weekend.

"Do you want praise for following through with your commitments?" he asked. She'd never seen him so sour.

"No, I just wanted you to know that the Brigade is still my priority."

He didn't say anything.

"I mean, he's just doing his job," Max said when Amy called him from her trailer.

"I guess, but he doesn't have to be such a dick about it."

Amy picked at the salad a PA had brought her from craft services. "Any word if that journal is going to take your paper?"

"No. Naheed keeps telling me not to worry about it, but I don't know. I think Richard is going to screw me over." Richard was one of the most senior members of the math department.

"He is not."

"He hates me. Well, he hates Audrey, and so me by extension."

"If he hates your PhD supervisor, then he shouldn't be allowed on your committee," Amy said. There was a knock on her trailer door. "I've got to go, but I'll see you tonight," she said. "You should listen to Naheed."

Max wasn't home when Amy got in from the studio. *Have you left yet?* she texted him.

She didn't hear back, so she made herself a grilled cheese sandwich and ate it while trying to memorize her knock-knock jokes for tomorrow's shoot. Her phone buzzed just as she was getting ready to leave for band practice.

Leaving in 5. A bunch of students came by freaking out about their final assignments.

I ate already. I'm heading over to Jason's, she wrote back. *We're like ships passing in the night*, she typed, but then deleted. Who was she to complain?

Fran didn't say anything about BIKES, but Jim couldn't help himself from telling Amy what he thought. "Their guitar work is sloppy, and their sound is muddled," he said over the craft table. He was picking the pretzels out of the party mix. "There's too much going on."

But that was the point, Amy argued. The point wasn't to be spare and perfect, it was to have a big, loud, messy sound. "It's about the experience," she said. She had heard Christophe say that in an interview once.

"It's self-indulgent," Jim said.

"Everyone loves BIKES," Amy said.

"No, *you* love BIKES," he said.

"Yeah, I do. It's really fun to play with them, and it reminds me that playing music can be fun."

"*Our* music is fun, Amy," he said. His voice was sharp, and Amy knew she had crossed a line.

"I know. That's not what I mean. It's just nice to play something different."

"You don't even get to play guitar," he said.

Amy wished she hadn't told Fran about the "tambo."

"Those big bands, they just use people like you."

"They're not using me, Jim. I'm a grown woman and I want to play with them, and they want me to play with them."

"As long as you're sure of that."

"And why do you think they wouldn't want me? Because I'm a shit musician?"

"I didn't say that!"

"Well, it's what you're implying."

"Amy, of course it's not. I just think that some big bands are run by big egos, and they just want accolades and don't really care how they get them."

"Well, that's not BIKES," she said.

"Okay, okay." Jim raised his hands in surrender.

What right did he have to make her feel insecure? And what did "people like you" even mean? She wasn't some naive twenty-year-old. And even if she were, who cared? She was playing with the biggest band in Toronto.

She wanted to tell Max what Jim thought about BIKES, but he wasn't home when she got in from the studio. She checked her phone—they had plans to order in—but he hadn't texted.

Amy ordered burritos and poured out the milk that had soured in the fridge, and threw out the container of fried rice that had a fuzzy layer of mould on top. The burritos arrived and there was still no text from Max, so she ate hers while scrolling through her phone.

"You said you were going to be home for dinner," Amy said when he finally got in. "You didn't even bother to text that you were going to be late."

"I had to finish up some marking," he said.

"And you couldn't have just brought it home?" Her voice was loud and sharp.

"Whoa, Ames, easy."

"Max, we had plans. We were going to have dinner, *remember*?"

"I'm sorry I was late, but I feel like you're making this a bigger deal than it is."

"It might not be a big deal to you, but it's a very big deal to me," Amy cut him off, letting the momentum of her hurt take over. "You're never home."

"What are you talking about? *You're* never home."

"I'm home right now, and we had plans tonight. It's been in your calendar for weeks."

"I'm sorry. We were just ordering in. I didn't think it was that big a deal."

"You stood me up. And it makes it clear how little this"—Amy waved to the space between them—"matters to you."

"What are you talking about?"

"We were supposed to have brunch on Sunday, but you barricaded yourself in your office."

"Your rehearsal went so late on Saturday night."

"So? I was still up for brunch."

"I lost track of time. You just had to knock," he said.

"It's my responsibility to remind you that we had plans?"

"I was distracted. I'm sorry."

"You're sorry for ignoring me? Or you're sorry that you were distracted?"

"Both, I guess."

"This whole tenure thing is getting out of control. You're not the only busy person around here."

"Since when does partying with BIKES count as busy?"

Amy stared at him, stung. "Are you joking?"

"Look, while you're doing shots with like, twenty-year-olds, I've got an MIT prof breathing down my neck about the funding we're applying for."

"Oh, right, your work is *so* important and mine is inconsequential."

"Ames, you get wasted at every BIKES rehearsal."

"That is not true."

"Ever since you started playing with them, you've been acting like one of my undergrads."

"Are you kidding me? I'm shooting a hit TV show all day and playing music with a huge fucking band at night. You know what? I think you're just jealous. I have fun doing my work. I can be really good at it *and* have fun. Besides, how is me having some drinks after band practice any different than you getting wasted with the Chalice of Champions at Grad House and having to crash in Waterloo?"

"I haven't done that in months," he says.

Amy left the kitchen. *What's going on tonight?* she texted Samantha.

Just getting ready to go out. Wanna come?

Amy sent back a thumbs-up emoji.

Kk. I'll text you the address.

She made small talk with the cab driver to keep from crying, and by the time she got to the bar, Amy was ready for a night out. The Jumping Owl was underneath a laundromat, its walls covered in carved wooden birds.

"Amy!" Sam shouted, throwing her arms around her. "Everyone, it's Fun Times Amy!"

Sandra handed her a beer and launched into a story about the date she went on the night before.

"Quick FYI, that guy at the bar is totally checking you out," Sam said into Amy's shoulder.

Amy looked over. There was a blond guy who was maybe twenty-five, and Sam was right. He was looking at Amy.

"Oh my god," she said.

Sam laughed, "Chill out! You're hot! You're fun! Of *course* he's checking you out. Now go and get him to buy you a drink!"

"I'm married," Amy said, laughing.

"Oh, who cares. Just go and flirt with the hot blondie."

Amy thought of Max, alone at home, the hunch of his shoulders over a pile of obscure lemmas, but then remembered him telling her she was acting like one of his undergrads, insisting that his work was more important than hers. She walked up to the bar and ordered three shots of bourbon. Without saying anything, she handed one to Blondie, clinked it with hers and threw back the shot.

She was a musician, not an undergrad student. She was a real fucking musician.

16

AMY WAS THE FIRST ONE AT THE RECORDING studio on Saturday morning. When others did show up, they stood around and shot the shit and opened beers, even though it wasn't even 11:00 a.m. Amy didn't know how Christophe and Jason justified paying for the space and technicians when they weren't recording anything, but it was nice not to have Ben insisting on maximizing their studio time.

Amy asked if they'd laid the bed tracks, but Christophe looked at her like she was nuts.

"We're doing a more organic approach," Jason said.

After a few false starts, Christophe and Jason decided to save "Astrid" for another day and Amy got to sing back up on "The Longest Morning."

It was clear that Daniel wanted to just get out of there. He was short and curt and impatient between takes. Emily had broken up with him, and though she insisted it wasn't breaking up, she was going to Montreal for a creation process with the cellist who had played with Do Make Say Think. Apparently, Daniel thought they were together-together, and was heartbroken. He didn't say hi to Amy, and she didn't push it. The last thing she needed was to be implicated in the recording going sideways.

"I want to do vocals again," Christophe said to the control room. "This mic sounds a little stale. I'm thinking a Neumann 67, but I'm open to options. Darren," he called to the studio assistant, "set me up with a few in the booth. I'll do a take with each."

The rest of them sat around while Christophe tried the new mics. Amy flipped through her phone and texted Emily to see how her new dance piece was going. She took some photos of the studio and posted them to Instagram.

"Yup, the Neumann," Christophe said after listening to the entire track four times. "There's such a vintage quality to the sound." And he made Darren set up the new mic on the floor.

After Christophe was satisfied, Jason got everyone back on the floor and said he wanted to try a Taylor Swift cover. Amy thought he was kidding.

"We should pay homage to her artistry," Jason said. His look challenged Christophe to say something, but he didn't. "I was thinking maybe 'Bad Blood'?"

"'All Too Well,'" Samantha said quickly.

"'Fifteen,'" Nathan said.

Christophe raised an eyebrow.

"Fuck off. I like Taylor Swift," Nathan said.

"'I Knew You Were Trouble,'" Sandra said resolutely.

"Oooh, good one," Nathan said nodding.

"Yeah?" Jason asked. "Vote?"

"I Knew You Were Trouble" won and Jason got Nathan and Jesse to sort out a horn line.

"If we're going to do this, we need a male lead, you know, so it's not too facile," Christophe insisted. "It'll add to the vulnerability."

Sandra rolled her eyes, and Amy thought she was going to walk out.

After an intense debate, Christophe conceded that Sandra could sing lead with Samantha and Amy joining in at the chorus. Robin suggested playing with the tempo, and Christophe eventually agreed that it sounded best slowed down, mournful almost.

"Yes! We should definitely add it to the Island set list," Jason said.

"Wait, we can pay royalties for a Taylor Swift cover, but we can't get paid for rehearsals?" Robin asked.

"You get paid for shows. It's in your contracts," Christophe said.

"Except Joseph gets paid for rehearsals," Robin said quietly.

The studio tightened and everyone looked at Joseph, and then at Christophe and Jason.

"He has a family," Christophe continued.

"We're all here because we want to be," Jason added. "We're all committed, and if you don't want to be here, you don't have to be here."

"I lost my bartending job because of our Montreal gig," Samantha said.

"And you just bought an SUV," Nathan said to Christophe.

"That wasn't with band money," Christophe said.

"Look," Jason said, "we're all in this together. We're a band, a collective. Sure, we could have fewer people, and make a few hundred bucks more a show, but what would happen to our sound? We'd sound like every other band."

"But I could pay my rent," Sandra said under her breath.

"Pardon?" Christophe asked her, his eyes sharp.

"Nothing," she said.

"Do you get paid for your kids' band rehearsals?" Nathan asked Amy.

Everyone looked at her. She shook her head.

"You get paid for shows, though, right?"

Amy nodded. "We get cut of the box office, and record sales. But we also have to pay for tours, and our manager and stuff."

"But you get paid when you're on tour?" Nathan asked.

Amy nodded again, not sure if this was the right answer or not.

"We're going to have hits on this record," Jason said. "We've got a shit hot producer, and we've got a photographer who's shot for *Rolling Stone*, and we've got some really great concepts."

"And Jay and I are already talking to BMO," Christophe added.

A bank? That *was* a big deal. The Brigade had landed Crayola, and a Canadian deal with Pampers Pull-Ups for "Sittin' on the Potty," and, a few years ago, Proctor and Gamble bought the rights to "Wash Your Hands" for a North American campaign, but they could never land a bank.

"It's going to be good," Jason said.

"And we've got the Island show coming up and everyone will be paid for that show," Christophe added.

"Sam, I've got a friend who's looking for a bartender," Jason said. "I'll give him your number."

"Let's get back to the music," Christophe said. "That's why we're all here, isn't it?"

Jason passed around beer. No one looked at each other and the quiet was unnerving.

"We good?" Christophe asked the room.

Robin took a sip of his beer and Sandra stared at the floor, but Amy and Nathan and Samantha nodded.

"'Kay, let's make the best album yet this weekend, and then we'll all be rolling in it," Jason said and asked Sandra to sing "I Knew You Were Trouble" again.

Everyone was buzzed by 5:00 p.m., and Jason ordered pizza. By eight, Daniel and Jesse were drunk, and the sound was getting sloppy. Still, Christophe insisted they keep recording. "You never know what will come out in the mix," he insisted, and sent Darren out to get more beer. "Not the shitty stuff!" Jason called after him.

They wrapped just before midnight, and other than singing backup on the Taylor Swift cover, Amy had only played the tambourine. She was hoping someone would offer to share a cab, but she was so much farther west than everyone, so she called her own taxi.

"Bring the receipt and we'll expense it," Jason said.

Sandra shook her head. "Good luck with that," she said, and Amy decided not to even bother trying.

It was late when Amy got home, but Max was waiting with a bottle of champagne.

"What's that for?" she asked, getting a glass of water. She felt greasy from all the beer and pizza.

"*Annals* accepted the paper," Max said, beaming.

"Pardon?"

"My paper. Mine and Hugo's. It's been accepted. Into *Annals of Mathematics*! I can include it in my CV for the tenure committee."

"That's amazing," Amy said. He was so clearly relieved, and so proud of himself, it was impossible not to soften, even if she still wasn't ready to let go of their fight about his work being more important than hers.

"I was thinking, maybe we could celebrate this week? Like really celebrate. Dinner in the market, maybe? The French restaurant?"

"Yeah," she said, knowing her shooting schedule was ridiculous. "We'll find a day." She really needed to go to bed.

"To *Annals*," he said, pouring the champagne.

Amy raised her glass. "To tenure," she added.

"Don't jinx it," he said.

"Since when do you believe in jinxes?" she asked, sipping her champagne, but he was not having any of it. "Okay, okay, sorry. To *Annals*," she said.

It was twelve thirty by the time everyone rolled in on Sunday, and Amy was already on her third coffee and second round of Advil.

"Let's track drums," Jason said once everyone was at the studio.

Why were they all there if they were just going to record Daniel? It made no sense, but Amy had a new round of Brigade jokes, so she tried to focus on her script while Christophe and Jason and Daniel argued about the drum tracks in the control booth.

"I almost forgot," Christophe said, as they wrapped for the day. "Photo shoot next weekend! We're meeting on the roof of the car mechanic on Dupont, just east of Dufferin."

Amy looked at the shoot schedule on her phone. Fuck. Of course she was scheduled to be on set—Raffi was coming in as a special guest. Maybe she could bow out early on Saturday, say her mom was having a crisis or something. She couldn't miss the BIKES photo shoot. She couldn't.

17

"YOU SHOULD GET A NANNY," AMY'S MOM SAYS over coffee in the living room. She had shown up on the front porch without any warning. Amy was terrified the doorbell had wakened Alice, but Alice stayed asleep.

"A nanny?" Amy asks, confused.

"So you can get back to work!" her mom says. "I wish I had gotten a nanny. I can't even tell you the number of opportunities I had to say no to when you were small. Those opportunities won't come back around."

"Mom, Alice is only four months old," Amy says, though she doesn't know why she bothers. Her mom has always been clear that Amy's arrival put the brakes on her artistic career, though Amy isn't exactly sure what it curbed. Mom still showed her work at galleries all over the place, and there are so many pictures of her dad holding her up as a baby at various gallery openings.

The Fun Times Brigade

"I can work with Alice around," Amy lies to her mom and sips her coffee.

"But performing?" her mom asks, as if she knows exactly what keeps Amy awake at night.

"Jim needs to finish his treatment before I need to worry about this, and when we're touring, Max will take his sabbatical," she says, forcing a confident smile, not sure if that is actually going to happen.

"It's harder than it seems," her mom says.

Amy is grateful that Alice starts wailing through the monitor.

After her mom leaves, Amy puts Alice down in her vibrating chair and googles *musicians who are moms* to remind herself that it's possible, that musicians can have kids and not abandon their careers. Beyoncé, Mariah Carey. Of course *they* can do it, they have huge teams of people. She looks up *indie musicians who are moms*, but other than Julie Doiron, she doesn't recognize any of them. Alice squawks and Amy feels guilty for being on her phone.

But before she puts her phone away, she orders baby headphones. Alice kicks and grabs at the air. "That's right, baby girl, these are for when you come to Mommy's shows!"

She turns her phone over and pulls Alice on her lap. "Here's a book from Grandma." She opens up the first page. "Guess you can't have too many copies of *Brown Bear, Brown Bear*."

Alice hits the page with her fist.

"We can do this," Amy says into Alice's wispy hair. "We're a team."

18

"WE'RE GOING TO THE TOP DECK," SAMANTHA said, grabbing Amy's arm as they boarded the ferry. They stood on the deck, the wind whipping their hair. Samantha pulled out her phone and took a selfie of them with the CN Tower in the background.

"What did Christophe say was the hashtag?"

"#IslandBIKES, I think," Amy said.

"'Kay, I sent it to you."

Amy took out her phone and posted it too. *#IslandBIKES here we come!*

It was petty, but she hoped Ben would see it. He had been pissed when she told him about the show, but it was happening. It was all happening. She was about to play a sold-out show with the biggest indie band in Canada.

The city got smaller and the green of the island got bigger.

"Excuse me," a woman said, touching Amy's arm. "Are you Amy from the Fun Times Brigade?"

The Fun Times Brigade

Amy nodded.

"Olive, Olive, look, it's Amy!"

A small child with tight braids and a dress that was covered in strawberries looked up with the wide eyes of a Brigade fan.

"You're Amy!" she said.

Amy pasted a smile overtop of her annoyance. She wanted to be BIKES Amy, not Fun Times Amy today.

"And who are you?" Amy asked, kneeling down. She smiled and nodded and asked the kid what her favourite song was, and hated that Samantha and Sandra were watching. The mom asked Samantha if she could take a picture of the three of them.

"Say cheese!" Samantha said.

"Look who's famous!" Sandra said after the mom and daughter moved to the back of the boat.

"Sure, with the under-six crowd," Amy said, embarrassed.

The sound crew was still running lines when they got to the stage.

"Are you fucking kidding me?" Christophe asked. "Load-in was supposed to be done an hour ago."

"It's fine, it'll be fine," Jason insisted. "We still have plenty of time to sound-check."

Amy found some shade with Samantha and Sandra, and Nathan went off to find a porta-potty.

"Literally the worst part of outdoor shows, right?" Amy said, but Samantha was on her phone.

"Can we have some water?" Nathan called out.

"Rider's not here yet," Jason said. "It's coming. Just, just... can we please just get through this?"

"Let's go already," Christophe called out.

Everyone stood behind their mics. Except there wasn't one for Amy. She stood off to the side. She didn't know who to ask about a mic—Christophe was in the worst mood, and Jason was talking with the head tech.

"What are you doing?" Sandra asked.

"I don't have a mic," Amy said quietly.

"Oh, for fuck's sake." Sandra walked to the front of the stage and yelled, "Amy needs a mic."

"No, I have it here. Eight mics," the sound guy called back, checking a clipboard.

"Well, whoever wrote that list was wrong, and we need another."

Amy wanted the stage to open up and swallow her whole. "It's okay," she started.

"No, it's not," Samantha said.

Someone found a mic and a tech came onstage and set up a monitor. Amy thanked him profusely, but he wouldn't even look at her.

The stage was so hot and Amy wished she had a hat. Sweat was dripping down her temples.

"We're going to pass out if we don't get water," Robin said from behind the keys.

"There's nothing I can do about that now, okay?" Jason snapped.

"Can you ask someone?"

"Like who?"

Like a manager, Amy wanted to say.

"We only have a half hour," Jason said. "Just, let's focus, okay?"

"Check check," Christophe said into his microphone at the front of the stage. "Okay, so I'm going to need more monitor. Check check. More monitor. Testing, la-la. Yup, more please."

Jason wanted more monitor, and Daniel said he couldn't hear the horns or the bass. As soon as they tried to play, there was a screech of feedback.

"Fuck!" Christophe yelled. "Fix that, please!"

First rule Jim taught Amy on the road was to keep the tech crew happy if you wanted a good show. This tech crew was clearly not happy.

"I'm starving," Sandra complained.

"The food is coming," Jason said. "It's literally on a water taxi right now. Now, can we please just do this so we don't sound like shit tonight?"

They made it through half of their opening song before the sound crew took a union break.

"They're two hours late with load-in and now they get a break?" Christophe said.

"It's fine. We sound fine," Jason insisted, and ushered them offstage.

There was water waiting for them, and they all put back two bottles each. Jesse poured one on his head and shook his hair like a puppy. The food wasn't waiting for them though. There hadn't been anyone to meet the water taxi, and it was on its way back to the mainland.

"Seriously?" Jason yelled into his phone.

Sandra slumped on a picnic table. Amy rummaged around in her bag and found a sesame snap.

"Thanks," Sandra said.

Nathan put in a McDonald's order, even though Jason insisted the Thai food was on its way back. Both orders arrived at the same time, and the gates had already opened.

Amy hated eating right before a show, but she was so hungry that she couldn't not. She had a spring roll and some fries and checked her phone.

Merde, Emily had texted.

Break a... vocal cord? Julie had written.

She hoped Max would send something, but he hadn't yet. *Your ticket is with Fran and Jim's at the will call table*, she wrote to him.

Amy watched the opening act from the side of the stage and had to remind herself to breathe. Samantha handed her a joint, but she passed it on to Sandra, and before she knew it, they were being cued onstage. Jason and Christophe walked on first, followed by the rest of them.

"Welcome," Christophe started into the microphone. The cheering came at the stage like a tsunami, and the mess of the afternoon instantly fell away.

Amy's mic was stage right of Daniel's drum kit, in front of the horns. The audience was pitch black, and the stage lights shone much brighter in contrast. At Brigade shows, they played outside in the afternoon, or the house lights were up so they could see everyone, every clapping kid, every crying face. But this was a black swath at the edge of the stage—a cheering, screaming black void. Amy could finally prove to Fran and Jim and Max that all the late rehearsals and groggy morning shoots and missed brunches were worth it. This was happening. This was actually happening.

Jason took a swig of his beer. "Are you ready, Toronto?" he yelled, and the audience screamed louder.

The set opened with Daniel on the kick drum, and it pounded against Amy's sternum. Her arms prickled with goosebumps. Samantha was next with the bassline, and Amy could feel the swell of it. She kept her feet rooted as the guitar took over from Sam's bassline, the backbeats layering, Nathan's trumpet at the ready. The build was nearly too much—Amy felt like she was going to explode.

The Fun Times Brigade

The next two songs were a blur, and Amy almost forgot the tambourine parts of "The Long Drive North" and then it was time for the Taylor Swift cover. Jason's guitar started, with Robin on keys. Sandra started singing soft and quiet into the microphone, an almost-whisper. Amy could feel the crowd pause, still. Samantha looked over at Amy and they both leaned into their mic stands to harmonize. Amy's lips were so close to the microphone she could taste the metal. The tambourine shimmied next to her hip. The drums kicked in and the music edged Amy out of herself and she was suspended inside the song. It was everything.

The crowd was deafening and Amy let it roll over her, consume her. She imagined Max and Emily and Julie and Fran and Jim standing together, swaying and clapping, and maybe even singing along.

At the end of the set, they exited the stage and then went back on, and the crowd sang so loudly to "White Squirrel" that Jason and Christophe held their mics over the crowd.

At the end of their third encore, Jason yelled "Thank you, Toronto!" and that was it. They were done. Amy looked out again at the black swath. She didn't want to leave the stage. She knelt down and ripped off the painter's tape that read MIC 9.

"Good show," Jason said as they all filed offstage. His shirt was dark with sweat.

Christophe high-fived everyone, and Sandra looked over at Amy and Samantha, beaming. "Now *that* was a cover," she said.

"It was perfect," Samantha said.

"Fucking perfect."

Backstage there was beer and pot, and Sandra had some blue pills, though Amy didn't need any—she hadn't ever had a post-show rush like this. Her phone was blowing up—photos of the stage from friends and acquaintances. *#IslandBIKES* was taking over Instagram.

"Come," Samantha said, pulling Amy's arm. "We need to celebrate. Also, you have to meet my new lady."

They snaked through the cheering crowd, getting hugged by people along the way. It was loud and packed. Jason had two girls hanging off his arms, and Christophe was holding court by the keg. "Party time," Robin said, tapping his plastic cup to Amy's. It was too loud to really talk, but they yelled anyway, and Amy took the joint Samantha passed her.

Amy checked her phone. Max was by the entrance. She excused herself and eventually saw him and Emily in the crush of people. She waved and they threaded their way toward her.

"You were amazing," Emily said, hugging her. Amy leaned into her and grabbed Max's hand and squeezed it.

"So," Emily said, "was it awesome?"

"Oh my god," Amy said beaming. "The best. The actual best. It was so good."

"You looked amazing up there," Emily said.

"You really did," Max agreed.

Amy *knew* he'd think differently about BIKES after he saw them perform.

"And Fran and Jim? Did they leave already?"

Max glanced at Emily.

"What?" Amy asked.

Emily did a weird half-smile. "They weren't here," she said.

"Pardon?"

Max and Emily didn't say anything, and Amy hated that her brain was foggy from the weed.

"Did they say they were coming?" Emily asked.

"Well, kind of. I mean, they said something about babysitting Levi."

Max looked at Amy.

"Well, I still thought they'd come, at least one of them. I mean, it's my first BIKES show." Was it because she'd skipped the wrap party for a BIKES rehearsal? Were they mad because she kept talking about how the show was sold out, or because she didn't stick around for drinks with Raffi?

"Jim hates BIKES," Amy said flatly.

"No—" Max started.

"He thinks they're—" Amy corrected herself, "*we're* sloppy."

"Maybe it's just not their scene," Emily said.

But she was their bandmate. Amy was a third of the Brigade and they couldn't even reschedule babysitting to come and see her play?

"Let's get drinks," Amy said, tugging on Max's hand.

"I've got to get the MIT notes back by noon tomorrow. I'm already a few weeks late," he said. "Besides, you don't need to be dragging around your boring old math husband."

"Em, you're coming, right?"

"I think I've had my fill of BIKES afterparties, and I don't want to ruin Daniel's night."

Amy tried to swallow her disappointment as she watched them walk to the ferry and reminded herself how weird people got whenever Max said he did math. This way, there wouldn't be any awkward introductions or stilted conversations about terrible Grade 11 math teachers. This way, she wasn't old and married and boring. This way, she could be BIKES Amy. This way she could get wasted and forget about Jim and Fran. She fingered the mic tape in her pocket and headed back into the party.

Amy didn't remember how she got home. Someone—Nathan maybe, or Sandra—had organized a water taxi, and someone must've put her in a cab. She woke up on the couch, still in her stage clothes, with mascara all over the throw pillow. She desperately needed water.

She filled a glass, but the room was spinning and she had to hold on to the counter. She drank a full glass, then another. She splashed water on her face and rubbed at her eye makeup with a tea towel. The clock on the microwave said 7:28.

She needed to go back to sleep. She lay down and pulled a blanket over her and the next thing she knew, Max was standing over the couch.

"Morning," she said, groggily.

"It's noon," he said.

"Did you get your notes in?" Amy asked, standing up. Her stomach lurched and she had to run to the kitchen, where she vomited in the sink. "Fuck," she said. She turned the tap on.

"I'm fine," she called to Max, and tried to breathe through her nose so she wouldn't puke again. "Just give me a few minutes," she said, but felt the lurch of vomit returning.

She puked again.

Amy eventually made it upstairs, drank more water, and turned the shower on as hot as it would go.

When she got out of the shower, Julie had texted her. *You got written up in the Star!*

Amy clicked on the link.

The Dovercourt Bicycle Collective, led by Jason Evans and Christophe Williamson, flooded Toronto Island and played encores until the noise curfew forced them off the stage, it read.

Amy scrolled down.

Sandra Kim paired up with Samantha Varga on bass and guest member Amy Scholl (known for her role with kids' band the Fun Times Brigade) on backing vocals for a stunning cover of Taylor Swift's "I Knew You Were Trouble" and imbued the song with a whole new meaning.

The Fun Times Brigade

Amy's phone started ringing.

"A whole new meaning!" Julie said without saying hello. "You were amazing!"

"Thanks," she said.

"I'm so sorry we had to leave without saying hi. We had to get back to the babysitter. Were you celebrating all night?"

"Yeah, kinda."

"And today?"

"Max and I were going to Aunties and Uncles, but I'm way too hungover," she admitted.

"A small price to pay for being married to a rock star," she said.

Amy laughed but felt a twinge of guilt at Max's closed office door. It came back in a rush—Fran and Jim hadn't come. The bridge of Amy's nose started to burn.

"Ames?" Julie asked.

She couldn't stop the tears. "Jim and Fran couldn't drop their musical standards for even one night."

"I'm so sorry," she said.

"It was my first show."

"Don't let that ruin your night," Julie said.

Amy closed her eyes.

"Was it fun?" Julie asked.

"It was the best," she said and tried to remember the black swath, the cheering crowd, the thump of the kick drum.

"So there you go. Hold on to that."

A kid screeched in the background.

"I've got to go. Callum's hungry," she said. "But I'm taking you for lunch tomorrow. Saving Grace. Noon. I will see you there."

"Okay," Amy said.

Callum was getting louder.

"Go," Amy said. "I'll see you tomorrow."

19

THE BRIGADE SUMMER CIRCUIT STARTED RIGHT after the Island show. They were originally going to fly to Winnipeg, then get on the tour bus, but Ben booked a show in Thunder Bay and decided it was cheaper if they got on the bus in Toronto and drove.

"Nope," Amy said to her computer screen. She was still hurt about Fran and Jim not coming to the show, and she didn't know how she could act normal for an extra fourteen and a half hours.

Please book me a flight to Thunder Bay, she texted Ben.
The bus is organized, he wrote back.
Please book me a flight to Thunder Bay, she typed again.
Come on, Amy.
I would like a full day with my husband before going on tour for two months, she wrote, even though Max would be teaching.

"Ames, are you sure this is the hill you want to die on?" Max asked her.

"I'm not dying on any hills. I just don't want to have to act as if everything is okay with Fran and Jim any longer than I have to."

"You're going to have to get over this."

"They didn't come to my show, and they didn't apologize."

"Fran asked how it went."

"In a text. That is not an apology."

Ben got Amy a flight. She landed two hours before the show, and her cab pulled up to the concrete-and-glass monolith an hour and a half before they were supposed to be onstage. She could tell Jim was upset that she was late, but she took her time tuning her guitar onstage and glanced at the set list—"The Rainbow March" then "Fishy Fishy" then "Sittin' on the Potty." Same old, same old.

"Let's do this, fuckers," Jim whispered before heading onstage.

Fran smiled and squeezed Amy's arm.

They walked onstage, the house lights blaring, little kids clapping. Amy wanted to go back to the Island. She wanted the dark swath of the audience. She wanted screaming fans, and a stage so full there was barely any room to move. She played her ukulele, smiling until her cheeks hurt. She swayed to "The Sleeping Song" and marched to "The Teddy Bears' Picnic" and told her knock-knock jokes, but it all felt so flat, so juvenile.

They finished with "The Crayon Song" and headed into the wings. Amy started for the stairs, but the stage manager caught her.

"There's an encore," she said.

Amy sighed and walked back out with Fran and Jim and they played "Reggie the Friendly Raccoon."

No second encore, Amy prayed as she walked back to the wings. This time the stage manager let her down the stairs and she had her makeup off and was back in her jeans before Fran and Jim had even had a chance to make it into their dressing rooms. Amy feigned a headache and skipped the meet-and-greet in the lobby afterward. She could tell Fran wasn't happy about it, but she made a production of taking Advil and went through the stage doors and straight to the bus. The air conditioning was cranked up, and she crawled into her bunk and pulled the blanket over her.

The bus was moving when she woke up, and Amy had no idea where they were or how long she'd been sleeping. She checked her phone. Eight o'clock. She'd been sleeping for four hours. Fran and Jim were in the back of the bus, behind the sliding door. Amy could hear Jim playing the guitar. She should go and sit with them. She would be with them for the next two months. She needed to make this okay. But she didn't want to move. She didn't want to pretend things were okay.

First show down, a thousand more to go, Amy texted Samantha.

We're missing you! Sam texted back with a photo. Nathan was giving the camera the finger and Amy could see Sandra's knees in the corner.

Missing you too! Amy wrote back and wished she was back in Toronto, playing the tambo in Jason's living room.

Amy skipped the next meet-and-greet, and was halfway through a beer in the back of the bus when Fran and Jim joined her.

"What's going on?" Jim asked.

"Nothing," Amy said, her heart thudding in her chest.

"Ames," Fran said. "Something's going on."

"I'm fine," she insisted.

"You're clearly not fine," Fran said.

"We're a family," Jim said, "and we're worried about you."

"We're a family?" Amy asked, incredulous.
"Of course."
"If we're *family*, then why didn't you come to my show?"
"What show?" They both looked genuinely confused.
"What do you mean 'what show'? The BIKES show. On the Island."
"*That's* why you're upset?" Jim asked.
"Of *course* that's why I'm upset." Amy could feel tears burning at the back of her eyes.
"I told you that we had to look after Levi," Fran said.
"Well why couldn't you change it? I mean, I know you think BIKES are sloppy, but it was a big deal for me." She willed the tears not to come.
"I'm so sorry, Ames. Arlo and Sina had a wedding," Fran said. "We couldn't just change it."
"One of you could've come," she insisted. "And you could've at least sent me a note—an apology, a *break a leg*, something."
"You're right. I should've. We should've," Fran said.
Fran and Jim looked at her, waiting. She wanted to say it was fine, she was fine, but it wasn't. She wasn't. She blinked hard to keep the tears at bay, and took her beer back in her bunk.

Stars are playing the Yorkton Music Festival, Samantha texted Amy while the tour bus pulled out of Portage La Prairie.
I'm playing Yorkton, she wrote back.
I know! I was texting with Torquil and he said you should play with them.
Amy's heart quickened. Torquil? Like, Torquil Campbell, the lead singer of Stars? *Really?* she wrote back.
Yes, really. You interested?
OF COURSE!!!!!
K, I'll send your number to Torq.

She got a text from Torquil before they stopped for dinner, asking if Amy wanted to sing two songs with them.

I'd love to! she wrote back and then texted Max and Emily the news with a string of confetti canon emojis. She put on her headphones and started learning the lyrics.

In Yorkton, Amy played the Brigade set in the middle of the afternoon, with kids perched on their parents' shoulders. She and Fran do-si-do-ed to "Old MacDonald Had a Farm," and she sang harmonies on "The Sleeping Song" with Jim. She told a knock-knock joke about flowers between "The Rainbow March" and "Sittin' on the Potty," and hoped no one from Stars was in the audience.

The Brigade didn't have to do a meet-and-greet—an upside to outdoor festivals—and Amy went back to the bus and changed into jeans and a vintage T-shirt Emily told her to knot in the front—the only clothes she had packed that would be appropriate for an indie rock show. She put her guitar on the Brigade bus and got her purse from her bunk.

"I'll meet you in Medicine Hat," she told Fran and Jim.

"You're not coming on the bus?" Jim asked. "We're going to stop at Galaxy Burger."

"I just want to stay and hear some music," she said. She hadn't told them that she was staying to play with Stars, and didn't want it to get back to Ben.

"How will you get there?" Fran asked.

"I've rented a car," Amy said.

"Oh," she said. "You're all sorted then."

Amy felt a brief moment of guilt for not saying anything earlier.

She spent the rest of the afternoon listening to music on the mainstage. When she stopped in the beer tent she felt like a

The Fun Times Brigade

teenager whose parents were gone for the weekend. She met the band backstage a half hour before the set.

"You must be Fun Times Amy!" Torquil said, shaking Amy's hand.

He introduced Amy to the band and they talked through the show—who would go where and when she'd go onstage for the two songs in the middle of the set. They gave her a tambourine.

"Let's run both songs quickly," Amy Millan suggested.

Amy nodded and tried to play it cool, singing harmonies next to Amy Millan and Torquil Campbell. Just as they were finishing up, the stage manager called the band onstage and Amy stood in the wings. Her legs were shaky, her stomach full of bees.

"What an evening, Yorkton," Amy Millan said into her microphone, and then she began dancing behind her guitar and Torquil was singing into his mic and the violinist was playing next to the saxophonist. Amy could barely believe this was happening.

After a few songs, the violinist stepped offstage and it was Amy's turn. She walked on and Torquil introduced her. "You might've seen her earlier on the Tots and Tunes stage, but we are delighted to have Fun Times Amy with us this evening," he said.

Amy should've asked him not to call her that, but she smiled to the audience. The crowd was so much bigger than the audience she had played for a few hours earlier.

"One, two, one, two, three, four," the drummer yelled from behind the kit and Torquil started singing.

Amy tapped the tambourine on her hip and waited until Amy Millan looked over at her and they launched into the chorus. Except Amy couldn't hear herself. Her monitor wasn't working and she had no idea if she was in tune. She kept singing, a hand to her ear, but she still couldn't hear herself. She hated that she'd missed the sound check because she'd been playing with Fran and Jim.

Before she knew it, the audience was cheering and Amy Millan was holding out her palm. "Amy Scholl, everybody." And Amy smiled and pressed her hands together at her heart and then walked offstage left. Someone handed her a beer that she drank fast while the band was finishing their set, and then she remembered she was going to have to drive. She left before the band was done playing.

How was it? Samantha texted while Amy was in a cab to pick up her rental car.

Good, I think. My monitor was fucked up, she wrote back.

Oh my god, festival monitors are the worst, right?

Amy'd never really had problems with her monitors at a festival—the Brigade was always on early in the day so their sound checks were before the gates opened.

The sun hung at the horizon, even though it was after ten, and the sky was still light. Amy hadn't ever seen the prairies from this angle. She was usually in her bunk or sitting at the back of the bus. She cranked the radio and opened the windows. It was going to be a long drive.

When she finally got to the hotel, she wheeled her suitcase down the hall, hearing the muffled clips of TV, a conversation, a toilet flushing. Cora usually dealt with the hotels, and the room was more expensive than Amy'd thought it'd be. Between it and the car rental, she realized how much she'd just paid to be able to play with Stars.

In her room, she flicked through her phone. Stars had followed her on Instagram. She looked at their posts and there was a video clip from the stage. She clicked play, and there she was, next to Amy Millan and her yellow guitar, in her jeans and knotted T-shirt, tambourine in hand. The clip was short, but she sounded good, even without a monitor, and she didn't look awkward or stiff. She reposted it. *Played an amazing show with Stars in Yorkton*, she wrote and tagged Amy Millan and Torquil. She put her phone down to open a bottle of wine from the mini fridge and by the time she picked up her phone again, the likes were piling up.

It was worth it. It was worth the drive and the car rental and the hotel room.

20

WHILE ALICE NAPS, AMY GOOGLES THE FUN TIMES Brigade and finds a YouTube video of a live show from their last tour. She watches her and Fran and Jim onstage at the Orpheum, their guitars all pointing stage left, leaning into the one microphone in the middle of the stage. The harmonies are perfect.

Would you look at this Vancouver magic?! she writes to Fran, and sends her the link.

It's weird, seeing the three of them so full of energy, so upbeat and cheery and suddenly Amy misses being onstage so much that she can't bear to watch it.

It's too hot to take Alice out for a walk, so when Alice wakes up, Amy streams the Brigade's third album, *Animal-riffic*. Amy props Alice up on the couch and sings along to "Going to the Zoo," waiting for her reaction.

Alice kicks her legs.

"That's right, baby girl. That's your mama singing!"

The Fun Times Brigade

Amy brings her guitar up from the basement and lays Alice on her play mat, the one with the pastel owls and mirrored chickadees, strums the open strings. She curls her fingers into a G chord.

"Okay, this is our biggest song," Amy says and starts playing "The Crayon Song." "Red met Yellow and they gave a high-five and they did a little dance and they did a little jive."

Her voice sounds like garbage, and her fingers, though they know where to go, feel swollen and clumsy. The pads of her fingers burn against the strings. Her calluses are gone. She can't remember not having calluses.

Alice stares at the owl near her left shoulder, and Amy stops mid-song and tries "The Rainbow March," but Alice doesn't even look over at her. She's too busy trying to put a dangling chickadee in her mouth. She tries "You Are My Sunshine" and "Fly Like a Butterfly." She used to have an entire auditorium—thousands of kids—rapt and hanging on her every word, but now she can't even get her own kid to listen. She knows she shouldn't take it personally; she knows Alice is just a baby, but it still stings. When she was pregnant, she had visions of calming Alice down with her songs, playing her guitar and doing singalongs in the afternoon. She's embarrassed she ever thought it would be that easy.

She leaves her guitar propped up against the couch and lies next to Alice.

"Should we do tummy time?" she says.

She has a fleeting thought about writing a tummy time song, but then Alice spits up all over the play mat. Amy cleans it up and props Alice up in the bouncy chair. "This is a guitar," she says, moving it out of the way. Apparently narrating even mundane things helps babies develop their language. "And this is a pick." She holds it up to Alice to see, but doesn't let her grab it. "It's actually Jim's pick," she says, looking more closely at it. "Your Grandpa Jim."

Amy nurses Alice to sleep after lunch and lifts her carefully into her crib. She takes the monitor to the living room, picks up her guitar, and plays a G chord. She glances at the monitor, but Alice doesn't stir. The strings are sharp under her fingers, but the weight of the neck in her hand feels good. She tunes, starting at the bottom and working her way up, the pegs tight, then yielding under her fingers. She plays a D chord, and retunes the B string, then plays D again, shifting to E minor, then C. Alice doesn't wake, so Amy plays Neil Young's "Heart of Gold." It's the first song she ever learned to play. She plays "Blackbird." She plays Indigo Girls' "Closer to Fine." She plays "If I Had a Hammer." She plays "Heart of Gold" again.

G, C, D, E minor. She has the buzzing feeling of a new song somewhere, in her fingers, in her throat, under her tongue, somewhere. She chases it, shifting through chords. G, C, D, E minor, G, C, D, E minor.

It's something about the tiny shell curl of Alice's ear, how she kicks at invisible ninjas and conducts orchestras, how she can see now—colour and shape and faces. How strong she is. How solid she is. How she loves Alice so much it has replaced the marrow of her bones.

G, C, D, E minor, G, C, D, E minor, but the buzzing dissipates and it's just Amy and her guitar and the baby monitor. Alice sleeps and Amy can't find any words that sound remotely interesting. Not even a single line to build on.

"Alice," she sings. "Alice, Alice, Alice." But that's not a song. That's just a name.

She hums, trying out something about smiling with your entire body. Her callus-less fingers ache. Despair fills her throat, but then she remembers the song she started on her phone. She opens the notes section, ready to figure out a melody, except it's not a song. It's a bunch of words—*Leaf green*

The Fun Times Brigade

A line of sparrows (guest flute? Clarinet??)
Violets as polka dots
Ants and peonies
Sun hats and sunscreen (title?)
Strawberries and
A snail named Simon?

Goddamnit. She tries not to think about her mom saying how many opportunities she gave up when Amy was born. She reminds herself that becoming a mom didn't keep Fran from making music.

Amy dials Fran's number and lets it ring and ring and ring. She waits for her voice on the answering machine, but it keeps ringing.

Max's face lights up when he sees Amy's guitar in the living room.

"Don't," she warns him. "I can't play. I can't write."

"It's been a while. You just have to get back into it."

"Stop," she says.

He holds up his hands. "Okay, okay. I just thought—"

Amy takes her guitar back downstairs. She doesn't need to be reminded of everything she can't do right now.

"Why don't we all go to Guelph?" Max asks over dinner, "for the music festival. Naheed and Rachel are going this year— they're camping with Alim, but we could just go for the day?"

"Royal City Folk Fest?" Amy says slowly. Where she met Fran and Jim? Where they've played every year since?

"It'd be so great. Alice would probably sleep in the stroller, or in a carrier. She'd love it, I'm sure."

"I don't think it'll work," Amy says. She doesn't tell him that she's been looking at the lineup, at first out of curiosity, then out of jealousy, for the last few weeks. "We're trying to get her used to her crib, remember? Besides, she'd scream the whole way there, and there's never enough shade."

And that's all true. Alice *would* hate the drive, and there isn't much shade, but mostly it's that Amy wants Alice's first festival to be one she's playing at. She wants to be the mom musician, nursing before a set, jiggling Alice on her hip afterward. She doesn't want to be wandering about aimlessly, watching people do what she used to do.

Max drops it, but the next night, opens up his laptop to show Alice a clip from the Brigade's TV show.

"No screens!" Amy says.

"Just one song. She should see her mom playing," Max insists.

Amy relents. "Fine, one song."

Max shows Alice a clip from the episode they shot in High Park, next to Grenadier Pond. He scrolls past the opening song, and the knock-knock joke Amy tells about trees, and Fran's lesson about flutes. It had been a ridiculously hot day and the makeup and wardrobe teams kept dabbing them with sponges. At least five crew members stepped in goose shit and one poor PA had to clean it up from the field between takes.

"Look at this," he says to Alice, holding her on his lap. "There's your mama."

Amy's wearing a seersucker dress and sitting on a gingham blanket with Fran and Jim singing "The Picnic Basket." Her smile is more grimace than smile, and, despite the makeup, she can see the dark circles under her eyes. The episode is from the show's last season, and she wishes Max had chosen something from Season 1, when things weren't so strained.

21

AMY, FRAN, AND JIM WERE IN COMOX WHEN THEY got the email saying their TV show hadn't been renewed.

"I can't believe it," Fran said, gutted.

Jim's face darkened, but Amy was ecstatic—no more ridiculously early mornings, no more forgetting her lines or telling stupid knock-knock jokes, no more hurry up and wait. And best of all, without the TV show, she wouldn't have to race from set to BIKES rehearsals. She wouldn't have any more hungover 5:00 a.m. call times.

"We'll still make royalties on the theme song every time it's played," Ben said in their daily post-show call. And it had been picked up by Nickelodeon in the States, so they were making money without having to do anything. Amy couldn't imagine a better outcome.

But Jim and Fran were upset, and Amy felt like she should hang out with them in the back of the bus. She could imagine Jim pouring them both a scotch, and Fran drinking a white wine spritzer. But she didn't. Instead, she lay in her bunk and decided she'd write a song for BIKES. Something about being on the road, something about wanting to be somewhere else.

She started writing, and by the time they got back to the mainland, she had a chorus: *Take me back to the city on the lake, to the house that holds my heart. Take me back to the story we're writing, to the stairs we climb together. Take me back. Take me back. Take me back.* She fleshed out the verses, then sent it to Jason before going onstage in Burnaby. She rushed to her dressing room after the encore to check her phone, but there was no reply.

A day passed and she still hadn't heard anything. Maybe Jason had lost his phone. Or maybe he was up north somewhere, doing a music retreat without cell service.

When she still hadn't heard back three days later, she texted Samantha. *Do you know if Jason's around?*

He was late for band practice yesterday, and the spare key wasn't under the rock, and we all had to wait outside until he showed up. Sandra threatened to quit the band. Haha, Samantha wrote back.

He was in the city then. He had cell service.

We're playing the Horseshoe this weekend. I wish you could be here.

Of all the venues in Toronto, that was the one Amy wanted to play the most.

What time? she asked.

On at 9, Sam wrote back.

Amy looked at the Brigade schedule to see if there was any hope of making it back to the city, but there was no way it would work.

Max called when she was onstage in Merritt, B.C., but didn't leave a message. Cell service was spotty leaving the venue, and reception on the bus kept cutting out as soon as he would answer. Finally, he just texted her the news.

I got tenure.

Yes!!! Amy wrote back. *That's amazing!!*

He sent her a screenshot of the email.

I knew it would happen. Waterloo's lucky to have you.

And I booked my flight to Germany today, he wrote. He was going to a prestigious math research centre for two weeks.

A few years earlier, Amy had overheard his PhD friends talking about some sort of legendary chalk made by a Japanese factory that was going out of business, and mathematicians all over the world were hoarding boxes of it. It took her a while, but she eventually found a box on eBay. It was ridiculously expensive, but she bought it anyway and paid extra for expedited shipping so it would arrive before Max left for Germany.

Jason didn't respond to her email, but after the tour bus stopped at a Tim Hortons outside of Calgary, Amy got an email from Christophe, with the whole band cc'd. He had booked them into a festival in Mexico.

"Mexico!" Amy gasped.

"Pardon?" Jim said from his bunk.

"Nothing," she said.

Mexico!!!!! she texted Samantha.

I know right? It's going to be a party! she wrote back. *Can you come?*

It was on Labour Day weekend and Ben never booked Brigade shows then because parents were too busy running around getting lunch boxes and backpacks ready for school. She'd miss her anniversary with Max, but he'd understand.

YES! Amy wrote back.

She sent a text to Emily.

Holy shit! That's awesome! she wrote back.
Jealous! Julie wrote when Amy texted her.

It was hard to find a good time to call Max with the time difference, but she stayed up late one night in a hotel room in Golden to catch him when he was getting up for the day.

"We were going to go to San Fran," Max said, his voice disappointed.

"We'll celebrate when I'm back," Amy said. "The next long weekend. Promise."

He was quiet.

"You think I shouldn't go?"

"I didn't say that. I was just looking forward to it, you know, celebrating our anniversary, and getting tenure, and having some time together before the fall semester starts."

Amy played with the zipper on her suitcase. "I miss you," she said.

"I miss you, too."

"How's Oberwolfach?" she asked.

"Good. Intense. We did the Black Forest hike this afternoon, and we stopped at a place famous for its Black Forest cake."

"That's about as authentic as you get. Was it good?"

"Yeah, it was. And I think we're finally making some progress. Hard to say. We're still deep in the figuring things out phase. How's the tour? Where are you again?"

"Heading to Revelstoke."

"How was your last show?"

"Fine. Same old."

"And Fran and Jim?"

"Fine, I guess," Amy said. "Mexico is a good dangling carrot to get through the rest of the summer. Oh, and did I tell you? Neko Case is recording in Vancouver and Samantha put me in touch with someone on her team."

Amy was about to get onto the bus after their Abbotsford show when she got a call from Ben.

"What were you thinking?" he said without even saying hello.

"Whoa, hello. I'm great, Ben, thanks for asking," Amy said. "And yes, today's show *was* sold out."

"I was just cc'd on an email from Ken Sherman."

"Okay," she said, kicking a stone against the tire of the tour bus. Ken was the guy Sam had put her in touch with to record with Neko Case.

"Ken Sherman, the manager for the New Pornographers."

"Yeah, and?" Amy said, wishing he'd get to the point already.

"It's a contract. For you to record with them."

"Yeah, I know. It's just one song."

"You don't see an issue with this?" His voice was harsh and clipped.

"With what? It's on our day off in Vancouver. I triple-checked the schedule. And I'm allowed to do whatever I want on my day off."

"The band is called The New *Pornographers*."

"Jesus, Ben. They're a band. They're not actual pornographers."

"And *you* are in a kids' band."

"Uh-huh."

"You do not see the problem here?"

"Come on, it's not like it's going to split sales."

"Oh my god, Amy. You cannot be in a band called the New *Pornographers*."

"I'm not going to be *in* the band. It's just one song."

"No. No way. Absolutely not."

"It's Neko Case," Amy said.

"If you want to sing on a Neko Case track, we can talk, but there's no way I'm ever going to let the words 'Fun Times Brigade' and 'Pornographers' be in the same sentence. Ever."

Amy's cheeks burned. That hadn't even occurred to her. "Fine. Fine. Whatever," she said quickly. "Let me handle it."

She hung up and opened her email. A contract to play with Neko Case and the rest of the band at the Miller Block studio. Fucking hell. She wrote back, taking Ben off the cc line, and said it wasn't going to work with her schedule. She wanted to punch something.

"We've got to go," the bus driver called out. "Surrey awaits."

"What the hell, Ames?" Jim said, after she threw her backpack onto her bunk. His eyes were blazing.

"Oh my god, did Ben get to you?"

"Amy!"

"It's not a big deal. It was just singing back up."

"But Pornography? They're called *Pornography*," Fran said from her bunk, her voice agitated.

"They're called the New Pornographers," Amy said, impatient. "It's just a band name."

"You could've put all of this at risk," Jim said waving his hand around the bus.

"You're being dramatic," Amy said.

"This is serious, Ames. You're late for every sound check, you clearly don't want to be onstage and now *this*?"

"That's not true."

"When's the last time you actually helped with a load-in?" he asked.

"Isn't that what a tech crew is for?"

"Jesus Christ, Ames. When did you turn into such a diva?"

She knew she was being awful, but she didn't care. She was tired of playing a kazoo onstage, of plastering on her cheery Brigade face. She was tired of this tiny tour bus, and their relentless schedule, and not being allowed to even go out for a drink after the show.

"What's going on, Ames?" Fran asked.

"What is going on is that you and Ben are ganging up on me and not letting me live my life!" She knew even as it escaped her lips how adolescent she sounded.

Amy went on autopilot for the rest of the tour, texting with Samantha whenever she wasn't onstage, and working on another song to send to Jason. On the drive from Sault Ste. Marie back to Toronto, Jim asked her to join him and Fran in the back of the bus. It was strangely formal, him asking. Amy took off her headphones and climbed down from her bunk.

Jim and Fran were sitting together on one side. Amy sat down on the other. "What's going on?" she asked.

Fran caught Jim's eye and gave him a small nod.

"We can't do this," Jim said, his hands on his knees.

"Pardon?" Amy asked.

"This isn't working," Fran said, looking Amy straight in the eye.

"What are you talking about?"

"This," Fran waved her hand between the three of them. "Us."

"The Brigade," Jim added.

"What do you mean 'not working'?" Amy asked.

"Amy," Jim said, his voice sharp. "You've been checked out all summer."

"You seem miserable," Fran said.

"Your music's been sloppy," Jim continued, "and you've been rude to the sound techs. You played the entire set in Regina with your uke out of tune."

"I did not!"

"You did."

"Then why didn't you say anything?" Amy asked, mortified. She'd had no idea her ukulele had been out of tune.

"It's obvious you're unhappy," Fran said.
"We need to take a break." Jim said quietly.
"You need to figure out what you want," Fran added.

What she wanted was to be back on the stage on the Island, with the kick drum pounding in her chest, the crowd roaring. *That's* what she wanted.

Green highway signs whipped past in a blur.

"We've spoken to Ben—" Fran started.
"Wait, what? You talked to Ben before me?"
"We had to, for logistics."
"So, what, no Sudbury show?"
Fran shook her head.
"And the United Way fundraiser?"
"Ben's handling all of it."
"Go, play with BIKES. Figure out what you want," Fran said.

Jim said nothing, and Amy could tell he wanted to say something, probably something disparaging about BIKES.

"Okay," Amy said. "Fine. I mean, so much for communication and making decisions as a group, but fine." Amy stood up, expecting them to tell her to stay, to sit and talk it out. But they didn't.

She went back to her bunk and tried to text Max, and then Sam, but she couldn't figure out what to write, so she put on her headphones and blasted Neko Case's *Blacklisted* album as loud as she could and stared out the window until they pulled into Toronto.

22

THE FLIGHT TO MEXICO CITY GOT IN LATE, AND Jason hustled the band to the festival green room—a tent set up over scrubby grass. BIKES was scheduled to play at 2:00 p.m.—a forty-five-minute set, which seemed a bit short to come all the way to Mexico for, but here they were.

Amy set her phone to roam and sent the blurry photos she took from the cab window to Max and Emily. She was hoping for something Mexican at craft services, but there were just picked-over trays of veggies and dip, and a few sandwiches with the crusts cut off. She was glad she'd packed a handful of granola bars in her purse. If there was one thing she'd learned from being on the road, it was to always have food on hand. She was embarrassed, though, of her bag full of snacks, so she went for a walk, and ate her granola bars surreptitiously.

It was chaotic backstage with publicists and managers and festival staff running around with clipboards. Christophe was furious about their rider being wrong again. "Honestly, I emailed the fucking promoter like twenty times. How hard is it to get a goddamn Snickers?"

BIKES' sound check got pushed, and, a few minutes later, the stage manager came by to tell Christophe it had been cancelled. Christophe tried arguing in terrible Spanish, but eventually threw his hands in the air.

"We're going to just have to play," Jason said as Christophe paced. "It's going to be fine."

"You want a sandwich?" Samantha asked Amy, holding out a plate of sad-looking egg salad.

"I'm good," she said. "I just need some water."

After introducing the band, Christophe asked the sound guys for more monitor. The crowd was sparse, but someone yelled out, "Go BIKES!" and Jason laughed into his microphone and asked how everyone was doing. "Woooo!" they yelled back.

Jason turned around. "Ready?" he asked, and Daniel's drumsticks counted them in.

They started the set with two of their biggest hits, but there wasn't the same energy as the Island show. It was too disparate, and the sound got lost in all the space. Amy felt awkward behind her mic stand and reminded herself that they could've brought anyone with them, but they'd asked her. She hit her tambourine—her tambo—against her hip and smiled over at Samantha. She was playing with BIKES on tour in Mexico. In Mexico!

The forty-five minutes went by in a heartbeat, and before Amy knew it, they were walking off, waving to the small, but enthusiastic audience.

"They promised crowds. That was not a fucking crowd," Christophe snarled, his bad mood snaking through the group. "That was a handful of people. Why are we even here? We're fucking BIKES. We play sold-out shows, not forty-five-minute sets for a hundred people. Do they know how much it cost to get us all here?"

"Let's ignore him," Samantha said, slipping her arm through Amy's. "You want to go back to the hotel, freshen up, and then come back when shit's getting good?"

It was rare that Amy didn't have to get right on a bus and go somewhere new, and she wanted to wander around the festival, but the thought of a shower was too good to pass up.

How was it? Emily texted when Amy was back at the Sheraton. Samantha, Sandra, and Amy were sharing a room.

Good, Amy wrote back. *We're heading back to the venue soon. Portishead is headlining! Epic party tonight!!!*

Amazing! Oh, and happy anniversary, Emily wrote. *Six years ago you were walking down the aisle!*

It feels like yesterday and like a thousand years ago, Amy wrote back.

She felt a twinge of guilt for not spending the weekend with Max. *Happy anniversary!* she texted him. *Let's book San Fran over Thanksgiving.*

"I feel weird," Samantha said from the corner of the bed.

"You need water? It was hot out there." Amy handed her a bottle from the mini fridge.

"Oh no, we're not allowed to take anything from the mini fridge," she said. "Christophe's cardinal rule."

"Okay," Amy said and found the water bottle she had picked up backstage.

"God. Oh my god. My stomach," Samantha said. She bolted to the bathroom and banged on the door.

"Give me a minute!" Sandra shouted.

"I don't have a minute," Samantha said.

Sandra came out in a towel. "What's your problem?"
But Samantha was already vomiting into the toilet.
"You okay?" Amy called to Samantha.
"No," she mumbled.
"Can I come in?" Amy asked. The bathroom smelled sour and she couldn't breathe through her nose. Amy got Sam a wet washcloth and put it on her neck.
"What the fuck," Sam moaned. "I didn't even eat any street food or anything. I only drank bottled water!"
"Move! Move!" Sandra came running into the bathroom and vomited into the toilet, almost missing the bowl.
Amy gagged and turned away, then got Sandra a damp facecloth, too.
"Rinse your mouth out," Amy told her, holding up a glass of water. "It's bottled," she said when Sandra hesitated.
"What was it?" Sandra moaned from the tiled floor.
"Those fucking sandwiches," Samantha said. "It must have been. The only other thing I've eaten was a bag of almonds on the plane."
Amy checked her phone. There was a series of texts on the BIKES group chat. "It looks like the guys are sick, too."
"How come you're fine?" Sandra looked up at Amy accusingly.
"I didn't have any sandwiches." She felt guilty for the granola bars. "I wasn't hungry," she added.
Amy found some Gravol in her toiletry bag.
"Oh my god, you're a fucking saint," Sandra said, taking the tiny pink pill.
"You're like our fairy godmother," Samantha said.
Amy got them both into bed. "You have water. The ice buckets are right next to you. Your phones are charging. Text me if you need anything," she said.

"Okay," they mumbled, but they were both almost asleep.

Amy took the Gravol to Robin and Nathan's room. Robin answered the door positively green. "I thought you were room service," he said. "We need more towels."

"Here," Amy said, handing him the Gravol. He took it, then ran to the bathroom.

Amy went down to the lobby. She needed to eat, but she didn't know if there was anywhere good close by. It seemed like a waste to get food from the hotel restaurant, but she was too tired to find anything else. The booths were large and covered in green pleather. She opened the oversized laminated menu. It was all spaghetti and gnocchi and pizza. She didn't come to Mexico City to eat spaghetti, so she ordered the only Mexican thing she could find—quesadillas from the kids' menu, and a margarita.

She checked the concert timelines. Grizzly Bear was playing now. And then Hot Chip. She still had her performer pass, but it was at least a forty-five-minute cab ride, and she was afraid she wouldn't be able to get a cab back to the hotel after.

Everyone is down with food poisoning, she texted Emily.

She waited to see the bubbles of her writing back, but nothing. She ordered another margarita. She was supposed to be partying with BIKES, and stumbling home as the sun rose, not eating a kid's quesadilla at the Sheraton. She tried taking a picture of her margarita to commemorate the trip, but the lighting was terrible. She scrolled through her photos and decided to post a selfie of her with Sandra, Samantha, and Robin from earlier, and added a bunch of hashtags: *#LivingMyBestLife #BIKESinMexico #ThatSunshineTho*. It felt a bit disingenuous, with all of them upstairs puking their guts out, and her sitting at a shitty Italian hotel restaurant, but the hearts started appearing and Amy downed another margarita, and the waiter told her about a bar on the second floor.

The next morning, everyone looked pale and wan and ordered plain pasta, no sauce, and ginger ale. Even Jason, who was usually so clean-cut, looked bedraggled. Amy ordered the kids' quesadillas again, and Christophe stumbled in, bleary-eyed and clearly hungover.

"What the fuck happened to all of you last night?" he asked, ordering a michelada before sitting down.

"Have you not looked at your phone?" Nathan asked.

"It died. I was at the venue till, well, till now."

Sandra rolled her eyes.

"We were all sick," Joseph said.

"Food poisoning," Nathan said.

"Rule number one, avoid street food," Christophe said.

"It was craft services," Jesse said.

"That's too bad," Christophe said. "Beth Gibbons was fucking ethereal, and you all missed a rager. I smoked a joint with Lady Gaga's publicist."

Samantha moved her chair so her back was to Christophe. "Thank you for saving us," she said to Amy. "Honestly, it never crossed my mind to bring Gravol."

"What'd you get up to? Did you go back to the venue?" Sandra asked.

Amy was embarrassed that she hadn't. "I had dinner and then went for drinks," she said. She didn't mention that they were at the hotel bar, with its tacky mariachi band decor.

Jason took care of the bill and told them to be down in the lobby in fifteen.

"Well, this is going down in books as the worst tour ever," Robin said in the cab on the way to the airport.

"Actually the worst," Sandra said.

Amy watched the palm trees and the orange-juice stands pass in a blur, disappointment heavy in her throat.

"Let's play New York," Samantha said to Jason.
"Yeah," Nathan said, "let's have a redo in Brooklyn."
"Just no egg salad sandwiches," Sandra said.
"Don't even say it," Robin moaned.
This was only the beginning, Amy reminded herself. This was just the first tour of many.

Amy slept for three days when she got home from Mexico—the summer tour and the BIKES trip had caught up with her, and she only woke to eat peanut butter sandwiches and gulp down glasses of water.

On Friday, Amy was cc'd on an email from Christophe about a meeting that night. A meeting, not a rehearsal.

What do you think it's about? Samantha texted.

I was going to ask you the same thing.

Maybe he's already sorted out a Brooklyn gig? Or maybe a music video? We haven't done one in a while.

They all piled into Jason's living room. There was no room on the couch, so Amy sat on the floor next to Robin. It was weird that there was no beer. They had to wait for Sandra to arrive, and Christophe wasn't annoyed when she showed up late. Amy looked at Samantha, whose brow was furrowed. Sandra saw them looking at each other and mouthed, *What's going on?* Both Amy and Samantha shrugged.

"We've decided we're going to get back to our roots," Christophe said finally, holding court in front of the fireplace.

"We're paring down our sound," Jason added. "We want you to know it has nothing to do with anyone's musicality or talent, or anything."

"It's entirely an artistic choice," Christophe said.

"Besides," Jason said, "you've all been going hard for so long."

Everyone looked confused.

"We're going back to the original members," Jason said. "Me, Christophe, Daniel, and Joseph."

"What?" Robin asked.

"So, no keys, no bass, no horns," Nathan said.

Christophe nodded. "Stripped down, really clean. We're interested in a really whittled sound."

Amy stared at her lap. What was happening?

"What the fuck?" Jesse said from the couch.

"And all dudes. Of course," Sandra said, quietly.

"But we just recorded an album," Nathan said.

Amy's heart started to pound in her throat. *No!* she wanted to yell. *I gave up the Brigade to do this. I wanted to do this.*

"Shouldn't we be touring the new record?" Robin asked.

"The album will speak for itself," Christophe said.

"It'll give you all time to work on your own projects," Jason added.

"I'm working on a libretto," Christophe said.

Sandra rolled her eyes.

"I heard Do Make Say Think is planning a West Coast tour," Jason said. "And Weakerthans are making a new album this year. I'm sure they'd love to have any of you play with them."

Christophe pulled out a bottle of champagne. "It's the end of an era," he said, popping the cork and pouring it into red Solo cups. "Let's celebrate all we've accomplished."

Sandra left without saying goodbye and Robin and Jesse lit a joint. No one, except Jason and Christophe, looked happy.

"At least you still have the Brigade," Samantha said, sipping her champagne.

Amy hadn't told her about the break.

"What am *I* going to do?" she continued.

"Play bass with every awesome band out there," Amy said. "You'll have no problem finding work. I'm a fucking kids' musician. What am I going to do?"

"Make music," she said. "That's what we do, right? We'll just make music."

PART THREE

23

ON MONDAY MORNING, AMY LOOKS UP A MOM and baby yoga class Julie suggested. She'll go to yoga, and when Max comes home from work and tells her about his day, she'll have something to talk about that isn't *Schitt's Creek*, or the consistency of Alice's poop.

She makes it to the class with ten minutes to spare—a veritable miracle, and she's grateful the foyer is air-conditioned. She leaves the stroller in the foyer and unclips Alice's car seat, trying not to wake her. Moms lay out yoga mats, and muslins, and pull out rattles and Sophie the Giraffes and water bottles. Amy sets Alice next to a mat near the front.

There's a knot of moms near the window who have backpacks instead of diaper bags, and one of them stands in Warrior pose nursing a baby. After a few minutes of eavesdropping, Amy realizes they're second-time moms. They've got older kids, which means, along with Goldfish crackers and errant raisins, they've probably got Brigade CDs in their minivans and let their kids watch Amy tell knock-knock jokes on TV. She waits for one of them to recognize her, but no one even looks in her direction, and she pretends to look for something in her diaper bag until the teacher dings a bell.

As soon as she's in her first Downward Dog, Alice wakes up. Amy tries rocking the car seat to get her to settle, but she starts escalating and Amy has to unbuckle her. Amy sits on her mat while every other mom does Upward Dog, and undoes her nursing bra. Alice takes forever to nurse, and, after she's burped, she's still fussy and refuses to be put down. Amy tries distracting her with her flannel bunny stuffie, but Alice is having none of it.

Eventually, Alice finds the ceiling fan and Amy is able to join the last few minutes of class. Alice is still mesmerized by the fan and Amy lies back on her mat for Savasana. The yoga teacher comes by and puts a lavender eye pillow on her eyes and covers her with a heavy blanket. It's so quiet, and so dark with the eye pillow and she feels her body sinking.

Amy bolts upright when the yoga teacher dings the bell—she must have fallen asleep. Alice is still staring at the fan and Amy feels guilty and terrified that she fell asleep beside her. Adrenaline surges through her veins and all the calm from the final pose is gone. Her pulse is still racing while everyone chants "Om" over the coos and whimpers of babies and the squeak of toys. "Take your time," the yoga teacher insists, even though the second-time moms are already at the door. How did they pack up so quickly?

She starts putting all of the toys back in her diaper bag, and the moms around her form a circle and introduce their babies—Eloise and Liam and Charlotte and Connor. It feels weird to say Alice's name and not her own, but no one else introduces themselves. All the kids are around Alice's age and are sleeping through the night. Amy doesn't say that Alice is still up at least twice, and usually three times.

Connor's mom tells them that he's been putting back an avocado a day. "Two if I let him," she says. "Our grocery bill is through the roof."

Eloise's mom says she just grabbed a piece of steak the other night. "Baby-led weaning, I guess," she laughs.

Amy can't keep herself from joining in and tells them about the pumpkin breast milk pancakes she's been making for Alice. "She just loves them," Amy says, even though really Alice just mashes them into her high-chair tray and throws them onto the kitchen floor. "And they're great for adding in whatever, bit of peanut butter, or cashew butter."

"Cashew butter! That's genius," Charlotte's mom says. "I was trying to figure out how I was going to get her to try cashews."

Amy feels proud of herself, even though she got the idea from Julie.

Conner perches on his hands and knees and rocks back and forth. "Look at you, getting ready to crawl!" his mom says.

"Whoa!" Amy says before she can catch herself. "He's six months?" Alice is only four and a half months, but Amy can't even imagine Alice sitting independently, let alone crawling.

"Six and a bit."

The perky ponytail mom stops packing up her diaper bag to say Liam also started crawling at six months. "What a nightmare!" she says, but her voice beams. "Be grateful you don't have a mover yet. Once they start, it's all over."

Amy hates how inadequate she feels. She picks Alice up and smells her bum. "Time for you to get a new diaper," she says. She stuffs Alice's muslin, her rattles, her caterpillar book, and her Sophie into the diaper bag. Alice starts protesting while she rolls up her yoga mat.

"I'll do that," the yoga teacher says. "You just clean up that baby bum."

The Fun Times Brigade

"Thanks," Amy says to the yoga teacher, buckling a now-howling Alice into her car seat, hauling it over one arm, and slinging the diaper bag over the other shoulder. Maybe those second-time moms are onto something with their backpacks.

24

THE DAYS AFTER BIKES ENDED WERE LONG AND lonely. Amy didn't touch her guitar, and it was strange, not having any Brigade shows to prep for, no emails from Ben, no calls from Fran, no set lists from Jim. She slept until eleven, sometimes noon.

Max was teaching three courses and prepping for a conference, so most nights Amy ate dinner by herself, then met up with Sam at whatever bar she was working at. Neither Max nor Amy mentioned rebooking their anniversary trip.

One Saturday in early October, Amy woke up without a hangover and convinced Max to go for brunch. It had been months since they'd done anything just the two of them. On the walk home, kicking through the leaves in the park, a mom ran over from the playground and asked Amy for a photo.

"No," Amy said, proud of herself for finally establishing a boundary. "I'm on a walk with my husband."

"Who even are you?" Max asked after the woman hurried back to the playground.

It took Amy a moment to realize that his voice was barbed.

"Aren't I entitled to go for a walk in a park without having to smile for someone?"

He didn't say anything.

"If you were accosted by students all the time, you'd also start saying no to photos."

"I don't even know who you are," he said.

"Max," Amy said.

He didn't answer.

"You're *mad* at me? Because I didn't want to take a picture with that woman's kids? Do you think they call Jim an asshole when he says no? It's sexist is what it is. They feel entitled to me. They feel like I owe them because they watch me sing in their living room. Well, forget it. I am done with that."

"It's not just that," he said quietly, and started walking again.

"Then what is it?"

"You're mad because BIKES didn't work out and you're taking it out on literally everyone," Max said. "Me, that woman, my mom the other night when she called, hell, our server."

"What do you mean, our server?"

"Ames, you were a dick!"

"I was not!"

"You were! Your tone was so rude. You want to talk entitlement? Jesus. That's you, Ames."

"What are you talking about?"

"You sleep until noon, and then go out drinking with twenty-year-olds. In the middle of the week! I know this has been hard, but grow *up*."

Amy was so angry, she was shaking.

"You're acting like a first-year. It's embarrassing."

Amy walked home without him, and texted Sam, her hands still trembling with rage.

Drinks tonight?

I've got a better idea, she texted back. *Kingston!!*

Wha? You really want to go to the show we were supposed to play before we got kicked out?

We didn't get kicked out, dumb-dumb. They took a different "artistic route," Sam wrote back. *There's room in the van and Daniel said we could come.*

Will it be weird?

Only if you make it weird. Come! It'll be fun.

Amy put a phone charger and a toothbrush in her purse and told Max she was going out of town for the night.

"So what, you're a roadie now?" he said, without looking up from his desk.

"Jesus, Max. They're my *friends*."

They could've watched the show backstage, but it felt too weird to not step out with the rest of the band, so Samantha and Amy stood a few rows back from the front of the stage. They sipped their third vodka tonics—Sam had stolen a roll of drink tickets from backstage—and watched Jason and Christophe towering above them.

Girls danced with their hands waving in the air while the guys nodded in time to Daniel's kick drum. Between each song, Amy smiled up at Jason, hoping he'd invite her onstage to sing backup for at least one song, but after the first encore, she knew it wasn't going to happen.

Backstage, Jason already had a knot of girls around him, and Christophe leaned against the door frame, talking to someone from the university paper. Sam and Amy flopped onto the couch, and Joseph rolled a joint and passed it to Amy. She didn't have anywhere to sing tomorrow, or the next day, or the day after that, so she took it from him and inhaled deeply. She looked over at him and smiled. "Great show," she said, the weed softening the edges of the room.

"It isn't the same without a full stage," he said and took a pull off the joint. He was slightly shorter than Amy was, and he smelled like cigarettes and pot smoke. "Off the record, I think it's bullshit, this whole paring down thing," he said. "You guys, and Sandra, the horns, you all gave depth to our sound."

When they finished the joint, Sam stood. "Let's go somewhere!"

The girl hanging on Jason's arm insisted they go to the Palace. Jason talked to the bouncer and they skipped the line of undergrads and went straight in. It was all Beyoncé and Rihanna and Nicki Minaj, and Amy could tell Christophe was not into it.

Joseph brought over a tray of shots. Amy was already tipsy from the vodka tonics, and high from the joint, but she took a shot glass off the tray and lifted it in an air-cheers before downing it. Christophe mumbled something about autotune and left, and Daniel bought another round of shots, and Amy let Sam pull her onto the dance floor. Joseph joined them, and Daniel and the tech joined their circle. It had been years since Amy'd gone out dancing like this. BIKES and the Brigade and Max being an asshole slid away, and the only thing that mattered was dancing and the hands that were on her hips and her back. Sam's? Joseph's? Amy didn't know and she didn't care.

Soon, her hair was dripping with sweat and her shirt was three shades darker.

Sam started making out with a girl with braids down to her ass, and Daniel disappeared with his tech, and it was just Amy and Joseph on the dance floor, dancing and dancing, and doing more shots, until the lights came on, bright and glaring from the ceiling, the black walls and floor suddenly grimy.

"Let's get out of here," Joseph said, and grabbed Amy's hand. They stumbled into a cab, and the cab ride to the motel was out of focus and blurry.

With the key card in his hand, Joseph leaned into Amy, and then they were kissing, hard and hungry against the door frame, and fumbling to get inside his room. It was dark, and they didn't bother turning the lights on. When their sweaty clothes were off, Amy pushed him back onto the bed, and soon he was licking her neck, and she was biting his shoulder, and then he was rolling a condom onto his cock.

When Amy woke up, there was a blanket on top of her, and Joseph was in the other bed. Eleven a.m., the clock radio glared at her in red. She blinked at the clock. Her hangover pulsed inside her skull and shame flooded her limbs. She had cheated on Max. With Joseph. Joseph, who had two kids at home.

She had a shower in the tiny beige bathroom, and scrubbed her skin, her scalp, last night's mascara streaming down her face. The industrial smell of the yellow motel shampoo made her nauseous. She gagged and rinsed her hair.

She towelled off with the only and threadbare motel towel and stared at herself in the mirror. What the fuck had she done?

Joseph was up when she got out of the bathroom. "Hey," he said, with a sleepy grin. "What happens on tour stays on tour, right?"

"Yeah," Amy said quickly. "Of course."

She needed to get out of there. But where could she even go? She let the door slam behind her and checked her phone.

I'm meeting with Stanley in the morning, and have office hours till five, Max had texted at 11:18 last night. *I'm meeting Salima to talk about her work after that.*

Amy walked over to the motel office and poured herself a cup of coffee. It was harsh and black, almost chalky. *Where are you?* she texted Sam. She couldn't bear the thought of being stuck in the van with Joseph for the whole ride back to the city. *I might take the bus home.*

"Hey," Jason said. He grabbed a banana from the fruit basket. He was in running tights, and his T-shirt had a ring of sweat around the collar.

"Hey," Amy said.

"Good night?"

She nodded noncommittally and sipped her coffee.

"Look, I'm sorry about the shift, you know, with the band," he said. Amy could smell his sweat.

"Yeah, totally. It's fine."

"It's not personal, but you know that. You're an amazing musician. Christophe and I really felt it was time to get back to our roots, you know?"

Amy nodded and felt a sharp acidic burn at the back of her throat.

"I think we'll head back in an hour or so?" he said. "Can you tell Sam? I'll tell the guys."

"Sure," she managed, and rushed out of the office, the bell dinging behind her. She vomited in the parking lot.

Max was still at work when Amy got home. She got into the shower, even though her hair was still wet from the motel. She turned the water to scalding and scrubbed until her skin was red. She threw her clothes in the washing machine. She sat in the kitchen and stared at the wall.

Lindsay Zier-Vogel

I'm tending bar at Little Hour tonight. Wanna come? Sam texted.

Amy turned her phone over, then picked it up again and opened Joseph's Instagram—it alternated between photos of him onstage and photos of his kids. They were three and five, maybe a bit younger. Amy looked at them playing in a pile of leaves; swinging on swings; the oldest in a soccer jersey, his foot on a ball; the youngest with chocolate ice cream all over his face. She stared at a photo of his wife from Mother's Day, the two kids kissing her cheeks. She had long dark hair, and a wide, easy smile. *Our queen, our sun, we are so lucky to orbit around your brilliance*, Joseph had written. Amy was a monster. She was a fucking monster.

25

AMY WAS UPSTAIRS WITH THE LIGHT OFF WHEN Max got home. She heard him drop his keys in the bowl by the front door, his heels thumping into the dining room, through the living room to the kitchen. She could picture him opening the fridge door and pulling out the takeout containers.

She must've dozed off because the next thing she heard was Max brushing his teeth, and then padding down the hall to their bedroom. She closed her eyes, and he tiptoed to bed. He got under the covers so carefully, so gently, so as to not wake her, and she lay there, wanting to roll over and wake him up. She almost did, but then decided it'd be cruel to tell him. It'd never happen again, so why would she say anything? She would never tell him. She would protect him from this, from her. It would be fine.

Max's alarm went off at six, and Amy closed her eyes and lay as still as she could. She heard him grind coffee. She heard the whistle of the kettle. She could see him eating his yogourt over the counter. What had she done?

The Fun Times Brigade

After Max left for the day, Amy texted Emily. She ate toast. She drank the rest of the coffee Max had made. She checked her phone. Nothing from Emily. She looked at Joseph's Instagram. There was a new photo of him and his kids. He'd posted it yesterday. They were eating pizza together, the youngest on his lap.

Amy had another shower and made the bed. She so rarely made a bed, and it was harder than she remembered, getting the sheets straight and taut. She was a grown woman who didn't know how to make a bed.

Her phone rang, and she panicked that it was Max. It was Emily.

"I left my phone charger in the studio and I just got this. What's up?"

But Amy couldn't tell her over the phone.

"Are you okay? I'm coming over," Emily said.

"No. No," Amy said. "I need to get out of here."

"Okay, then come to the studio," she said. "Get in a cab. I'll text you the address."

The studio was in a converted church, and light streamed through the stained glass, a kaleidoscope of reds and oranges and yellows falling on the black dance floor. Emily was moving in the centre of the space when Amy arrived, kicking one leg behind her, high, like a blade. She stopped when she saw Amy's face and ran over to hug her.

Amy sobbed into Emily's shoulder while Emily rubbed her back.

"You're okay. Everything's going to be okay," she said into Amy's ear.

But it wasn't. It really wasn't.

"I, I can't even say it," Amy started.

"Say what? It can't be that bad."

Amy started crying again. "No, it is. It's worse than bad."

"Ames." Emily's voice was steady.

"I slept with Joseph," she managed between sobs.

"Joe, from BIKES?"

She nodded.

"Oh," Emily said. "Yeah, that's not great."

"I'm married. Married. What am I going to do?"

"Is it, like, a thing? You and Joe?"

Amy wished Emily would stop calling him Joe. "God, no. We were wasted. Like, I barely even remember anything. I went to Kingston. Why did I go to Kingston? I wasn't even playing. And then we just got wasted. Oh my god. He's a dad, for fuck's sake. He has kids." Amy pressed the heels of her palms into her eye sockets.

"I mean, he's kind of notorious," Emily said.

"What do you mean?"

"This is kind of his thing. He's Super Dad when he's at home. And then on the road, he's well, you know."

"He just sleeps around?"

"It's not your fault he's slutty. You used a condom, right?"

Amy nodded. "I feel like such an idiot."

"You're a musician who got drunk on the road. That happens, right?"

"Cheating on your husband doesn't just *happen*."

"I mean—"

"Max is going to kill me." Though that wasn't it; it was that Max was going to be so hurt, so very hurt. Amy couldn't bear it.

"Have you told him?"

"God no."

"But you're going to," she said, and Amy didn't know if it was a question or not.

"I have to," Amy said. "Right?"

Emily nodded slowly.

"I am the worst. I am the fucking worst," Amy said.

"You're not the worst," Emily said, rubbing her arm. "Let's turn the tables, what if Max slept with someone, at a conference or something. A one-off. How would you feel?"

"But he wouldn't."

"But let's say he did."

Amy started crying again. Max would never cheat on her.

"Oh, sweetie," Emily said, rubbing her back.

When Amy stopped crying, she made Emily show her what she was working on.

"It's going to be a group piece, but I'm just figuring out the material," she said and started in the centre of the studio, unfurling her body, and jumping, without making a sound. For ten minutes, Amy was almost able to put aside Max and Joseph and the catastrophic mess she'd made.

When she was back home, Amy decided to make something elaborate and time-consuming for dinner, something to keep her mind occupied. She flipped through Max's cookbooks and stopped at a page with an agnolotti recipe. It had been so long since she had cooked anything; she didn't remember where they kept the flour, or the parchment paper. She didn't even know if they owned a rolling pin.

She put the radio on as loud as she could, and listened to CBC, mixing an egg into a well of flour, kneading the dough, then rolling it out. She grated leftover bits of cheese she found in the fridge for the filling, and tried to follow the instructions for folding the dough into finicky little envelopes. It took a lot of mangled pockets before she got the hang of it, and she was putting the last few into the boiling water when she heard Max's key in the front door.

"Whoa!" Max said, coming into the kitchen. "Did you make pasta from scratch?"

Amy nodded, unable to speak, unable to breathe. She turned away from him and checked on the stove.

"How was Kanata?" he asked.

"Kingston," she said.

"Right."

She fished the floating pasta out of the water.

"White or red?" Max asked.

The thought of any alcohol made Amy's stomach turn, but she didn't want anything to seem off. "Red's good," she said.

They sat down to eat, and the news came back on the radio, the same news she'd been hearing every hour on the hour—the windstorm that had taken out power in the Maritimes, the six-car pileup on the QEW, the new safe injection site that had opened in Vancouver.

"It's good," Max said, biting into his pasta.

The pasta was too thick, and the filling leaked out of a bunch of them.

"You okay?" he asked.

Amy speared an agnolotti and nodded.

The weather came on the radio and Max told her about the department hiring another logician. "Stanley keeps promising to hire someone in topology, but instead, we're getting another logic person. God, isn't Spencer enough? Stanley keeps saying next year, next year, but when? I'm the only person doing this? It's Waterloo, for Christ's sake. I should have someone else in my field. It'd be nice to not have to teach every topology course for once. Or at least have a potential collaborator nearby," he said.

Amy put her fork down. "I made out with someone."

Max looked at her.

"Pardon?"

"In Kingston. We were really drunk."

"What? Who was drunk?"

"Me. And Joseph."

"Who's Joseph?"

"From BIKES."

Max didn't say anything. She couldn't read his face.

"It was stupid. We were really drunk. I was really drunk."

"Okay," Max said slowly. "Okay."

"I slept with him," Amy blurted out before she could stop herself. "I was so drunk, Max. I didn't even know what I was doing. I, I don't know, I can't explain it. It just happened, but it'll never happen again. Never."

He looked at her. "What?"

Amy looked away and didn't say anything.

"You had *sex* with someone?"

She still didn't say anything. She was still, so still, as if being still would make it all go away.

"Who the fuck is this guy?"

"Just a musician. He's—I don't know. I don't really know him."

"Have I met him?"

"No, not really—he played the Island show."

"Did you sleep with him that night, too?"

"God no. No. Max, this was one time. I swear. It was a mistake. A horrible, horrible mistake."

"Partying like a twenty-year-old." He said it so quietly Amy could barely hear him. "You couldn't be content to just play in a hugely successful kids' band. You had to go and be the *cool* musician, in the *cool* band, and sleep with some wannabe indie rock star."

Amy sat in her shame. She said nothing. There was nothing to say.

He picked up a roll of paper towels and smashed it against the edge of the table. "What the actual fuck?" He whipped the paper towels across the kitchen. They bounced off the fridge door and rolled onto the ground. "You had an *affair*."

"It wasn't an affair. It was just one night. One stupid, stupid night. Look, you can check all my emails, my texts." Amy thrust her phone at him. "It wasn't an affair. Look. I don't even have any texts from him. Only group texts about BIKES shit."

Max pushed his hands through his hair, his eyes wild.

"It's not an affair, I swear. I was so drunk, Max. So was he. It didn't mean anything."

"And that's supposed to make me feel better? That you were wasted?"

Amy closed her eyes and wished she could make it all go away.

He got up from the table and walked to the front door.

She followed him. "Where are you going?" she asked, her voice desperate.

"Out."

"Where?"

"I don't know." He slammed the door behind him.

She wanted to run after him, pleading for him to come back, but she couldn't. She couldn't ask him for anything.

He came back after midnight. Amy didn't ask where he had been, and he didn't say. She was on the couch, where she had been since he'd left. She'd talked to Emily, who'd assured her he'd come back, that everything was going to be okay. She'd put on old episodes of *30 Rock* and sat, waiting, hoping, praying, that Max would come home.

He walked right past her and got a blanket and sheets from the linen closet.

"No," Amy said, as he started to make the couch in his study into a bed. "I'll sleep in the living room."

He closed the door to his study and Amy sat in the hall and cried as silently as she could.

It took her forever to fall asleep, but she must've eventually. When she woke up, the house was eerily quiet. She went downstairs and Max's suitcase was by the door.

"Max, what's going on?" she called out, unable to keep the panic from her voice.

"I'm going to stay with my parents for a bit," he said from the living room.

"Wait, what? You're going to Florida?"

"I can't be here."

"But, but, oh my god. What about teaching?"

"Naheed is going to cover my classes."

Had he told Naheed? The thought of people knowing what she had done made Amy's stomach bottom out. "Oh my god, Max. I'll go. I'll leave. You stay."

He shook his head. "I need space. I need some time."

"What can I do? I'll do anything."

He said nothing. A cab pulled up and honked once. Max rolled his suitcase outside and carried it down the steps.

"I love you," Amy called from the front steps as he loaded his suitcase into the trunk. "I love you!"

He didn't turn around and the cab pulled off the curb. Amy sat on the steps, sobbing long after the cab had disappeared.

"You okay?" a neighbour asked from the sidewalk. He was picking up his dog's shit in a green plastic bag.

She needed a time machine. She needed to go back to Kingston and not get into that motel room, not get into that cab, not have those shots at the club, not even go to the club. She needed to not even go to Kingston, where she wasn't even playing, with a band that didn't even want her. What was she thinking? How could she have done this? "I'm fine," she replied, and closed the door behind her.

Emily called around noon, but Amy couldn't answer. She couldn't tell her that Max was gone.
I'm okay, Amy texted instead.
For real? she wrote back.
No.
I can come over.
You have rehearsal, she wrote.
Rehearsal can wait.
I'm okay. I think I just need to be alone for a bit.
Okay, just say the word, and I'll come, Emily wrote.
But if she came over, Amy would have to tell her Max was in Florida, and she couldn't bear to say out loud that he was gone.
She texted a frantic apology to Max, and then another. She tried calling his sister, but it went to voice mail, and she didn't know if he had even told her, so she hung up. She left voice mails on his phone instead. "Max, I'm sorry. I'm so, so sorry. I will do anything to make this right. It was one stupid night. It was the biggest mistake of my life. Max, I'm sorry. God, I'm sorry." Over and over on a loop.
She cried herself hoarse and got a text from Emily, reminding her to have dinner. She hadn't eaten anything since last night's few bites of pasta, but she wasn't sure she could keep anything down. She sat in Max's office, staring at his indecipherable scribbles on a lined piece of paper—triangles and cursive M's, and upside-down L's. There was a photo from their wedding on his desk. Amy was smiling, and Max was beaming under the chuppah. They looked so happy. They *were* so happy. What had she done?
And then she couldn't breathe.

The Fun Times Brigade

She panicked. *Breathe*, she willed herself. *Breathe*. But she couldn't get a single breath in.

Amy rang the doorbell as the cab pulled away from the curb.

Fran answered. "Amy?" She stood in the door frame in her nightgown.

"I—I didn't have anywhere else to go," she said, her voice cracking.

"Amy, what's wrong?"

But she couldn't speak. She just sobbed into her hands.

"Come. Come in, here we go. Here we go." Fran took Amy's elbow and guided her into the living room. "Okay, you're okay, just sit."

Amy curled into a ball on the couch.

"F, who was ringing the doorbell this late?" Jim called from the top of the stairs.

Fran slipped Amy's shoes off, and Jim walked into the living room in his pajamas. "Ames?" he asked.

"Okay now, what's happening? What's going on?" Fran asked, pulling a blanket over Amy.

"I think I had a panic attack," Amy said. "I'm so sorry. I didn't know where else to go."

"You don't have to apologize," Fran said.

"Max," Amy managed eventually and choked out the whole story.

"Where is he now?" Fran asked.

"Florida," Amy said, and she started sobbing again.

"You're going to get through this," Fran said.

"But are *we* going to get through this? Me and Max?"

"One step at a time," Jim said. "One step at a time."

Fran rubbed her back. Jim handed her a Kleenex, and she eventually caught her breath.

"Jim, can you make sure there are fresh sheets in the guest room?" Fran asked quietly.

"No, no. That's okay," Amy said standing. "It's late. I should go."

"Don't be silly," Jim said.

Fran found her an old Brigade T-shirt, and a pair of Arlo's track pants. "Here," she said, handing Amy a toothbrush still in its package.

Amy brushed her teeth with tears falling down her cheeks. She splashed water on her face, hoping the cold water would stop the tears. It didn't, and she curled up on their guest room bed and sobbed into her pillow. Fran knocked on the door, then crawled into bed next to her. "You're okay," she said over and over again, rubbing her back. "You're going to be okay."

26

"HI," AMY SAYS TO A MOM SITTING ON THE EDGE of the sandbox. She plunks Alice down in front of her. The yoga class was cancelled this week, and she promised herself that she'd go to the park when Alice woke up and talk to whoever was there.

"Hi," the mom next to her says, smiling. Amy is relieved. Maybe it really is this easy.

"How old?" the mom asks, gesturing to Alice.

"Twenty-two weeks," Amy says, and then wonders if she should've said almost five months. Did she sound ridiculous counting her baby's age in weeks? Alice wobbles and Amy props her up against her shin. "Yours?"

"Nine months," the mom says. "Oh, sweets, let's not eat the digger." She grabs the plastic toy from her kid, who starts wailing. "I mean, I guess it's good for his immunity, right?" she says to Amy, handing it back to her kid, who puts it back in his mouth. Amy nods and tries not to be horrified. This is essentially a large litter box, but she doesn't say anything.

They trade stories about sleep and poop and nap times.

"Living the mat-leave dream," the mom tells Amy. "A whole year without last-minute projects, or being cc'd on a thousand emails, or four-hour meetings that should be emails."

The dream? Amy's days stretch on interminably, and she's so impossibly lonely. She still can't manage to write a song, and Alice is up at least three times a night. But she nods and manages a "yeah."

"Don't get me wrong, I love my job, but it's so nice to have a break, you know?"

Amy doesn't know. She doesn't want a break from her work, but she also doesn't know how she's going to go back to it, either. Both things feel impossible. But this is the first conversation she's had with someone who isn't Max all week, so she smiles and nods.

"Beth!" the mom calls out and waves to a mom pushing her stroller into the park.

Beth sits on the other side of the mom. Her kid looks about the same age—nine months or so. Amy tries to imagine Alice at nine months, enormous, and sitting, and crawling through the cat-poop sand.

"How's Brad?" Beth asks the other mom, who rolls her eyes.

"Honestly? I don't understand how he can sleep through the baby screaming in the next room. But he just lies there, snoring."

"I've never wanted to divorce Rory more than I have in the last nine months," Beth says.

Amy remembers Julie telling her that trashing husbands is a mat-leave rite of passage. Max isn't perfect, but there's no way she'd complain about him to strangers. As the park moms continue complaining about their husbands, Alice tips over and face-plants in the sand.

"Oh, oh, baby girl," Amy cries, picking her up and wiping the sand off her face. "Oh, I'm so sorry."

Alice wails and Amy bounces her up and down. "You're okay. You're okay."

Alice whimpers.

"I think I'll get her home," Amy says. The moms don't even pause their conversation.

She gets Alice settled in the stroller and pulls out her phone as she passes the swings. *A, you were right about the husband shit-talking,* she texts Julie. *And B, I need to find some good baby-friendly activities asap.*

But when she goes through the list Julie sends back—story time at the library that she never wants to go back to, a Mommy and Me boot camp, a La Leche League meetup—she knows she's not going to do any of them. It'd just be a repeat of the park, anyway, and besides, she's not sure she wants friendships based on something as new as being Alice's mom.

When Alice goes down for her afternoon nap, Amy turns on another episode of *Schitt's Creek* and decides that David can be her mat-leave friend.

27

WHEN AMY WOKE UP, SHE DIDN'T KNOW WHERE she was, and then it hit her like a truck. Max was in Florida, and she was at Fran and Jim's. The clock on the side table said 10:32. She changed into an old pair of Jim's jeans and brushed the sleep off her teeth.

Jim was standing at the stove over a pan of bacon. Fran handed Amy a cup of coffee. "Did you sleep?' she asked.

Amy nodded.

Toast popped up from the toaster on the counter, and Jim handed her a plate. Scrambled eggs, bacon, toast. Amy didn't think she'd be able to stomach anything, but as soon as she took a bite, she realized how hungry she was. After breakfast, she started putting her shoes on.

"Where are you going?" Fran asked. She was sitting in the living room. She patted the couch next to her. "*Fried Green Tomatoes* or *Thelma and Louise?*"

"It's not even noon," Amy said.

"I've got nothing on. You?"

Amy shook her head.

"So which one first?"

They watched *Fried Green Tomatoes*, and, after Kathy Bates smashed her car into the red convertible in the Winn-Dixie parking lot, Amy checked her phone. There was a text from Emily checking in on her and a photo of Ollie sitting on a potty from Julie. Sam texted *Missed you last night, loser!* with a blurry selfie of her and Sandra at a bar. There was nothing from Max.

"Why don't you put that away for a bit," Fran said gently, taking the phone from Amy. She put it on the side table, but Amy wanted it back. She wanted to make sure the ringer was on in case he called, in case he texted, or emailed.

When Jim got home from the grocery store, the three of them watched *Thelma and Louise*, and Amy fell asleep and woke to the late afternoon sun pouring through the window. She could hear Fran playing the guitar in the basement.

She grabbed her phone. There were fifteen texts from Emily and three missed calls, but nothing from Max.

Where are you?

I'm on your porch. Why aren't you answering?

Are you okay? Tell me you're okay.

Ames, I'm freaking out here.

I'm at Fran and Jim's, Amy texted her back. *I'm sorry. I'm okay.*

Amy helped Jim make chili, and, after dinner, Fran pulled out her knitting while Jim stood at the record player and asked what Amy wanted to listen to. The thought of having to make even this small decision was impossible.

"How about the McGarrigle sisters," Fran said, saving her. "Their second album."

Jim pulled a record out of its sleeve and set the needle over the spinning LP. The waver of the McGarrigles' voices was dated, but their harmonies were perfect, so perfect. Jim handed Fran a glass of wine and poured Amy a finger of scotch, then stood at the wall of books, and handed Amy a copy of Anne Carson's *Autobiography of Red*. He'd been trying to get her to read Anne Carson for years.

"Or this," he said, passing her a Gwendolyn MacEwen first edition.

Fran's needles clicked, and the record spun, and Jim sat in his chair with his scotch, working on a crossword puzzle. Words swam on the page. Amy didn't deserve this—their kindness, their generosity.

"I'm sorry," she said, her voice cracking. "For all of it. For everything." Tears spilled over. "I was horrible this summer. Even before the tour. I was an asshole. And here you are, nothing but kind and taking me in when I'm a mess."

"You were kind of horrible," Jim said, nodding.

Fran swatted his knee.

"She said it," he said, not unkindly.

"I was," Amy said. "I'm a horrible person."

"You're not horrible. Your *behaviour* was horrible," Fran said.

"You're young," Jim added.

"I'm thirty-six," Amy said.

"You needed to figure out what you wanted," Fran said.

"And hurt you in the process."

They didn't say anything.

"I'm sorry," Amy said, and stood up. "I'm sorry. I shouldn't be here."

Fran shook her head. "Don't be silly. This is exactly where you should be."

"But I hurt you."

Jim nodded. "And you've apologized." He stood up and flipped the record to the other side. There was a hiss of the needle before it caught the music. "You're family."

Could they really accept her apology just like that? She didn't know what else to say, so she stared at the Anne Carson book and tried to read.

After listening to Rufus Wainwright's first album, Jim stood up. "Don't stay up too late," he said standing, and kissed Fran good night. Their closeness, their intimacy was almost unbearable.

"I don't think I've ever told you, but I left Jim for a while," Fran said, after the bedroom door had closed upstairs.

Amy looked at her, stunned. "Really? When?"

"After Arlo had moved out, before we bought the bookstore." She took a sip of her wine. "Jim and I got together when I was twenty-one and I hadn't ever been with anyone else. I mean, I had slept with a bunch of guys, but I had never been in a relationship until I met Jim, and then our music took off and I didn't even think about not being with him. My whole identity was tied to him and our music and our success as musicians."

"So, what happened?"

"After our label dropped us, he was impossible to be around. He blamed me for everything and was constantly picking fights. I didn't want to have to keep smoothing things over, so I left."

Amy was shocked. They had always seemed like such an inseparable unit. "Where did you go?"

"I found a sublet in Cabbagetown. A woman I knew was on sabbatical and needed someone to water plants and take care of her cat who had diabetes. I hated that cat," she said, laughing. "I hated that I had gotten roped into taking care of someone else yet again, something else, I guess, but that cat was my ticket out. I didn't want to be Fran of Fran & Jim anymore. I didn't want to be tied to all of that. I don't even remember what I did—smoked a lot of grass. Went on ridiculously long walks. Tried my best not to think about Jim, or music."

"So, then what happened?"

"We bought the bookstore."

"Just like that?"

"Well, no. I moved back in when the sublet was over. We were both really shaken up by being apart. It reminded us that we couldn't take each other for granted. It took a while before we found our way back to each other, and we talked a lot about who we were when we weren't playing music, who we wanted to be, as individuals, and as a couple. And then one day we were walking through Kensington Market and saw a For Sale sign at a health food store. We didn't want to run a health food store, but thought we could maybe run a used bookstore—we had so many books anyway, and were friends with people who were always getting rid of books. And Jim's mom had died, so we had a little bit of money. I needed something new. We both needed something different."

After Fran went to bed, Amy sat on the couch in the quiet, wondering if this was Fran's way of telling her Max would come back. Or that, like Jim, she could find her way out of this. Or maybe Fran was just telling her that marriage was hard. She didn't know.

Sina dropped Levi off the next morning. He was two and a bit and so much bigger than the last time Amy saw him. Max and Amy used to talk about having kids. In the early days, they'd lie in bed and imagine what their kid would look like—Max's curls, Amy's long legs. They imagined taking them to conferences in Europe and walking around cobblestones, and on tour, dancing in the front row of Brigade shows.

The Fun Times Brigade

But they hadn't talked about it in so long. They hadn't really talked about anything in so long. "I think I'm going to nap for a bit," Amy said.

"Of course," Fran said. "We'll be quiet, right, Levi? Right, stinker?" She tickled him.

In the guest room, Amy found a video of Max on YouTube, and watched him stand in front of a wall of chalkboards at a conference in France, a piece of chalk in his hand. His hair was longer, and he already had chalk dust on his pants.

"When we're talking about the free loop space of the manifold, we're going to be referencing all possible loops," he said in front of the chalkboard. "We're not making restrictions with transversal intersections."

The sound of his voice was almost too much to bear. Tears rolled down Amy's cheeks. She stopped the clip. She picked up her phone, and texted him, and then held the phone in her hand, hoping desperately to see the three bubbles of him typing back, but nothing. Of course he wasn't writing back. Amy scrolled to his parents' number and pressed the call button before she could stop herself. The phone rang, and she could see their old rotary phone jangling in the corner of their bright yellow kitchen.

"Hello?" said his mom's voice. Amy opened her mouth, but nothing came out.

"Hello?"

Shame flooded Amy's limbs.

"Who is it, Mom?" Max. In the background. Max! *Oh god, Max.*

"Hello?"

"It's probably a duct-cleaning scam," Max's dad said before Amy hung up.

After Sina picked up Levi, Fran left for a doctor's appointment, but not before she handed Amy a phone number. "Debbie's a couples' therapist," Fran said. "She's in my knitting group."

Amy thanked her and put the piece of paper in her pocket. She curled up on the couch and tried to read the Anne Carson.

"You know, I fucked up with Fran once," Jim said, joining Amy in the living room. "I mean, I didn't sleep with some wanker from a hipster band, but I almost lost her."

"She told me," Amy said.

"I took her for granted. I didn't listen to her. Hell, I didn't even listen to myself. All I wanted was bigger record contracts. I wanted bigger venues, and more shows. I lost myself and it very nearly ruined us."

Amy blinked hard. Ever since that stupid afterparty with Emily, all she'd cared about was BIKES. She cringed at all the nights she was out partying, hoping Jason would see her as an equal, hoping Christophe would recognize that she was an actual musician. Of course, they never did.

"I can't even tell you how hard those six months were," Jim said.

"Do you think Max will stay in Florida for six months?" Amy asked. She couldn't handle six months. She wasn't sure she could even handle six more minutes.

"No, no, I didn't say that. I'm just saying it'll take some time. Healing takes time. And it wasn't just Fran. I had to heal, too."

"How? How do you do that?"

"I took a woodworking course," he laughed. "I needed to do something that wasn't music, something that kept me occupied and not missing F."

"But how did you make it right with her?"

"I apologized and started listening. We started having dinner together. Actually sitting and eating together. Other than barbequing, I'd never really cooked before, and I knew that F hated it. So I took on meals. I think the first thing I made was scallops. I cooked the living shit out of them—they were hockey pucks."

The Fun Times Brigade

Amy laughed.

Jim handed Amy his guitar and got another that was leaning against the wall in the dining room. "I don't know much, but I know that music fixes everything," he said.

Jim tuned his E string, and Amy did the same. She hadn't touched her guitar all fall. They tuned each string in tandem, then Jim started playing the Mamas & the Papas. Her fingers felt thick on the strings, clumsy, but Jim didn't seem to notice. When Fran came back, they were playing Gordon Lightfoot's "Sundown." She got her guitar and joined them. The pads of Amy's fingers hurt, but she didn't want to stop playing. She didn't want to stop singing. Their harmonies were as perfect as they always were.

The next morning, Amy woke up to a half-formed song. It had been so long since she'd written anything, she almost didn't know what to do. She tiptoed out of the guest room and found some scrap paper in the kitchen. She sat cross-legged at the kitchen table and scribbled what she could remember.

High up in the bright blue sky, a pair of blue jays flying by.

Sparrows, crows, a robin sings, the sky's filled with all sorts of things.

From the tallest branch in the big oak tree, the cardinals weave a nest...me, bee, key??

She crossed it out.

With perfect scarlet pointed crests, the cardinals weave a little nest.

Sticks and stems and leaves and clay, they make a nest for eggs to lay.

Amy grabbed her phone and looked up the colour of cardinal eggs. Greyish and speckled.

More about eggs here????

Lindsay Zier-Vogel

With one big crack, the birds come out, they squawk and stretch and look about.

These baby birds will learn to fly, their tiny wings catching the sky.

They will be brave, they will be strong, they will learn to sing their song.

Amy heard Fran getting up, and then Jim's footsteps down the hall, so she put the kettle on for coffee.

28

IT RAINS ALL DAY MONDAY, AND ALICE BARELY naps on Tuesday, and Amy knows she has to get out of the house on Wednesday. In the morning, she texts Fran, but Jim's had a rough night, so she can't go over there, and Amy can't bring herself to go back to the library, so she registers for another baby yoga class.

Amy rolls out her mat next to the second-time moms, who don't bother with her and her enormous diaper bag. Their babies mouth yoga blocks and the edges of mats while they talk about City swimming registration (a nightmare), letting their four-year-olds wear pull-ups at night (the bladder is slow to develop), packing lunches for their kindergarten kids (the most thankless job of them all), and their husbands getting vasectomies (not even an hour-long procedure). It's like listening to people talking about travelling somewhere impossibly far away.

Alice wakes up mid–sun salutation again and takes forever to nurse. Amy gives in to it this time and leans against the studio wall. Another mom pulls a bottle out of a Thermos for her screeching baby and sends a commiserating smile Amy's way. Amy convinces Alice to gnaw on Bun Bun's flannel ear and manages to do at least a third of the class. She doesn't let herself fall asleep during Savasana and packs up quickly after the teacher dings the bell. She doesn't want to get caught up in another passive-aggressive bragging competition.

Amy doesn't want to go home, though; not yet, and besides, Alice won't nap again for a few more hours. She stops in at a coffee shop where she used to edit liner notes and work on song lyrics. She can't get the stroller in the door by herself, though, and a woman carrying a baby holds it open while Amy bashes the wheels up the stairs.

"Thanks," Amy says.

"No problem."

"You were just at that yoga class, right?" Amy asks.

The woman nods.

Amy orders coffee and sits at the table next to the yoga mom.

"How old?" Amy asks.

"He's five months next week."

"No way! Alice turns five months on the second."

"Is her birthday April second?"

Amy nods.

"Oh my god, they're birthday twins!" the mom says.

"That's wild! Did you have him at St. Joe's?" Amy asks.

"We were going to, but I had him at home, actually. By accident, kind of."

"By accident?"

"We had midwives, but by the time they showed up, I refused to put on shoes," she laughs. "I gave birth on our shower curtain and a pile of tea towels."

"Oh, wow," Amy says.

"Birth is fucking nuts," she says.

Alice is drooling all over her onesie, so Amy digs around in the diaper bag and pulls out a bib. "There you go," she says, Velcroing it around her neck.

"Any teeth yet?" the mom asks.

"Not yet, but she's got gobs of drool."

"He hasn't cut any yet, either," she says.

Alice gnaws on Amy's finger, and Amy wishes she had washed her hands, or at least used the hand sanitizer that's in the diaper bag.

"So, what did you think of that class?" the mom asks.

"It was good," Amy lies. "Well, it would be if I could actually do it."

"Every week I hustle to get there, and every week I pay to feed my kid on a yoga mat."

"I hear that," Amy says.

"At least it gets me out of the house."

"Totally."

"And my wife keeps saying maybe I'll find my people."

"I know! Everyone keeps saying 'find your people,' but how are you supposed to find your people when you're so goddamn tired?"

"Right?"

"And now I'm in nap jail. It's impossible to do anything and get her sleeping in her crib."

"He's totally going to fall asleep on the walk home and it's going to be a nightmare afternoon."

Amy nods and wipes drool off Alice's chin and realizes she doesn't even know this woman's name.

"I'm Amy," she says, extending her hand.

"Fiona," she says.

And then it feels awkward, like a date that got self-conscious and uncertain of where to go next.

"This is Henry, by the way," Fiona says.

"Alice," Amy says.

There's another long, awkward pause, but Amy smells Alice's head for courage and asks if Fiona wants to hang out some time.

"I was going to ask you the same thing," she says, smiling, and they exchange numbers.

Fiona and Henry leave and Amy beams in the coffee shop. *I think I made a mom friend today*, she types to Max, then changes it. *I made a mom friend today*, she writes and presses send.

"I made a mom friend!" she whispers to Alice before strapping her into her car seat.

Amy and Fiona start hanging out, first at a coffee shop near Fiona's house, and then at the coffee shop near Amy's house, trading stories about how rough the night before was, and sipping lattes over their strollers. The first time Alice starts scream-crying and they have to leave in a hurry. The second time Henry does.

Why don't you come here? Amy asks the next time they plan to meet up. *Then no one can give us stink eye.*

She cleans the house the night before, and debates making muffins in the morning, but then Alice wakes up early from her first nap and there's no time.

In the living room, Henry grabs a ball and sticks it in his mouth. "No, no, that's Alice's," Fiona says.

"It's fine," Amy says and pours them both coffees. Henry gums Alice's board books. Amy tries to make a mental note of which ones, so Alice doesn't put them in her mouth, but she loses track after the third Robert Munsch book.

"Wait, that's you?" Fiona asks, pointing to the three framed Brigade posters hanging in the hallway.

"Yeah," Amy says, and can feel her cheeks begin to flush.

"I *knew* you looked familiar! I've totally watched your show with my nieces. I remember my sister-in-law saying the Fun Times Brigade was the only kids' music that didn't make her want to stab her eyes out."

Amy laughs. "The biggest compliment of all."

"And you played with the Dovercourt Bicycle Collective."

"For a hot minute," Amy says, shocked. No one ever remembers her for that.

"You played their big show on the Island."

Amy nods. She has a flashback to that wall of sound, the black swath of the audience, Daniel's kick drum pounding in her sternum. She's embarrassed by how good it feels to be remembered for playing that one BIKES show.

"Lisa and I got engaged that afternoon," Fiona says. "That whole day was perfect."

Amy almost tells her about Christophe having a tantrum over the late sound check and the rider that crossed the lake twice, but Fiona doesn't need to know any of that.

Alice and Henry gum toys next to each other, and Amy and Fiona take photos of them. "Alice is his first friend," Fiona says.

Alice reaches for his ear. "Gentle, gentle," Amy says, pulling her hand away. "Henry's her first buddy, too."

Amy starts seeing Fiona at least once a week, sometimes twice, and she stops needing Max to understand her days with Alice. She stops feeling desperate for Fran to invite her over to sit on their porch. She has Fiona, who gets the long, mundane hours that are sometimes delightful and often a slog. She understands what it is to be jealous of their partners' jobs, to long for their previous lives, but also to love their kids so much. They text nonstop—trading purée recipes and links about how babies

The Fun Times Brigade

who sleep less are more intelligent, and breastfeeding memes that are so ridiculous Amy ends up laughing out loud and waking up Alice.

29

AFTER SIX DAYS OF SLEEPING IN FRAN AND JIM'S guest room, Amy decided it was time to go home. Fran and Jim both tried to get her to stay, but she was afraid if she didn't go then, it would only get harder. She was set to take the streetcar, but Jim insisted on driving her.

"Thank you," Amy said, tears welling up when he pulled up on the curb in front of her house.

"Of course, Ames. We're here if you need us. I've got a dentist appointment this afternoon, and Fran's watching Levi, but you've got a key."

Amy hugged him goodbye.

"Practice tomorrow?" he said.

"Practice?"

"It's time we start playing again, don't you think?" he asked.

Amy nodded slowly. "Okay."

"Noon?" he asked. "Or maybe one? I don't know what Fran has on in the morning."

"Whenever," Amy said. "I'll be there whenever."

The house rang with quiet when Amy woke up and the morning stretched long and empty in front of her. She walked down to the coffee shop and sat in the window with her latte, not ready yet to return to the empty house.

A kid, who was maybe three or four, ran a red fire truck under her chair.

"Hey, buddy," she said. He looked up. "Nice fire truck."

"I'm going to the doctor to get a shot," he whispered, clutching his truck in his fist.

"Well, that's going to take some bravery."

He nodded solemnly. "It's going to protect me and my little sister," he said.

"That's true. That's a pretty big job."

"Mason," his mom called, "please leave that lady alone."

"I don't mind," Amy said, but Mason joined his mom in line and Amy went back to her latte, wishing she had thought to bring a book. All she had was her phone. She looked through old text messages from Max, scrolling and scrolling until she found one that said *Love you. Love you too*, she had written back.

The kid tapped Amy's knee. "Do you want some cookie?" he asked, thrusting the paper bag at Amy.

"I'm okay, but that's super generous."

"Mason! Oh my god, we're going to be late! Leave the poor lady alone."

"No, that's fine," Amy insisted, but the mom rushed the kid out the door. "Good luck with your vaccine," she called after him.

"I think we should write a song about getting shots," Amy said to Fran and Jim when she went over that afternoon.

"Vaccine, Jolene," Fran rhymed off. "Seen, been, lean, keen."

"It can be a kids'-song fuck-you to the anti-vaxxers," Jim laughed.

There was a pause that started to feel awkward. They hadn't played as a band since the summer. Shame flooded through Amy again, and she bent over her guitar, retuning her already in-tune E string. Jim started picking a melody. It was pretty, and Amy hadn't heard it before.

He looked up at her and sang, "High up in the bright blue sky, a pair of blue jays flying by. Sparrows, crows, a robin sings. The sky's filled with all sorts of things."

"That's lovely," Fran said, adding in chords to his picking.

"Wait," Amy said. "Where did you—"

"I found it in the kitchen," he said.

"What's going on?" Fran asked.

"Ames wrote us something new," Jim said, still playing.

Amy didn't know what to say.

Jim turned the scrawled lyrics toward Amy and Fran.

"What an absolutely charming song," Fran said.

"Well, come on now, let's figure it out," Jim said.

They sang the chorus a few times until Fran picked up on the words, then they started figuring out the verses, filling in the holes where Amy had been stumped.

"They will be brave, they will be strong. They will learn to sing their song," they sang together, Fran taking the half-step harmony.

"We've got a keeper," Fran said when they got to the end.

"Maybe even the title track of a new album," Jim said.

Amy could feel her face getting red. She excused herself to go to the bathroom to splash water on her face. When she came back, Jim wanted to play some classic folk songs, "and some Grateful Dead, because I feel like kids will love early-seventies Jerry."

The Fun Times Brigade

They played and jammed and riffed on Grateful Dead lyrics to make them kid-friendly until Fran was laughing so hard she snorted. For two and a half hours, Amy didn't think about Max, or how badly she'd fucked up. It was just her and music and Fran and Jim, and the potential of a new Brigade album burbling in the background.

Amy was loading the dishwasher when she heard someone at the door. She tensed and grabbed her phone.

It was Max.

"Oh my god," she said, when she saw him in the front hall. "Max!" Amy went to rush toward him, to hug him, to smell him, but stopped herself. He didn't meet her gaze.

"You're home," Amy said.

"I'm teaching tomorrow," he said. He wheeled his suitcase into the living room.

She wanted to ask him a million questions—how was Florida? How were his parents? Did he tell his parents? Was he going to leave her? Did he want a divorce?

"Do you want Thai? There's leftover Thai. And Jim sent me home with some chili," Amy said.

"Jim?" Max asked, looking up.

"I stayed there for a bit," Amy said.

He didn't say anything but opened the fridge and pulled out Jim's chili. He stuck it in the microwave. Amy didn't know what to say, so she stood there, hovering. Time, patience, Jim said—that's what Max needed.

"We worked on a new song today," Amy said tentatively.

"We? Like you, Fran, and Jim?"

She nodded.

"So, the Brigade is a thing again?"

"I think so," she said.

He didn't say anything.

"How're your parents?" she ventured.

He shrugged and ate his chili while Amy wiped down the counters to keep herself from wrapping her arms around him.

The next morning, Max was up early, but Amy was already awake and put on coffee while he was in the shower.

"You don't have to," he said, but she poured it into his travel mug.

She spent the morning cleaning the house, and working on the vaccine song, but she couldn't focus. She went on a walk and did a load of laundry and found the number of Fran's therapist friend in her jeans' pocket.

She made dinner—penne and jarred sauce from the cupboard, and hoped Max would be home for dinner. She checked her phone, but he hadn't sent anything. She pictured him on the 401, driving with one hand on the top of the steering wheel the way he always did when he was on the highway. She pictured his car smashed into the guardrail, crushed by a transport truck, accordioned. If she lost him now, when things were this bad, she would never forgive herself. He couldn't die. Not now. She was crying when she heard the key in the lock. She wiped her eyes and stirred the sauce.

Amy put out bowls and ladled the sauce onto the noodles. Max sat across from her, but got up one bite in. She was expecting him to go upstairs to his office and close the door, but instead he got the parmesan from the fridge. They ate, in silence, but together. It was progress, Amy told herself.

She started baking when Max was at work—puff pastry from scratch, croissants, macarons, choux pastry. The fussier the project,

The Fun Times Brigade

the better. The more time it took, the better. When she was baking, she had to focus on levelling measuring cups, on getting butter laminated evenly between sheets of dough, on not letting the sugar burn. When she was baking, she couldn't think about Max, or what was going to happen with them.

But when she wasn't baking, it was all she could think about. I'm a cheater, she almost told the barista, the guy in the grocery store restocking yogourt, the mom who stopped her in line at the convenience store while she was buying tulips to take over to Fran and Jim's. Amy smiled as the woman took a picture of her and her daughter, but Amy felt like it was written all over her face—cheater cheater cheater.

She couldn't tell Julie, though Julie kept calling and wondering when they could hang out. She'd been engaged before she married Arun, and the guy cheated on her right before their wedding. She'd never forgive Amy, and Amy didn't deserve forgiveness, not from Julie, and not from Max.

Max started going to the gym. He didn't tell Amy, but every day when he got home from work, there'd be a T-shirt still damp with sweat in his gym bag, clothes he would put in the laundry. Amy had never done his laundry, but now she was desperate to wash his clothes with hers, to fold them, carefully, and put them in his drawers. She didn't even know which drawer he kept his T-shirts in, until one day when he was at work, she opened all of his drawers to see where his clothes were and sobbed over the folded jeans, the T-shirts, his paired-up socks. She couldn't bear the thought of these drawers being empty.

"We should probably talk," Max said. It had been two weeks since he'd arrived home from Florida.

Amy's stomach flipped. Talk—this is what she'd wanted—but suddenly she didn't know what to say.

"So," he said.

"So," Amy said.

"I don't know where to start."

"Me neither," she said. "But I just need to say one more time that I'm sorry. God, Max, I'm so sorry. I'm so, so sorry," She felt the pressure of tears behind her eyes.

He shook his head, and Amy tried to keep the tears at bay, but couldn't keep them from streaming down her cheeks. "I fucked up. Oh my god, I fucked up," she said. "I'm so sorry."

He stared at his coffee cup, knotting his fingers together.

"I just don't know how I'm going to get over this," he said eventually, his voice breaking. "I want to. I mean, sometimes I don't, but I want to, but then, I don't know how."

Amy went to reach for him, but he held up his hand. She wanted to tell him about Jim taking up woodworking and teaching himself to cook. She wanted to tell him about how Jim and Fran found their way back to each other. She wanted to insist they could, too. "I'll do anything," she said instead.

"But what could you even do?"

"Fran has a therapist friend. A couples' counsellor," she said. "We could start there?"

He shook his head. "I don't want to talk to a stranger about this," he said.

"It's not a stranger, it's someone who knows how to guide couples through things like this," Amy said.

"I don't know," Max said. "I don't know."

Amy left the number of the counsellor out. She waited a day, two days, but nothing.

She sent Max the link to Debbie's web page that promised she had been *helping strengthen partnerships for over twenty years.* She hoped he could overlook the stock images of grinning couples.

The Fun Times Brigade

He came home one night looking even more exhausted than usual. "Fine," he said, over dinner.
"Pardon?"
"The couples' therapist."
Amy felt a bubble of hope behind her sternum. "Okay," she said. "Do you want me to book it? Want to look at your schedule and send me some dates?"

30

AMY CHANGED HER OUTFIT THREE TIMES—SHE didn't want to look like a cheater. She wanted to look like someone who wanted her marriage to work. Were jeans too casual? Was a dress too much?

It doesn't matter what you wear, Emily texted her after Amy sent her another photo of her outfit. *Just make sure you bring water. And eat something beforehand.*

Max came home from work early, and they drove there together, sitting in silence as the radio blared the traffic report every fifteen minutes. Debbie's office was in a narrow old Victorian. The main floor had a Subway and the overwhelming bread smell followed them up the stairs to the second floor, and then waned as they climbed to the waiting room on the top floor. Max stood near the window, worrying at the skin next to his thumbnail. Amy wanted to grab his hands and make him stop, but instead she flipped through a months-old copy of *The New Yorker*.

"Max and Amy?" Debbie said at four on the dot, opening the door to her office.

There was a long, tufted couch in front of a glass coffee table. There were two Kleenex boxes and a chair—Debbie's chair, Amy realized. She tried to catch Max's eye, but he stared straight ahead.

"Tea?" Debbie asked.

Max shook his head, but Amy nodded. She needed something to hold on to.

"Lemon verbena, chamomile, or mint?" Debbie asked.

"Lemon would be great," Amy said.

Debbie handed her a plain black mug and laid out the ground rules. When they had agreed to creating a respectful, safe space, she began by asking them what their courtship had been like. It was funny to think of those early drunken days as a "courtship," but Amy didn't say that out loud. Then Debbie asked what had brought them there.

But Debbie knew why they were there. Amy had put it in her email.

Max looked at Amy. She had to say it. "I," she started. "I cheated. One night. I was super drunk. I cheated and I'm sorry. God, I'm so sorry. It was stupid and I still can't believe I did it." Tears streamed down her cheeks. She hadn't even made it ten minutes before crying.

Debbie nodded slowly and wrote something down on her yellow legal pad.

"And Max, how did that make you feel?"

"Uh, shitty," he said.

"Of course. That is a huge breach of trust," Debbie said.

"I'm sorry. God, I'm so sorry," Amy said, getting another Kleenex. "I'm sorry I broke us. I'm so, so sorry."

"And Max, can you hear Amy's apology?"

He nodded quickly.

"It's okay if not," Debbie said.

"I know she's sorry, but sorry doesn't change anything."

"No," Debbie said gravely. "No, it doesn't. Amy, is the affair over?"

"It wasn't an affair," she said, her voice higher pitched than she intended. "It was one night. One stupid night. And of course I'm never going to do it again. I'm never in touch with"—she couldn't bear to say his name—"him."

"And Max, you're not a musician?"

He shook his head. "I'm a professor," he said.

Debbie nodded and asked him what he studied and where, and Amy was annoyed by her calm, placid tone.

"So, Amy, you can commit to no more contact—is that what I'm hearing?"

"Yes," she said. "Of course."

"Okay, that is a great first step," Debbie said. "So, together, we will learn how both partners have played a role in contributing to the current state of your relationship, but first—"

"Wait," Max interrupted. "She cheated. Not me."

"Yes," Debbie said. "And that was a breach of trust, but it takes two people to create the conditions in which a transgression like this takes place."

Amy felt Max stiffen beside her. Neither of them said anything.

"Okay, then," Debbie continued. "Let's establish predictable patterns so we can figure out how you communicate, especially about challenging things. So, how do you talk to each other when things feel hard?"

But they didn't, not really. Amy was always performing, or rehearsing, or touring, and Max was working or at a conference. They had communicated by email in the early days, and now by text. Sometimes over the phone when Amy was on tour, but not recently.

The Fun Times Brigade

Max didn't say anything. He was punishing Amy, making her do all the work. She deserved it. She was the reason they were there, so she said a bunch of things about texts and emails, and Debbie took notes.

"We're almost out of time," Debbie said when Amy had finished mumbling.

Out of time? Already? They hadn't even done anything or gotten to anything that was going to fix this.

"Now, some couples make boundaries to only have these discussions in this room. Others don't need those limits. You can decide that together." She paused, and it took Amy a moment to realize she was asking them to make that decision right now.

"I'm fine either way," Amy said.

"Here is good," Max said.

Debbie nodded and made a note on her legal pad. "Now thank each other for taking the time to focus on each other and improving the connection in your relationship," Debbie said. She looked at them expectantly.

Max didn't look Amy in the eye, but they both murmured thanks to each other.

"Great, so I'll see you next Wednesday. And try to hold that limit, try to keep conversations about this"—she made a circle motion with her hand—"till we meet again."

They walked down the three flights of stairs, the smell of Subway bread getting stronger and stronger until it was a thick fug on the main floor. It was a relief to get out onto the sidewalk.

"So?" Amy started.

Max didn't say anything and walked ahead of her to the car.

After their second appointment, Amy started hearing Debbie's voice in her head while she kneaded brioche dough, while she showered, while she walked to the coffee shop after Max left for work. "Without looking for blame or finger-pointing, let's talk about underlying causes," Debbie said in Amy's head.

"Why do you think you turned to BIKES to find artistic validation?" she'd ask while Amy was putting in a load of laundry. "How did you feel when Max was working toward getting tenure?" she'd ask when Amy was unloading the dishwasher. "How did it feel when Max insinuated that his work was more important than yours?" she'd ask when Amy piped her second attempt at macarons onto parchment paper.

And Max would talk about all the brunch dates she'd been too hungover for, the time she was an asshole to the woman in the park, the nights she was out partying with Sam while he was at home marking or working on a paper. Of course, he'd only ever talked about those things in Debbie's office or in her head. Outside of their appointments, they talked about when they were going to be home, or if the car needed gas or not.

Amy couldn't stop replaying Debbie saying that she needed to stop beating herself up. "You made a mistake," she had said near the end of a session, before Max and Amy had to look each other in the eye and thank each other for making the time and space to heal, "but by focusing on the mistake and letting yourself be consumed by the shame of it, you're focusing on you, not on Max, and not on your relationship."

But Amy didn't know how to apologize without making it about her. She didn't know how she was supposed to let Max know how deeply she regretted that night in Kingston, how much she hated herself for it, if she wasn't allowed to talk about it.

"The shame isn't serving you," Debbie said, and every time Amy wanted to apologize again to Max and cry over dinner, she told herself that shame wasn't serving her, that it wasn't serving them. She didn't know if it was true, exactly, but it meant she didn't have puffy eyes for the Brigade meeting with Ben, and her throat wasn't hoarse when they played the new bird song for him.

The Fun Times Brigade

In November, Jim convinced Ben to draw up new contracts, insisting there be a clause about getting paid extra for meet-and-greets and autograph sessions. Amy tried thanking him, but he waved her off. "We should've done this years ago," he said.

They did a holiday fundraiser for Levi's preschool, and Amy showed up so early that they hadn't even set up the chairs. She hadn't realized how much she'd missed hearing kids sing along to "Menorah Menorah" and "The Silliest Reindeer." She felt more like herself on that stage than she had in months, years, maybe. She wasn't ready to leave after their final song, and hoped that somehow the small but mighty crowd in the school gymnasium would insist on an encore.

Backstage, in the staff room they'd set up as a green room, Amy felt reality seeping back in, like cold water filling a pair of rubber boots. During their last appointment, Max had said Joseph's name, and it was still haunting her. "I know she's not going to sleep with Joseph again," he had said, "but how do I know that she won't sleep with someone else?"

"You don't," Debbie said.

Dammit, Debbie. Amy wanted Debbie to say of course she wasn't going to ever cheat again, that it would never ever happen again, because it wouldn't. It would never happen again.

"You have to trust that now is different than then," Debbie continued. "You grew apart from each other and stopped valuing each other as individuals. You stopped valuing each other's work," she said. "But you're in a different place, and, Max, you have to trust who Amy is now, who you are now, who you are as a couple."

"How was it?" Fran asked, handing Amy a wipe to take off her makeup.

"Good," Amy said, rubbing off her eyeliner. "It felt really good. How about for you?"

She smiled. "Good."

"We fucked up the final verse of the reindeer song," Jim said, coming in with his guitar.

Amy laughed.

"We did!" he insisted.

"I know. I know," Amy said. It even felt good to get Jim's post-show notes.

Ben booked them a gig in Oakville, another careful, gentle show, where they figured out the bridge for the bird song, and sang "The Vaccine Waltz" for the first time.

"The new songs are a hit," Ben said after the meet-and-greet.

Ben and Amy were careful around each other, more formal and polite than they'd ever been, even in the early days. She kept waiting for him to say *I told you so*, or something about BIKES, but he hadn't so far. They were in some sort of peaceable stalemate that Amy was pretty sure Jim and Fran had orchestrated.

Amy hugged Jim during load-out.

"What's this for?" he said, setting down his guitar case to hug her back.

But she didn't need to say anything. He knew.

Amy baked croissants before their Tuesday afternoon Brigade rehearsal, filling half with almond paste, and half with cheese. She took a batch over to Fran and Jim's, which they devoured before working on a new song Fran had started about a tree named Sadie.

"You're going to have to open a bakery at this rate," Fran said.

Amy texted Max to let him know she was on her way, but there was no message from him, and she tried not to get frustrated that he hadn't texted her when he left work. He was in a terrible mood when he finally got home, and Amy didn't bother saying anything. He left his bag by the door and kicked his shoes off in a heap.

"You okay?" Amy asked from the kitchen.

"Fucking Richard is doing it again," he said. "Naheed heard him shit-talking Xingshi—how he wasn't churning out enough research. The guy doesn't even teach his own classes. He makes his TAs do it all and never does any committee work. We could all publish a lot more if we did that, but that's not the fucking job."

"He's an asshole," Amy commiserated.

"An asshole with a lot of sway in the department," he said. He opened the fridge and stared at the shelves.

"There are cheese croissants, and I was going to make salad for dinner," Amy said, pulling out plates.

"Jesus, Amy, croissants aren't dinner," Max said, slamming the fridge door shut. "Why is it always up to me to figure out meals? And get groceries? And when's the last time you cleaned the bathroom?"

"Whoa, okay. I can clean the bathroom," Amy said, stung.

"I know you can, but you *don't*. You never do."

"I'll clean the bathroom. I'll get groceries. I'll make dinner. Also, I've been the one making dinner, if you haven't noticed."

"Guilt dinners," he said.

"I'm making dinners because I'm home. I'm not always home."

"Oh, I know."

"You're never home, either, Mr. Important Professor who still can't be bothered to text when he leaves work."

"You know what? I *am* important at work. I've got three master's students and four undergrads with NSERCs to supervise, and I'm trying to finish a paper with Hugo. And now I'm going to have Richard on my case about research."

"Don't worry, you've made it *very* clear how important your work is, while I'm just over here singing about potties."

"Look, Debbie says I'm supposed to talk about my feelings, and this is how I feel," Max said. "And also, we never even celebrated me getting tenure."

"I was on tour! I sent you that special chalk."

"But we didn't *celebrate*," he said.

"Well, when's the last time we celebrated something I've done? I've put out eight albums and when have you celebrated any of them?"

They stared at each other, furious. Eventually, Max took his croissant to his office, and Amy ate hers over the sink.

"Good!" Debbie said when they told her about the fight. "That's wonderful! That is a huge step."

Amy and Max were both shocked.

"Really," Debbie continued. "You talked about your feelings. Directly. To each other! No texts, no emails! This is progress!"

Max laughed nervously.

"So, in addition to finding value in each other's work, one takeaway here is that eventually you need to do some celebrating. Tenure, albums, making it to Friday, whatever."

They had homework to do—they had to celebrate something—so, on Friday night, they ordered pizza and watched the newest Spider-Man movie. Amy had already seen it in a hotel in Victoria, but Max hadn't, and she didn't want to spend an hour looking for something they both hadn't seen and then end up arguing and not watching anything. She wanted to be able to report back to Debbie that they had done what she had asked them to.

They watched it, next to each other on the couch, not talking, but not fuming, either. Max still slept in his office that night, but said, "Have a good show," before Amy left the next morning. It wasn't much, but it felt like the needle had moved, even just a little bit.

31

ALICE IS FIVE MONTHS OLD AND TEETHING AND no one is sleeping, and Amy hasn't been away from her for even a few hours, but she promised Emily months ago that she'd be at opening night of her show.

"We'll be fine," Max insists. But it's not them Amy's worried about.

Amy feeds Alice one more time, even though she's clearly not hungry, and she spits up all over Amy's top. Amy changes into a black T-shirt that clings a bit too much to her stomach, but she has nothing else that fits. She kisses Alice and says goodbye to Max, double-checks that she has her wallet and keys, then kisses Alice again.

"My girl, my girl." She doesn't want to leave.

"You're going to be late," Max says.

"I'm going."

"We're going to be fine."

The Fun Times Brigade

Amy kisses Alice one more time and locks the door behind her. Her hands swing beside her, empty and useless without the stroller, and she wishes she had invited Fiona so she didn't have to go alone. Halfway to the station, she almost turns around and goes home, but she gets a text from Emily—*Can't wait to see you!!!!!!!*—so she keeps walking, one foot in front of the other, sidewalk square after sidewalk square.

Even though the subway is fairly empty, Amy hasn't seen this many strangers in months. She brought her Stevie Nicks biography, but she can't focus, so she flips through photos on her phone—Alice looking out the living room window, Alice smiling in her crib, Alice in the stroller on a walk yesterday. It makes her miss her more and less all at once.

She gets out of the subway and suddenly feels the tingle of milk starting near her clavicle. She focuses on a tree branch, a car. She recites licence plates out loud to keep the milk from coming.

There's a ticket under her name at the box office, and, after she finds her seat, she texts Max that she's there. She wants to ask if Alice is asleep yet, but the house lights dim and the stage manager comes onstage and asks everyone to turn their phones off. Amy checks hers one more time. *Text me when she's down*, she writes as fast as she can and turns her phone off.

In the centre of the stage, there are eight dancers with their backs to the audience, all muscle and sinew poking out of their black costumes. They begin to move—slowly, coiling and uncoiling like a moving, spinning game of Red Rover in which gravity doesn't seem to exist. There is no music, just the sound of feet on the floor. Dancers fly off the pinwheel into the wings until there are only three dancers left onstage. They stand there, in the muddled blue light and Amy can hear them breathing. It is unbearably intimate and makes her ache for Alice's tiny little puffs of air while she sleeps—the sound Amy can hear from across a room, from across the house.

Light blooms on the floor, and the dancers scatter through it. They jump and land without making a sound. It's ambitious and physical, this strange world of flung bodies and spiralling light. A cellist enters, the guy Emily was sleeping with the last time they talked. A violinist joins the cellist and the dancers spin around the musicians and Amy tries to focus on Emily's choreography, on the dancers and their wide-open bodies, but can't help but wonder what Alice will look like at five, at eight, at twelve, at twenty-five. She pictures her in dance class—not princess ballet classes with pink tutus and sequined slippers, but creative movement, where she will dance with scarves and be a tree and a snowflake and a butterfly emerging from a chrysalis.

Amy wonders if Alice will play piano, or guitar. She wonders if she will love numbers like Max or write poems in journals marked PRIVATE DO NOT READ. She wonders if she will play baseball or soccer. Her heart swells at the thought of Alice kicking a soccer ball, fierce and full. Her ribs ache at the thought of Alice, her tiny little Alice, running the length of a field, driven and focused.

The piece ends in a fury of spinning dancers and wild strings and the stage fades to black. The lights snap on and the dancers stand in a row, smiling and sweating, their chests heaving. They bow and the audience stands, cheering and clapping. The dancers open their hands to the wings and Emily walks out looking positively radiant. She presses her hands together at her lips and nods her head.

Amy checks her phone as subtly as she can when the house lights come up. Max has sent a photo of Alice in her sleep sack, and she feels the lightning tingle of a letdown again. She tries to think of something else and realizes she's holding up the whole row. "I'm sorry," she says, shoving her phone into her purse and moving to the aisle.

She finds a bathroom, and then stands around in the lobby, waiting for Emily. Everyone knows everyone—hellos and kisses and "Wasn't that amazing" flung across the tiny space. Amy stands in the corner and scrolls through her phone, trying not to feel out of place.

"Amy!" Emily waves to her from across the lobby, and Amy makes her way over to her. She looks stunning in a hot pink jumpsuit and matching lipstick.

"That was amazing. That was fucking amazing!" Amy says, hugging Emily.

"It's surreal! This is all just so crazy!" Emily is wide-eyed, and Amy misses the post-performance high, the buzz, the adrenaline. "It means so much to me that you came!"

She introduces Amy to one of her patrons, an elderly woman with a lot of rings, and to a knot of her dancers, then the lighting designer. Emily presses a glass of Prosecco into Amy's hand, and someone she's never met makes a toast in Emily's honour. Everyone raises their glasses and drinks to her brilliance.

After the toast, Emily pulls Amy aside. "Just before the show tonight, I got an email," she whispers over her drink. She waves to someone, then leans close again. "A presenter from Italy watched rehearsal earlier this week. She wants to show the work there. In *Italy*. At the Venice Biennale."

"Holy shit!" Amy says.

"Right? I'm freaking out. It's not official-official so I can't tell anyone, none of the dancers, or musicians, but can you believe it?"

"That's amazing." Amy hugs her tight and swallows the envy that heaves in her throat.

The cellist waves Emily over. "Go," Amy tells her, ashamed of this flare of jealousy.

"You'll stick around?" Emily asks.
Amy nods, even though she knows she won't.
"I love you," Emily says. "Thank you so much for coming. It means the world to me."
"Love you, too."
"Give Alice a kiss for me," she says.
"Come over soon."
"I will. I totally will."
Amy checks her phone, but there's nothing from Max.
Is she asleep? Amy writes to Max.
"Amy! Is that you?"
She looks up from her phone to see Sandra walking toward her with her arms open. Amy hasn't seen her in years. Her hair is cut in a short bob, and she's wearing denim coveralls that somehow look majestic.
"You're a *mom*!" Sandra says, hugging Amy, careful not to spill her plastic cup of wine.
"Yeah," Amy says. "Alice." It's been so long since she's had to make small talk, she doesn't know what to say. "She's five months."
"I was just thinking about you this week. I'm putting together a solo EP and want to feature really rad women. Sam's coming in from Montreal and I've already recorded Sarah Harmer. Julie Doiron has agreed to be on it, and Kathleen Edwards. Feist is recording remotely."
"That's a lineup!" Amy says, trying to keep envy from hijacking her voice.
"Right? I'm stoked. So, what are you doing next Thursday? Can you come record?"
Amy stares at her. She hasn't played with anyone since BIKES, except Fran and Jim. She hasn't been in a recording studio since before she got pregnant with Alice. "Um, yeah. Totally. Wow. Thanks for asking."

"Of course," she says.

Someone calls her name and Sandra squeezes Amy's arm. "I'll send you the details," she says. "It's so good to see you!"

"You, too!" Amy says. She drops her plastic cup in a blue bin and makes her way through the impossibly beautiful crowd to the door. She's buzzing with the potential of Sandra's offer as the subway takes her west, over the river, and then underneath the downtown towers. But as the escalator carries Amy up to the bus platform, she starts worrying that Fran and Jim will see this as BIKES all over again.

"Should I do it?" she asks Max when she gets home.

"They're not going to say no," he says.

She knows they won't say no. "Maybe I shouldn't."

"Do you want to do it?"

Amy nods.

"Then they'll understand," Max says. "It's only one day."

Amy calls Fran in the morning, but she doesn't answer, so she texts her, but still doesn't hear back.

Your mom okay? Amy texts Arlo.

They've both caught a cold.

Are they all right?

Yeah, just laying low. Sina took them over some broth.

Sandra sends the lyrics and a recording of the two songs she wants Amy to do harmonies for. *A tight harmony*, she writes, *Three-part—you, me, and Sam.*

Amy listens to the tracks while Alice naps, and calls Fran again. She needs to talk to her before Thursday.

32

IN THE NEW YEAR, BEN BOOKED THE BRIGADE A small East Coast tour. It was strange to be away from Max when things were still so fragile, but it felt good to be back on a tour bus, playing sold-out auditoriums. Amy wanted this. She wanted full audiences, and professional sound crews, and Cora, their tour manager handling all the logistics. She wanted a king-size hotel bed at the end of the night all to herself.

One night in Halifax, Fran crashed early and Jim and Amy sat in her room, ordered room-service hamburgers, and drank scotch.

"It'll put hair on your chest," Jim said, taking a sip.

"You can really taste the bourbon casks," Amy said.

Jim nodded. "How are things with Max?"

"Okay, I think," Amy said. "We're seeing Fran's friend, Debbie."

"Good for you," he said.

The Fun Times Brigade

Amy took a sip of her whisky. She couldn't believe she had almost given up touring, and late-night whiskys with Jim.

"Fran and I never did couple's counselling, though I think we probably should've."

"It's hard," Amy admitted. "And exhausting. She told me I had to stop living in a shame spiral or I'd never get on with my life."

"That sounds like pretty good advice."

Amy nodded. "And we're working on this feedback wheel thing so that we can stop being defensive and have, you know, meaningful resolution. Still, I don't know how we're going to heal-heal. Like, actually heal," she said. Sleep in the same bed was what she meant. That seemed like a thousand appointments away.

"You'll get there. Slow and steady."

Debbie said they had to accept each other's strengths and weaknesses. Amy still hated when Max forgot to tell her when he left late from work, or got so into his work that he forgot about everything else, but then she thought of him sitting with his nephews playing a long-division game he'd made up for them, or hearing him on the phone with Naheed walking through a theorem he was working on, and she missed him so much it made her chest ache.

Jim and Amy finished their burgers, and he found a package of cashews in the mini-bar.

"Or there's a tin of mixed nuts," Jim said.

"Are there chips?"

He threw Amy the tube of Pringles and picked up her guitar. "The ending of the tree song needs some work," he said, and Amy got her rainbow uke from her suitcase.

The BIKES album came out while the Brigade was in Fredericton. Samantha forwarded the email from Jason with a link to buy the album. Amy couldn't believe that, even though she was on it, she still had to buy a digital copy.

She waited until after the Brigade show to listen to it, and sat in the doorway of the theatre with her headphones in. The mix was off, and the drums were sloppy, and you could tell Daniel was drunk. The Taylor Swift cover hadn't made it on, and all the things that had felt funny and silly—the toy piano outro on "Dovercourt, Sweet Dovercourt," and all of them yelling the chorus of "White Squirrel" just seemed embarrassing and adolescent.

We're all going to Jason's for a listening party, Samantha texted. *You have to come!*

Can't, Amy wrote back. *I'm out east.*

She went to bed early that night and woke up to a series of texts from Samantha. *You're not missing anything*, she had texted. *Jason couldn't get a sponsor, so the beer is garbage and Christophe didn't even bother showing up.*

Emily sent a review of the album with the grimace emoji. *Yikes*, she wrote. It turns out Amy wasn't the only one who thought it was a mess. Critics also thought it was a hack job. They called it BIKES' "nail in the coffin" album.

Amy didn't mention the BIKES album to Max, or Debbie. There was no point in bringing it up. It was in the past and they were moving forward, even if it was at a snail's pace.

"How was the tour?" Debbie asked.

At first, Amy thought she meant the actual shows, but then realized she meant how was it for both of them.

"Good," Max said. "I mostly just worked."

"And Amy?"

"Good," she said. "I missed Max."

Debbie beamed. "You can tell him that if you'd like."

Amy flushed and turned to him. "I missed you," she said.

He met her eyes then looked away. "I missed you, too."

Debbie smiled and wrote something down on her yellow notepad.

"I'm sorry I've made you feel like your work doesn't matter," Max said, without looking up. "It matters. I know it matters."

Amy's eyes filled with tears. She reached for his hand, and then instinctively pulled it away, but he put his hand on hers. No one spoke, and Amy wanted Debbie to disappear so they could have this moment, just the two of them.

"Thanks," she choked. Max squeezed her fingers.

"Well, then," Debbie said, beaming.

Amy grabbed a Kleenex.

Just as their time was up, Debbie said, "Your homework this week is to start prioritizing each other. Sit down with your schedules and find two times where you can connect. A dinner out, maybe. Brunch? You said brunch was something you do."

On Thursday night, as Amy was loading the dishwasher, Max asked if she wanted to prioritize each other.

"Pardon?" she asked.

"Would you like to prioritize each other?" he asked, pulling out his phone.

It took Amy a moment to realize he was making fun of Debbie.

"Yeah," she said, smiling.

"Saturday night? Dinner?" he asked. "Or brunch? Brunch is *something we do*," he said.

"Sunday?"

He nodded and put it into his calendar. Amy's heart swelled.

"Thank you for taking the time to improve the connection in our relationship," he said mock gravely.

"No, thank *you* for taking the time to improve the connection in our relationship," Amy said, and laughed for the first time in as long as she could remember.

They had been seeing Debbie for almost five months when she asked them to come up with couple's goals: things they wanted to do together, big and small.

"I want to clean out the garage," Max said.

The garage? *That* was his couple's goal? Amy tried to keep from laughing.

"Amy?" Debbie asked.

"Travelling," she said. "Just the two of us, not tacked on to a conference, or a tour, but actually travelling."

"Keeping our Friday-night pizza date," Max said.

"Hosting something, maybe Easter brunch or a Seder, or something," Amy said.

"Great, these are great," Debbie murmured, taking notes.

"Starting a family," Max said quietly.

"Amy?" Debbie asked.

Amy looked at Max.

"Do you want to do that?" Debbie asked softly.

"Yes," Amy said, afraid her chest might burst. She didn't know how it would work with the Brigade picking up again, but she grabbed Max's hand.

"Let's put it on the list, and circle back later," Debbie said. "What else?"

Amy and Max didn't talk on the drive home, which wasn't rare, but the silence felt different. Max wanted to have a baby. After all of this, he still wanted to have a baby. They were going to be okay.

The Fun Times Brigade

One Friday night, after rewatching *The Bourne Identity*, they were both tipsy and had sex for the first time since before Kingston. It wasn't the best sex they'd ever had—it was sloppy and drunk—but after that, they started sleeping in the same bed, which felt like an even bigger milestone.

When the weather got warm, they organized the garage, and only argued once, about where the shovels should go. They hosted a Seder for Max's sister and nephews. Amy made dinner when she was home instead of always ordering in, and they kept a running grocery list on the fridge. After the Brigade's summer tour, and Max had handed in his summer-semester marks, they even booked a trip to San Francisco.

"We're doing it," Amy said to Max, squeezing his hand as the plane hurtled down the runway. "We're doing the things."

33

AFTER THEIR TRIP TO SAN FRANCISCO, AMY started taking folic acid and B6, and charting her cycle, slipping a thermometer under her tongue on the tour bus. Eventually, she started seeing the patterns emerge on the app on her phone—the pink fertile window, with a flower on ovulation day, *the* day—but she'd be a thousand, two thousand, three thousand kilometres away from Max.

After months of negative tests, Amy gave up tracking her cycle. There was no point in staring at pink calendar squares if she was going to be in St. John's, or Victoria, or somewhere in the prairies. But the desire to be pregnant was a fog that blanketed everything. Every conversation, every show, even the long days in the recording studio recording their folk album, were muted with Amy's need to have a baby. It was the lens she saw through during every show, looking out to an audience of babies that weren't hers.

The Fun Times Brigade

Right before Amy got on the bus for Thunder Bay for the second leg of their *Sunshine & Rainbows* summer tour, something felt different. Her body felt different. She'd peed on so many sticks for so many months, cried in so many hotel bathrooms and green room bathrooms, and once in a porta-potty in Saskatchewan, that she braced herself for a single line—an em dash to nothing—even though she knew something was different this time.

She bought a box of pregnancy tests and peed on one before dinner. She set the timer on her phone and stared at the grout between the tiles. She looked at it after two minutes. Only one line. She hated that fucking line.

She had been so sure. This time had felt different. It had, but she wasn't pregnant.

She and Max split a fancy bottle of red that night and ate the steak rarer than usual, and, when she woke up in the morning, she peed on the extra stick that came in the package before she left for the airport. She didn't want it waiting for her when she got home, reminding her that she wasn't pregnant. And then, while she brushed her teeth, two lines showed up. She shook it as if that would make it correct itself. Two lines—a plus sign. She was pregnant.

"Max!" Amy shouted from the top of the stairs.

Max was in the kitchen, getting breakfast. "I can't hear you."

"I'm pregnant!" she shouted.

She heard something drop in the kitchen.

"Max?"

He ran to the stairs. "What?"

Amy nodded, holding up the test. "Two lines."

"But there was only one yesterday."

"You're supposed to do it in the morning when the hormone thing it tests for is the highest. I should've known."

He took the stairs two at a time.
"We're pregnant?"
"Well, I am."
He kissed her. "Holy shit! We're having a baby!"
"Hopefully."
"What do you mean hopefully?"
"I could miscarry. It's still so early." Amy started crying. The thought of losing the baby she had only known about for less than a few minutes made her terribly sad.

He held her tight. "You're pregnant," he said into her hair.

She closed her eyes against his shoulder. She was pregnant.

It felt surreal eating toast while cells divided furiously inside her. The baby was a zygote still, the size of a poppy seed, according to the app she and Max both downloaded.

"I wish you didn't have to go," Max said when he carried her suitcase to the door.

She nodded. "Me, too."

Amy kept it a secret from Thunder Bay to Medicine Hat, but she started vomiting in the mornings through the Rockies and she couldn't not tell Fran and Jim, though by then, even the bus driver had guessed.

"But don't worry," Amy insisted to Fran and Jim. "I'm just going to take three months off and I'll be back onstage."

But Fran wouldn't hear of it. "You're going to need more time," she insisted.

"I'll be fine. I'll bring the baby on the road, with a nanny, or Max."

Fran looked at her. "Amy Scholl, you are not going to be on the road with a baby at three months. Six, maybe. Nine, possibly."

"You had Arlo on the road."

"And I wish I hadn't. My breasts leaked onstage, and I'd be able to hear him crying from god knows how far away, and performing was the last thing I wanted to be doing. You need to stay home. You need to heal and be with your baby and let people take care of you."

"Like who, my mom?"

"Max, me, and Jim. Julie, Emily, Max's sister."

Amy was still skeptical. "I'll write songs during naps."

"Write us a whole new set," Jim said.

"Or you could just be a mom for a bit," Fran said, glaring at Jim.

But Amy wasn't going to give up the band, not again. She was going to be an artist and a mom. She would do both. "Our live album will be in post, and I'll work on new material," Amy insisted, smiling until a wave of nausea hit and she lurched to the tour bus bathroom.

"I'm okay," she called out after she vomited up her breakfast. "I'm okay." And she put an alarm in her phone to remind her to eat crackers every hour on the hour.

34

MAX TEACHES ON THURSDAYS, SO AMY ASKS HER mom to watch Alice while she goes to record with Sandra. She gets everything organized—extra wipes and diapers, a schedule of Alice's afternoon. If Amy nurses her before she goes, Alice will be fine until she gets back.

Amy tries Fran again, but she still doesn't answer, so she puts on makeup while Alice kicks in her bouncy chair. "What do you think, baby girl?" Amy asks. She hasn't worn mascara in so long that her eyelashes feel strangely thick and heavy. She starts to worry that she looks like she's trying too hard, so she wipes off her dark lipstick and puts on something more neutral. "How's this?" she asks Alice. Alice kicks and grabs at the giraffe dangling over her chair.

Her phone rings as she's carrying Alice downstairs, and she's flooded with relief. She'll be able to tell Fran and Jim before she goes.

But it's her mom. "Hey, you on your way?" Amy asks.

"I just got a call to teach at the School of Contemporary Art! I mean, just a first-year drawing class, but still! Dalia, who is the usual sub, is out with the flu. I've been on the roster for years, and they finally called me in!"

"That's great," Amy says. "Congrats."

"So, I'm free next week if you need me."

"Wait, what? It's today?"

"I should've left ten minutes ago," she says.

"Mom! I asked you about this last week!"

"I know, kiddo. I'm sorry. It's a very last-minute thing."

Amy hangs up without saying goodbye. What is she going to do? Max is an hour away without traffic. She tries Emily, but there's no answer. She tries Arlo, then Sina, but they don't pick up, either. Max's sister has a nanny for the boys, but Amy doesn't even know if she's around while the boys are at school. She looks at her phone. She could ask Fiona, but it's too much to ask her to take care of two babies. "Fuck!" she yells at the ceiling.

Amy texts Julie, and Julie says she can duck out of a meeting and be there in forty-five minutes.

You're the best, but I have to leave now.

She has to bring Alice with her. She has no choice. She'll be that mom, she tells herself, that musician mom, like Fran was, bringing her kid to the recording studio. But then she remembers Max has the car. How is she going to get Alice over there?

Julie sends over a YouTube video about how to secure the bucket seat into a car without the base. Amy watches it three times and then calls a cab.

Amy's never been to Shanly Street Studios before. It's a converted Victorian house with peacock wallpaper and narrow hallways. She can barely carry Alice down the hall without bumping her car seat into the wall. At least she fell asleep on the ride over. Amy covers the car seat with a muslin and prays that she stays asleep until she's done.

"Amy!" Sandra yells. "Oh shit!" She lowers her voice. "Sorry. I didn't know you were bringing the baby."

"My babysitter bailed last minute," Amy says. She can't admit it was her mom.

"That's the worst," Julie Doiron says. "Julie," she extends her hand as if Amy doesn't know who she is.

Amy puts Alice's car seat down and shakes her hand. She doesn't mention that they met before at a long-ago BIKES rehearsal.

"Amy!" Sam says, a coffee in hand. "It's been ages!" She gives Amy a sideways hug. She's shaved half her head and dyed the other half purple. "And this is Alice?" she says, lifting up the muslin.

Don't, Amy wants to say, terrified she'll wake up.

"What a cutie."

"You're the best for coming to do this," Sandra says. "Seriously, I'm so tired of dudes taking up so much space in this industry."

"Amen," Sam says over her coffee.

Sandra leads them into the studio and introduces Amy to the producer, Runa. "Pleasure," she says, shaking her hand.

Amy puts Alice in the corner of the control room and prays she stays asleep.

"I think it's so amazing that you're making your baby part of your artistic world," Runa says. "That's so cool."

"I'll keep an eye on her," Julie says.

Amy's so grateful she wants to cry, but instead, she smiles and thanks her.

The tech gets Sam and Amy set up in the booth, and Runa has them test their mics.

"Perfect," she says through the speakers. "Let's start with 'Dark Windows,'" she says.

Sandra's voice comes through the headphones, with Sam's bass track, and Julie on lead guitar. Amy wants to ask Sam if she's playing on all the songs, but doesn't want to seem ungrateful.

"I'm waiting outside your apartment, and the windows are all dark," Amy sings into the microphone, harmonizing with Sandra's lead vocals and Sam's octave harmonies.

"Great," Runa says after the run. "Let's do it again, but I want more connection."

They start again, but Runa stops them before the end of the first verse. "So, I'm loving the energy, but I want you to really be there. Don't perform it, *experience* it. I need you to be Sandra, standing there, waiting, so desperate."

They try again, but Sam keeps fucking up on "dark" and "park." Don't say the *K*'s, Amy wants to tell her.

"Phrasing's a bit strange," Runa says from the control room. "It's a tricky line to get. Let's try it again."

This would be a piece of cake with Fran, but Sam is pitchy, and it's throwing off Amy's half-step harmonies. She just wants to sing it by herself. She'd nail it if she could just do one pass on her own.

"And I can see you, standing there," they sing. Amy can feel her ear being pulled down to the melody.

"Look, I know it's a tough harmony, but I need you to be an extension of Sandra's voice," Runa says.

"Jesus," Sam says under her breath.

Amy wants to tell Runa to ease up. Sam's going to crack, and they won't have anything they can use. She can see Sandra and Runa talking in the control room. She tries to figure out what they're saying, but they just look annoyed.

"Three-part harmony's not an easy one," Amy says quietly to Sam. "We've got this."

They do another pass, but Amy can tell from Runa's face that she's still not happy.

"Tell us what you need," Amy says. "What can we do?"

"Just try again, and we'll see what we get," is the answer from the control room.

Sam stops in the middle of the second chorus of their best take and yells, "Fuck me!"

Amy clenches her jaw.

"Again for tuning," Runa says.

Amy can see Julie rocking Alice's car seat. Amy hopes she's still sleeping.

"We can do this," Amy tells Sam. "We're going to nail it next take."

Amy's mid-chorus when she sees Julie taking Alice out of her car seat. She misses the beginning of the second verse and hopes Runa didn't notice.

"Amy," Sandra says after the next take. "Alice is up."

"Is she okay? Can we do one more pass?"

"Standby," Runa said.

Sam and Amy do another take, but Alice is raging in Julie's arms.

"Amy, you need to come in here," Runa says.

Julie is bouncing and shushing Alice, but Alice is in full-bore scream-mode.

"Sorry," Amy says, taking Alice from Julie. "Thank you." Alice's face is blotchy and red. Amy bounces her and kisses her face. "You're okay, you're okay, baby girl. Mama's here."

Amy can feel Sandra's impatience.

"Maybe take her in the hall?" Runa asks.

"Of course," Amy says.

Julie gives her a commiserating smile.

"I just need a sec," Amy says.

The Fun Times Brigade

She bounces Alice around the hallway. "Come on, come on, baby girl. We've got this. Come on." She whisper-sings "The Crayon Song" and eventually Alice's screams turn into whimpers.

Amy slides down the peacock wallpaper and sits on the floor and then realizes she can't breastfeed in her jumpsuit. "Fucking hell," she says under her breath. She slides both arms out of the sleeves so the top of her jumpsuit is around her waist. Alice latches, her face is still blotchy red from screaming. Amy sits half-naked while she nurses and reminds herself that this isn't Alice's fault. If her mom hadn't bailed, this would all be fine.

When Alice is done, Amy takes her back in the control room, but Alice refuses to go back into her car seat. Julie offers to hold her, but Alice will only be held by Amy. There's no way she's going to be able to sing the second song with Alice on her hip.

"We're back in the studio tomorrow," Sandra says.

"We'll be doing backups for three tracks," Runa adds.

Amy smiles and tries to blink the tears out of her eyes. "I'll see if I can get a sitter," she says as brightly as she can.

She slips out mid-song so she doesn't have to see Sandra or Runa promising each other that they'll never let babies ruin their careers. Amy buckles Alice into the back seat of a cab and wonders if her mom was right—maybe it is impossible to have an artistic career and a baby.

"I don't think we'll be coming back tomorrow, eh?" Amy says, tears streaming down her face. "And that's okay, right, baby girl? Mama's probably on one track at least, and we'll have a good day, just the two of us. We'll be okay."

35

"WELCOME, OTTAWA!" AMY SAID INTO THE microphone, beaming at the audience, her pregnant belly touching the mic stand, the stage lights hot and bright. The National Arts Centre was packed and a voice in the back yelled, "We love you!"

"We love you, too," she said, laughing.

"It's so good to be here," Fran said into the microphone stage left.

Jim was at the middle mic and played the opening chord of "The Rainbow March" then glanced over at Amy and Fran.

"One, two, three, red!" they sang, Jim's tenor anchoring Amy's and Fran's voices. "One two three, orange. One, two, three, yellow! All the colours saying hello!"

Amy marched in her bright red Converse. She had a matching red kazoo in her pocket for their version of "You Are My Sunshine," that, according to the set list taped to the floor in front of Jim, was still a few songs away.

"All right, friends, everybody on your feet," Fran called out before the second chorus, and the entire concert hall marched and sang together while Fran and Amy swished their skirts in time with the music. The house lights were bright enough for Amy to see the audience, their small, earnest faces, their heart-bursting enthusiasm. Amy looked over at Fran, and Fran smiled back at her. Jim winked at the two of them.

"One, two, three, green! One, two, three, blue!"

They let the audience sing the final verse, and Amy stood behind her microphone, and beamed. She would never get used to the fact that two thousand people were singing a song she'd written with Fran and Jim on their porch.

"Whew!" Fran said at the end of the song, miming wiping sweat off her brow.

"Knock-knock," Amy said into the microphone while Jim and Fran got new guitars from the guitar tech in the wings.

"Who's there?" the audience called back.

"Lettuce."

"Lettuce who?"

"Lettuce sing you one more song!"

The kids laughed and the adults groaned, and Amy started the intro to "Puddle Jumping."

"Plonk went the rain, and plink went the rain, and our rain boots started dancing."

Amy and Fran and Jim did their rain-boot choreography in front of the mic stands—right foot, left foot, click the heels twice.

"And our umbrellas started spinning," the audience sang back to them, kids in the aisles twirling.

It was their second-to-last show before Amy went on mat leave and Jim and Fran wanted to go out for dinner afterward. They usually went to a tiny seafood place on Bank Street, but Amy couldn't eat oysters or tuna or swordfish, so they took a cab across town to a place Arlo had recommended—all farm fresh and local, he'd promised, though Amy wasn't sure what would be fresh and local in February in Ottawa other than maybe carrots and potatoes.

Amy's morning sickness had let up in her third trimester, and she finally felt the glow of pregnancy, the joy of it. She felt lucky, so lucky as she opened the menu, ecstatic to be able to eat again.

Jim ordered sparkling water for the table.

"No, no, get wine! Just because I can't have any doesn't mean you can't," Amy insisted.

Fran did, and they ordered appetizers to share.

Jim fidgeted with his napkin while Amy spread butter on a roll. "You okay?" she asked him. He gave her a tight smile and the server refilled their water glasses and brought another bread basket.

Jim was quiet throughout dinner, and Fran compensated by being extra upbeat. He was usually only grumpy after a bad show, but it had gone so well.

After they finished eating, Fran looked at Jim and raised her eyebrows.

"What?" Amy asked. "You're being weird. Both of you."

Jim shook his head.

"Jim," Fran said.

"F," Jim said.

The server cleared the table and handed them dessert menus.

"Okay, you're freaking me out," Amy said. "What's going on?"

"We have some news," Fran said when Jim still wouldn't say anything.

"Good news or bad news?" Amy asked, though she already knew it couldn't be good news.

"I have cancer," Jim said.

The restaurant fell away. The plates and the conversations of strangers next to them, and the clatter of metal in the kitchen behind Fran—it all disappeared. All Amy could see was Jim's sad, drawn face.

"Wait, what?"

"Colon cancer," Fran said.

"But you're so young."

"Sixty-five isn't young, Ames."

Just a few hours ago, he had been onstage making the kids laugh at his "Five Little Monkeys Jumping on the Bed" faces. He wasn't old.

"We've still got a lot of questions to answer before jumping to any conclusions," Fran said, reaching for Jim's hand. "He's got a series of tests when we're back, and then we'll see what the treatment options are."

"Surgery to start," Jim said.

"It's just laparoscopic," Fran added. "And then that might be it, or they could do radiation after that. We have lots of options."

Amy looked at Jim. He had been tired lately, but she had been so wrapped up in her own exhaustion, she hadn't thought much of it. "We'll cancel our Toronto show," she said. "Let's just call it."

"No, no," Jim said. "We'll do Toronto."

Amy looked at Fran, who nodded. Amy reached for Jim's hand.

"I'm going to be okay," Jim said resolutely.

"Surgery for Jim, and you'll pop this baby out," Fran said.

Amy tried to smile. She squeezed Jim's hand and he squeezed back.

"We'll regroup in the new year to get our live album out in the spring," Fran continued.

"Your mat leave is perfectly timed," Jim said, smiling.

And then five weeks later, just before her due date, Amy's water broke. It was 4:00 a.m. and she thought it was the hot water bottle leaking, the way it had a few weeks earlier. But when she stood up, the water kept pouring out of her—on her waddle to the bathroom, and then back to the bedroom.

"It's happening," Amy told Max, shaking him awake. "We're having a baby." They called the midwife, but she said to call back when the contractions started. They ate breakfast—nothing. Amy changed the towel in her underwear every half hour—still nothing. She was still and quiet on the couch, waiting to feel something. But nothing happened. Max hovered and Amy wished he would go to work, but then she'd be alone and she didn't want that, either.

When the contractions arrived shortly after lunch, they hit her like a truck. By the third, or fourth, she knew it was a runaway train. She made Max close all the blinds. She made him call the midwife, but Ariana was calm, too calm. Amy wanted energy. She wanted mobilization. She buried her head in a pile of towels and blankets on the couch that she called her rat's nest. She plugged her ears and hummed to make the pain recede. Max called Ariana again, and when Amy couldn't hold the phone, Ariana told Max she'd meet them at the hospital.

She refused to get into the front seat. Max insisted she put her seat belt on, and she told him to fuck off. When they arrived at the hospital, Max tried to get her to sit in a wheelchair. Amy refused—her insides were splitting from themselves and she wanted out of her body. She pushed the wheelchair toward the elevator, pausing every few minutes to get through another contraction.

Ariana was waiting for them, and while Max handed over Amy's health card and filled out forms, Ariana got Amy to a room.

"Ride those surges," Ariana said in a voice that was still too calm. Amy wanted to be drowned out, not soothed.

Ariana suggested she bounce on the turquoise exercise ball Max carried in from the car, but Amy just wanted her rat's nest. Ariana insisted and, eventually, Amy bounced between contractions, then went back to her nest. Ariana tried to get her to try the birthing stool, and Amy told her to go fuck herself. Amy saw a flash of embarrassment on Max's face and rage coursed through her. They could both go fuck themselves.

"You're fully dilated," Ariana said after two, six, twenty-eight hours. "Listen to your body."

It was time to push, and, strangely, the pain disappeared between contractions. The pain had become a constant, a wall, a room, and Amy didn't know what to do without it. She was lucid in the moments between pushes. She was clear-headed. She was Dr. Jekyll. She started cracking jokes.

"Knock-knock."

"Who's there?"

"Radio."

"Radio who?"

"Radio not, here I come."

Amy pushed for three days, a week, a month. How long had she been there? How long would she be there? At one point, she blacked out from holding her breath and pushing so hard.

"You're amazing," Max said into Amy's ear. "You're bringing our baby into the world."

She wanted him to shut up.

A splitting open. A searing white-hot blinding. A scream, Amy's first, then the baby's. And she was there. Gunky and smeared with red, with swollen eyes and wrinkled toes like she had been swimming for too long, and the longest fingernails.

She lay on Amy's chest, still connected, the umbilical cord stretching up Amy's body.

The second midwife, whose name Amy didn't know, showed Max the placenta, and Ariana stitched Amy up and stuck a needle in her leg to stop her from bleeding.

"Alice Marie Scholl-Saltzman," Amy told her. Alice's eyes opened for a brief moment, navy blue and wise. She was still curled up, and it was impossible that she had been inside Amy just minutes ago.

Amy wept, from the exhaustion, from the joy of Alice's arrival—Alice, who was already looking for milk Amy didn't even know she had. Max cried and kissed Amy and kissed Alice. Her tiny, soft skull, her impossibly small ears.

There was a blur of calling Fran and Jim, and Max's parents and sister, and Julie and Emily, and Amy's parents—first her mom, then her dad. Ariana made Amy pee to make sure her organs were moving back to where they needed to be. When she couldn't, Ariana made her stand in the shower until urine and blood swirled down the drain. Amy's thighs trembled like she had just run a marathon, and she couldn't bear to be this far away from Alice. She sobbed, and Ariana wrapped her in a robe and walked her back to the bed that was taut with clean sheets.

Ariana and the other midwife checked boxes and got Max to sign things and Amy lay there, with Alice's skin against her skin, her tiny little grunts, her balled-up fists. Max handed Amy granola bar after granola bar. She drank as many cups of water as he could carry from the bathroom tap.

"All right, you're good to go," Ariana said.

Go? Go where? Amy wanted to ask.

It was time to go home. But she didn't want to go anywhere. She wanted to stay in this oasis of overbleached white sheets with Alice on her chest. She didn't want to put on clothes, or shoes. She didn't want to move. Ariana got her dressed while Max put Alice in the sleeper Amy had bought for her when she

The Fun Times Brigade

was performing in Saskatoon. It was bright blue, the colour of a prairie sky. It was so small, but it was still too big for her.

Max went to get the car, and Ariana wheeled Amy and Alice out through the foyer. It was the middle of the night and the sky was purple orange, and thick with clouds. "This is your first sky," Amy told Alice, wiping away tears and apologizing to Alice that she couldn't see the moon.

36

AMY NEEDS TO TELL FRAN ABOUT HOW AWFUL IT was, trying to record with Alice in the control room. She needs to hear one of her horror stories from when Arlo was a baby, but Fran doesn't pick up when Amy calls. Eventually, Fran texts her back and asks if she wants to come by after lunch on Friday.

Amy knocks on the screen door, but quietly so she doesn't wake up Alice.

Here! Amy texts Fran and hears her phone ping from inside.

"Ames!" Fran walks out of the kitchen toward the door.

She hugs Amy with the ferocity of all of her hugs, so tight that their bones are pressed together, and Amy's grateful she nursed Alice before coming over or they'd both be covered in milk. Fran's hair is down instead of in its signature braid, though it carries the kinks of a previous braid, last night's or maybe this morning's.

The Fun Times Brigade

"Jim's just upstairs," she says. "He's a little slower today than usual. It's taken him a bit longer to recover. That cold was a doozy."

"But you're both okay?"

She nods. "Do you want to sit out here until the little munch wakes up?" Amy nods and Fran helps her lift the stroller up on the porch. "Coffee? I just made a fresh pot. You probably need coffee."

"Do I look that tired?"

"No! You look amazing. I just remember those early nights. God, they were awful."

"They are."

"It'll pass."

Will it, though? Amy wonders.

"I could go for some coffee, too," Fran says. "Jim had a hard time settling last night." She goes inside to get it, and a garbage truck rumbles down the street and Amy's afraid it's going to wake Alice. The brakes squeal, but Alice keeps sleeping.

"I don't know how they sleep through it all," Fran laughs, careful not to let the screen door slam behind her. She hands Amy a mug. "Arlo would sleep straight through an electric Zappa set like it was wind through the trees."

"So last week, I had to channel my inner Fran—" Amy starts.

"Sorry, one sec," Fran says, standing and turning to the door. "Oh, that's him. I think I hear him. Jim?"

Amy hears a cough.

"The kettle just boiled, hun. There's tea waiting for you," Fran calls through the screen door.

Amy's never seen Jim drinking tea, but he carries out a mug with both hands. He's wearing pajama pants and a T-shirt from their *Big Band* tour. He's skinnier than Amy was expecting, but swollen somehow, and too pale for the end of August. Fran takes his tea and Amy hugs him hello. Fran makes sure he has a pillow behind him.

"I'm fine, F," he insists.

"I hear we both didn't sleep last night," Amy says.

He shoots a look at Fran.

"It's Amy," she says. "She's not sleeping, either!"

"How's our little bug?" he asks.

"Sleeping now," Amy says, "but she was partying all night."

"It's a good thing they're cute, eh?" he says.

Amy nods. She wants to tell them about trying to record with Sandra, but Alice stirs under her muslin and Amy hears her whimpery waking-up sounds. Amy unclips her from her stroller.

"There we go. There's my girl. Do you want to say hi?"

"Look at her," Fran says.

"She's so big!" Jim adds, holding out his hands.

Amy knows she's going to fuss, but she passes Alice over anyway.

"Well, hello there, little one," Jim says. "Look at you. Look at those big eyes. You're taking it all in, eh?"

Alice's face splits into a wail and Amy takes her back, unclipping her bra and putting her on her breast in one fluid motion.

"Look at you, super mama," Fran says. "I mean look at those chubby little legs. Do you remember those days?" she asks Jim.

"It was all such a blur."

"What he's saying is don't go on tour with a baby," Fran laughs.

Amy starts to tell them about Sam being unable to hold the harmony, but Alice pops off and she has to convince her to relatch. "Come on, come on, baby girl," Amy says, still trying to get her back on.

"Jim—" Fran says.

"F—" He looks at her sharply.

"What's going on?" Amy asks.

"The radiation wasn't quite as effective as the doctors had hoped," Fran says.

Amy stops patting Alice's bum. "So, what does that mean?"

"Chemo," Jim says.

"It's par for the course," Fran insists. "Our oncologist is really optimistic about it, and there's a bunch of clinical trials she's looking into."

"Oh," Amy says.

"First, we've got to get his platelet count up, and make sure his white blood cell count is strong, and then we start. Probably next week, and we'll be wrapped by the new year, with plenty of time to get the album out."

Jim smiles. "It's about time we find out what my chin looks like, eh?" he laughs. "And I guess F won't be after me about my caterpillar eyebrows."

"You might not even lose your hair," Fran says. "The oncologist said there's a special cap you can wear."

Amy looks at Fran, but she's smiling. Jim doesn't seem particularly fazed. If they're not worried, she shouldn't be either.

Alice belches like a teenager and makes them all laugh.

"Ames, you were saying something before?" Fran asks.

"Oh," she says. She can't tell them about recording now, not with Jim's chemo news, so she tells them about how Alice went from the fifteenth percentile for weight to the twentieth.

"Nicely done, mama," Fran says. Amy hands Alice over to her and goes inside to use the washroom. She pauses by the screen door, in case Alice starts screaming, but she's quiet.

When she comes back, Jim's singing Alice Joni Mitchell's "All I Want." Fran joins him, and Amy waits behind the screen door.

It's just chemo. He's going to be fine. They got out most of it with surgery and radiation shrunk even more of it, and the chemo will get rid of even more, and they'll still have time to rehearse for their album launch in the spring.

Amy opens the screen door and joins them for the final verse.

PART FOUR

31

SUMMER EASES INTO FALL, AND AMY DOESN'T have to worry about Alice overheating or getting a sunburn. They meet up with Fiona and Henry, and Alice laughs, drooling through the bibs Amy Velcros around her neck five times a day. Alice loves bouncing up and down in her Jolly Jumper so much, Amy googles, *How long is too long in the Jolly Jumper?* Max starts sleep-training Alice, and the bedroom feels huge and empty without the bassinet. Amy stumbles down the hall to feed Alice in the middle of the night, sitting in the uncomfortable glider, but Max is back sleeping in their bed, and Alice is getting used to sleeping on her own.

Progress, Amy thinks, stumbling back down the hall, slipping into bed as gently as she can. This is progress.

Max finally gets Alice to take a bottle, and Amy fills the freezer with baggies of pumped milk, and Jim starts chemo. Amy keeps his appointment schedule in her phone. He struggles to keep his white blood cell count up at first, and his doctor says no visits from young kids—Alice or Levi—because Jim can't be exposed to germs. Alice isn't in daycare, Amy wants to protest—she barely interacts with anyone other than Amy and Max, but Fran is at capacity, so Amy orders all of the poetry books that were longlisted for the Governor General's Literary Award, and after Fran tells her how cold Jim gets during his treatments, Amy buys him a beautiful knitted blanket on Etsy, even though she knows Fran would balk at the price and insist on knitting one herself.

Fran keeps saying everything is fine, so Amy starts touching base with Arlo a few times a week to find out how Jim is really doing. Arlo texts Amy about Jim's mouth sores and the nausea, so Amy gets cookbooks from the library and makes her way through the soup chapters, delivering Mason jars to their front porch, the next best thing to being able to see him. The purées are the easiest for Jim to get down, and Amy makes sure to add lentils and Max's homemade chicken stock for extra protein.

I let Mum sleep and took Dad in today, Arlo texts one afternoon. *Doc says things are going well. Got some anti-nausea meds that seem to be working. Dad says hi and he loved the squash soup you brought last week. Mum, too.*

Amy makes another batch while Alice naps, and leaves it on their front porch that night in a cooler. The lights are off, and the house is quiet. She doesn't even open the screen door in case it squeaks and wakes them up. *Love you,* she writes on the metal lid of the Mason jar and makes a note to tell Arlo the porch light is burned out.

Max and Amy usually do something special for their anniversary, but this year Alice is teething and neither of them have slept in days, so they decide to hold off celebrating. In early October, Max surprises Amy with a weekend getaway in wine country. *A belated anniversary weekend,* he writes in the card.

Amy texts Arlo and makes sure he'll be around if Jim and Fran need something. She texts Fran, who insists they'll be fine. *Go, have fun with your fella and your babe*, she writes.

"Debbie would be proud of us," Amy says to Max on the drive up.

Max looks at her.

"For celebrating!"

And he laughs. "We should go for brunch in her honour."

After they cover the windows with navy bedsheets, set up the monitor, and get Alice down in the Pack 'n Play with Bun Bun, Amy and Max sit in the living room and eat the charcuterie they picked up before they left the city.

Amy raises her glass, "To eight years," she says.

"Eight years," he says. "Can you even believe it?"

They open a second bottle and trade the same stories they tell every year—how Fran confused the officiant with Max's mom before the ceremony, how Max's sister Jill was pregnant and miserable she couldn't drink, how Emily taught one of Max's PhD friends how to sabre a champagne bottle.

The next day, they make it to two wineries before Alice starts to melt down. She screeches during the tasting and Amy leaves her half-sipped flight and straps a furious Alice into the carrier. Amy pictures walking up and down the rows of grapes, but there's an electric fence protecting the vines, so she walks along the perimeter of the parking lot, and whisper-sings "The Crayon Song" until Alice falls asleep.

Their dinner reservation is so early that the wait staff are still setting tables, but Alice is in a good mood, and Max and Amy take turns spoon-feeding her kale-apple-pea-and-banana purée while they eat oysters. Max must've told the restaurant that it was their anniversary, because the wait staff bring complimentary champagne, and when they're done, their server comes out with a slice of carrot cake with CONGRATULATIONS written in chocolate on the plate.

Max is driving, so Amy finishes off the bottle of wine, and on the way back to the Airbnb, it starts drizzling—a light, misty rain that turns the sky a pale mauve. Amy finds the local classic rock station, and Neil Young sings about a town in north Ontario. She's not sure she ever could've imagined this when she stood under the chuppah with Max, or during that horrible year when everything was falling apart. She's not sure she could've imagined this even a few months ago, when Alice was still so tiny and needy and everything was so terribly bewildering and she and Max felt like they were on separate islands. They're not anymore, though—they're a family, a unit. Amy watches the windshield wipers clear the glass and reaches over and squeezes Max's hand.

Max puts Alice down, and Amy takes the rest of a bottle of pinot noir out to the porch with a quilt. The rain is misty but still not heavy enough to be full raindrops. She pours herself a glass and posts a photo of her wearing Alice, holding a wineglass at the second winery.

Before she puts her phone down, she gets a text from Fiona: *Hope you're having a great trip (and that Alice sleeps!)*

So far she's been sleeping like a champ, Amy writes back, and adds the fingers-crossed emoji.

Amy is looking for a photo to send to Fiona when a text from a number she doesn't recognize pops up.

Amy, it's Sina.

Arlo's wife? She's never texted Amy before.

Hey, Amy writes back.

I just wanted you to know that Jim isn't well.
What do you mean?? I talked to Fran yesterday. Arlo, too. They both said everything was okay.
It's spread to his liver. And his lungs.

Amy pictures a drop of food colouring in milk, the colour radiating. Spreading. Amy's heart starts racing.

But he was responding to the chemo, she writes.

Sina doesn't write back.

That's what Arlo said. Fran, too.

I'm in Prince Edward County, Amy writes. *I'll load the car up now. I'm coming home. Tell them I'm on my way.*

No, don't. He's stable. They've admitted him into a room at Mount Sinai. I just thought you should know. Kids are allowed now, by the way. We took Levi to see him this morning.

Amy goes inside and starts packing up all of Alice's toys from the living room, grabbing the ball that had rolled under the couch, the squeaky giraffe from the dining room table.

"We have to go," Amy says, when Max closes the bedroom door behind him. "I'll get Alice's stuff. You pack the bathroom."

"What are you talking about? What's going on?"

"Jim," Amy manages.

"What?"

"Jim." Amy shows him her phone. "We have to go."

"We don't have to go tonight."

"We do! The cancer's everywhere."

He takes her phone and puts it on the coffee table. "Ames, we can't go now."

"We have to."

"It's so late," he says. "There's no way the hospital would let us in."

Amy crumples onto the couch. "Arlo said Jim was fine. He said that yesterday. So did Fran! I never would've left the city if he wasn't fine."

The Fun Times Brigade

"You didn't know," Max says, putting his arm around her.

Ever since that dinner in Ottawa, she'd assumed he'd be fine, that this was all just temporary, that she'd have a baby and he'd get treatment and everything would go back to normal.

"When did they find out? And why didn't Arlo tell me?" Amy sobs. "Or Fran? Why didn't they tell me?"

"I don't know," Max says. "Maybe they were trying to protect you. Maybe they were protecting themselves."

"Was anyone *ever* going to tell me? I haven't seen him in weeks!" Amy says.

"That's not your fault. His oncologist was trying to keep him away from any germs."

"But it's not like Alice is in daycare. I should've just gone anyway. I should've called his doctor and explained—"

Max hugs her tight.

"We'll leave first thing and go straight to the hospital," Max says into her hair. "I'll pack everything up out here and as soon as Alice is up, I'll do the bedroom." He pours Amy another glass of wine. She takes a big gulp and finishes packing up Alice's toys.

Amy falls asleep in the car and wakes up with a crick in her neck and drool on the seat belt. "Where are we?" she asks.

"A few minutes away," Max says. "I just need to find parking."

"It's okay. It'll be a fortune. Just drop me off."

Max pulls the car over. "Are you sure? I'll come with you."

"I'm good," she says.

"You sure?" he asks.

"Yeah. It'll be okay. You can unpack the car, start some laundry, maybe."

"Okay. I'll get Alice a bottle when she's up."

But Amy needs Alice with her. "I'll take her," she says.

"You sure? There's plenty of milk in the freezer."

She nods and opens the car door. Amy puts on the carrier and unbuckles Alice from her car seat. She manages to get her in the carrier without waking her up.

"Okay, text when you want me to pick you up," Max says, clearly not wanting to go.

Amy nods and slings Alice's diaper bag over her shoulder.

"Love you," he calls out.

"Love you, too," she says.

The revolving door turns slowly, gathering a man in a wheelchair, a woman with an IV, another woman herding three kids in matching peacoats, an elderly man in a leather jacket. Amy joins them, and they shuffle until they are spit out in the lobby of the hospital. It smells like antiseptic, and there's a Tim Hortons and a bookstore with a table of easy reads. Amy hasn't been to a hospital since Alice was born. She checks her phone—Room 517 in the northeast wing. She gets a squirt of hand sanitizer from the dispenser and heads to the bank of elevators.

The hallway is grey and white and filled with beeping and suctioning, and Amy wants to run back to the elevator and take Alice as far away from here as she can. She tries not to look in the opened doors, but she can't help herself—socked feet, IV poles, visitors curled in uncomfortable chairs at the ends of beds. She presses her lips against Alice's sleeping head.

She pauses in the door frame of 517. Fran's bag is on the windowsill—no Fran, just her bag and some knitting. One bed is empty and lying on the bed by the window is an elderly man. He is bald, his skin a yellowish-grey. He is impossibly old. He can't be Jim. Jim was doing the hokey-pokey onstage in February. They were putting their right foot in and taking their right foot out. This is the wrong room.

But it's Jim. His hair is wispy from the chemo, and he doesn't have a beard. His chin looks so vulnerable, so terribly naked. Amy steps into the room and sways with Alice to keep herself from crying. It's too intimate, watching Jim sleep. Watching babies sleep is one thing, but watching adults sleep feels like a violation. She wants to wake him up and get him to tell a story about playing with Frank Zappa or Joni Mitchell. Instead, she watches IV fluid dripping from the bag down into the tube that snakes into his old-man hand, the hand that's played a thousand, a million, songs on his guitar.

The sheets above his chest rise and fall, and stutter, and then rise again. Amy stares at the sheets, terrified the starched white will stop rising and falling, rising and falling.

"Amy!" Fran walks into the room holding a Tim Hortons cup. "What are you two doing here? Isn't this your anniversary trip weekend?"

"I got a message from Sina," Amy says.

"Oh, Sina—she's been a bit of a negative Nancy about all of this," Fran says. "I know he doesn't look great today, but his oncologist says we can do another round of chemo, then start an immunology protocol."

"Oh," Amy says.

"He's definitely more tired than usual, but he had a great morning."

Fran sits, and Amy stands next to her, Alice's sleeping weight heavy in the carrier. She doesn't know what to say, so she sways.

"Ben was by yesterday," Fran says, nodding to the flowers on the windowsill.

Neither of them says anything and a machine next to Jim beeps gently.

"The room's quiet," Amy says eventually.

"And the light is beautiful," Fran says, gesturing to the window.

"You hungry?" Amy asks, wishing she had thought to bring sandwiches, or something, anything. All she has is a handful of granola bars and a container filled with almonds.

Fran takes an almond. Amy tries to open the wrapper of the granola bar quietly so the rustling doesn't wake Alice or Jim.

"It's like we're on tour," Fran says.

"Except we don't have to wait to shit at a gas station."

Fran laughs and it's a relief to see her face loosen, if only for a moment.

"And how's our baby girl?" she asks.

"Good. Great," Amy says.

"Any more teeth?"

"Only the two," she says.

A doctor comes in, holding Jim's chart to her chest the way a lifeguard holds a flutter board, and asks to speak with Fran. They stand just outside the door and talk in hushed voices in the hall, the kind Max and Amy use around Alice when she's sleeping. Jim's IV drips and the heart monitor peaks over and over again. His wrists are too big, his hands are too big, and the skin on his neck is slack, making his head look too big. Amy tries to find the parts of him that still look like Jim. She settles on his ears, with the tiny dot from the earring he wore in the seventies.

Alice shifts in the carrier as Fran comes back in. "She's so great," she says. "Only woman oncologist here."

Alice opens her eyes and blinks.

"Look at you, sweetie," Fran says. "Look at those beautiful peepers!"

Amy unclips the carrier and Fran reaches for Alice. She holds her on her hip, and they look at the flowers on the windowsill until Jim starts to stir. Fran hands Alice back to Amy and goes to his bedside.

"You have visitors," Fran says in the same voice she used with Alice. "Look who's here!"

"Ames," Jim croaks.

Amy hugs him with Alice on her hip. He smells sweet—the sweet smell of the very sick.

"It's so good to see you," she says, the backs of her eyes burning.

"Good to see you," he says. His lips are dry and his voice is a ghost of its former self.

"Alice, say hi to your Grandpa Jim," Amy says, waving Alice's hand at him.

"You need some water, sweetie," Fran says, bringing a Styrofoam cup to his mouth and bending the straw toward his lips. While Fran dabs his mouth and smooths his wispy hair back, Amy looks away and pretends to get something from Alice's diaper bag.

"There we go," Fran says. "You hungry? Your lunch came while you were sleeping."

Jim shakes his head. "I want to see my little bug," he says, so Amy sits Alice on the railing of his bed.

"Here's your Grandpa Jim, baby girl," Amy says, and decides to bulldoze the situation with as much baby joy as possible. "She's got two teeth! And she's sitting up and thinks raspberries are the funniest thing ever."

She tells them about Max sleeping-training Alice, and lists the foods she eats now—barley and rice cereals, sweet potatoes, avocados, pumpkin pancakes, bananas, peaches, mashed-up hard-boiled eggs. She talks and talks to fill the space between each of Jim's laboured breaths.

After Max picks them up, and gets Alice down for her afternoon nap, Amy sobs in the kitchen. "He's dying," she tells Max.

"You don't know that," he says. "You said they can do another round of chemo, and they can still try immunotherapy."

"Stop. You and Fran and Arlo can just stop already. It's bad. It's really bad." She feels so stupid for not realizing how bad it was.

"I'm so sorry," Max says.

Amy presses the heels of her hands into her eyes, fireworks bursting on the backs of her eyelids. "Fuck. Fucking fuck."

38

ALICE SLEEPS FOR THE LONGEST STRETCH SHE'S ever slept, but Amy still wakes up every three hours. She ends up falling back to sleep after watching the light begin to creep around the edges of the blackout blind and wakes to Max and Alice in the doorway.

"Hey," Max says, his voice quiet and careful. He's already dressed for work. Alice is dressed, too, and has something green on her face.

"What's that? On her cheek?"

"Whoops, I didn't get it all," he says.

"You fed her?" Amy asks, propping herself up on her elbows.

"We wanted to let you sleep."

"I have to nurse her first," Amy snaps. "Always. Milk first, then food."

"I'm sorry. I should've woken you up. I just thought you needed more sleep."

The Fun Times Brigade

Amy takes Alice from him and tries to get her to latch. She won't. Of course she won't. She's full.

"See?" Amy says.

"I'm sorry," Max says.

Amy jiggles her breast in front of Alice's mouth trying to get her on.

"I've got an eleven o'clock class, but I can reschedule my meeting this afternoon," Max says.

"I'll be fine," Amy says.

"Okay. I've got to go. Your coffee's ready, and I made you some lunch. It's in the fridge."

Amy's phone buzzes while she's standing over the sink eating her toast. *How was your weekend?* Fiona writes. *Still on for coffee this morning?*

Amy totally forgot that they had plans. *Alice woke up sick,* she lies, and finds the emoji with the Kleenex.

Poor Alice. Poor you! Fiona writes back.

Amy feels guilty for lying but doesn't have time to dwell on it. She can't take a cab because she doesn't trust the way she strapped the car seat in last time. She can't take the stroller because only a few of the subway stations have elevators, and the ones that do are always broken. Amy wears her instead, and packs everything she can think of—hand sanitizer, rice husks, as many toys as she can fit in the diaper bag.

The noise of the subway startles Alice and she starts crying—loud, insistent wails. She screams and Amy bounces and murmurs into her hair. People glare at Amy, as if she's not doing anything to calm her. Six stations later, Alice is still screaming, and Amy wants to turn around and go back home. Alice finally settles two stations from their stop, and by the time they're heading up the escalator, she's cooing and smiling at strangers who wave with their fingers and wink at her.

I'm sorry about this morning, Max texts as Amy and Alice leave the station.

No, I'm sorry! I was such an asshole, Amy writes back.

I've got class until noon, but I'll keep my phone on. Text if you need anything. Give Jim and Fran a hug for me.

The elevator is packed with doctors and nurses and people in suits—a very different crowd from yesterday. How was it just yesterday? Amy walks down the same hallway, refusing to let herself look in the open doors. She pauses outside 517, taking a deep breath, inhaling Alice's milky baby hair smell, and knocks on the frame. "Morning!" she calls out.

There's one empty bed, the same one as yesterday, but Jim's spot by the window is empty, no bed, nothing. Fran's bag isn't here either and there's no knitting. The flowers are still on the windowsill, but that's it. Amy's heart starts racing. Did he die overnight? No, that's impossible. She checks her phone, nothing from Arlo or Fran. But where is he?

Alice squawks as Amy runs to the nurses' desk. The nurse is on the phone and holds up a finger. Amy searches the board behind her for a clue, but it's written in a code Amy doesn't understand, all letters and names that aren't Jim's.

Amy texts Fran, desperate to see the bubbles that show she's writing back.

"Can I help you?" the nurse finally asks.

"Room 517. Jim Powell. He's not there. He was there yesterday."

"Jim. Yes." She looks at a clipboard and Amy's heart pounds. "He's down for some tests."

Her throat floods with relief. "Oh, thank god."

"He should be back up"—the nurse glances at the clock—"in the next hour or so. Are you family?"

Amy nods.

"You can wait in his room if you'd like. Or there's a lounge on the fourth floor."

Amy's hands are still shaking when she walks back to Jim's room, her heart still pounding.

"All right, baby girl," Amy says, putting the diaper bag down and unstrapping Alice from the carrier. "Grandpa Jim's okay. Let's get you settled in."

Amy reads *Each Peach Pear Plum* and makes Alice's giraffe squeak, then she changes her diaper. Amy checks her phone, but nothing from Fran. She stands Alice up on the windowsill and they look at University Avenue—cement trucks, taxis, ambulances pulling into the children's hospital across the street. Alice starts rubbing her eyes. She needs to sleep, but Amy doesn't want to leave now, so she straps Alice back in the carrier and paces the room, but Alice grumbles and whimpers and arches her back. Amy walks the halls, up and down, shushing and bouncing. She keeps her eyes on the tiles, grey and flecked with blue, so she doesn't look into anyone's room.

Amy finally gets Alice to close her eyes and bounce-walks back to 517. She sways in front of the window and tries to focus on the traffic, the curve of turning cars at the advance green, the weaving of a bike courier in and out, in and out.

"Amy?" Fran stands in the door. "Oh, sorry, is she asleep?" she whispers.

Amy nods, and a pair of orderlies wheel Jim in. He's asleep, too.

"How long have you been here?" Fran whispers while the orderlies rearrange Jim's oxygen tank, his IVs, attaching the monitor to his finger to read his pulse.

"Not long," Amy lies. "The nurse said he was having a few tests."

"Just a CT scan," Fran says. "All routine."

Alice shifts in the carrier.

"He's got some colour in his cheeks today," Fran says. "He's on the upswing."

His cheeks are grey. Amy doesn't know how to tell Fran that this is not upswing.

"Are you staying for a while?" Fran asks.

Amy nods. "Of course."

"Would you mind staying here so I can grab something to eat?"

"Of course," Amy says.

Fran walks into the hallway, her narrow shoulders sagging. Amy sways next to Jim's bed. His skull is so round, and without eyebrows, he looks like one of her mom's papier-mâché creatures before she adds yarn. It seems impossible that this is the same person who would wake them up in the middle of the night on the tour bus because he'd figured out a new guitar part for a song they were working on.

Alice shifts in her carrier. Amy wants her to know the Jim who swears like a sailor before getting onstage, the Jim who taught her what a load-in is, how to figure out monitor levels, how to fake it if her guitar was out of tune onstage. She wants her to know the Jim who stood at the Royal City Folk Fest all those years ago and saw Amy sing "Baby Beluga" and decided with Fran that she was their plus-one.

"That's just what I needed," Fran says, walking back into the room. "You know, Timmy's egg sandwiches really aren't that bad."

Amy puts on her cheeriest face, the one she used for all ninety-six episodes of their TV show. She waits for Fran to call her on it, but she doesn't.

"And I picked up this for Alice," Fran says, holding up a plush *Very Hungry Caterpillar* toy.

"She's going to love it!" Amy says, swaying to keep Alice asleep.

The Fun Times Brigade

Fran tells her about Levi's kindergarten teacher, about his Mickey Mouse–themed birthday party, about Sina's new boss, and the permit drama the couple who bought their bookstore are having with their renovation. It almost feels normal for a moment, standing and swaying and chatting with Fran, except the monitor beeps, and Jim is lying there with his proportions all wrong.

When Alice wakes up, Fran passes her the caterpillar toy. Alice immediately starts chewing on its antennae.

"Look at those chompers," Fran says.

Fran wants to hold Alice after Amy unclips her.

"Mamamamamama," Alice babbles from Fran's knee, holding on to the caterpillar.

"Listen to you, you chatty little munch," Fran says, bouncing her.

Amy's afraid that Alice is going to wake Jim up with her squealing and babbling, so she packs her up and apologizes over and over again to Fran.

"It's okay," she insists. "I'll tell him you were here as soon as he's up. It'll mean the world to him."

39

I'M JUST GETTING ALICE DRESSED AND WE'LL BE by soon, Amy texts Fran the next morning. *Want me to bring lunch?*

We're heading home today, Fran writes back.

Best news!! Amy writes back. "Max! They're going home!"

"That's amazing," he says. "Wait, it's amazing, right?"

"Why wouldn't it be amazing? Jim's being discharged. How is that not amazing?"

"Because, you know—"

"No. What do you mean?"

"Maybe there's nothing more they can do for him there."

"He was so much better yesterday. Fran said he was on the upswing."

But Max is right.

Palliative care, Arlo says when Amy calls him to find out when they're going to be home.

"He'll have a nurse that comes three days a week, and a PSW will come to help Mum out."

"A PSW?"

"Personal support worker," Sina calls out. Amy hadn't realized she was on speakerphone.

"Oh."

"It's still way better than the hospital," Arlo says, his voice carrying Fran's optimistic edge. But Amy doesn't believe him. How can being at home without doctors or equipment or resuscitation machines be better than being at a hospital?

Arlo says today isn't a good day to go over because they're getting set up, so they go, all three of them, the next day. There's a hospital bed in the living room, shoved between the bookshelves and the couch. "They couldn't take the bed upstairs," Arlo whispers. "Mum's freaking out about it. Tell her it's fine."

"I'm thinking maybe we should just move the dining room table out and put the bed there," Fran says, her hands a flurry.

"It's great where it is," Amy lies. "He's surrounded by all his books."

Jim is so tiny in the hulking hospital bed, and Amy feels like an idiot for thinking that being discharged was a good thing. Max ducks out of the living room with Alice, and Amy knows he's fighting tears. She wants to disappear into the kitchen with him, but she makes herself stay. There's an IV pole next to Jim's bed, and the soft pocket on the inside of his elbow where the IV needle disappears makes Amy's knees buckle. He's awake and Amy kisses his cheek.

"Like my new digs?" he asks. His voice is like sandpaper and Amy gets him his water glass, angling the bendy straw to his lips.

"Thanks," he says.

"The light in the afternoon will be nice," she says.

"That's what F keeps saying," he says.

"I'm just glad to be out of that hospital room," Fran says, her voice forced and cheery. "It was so loud there, wasn't it Jim?" She pulls his blankets up on him. "All the beeping and the intercom paging."

"Stop fussing," he says, waving her off.

Hurt flashes across her face and is replaced almost instantly with a smile.

"Hello there, sir," Max says, handing Alice over to Amy and coming alongside Jim's bed.

"Nice to see you. Wish it were in slightly different circumstances, but this'll do." Jim smiles, but it looks more like a grimace. "And how's our little bug doing?"

Amy holds Alice up. She kicks her legs.

"Fierce little thing," Jim says.

She puts Alice down on a tiny bit of empty floor with her Sophie the Giraffe toy in front of her. "Go get it," Amy tells her. "She's started army-crawling," she says as brightly as she can.

"I think it's time for Jim to get some rest," Sina says, coming into the room.

"I'm all right," Jim insists. "They just got here." But Sina's right. He looks exhausted.

"We'll be here when you wake up," Amy promises.

Fran kisses Jim's cheek, and they all retreat to the kitchen.

"Do you want some tea, Ames? Max?" Arlo asks, filling the kettle at the sink.

She doesn't but says yes anyway.

"Tea, Mum?" Arlo asks.

Fran stares at the counter and says nothing. Amy wants to go and put her arm around her, but she's afraid Fran will break if she does. Fran nods without turning around.

Alice smashes her Sophie the Giraffe into the table, making it squeak. Max takes it away, but she starts crying, so he gives it back. "Just no squeaking," he says.

The Fun Times Brigade

Of course, she smashes it again into the table.

"I think this is where we'll take our leave," Max says.

Amy doesn't want them to go, but she also doesn't want Alice to be the reason Jim wakes up. Arlo and Sina leave shortly after Max and Alice, and Fran and Amy drink tea in the kitchen. Amy can't think of anything to say, so they just sit, sipping their tea, Amy's stomach fist-tight.

Jim's sheets rustle and Fran is up like a shot, checking on him from the hallway. "He's fine," she says. "Every time I heard him last night, I had to race down the stairs, so I ended up sleeping on the couch."

"I know that feeling," Amy says, but then wishes she hadn't. Being up with a baby at night is the opposite of being up with your dying husband.

They settle back into silence.

"Do you need anything?" Amy asks eventually.

"I think we're okay," she says. "Sina's filled the fridge. It's kind, but Jim can't keep much down and I can't really, either."

"You have to eat, though."

"I know, I know. I just—I'm nauseous all the time. I have been having toast every morning. I had eggs earlier."

Amy makes them a late lunch—sandwiches and some vegetable soup she finds in the cupboard. Fran insists on waking Jim up to eat. Amy spoons broth into his mouth while Fran crumbles crackers into hers. She barely touches it and Jim's back to sleep before Amy can finish washing the dishes.

"Try to rest tonight," Amy tells Fran at the door. "And text if you need anything."

"I will," she says, though Amy knows she won't.

"I'll be over tomorrow morning," Amy says and kisses her goodbye.

Fran nods, and Amy lets herself out, sobbing all the way to the streetcar.

Amy gets a text from Fiona trying to reschedule their coffee date, but she doesn't write back. She should. She should tell her why she can't meet her, but she can't. She can't even tell Julie or Emily what's going on, though Julie eventually calls Max and he tells her.

She and Alice visit Fran and Jim every day. Amy takes over croissants that she finds rock-hard on the counter the next day, and lattes that Fran barely sips, and blueberry muffins Amy bakes after Alice goes to bed. Ben comes by every other day with paper bags filled with fancy salads and smoothies and beet juices. Amy puts them in the fridge and Fran insists she take them home when she leaves for the day.

"You have to eat something," Amy says, and Fran promises she'll make oatmeal, or toast, or have whatever she spoons out for Jim.

Sometimes Alice falls asleep in the office in Levi's old Pack 'n Play, a dusty shelf of their JUNO awards looking over her. There's no blackout curtain, or monitor, or sound machine, but Alice clutches Bun Bun and sleeps anyway.

Amy sets the table in the kitchen if Jim is sleeping, and they have picnics on one of Fran's old sarongs in the living room when he's awake, even though Fran picks at her food, and the only things Jim can eat are soup, or smoothies, or a half a can of Ensure.

"Slow and steady," Amy says, lifting the spoon for Jim. "That's what you used to tell me."

"I'm not sure fixing your marriage and finishing soup are the same thing," he says, and laughs, a short scratchy bark.

The circles under Fran's eyes get darker and darker. Amy tries to get her to nap, but she refuses, so Amy sends her down to the pharmacy to get a flu shot, and another day, she sends her to get more adult diapers, not because Amy can't bring them, but because Fran needs the fresh air.

The Fun Times Brigade

Some days Jim sleeps fitfully, and Fran snaps at the PSW, and Amy tries to keep Alice quiet in the kitchen, or upstairs in the office. On good days, Jim is propped up in clean pajamas, the sheets fresh from the PSW's visit when Alice and Amy arrive. On good days, Jim's cough doesn't rattle the house, and he's working on a crossword puzzle, and Fran knits, and there's a record spinning on the turntable. On good days, Jim reminds Fran and Amy that music fixes everything, and they play—ukulele mostly, the guitar is too heavy for Jim now and he gets frustrated when his fingers won't play what he wants them to. They don't play any of their songs, but old folk tunes—"Teach Your Children," "Goodnight, Irene," and "Four Strong Winds"—and when they're playing, Amy can mostly tune out the hospital bed, and pretend they're just jamming like they always have.

"Oh, we ain't got a barrel of money," Fran starts.

"Maybe we're ragged and funny," Jim and Amy join in.

"But we'll travel along, singing a song, side by side."

Alice sits and bangs the caterpillar stuffie against the carpet. Fran gets her a wooden spoon and she smashes it against the couch cushion.

"We always did need an in-house rhythm section," Jim wheezes.

Alice bashes the cushion and squeals.

"Through all kinds of weather, honey, what if the skies should fall? But as long as we're together, it really doesn't matter at all—"

40

DAD'S GONE, AMY READS ONE MORNING NEAR the end of November. It's four thirty in the morning, and she's just finished nursing Alice.

Amy blinks at the screen. Dad? Her dad? But it's from Arlo. Arlo's dad. Jim.

Mum called. She went into the kitchen to make tea and he was gone when she came back.

This can't be. This isn't right.

I'll call you in the morning, Arlo has texted, but there's nothing more.

Amy stares at the wall in the bluish glow of her phone. She was going to take Alice over this morning with a record she found—a beat-up Valdy album. She was going to put it on in the living room. She was going to hear Jim tell the story of meeting Bruce Cockburn at Mariposa, how he introduced them to Valdy, how they smoked a joint with Neil Young.

Jim.

Jim.

Her legs are heavy. Left. Right. They are lead. She can barely walk to the bathroom.

She turns the shower on hot, so hot, and almost climbs in with her pajamas on. She leaves them in a pile.

Jim is gone, she thinks. His name floats, then sinks.

The water soaks her hair, fills her ears.

"Ames?" Max opens the door. "Amy?"

She lets the water beat against her eyelids. He pulls back the shower curtain. The bathroom is thick with steam.

"You've been in here for forty-five minutes," he says. "What's going on?"

She shakes her head. She can't say it. If she says it, then it's real. She wants to rewind to nursing Alice in that uncomfortable glider at four in the morning, when everything was still fine. Except it wasn't fine then, either.

"Jim?" Max asks.

She lets the water pour down her face.

"Oh god, Amy, I'm so sorry. Oh Ames." He starts to cry, but she can't see him cry. It's too much.

She will never hear Jim's voice again—it hits her like a fist to her gut and she crumples to the floor of the tub. She hugs her knees, the water drumming against her spine. Max tries to put a hand on her back, but she flinches.

"I think Alice is up," Max says. "I'll get her and then I'll cancel my classes."

"I'll get her," Amy says. She shuts off the water and towels off. She pulls her pajamas back on, her hair dripping water down her back.

Alice in her sleep sack, kicking with both legs, laughing at her mobile. Amy opens the blackout blind. The sky is starting to lighten.

"Mamamamamamamamama," Alice babbles in her crib.

"Baby girl." Amy picks her up and holds her, pressing her warmth against her body. "Good morning, sweet pea."

Amy nurses her next to the window, lips pressed against the top of her head. She breathes in her sleepy baby smell. She watches a squirrel run the length of a branch, then headfirst down the trunk of their neighbour's oak tree. It's lost most of its leaves, but some refuse to fall.

"Can I get you coffee?" Max asks. "Breakfast?"

Amy still hasn't texted Arlo back. She hasn't sent anything to Fran. What is she supposed to write—*Sorry?*

Instead, while she nurses Alice, she texts both of them. *On our way over.*

No one answers their knock, so they let themselves in. The house is quiet, and the hospital bed is still in the living room, empty, stripped to its mattress.

"Fran? Arlo?" Amy calls out.

Max unclips Alice from the carrier, and Amy takes her from him. But Alice whines and wriggles and arches her back, and Amy has to put her on the floor.

"Amy?" Arlo calls up from the basement.

"Hey," Amy says. She feels a slippery panic loosening in the centre of her chest. She picks Alice up and carries her to the kitchen. Alice fusses and Amy pulls a baby sock out of her pocket. Alice sticks it in her mouth.

"Hey, man," Arlo says to Max, coming up the stairs to the kitchen.

Max hugs him. "I'm so sorry," Max mumbles into his shoulder.

Amy hugs Arlo next. Where is he? she wants to ask. The hospital? The morgue? The funeral home? She wants to be with him. She wants someone to be with him, one of them.

"How is she?" Amy asks when he lets go.

He shakes his head, and the kettle on the stove begins to whistle.

"I'll take her up some tea," Amy says, pulling Fran's favourite mug down from the cupboard.

Max sets Alice on his lap, and Arlo gives her a napkin to play with. Amy carries Fran's mug up the stairs. The bed in the guest room is unmade, but Fran's not there. She's not in the office, or the bathroom, so Amy taps on the door frame of their bedroom. "Fran?" Amy calls out.

Fran sits on the corner of the bed, staring out the window. Amy sits next to her, wanting to say something, but all the words cling to the roof of her mouth, like the peanut butter they used to eat by the spoonful in the back of the tour bus. They sit and Amy rests her head against Fran's.

"I'm so sorry," she says, hating the smallness of her words, the nothingness of them. She hands her the tea.

Fran wraps her fingers around the mug and keeps staring at the window. A garbage truck pauses, then lurches forward, then pauses again.

"You know, I didn't think he'd die," Fran says eventually. "I know that doesn't make any sense. I knew how sick he was by how the nurses would look at me, how they got gentler and gentler with him. I mean, I knew it was happening, but I didn't think he would ever actually—"

"Me neither," Amy says.

Fran takes a sip of her tea. "I keep waiting to wake up from this nightmare and see him in the kitchen, looking up barbeque sauce recipes, or pouring another cup of coffee. Hell, even propped up in that stupid bed, complaining about not being able to eat a hamburger."

"He really loved hamburgers," Amy says.

Fran nods. Amy puts her arm around Fran's shoulders.

"I wasn't even there when he died," Fran says, her face crumpling.

"You were. You were so there for him," Amy says.

"But I wasn't there-there. I went to the kitchen to make tea. And when I came back, he was gone."

"Oh Fran. He probably waited until you left the room. He probably didn't want you to see him go."

Now they're both sobbing.

"He knows how much you loved him."

"But I wasn't *there*."

Amy rubs Fran's back. Her vertebrae are so close to the surface.

Amy stares at the photo of the two of them on the dresser—Lake Louise gleams green behind them. She remembers Jim's hands making an F chord, then sliding into a C; the curve of his shoulders as he hunched over his phone onstage, customizing his earpiece; the angle of his knees at the back of the tour bus, a glass of whisky sweating on his jeans.

"That was the last song he sang," Fran says.

"Song?" Amy asks, not following.

"When you were here last Thursday, or was it Wednesday?" she says. "We ain't got a barrel of money. Maybe we're ragged and funny."

"But we'll travel along, singing a song, side by side," Amy finishes for her.

"That was the last song," she says.

"At least it wasn't 'Sittin' on the Potty,'" Amy says, and then freezes. But Fran laughs, a short, sad bark.

Alice wails from downstairs. Amy wants to bolt and get her, but she makes herself stay.

"How's our little girl today?" Fran asks.

"Okay," Amy says. "She's probably nearing nap time."
"Amy?" Max calls from the bottom of the stairs.
She pauses.
"Go," says Fran. "I'm fine."
"No, you're not," Amy says.
"No, I'm not," she says, "but there's nothing you can do. Tell Arlo I'll be down in a bit."

Max has Alice strapped into the carrier. "I'm going to try to get her to nap," he says.

Amy kisses Alice's head and asks Arlo what she can do.

"Sina just sent over a list," he says, scrolling through his phone. "An obituary. Something for the funeral home. A photo, probably a bunch. We need to call Ben. The bed needs to go back."

Arlo starts on the obituary, Sina deals with the funeral home from their place, and Amy calls Ben.

Ben arrives wide-eyed and frantic. Amy has never seen him like this before. Arlo sets him up at the dining room table, and he starts going through Sina's list.

When Fran comes down, Arlo offers to make food. She shakes her head, but he insists that she needs to eat something. He makes toast and scrambles eggs for all of them.

"I want the photo of him from out east," Fran says. "You know the one."

"From Halifax?" Ben asks over his computer.

She shakes her head. "From, damn it, what was it called? That ocean thing, the tides, damn it, you know—" she says to Amy. "Remember?"

"The Bay of Fundy?" Amy asks.

"Yes. That picture."

"On it," Amy says. She still has it on her phone.

Fran eats three bites of toast and goes back upstairs. Amy starts to go with her but Fran waves her off. "I'm going to try to sleep," she insists, and Amy lets her go.

Amy finishes her eggs and finds the photo. Jim is standing on the beach and the tide is out, a tower of rock with evergreens perched on the top next to him—blue sky, red rocks, a beach that stretches on forever. He's holding his hat and squinting into the sun. He looks so happy. He *was* so happy. It was their first East Coast tour after their hiatus, and it was the first time in years that it had just been the three of them without call sheets and load-ins and ticket sales and media interviews to worry about. Amy can't bear to look at it—the sparkle in his eyes, his bushy beard, his smile.

"I'll wait till the obituary's done, and then I'll send out a press release," Ben says.

"A press release." Arlo shakes his head.

"I know. I'm sorry," Ben says.

Arlo half throws his plate in the sink. "Okay. I've got to finish writing this."

Amy washes up the dishes and cleans off the counters. She hangs the tea towels up to dry. She sweeps under the kitchen table. She takes the recycling out.

Did Alice fall asleep? she texts Max.

He sends back a photo of her little hat tucked into his coat. *Everything okay there?* he asks.

No. But yes.

Tell me if there's anything I can do.

Coffee would be good.

Max arrives with a tray of lattes and a cranky Alice. Amy nurses her, and then Max takes Alice home, and Amy reads over the obituary. Ben does another pass before showing it to Fran.

"Fine," she says, staring at the screen.

"Mum," Arlo says, "it doesn't have to be fine. We can add whatever. We can make changes."

"It's fine," she says, her voice flat.

She goes back upstairs, and this time Amy follows her. Fran curls up on the guest bed and Amy lies next to her. They don't say anything, and eventually they both fall asleep.

Amy is back home when the press release goes out and her phone starts blowing up—Julie, Emily, her mom and dad, Max's parents, Robin, Nathan, Jesse, Samantha, Sandra, musicians she met at festivals, sound techs, producers from their TV show. All the words are so sad and lovely, and Amy can't read any of them. They are a jumble of letters and dings and more dings and little red numbers multiplying. The press want quotes, and Amy stares at emails from journalists and producers and requests to come on this morning show and that news show.

"You can't die," Amy tells Max when he finds her sobbing in their bedroom.

"Hey, it's okay. I'm okay."

"But you can't. No speeding, no biking without a helmet, and you have to get your moles checked. Make an appointment."

"Okay," he says quickly. "I will. I'm okay, though, Ames. I'm not sick. I promise, I'm right here."

The next day, flowers start arriving, filling the house, tiny cards in florists' unfamiliar handwriting, *Sorry, so sorry*. Stems jammed into green cubes of wet foam. Amy hates them. While Max gives Alice lunch, she takes all the flowers out of their vases and piles them up outside in the yard.

"What are you doing?" Max asks. "It's cold out."

But Amy doesn't answer. She just piles the carnations and the lilies and the stupid ferns, and the roses, and the gerberas with their forced cheer. When she gets inside, Max puts a sandwich in front of her. He's cut it in triangles like she's six.

Amy texts Fran but she doesn't write back. She texts Arlo and he says she's sleeping. She asks if she should come over, even though she means *Can I come over?*

She's okay, he writes.

But Amy knows Fran's not okay, and she wants to not be okay with her.

Mom and Bill come over with newspaper clippings with the words that Arlo wrote, quotes lifted from Ben's press release, and the photo of Jim from the Bay of Fundy. There are articles with photos of the three of them—one with their first JUNO award, one from their *Big Band* album promo shoot, one of them onstage at Roy Thomson Hall. There are quotes in bold from the governor general, from Joni Mitchell, from a five-year-old named Gus.

"It's really a great photo of Fran, isn't it?" her mom says. She wants Amy to read the articles. She wants to talk about them, but words jam in Amy's throat and she can't swallow and her throat fills until eventually she runs upstairs and vomits.

"Maybe you should have a shower?" Max suggests after they leave.

But she doesn't. Instead, she stares at the photos of them on the newsprint—a blurry, grainy Fran, Jim, Amy, her ukulele, Fran's tambourine, Jim's guitar. Their names parading underneath in a small italicized font—*Fran and Jim Powell, and Amy Scholl of the Fun Times Brigade onstage at Roy Thomson Hall.*

It was surreal the first time they played there—it was where Beethoven and Mozart and Handel's *Messiah* were played. The acoustics were incredible, a lighting grid that was positively awe-inspiring, and the enormous pipes of the organ like a piece of modern art behind them. It was the best sound check they'd ever had.

It hits Amy like a screech of feedback—they will never sound-check again. They will never stand onstage, Jim's right foot keeping time, driving the sound techs crazy by singing into the same mic in the middle of the stage.

After Alice wakes up, Amy nurses her, then pumps a bottle, and goes over to Fran and Jim's. The bed is gone from the living room, which is full of flowers.

"Mum's upstairs," Arlo says. "Sleeping, I think."

Amy tiptoes upstairs and looks in the guest room. Fran's back is curled away from the door, and Amy wants to go in and see if she's actually sleeping, but she doesn't want to wake her if she is, so she goes back downstairs, where Arlo and Sina have taken over the dining room table.

"The funeral is Saturday," Sina tells her.

The day after tomorrow. *It's too soon*, Amy thinks, but then, when else would it be?

"Here's the guest list," Sina says, handing Amy a spreadsheet.

"Guest list?" she asks.

"Well, a list of people so they know when and where. Let me know if I'm missing anyone."

Amy scans the list—names she knows, names she vaguely knows, a few names she's never heard before. Amy texts the address of the funeral home to Julie and Emily and Max. *11 a.m.*, she writes, then puts her phone away.

"And here's the order," Arlo says, handing Amy what looks like a set list. She wonders if they thought of asking her about it, but something has shifted, some invisible tectonic plate has moved.

Arlo is going to emcee it—emcee, like it's a wedding, or a bar mitzvah. Levi is going to speak, then Ben, then Fran.

"If you want to say something, you can speak before Mum."

"But you don't have to," Sina adds.

"Of course I will," Amy says.

She scribbles a note for Fran. *Love you*, she writes and slides it under the guest room door. She realizes when she unlocks the car that she forgot to sign it. Fran will know it's from her, Amy tells herself, pulling her seat belt across her chest. But she wonders, as she flicks on her turn signal, if she will.

41

WHEN AMY ISN'T NURSING ALICE, SHE WRITES scraps of stories—about their Nova Scotia road trip, about Jim's surprise parties, about how much he loved Fran, about how much he loved music—recording, performing, rehearsing, even sound checks—but none of it really captures him.

"Maybe I shouldn't speak," Amy says to Max.

"Are you sure you won't regret it if you don't?"

She knows he's right, and she sits at the kitchen table and stares at the blank page, Max's indecipherable math printed on the back.

"Tell the story about how you met," Max says.

But that's more about her than him.

Amy opens Facebook and, even though she knows she shouldn't, she scrolls to the post about Jim—underneath are a lot of crying emojis, and *We miss you Jim*s.

Jim is still here in spirit.

Luv luv luv you guys.

The Fun Times Brigade

My 8yo daughter is inconsolable.
I saw them play Regina. Best Christmas gift for my twins.
My mom listened to Flying Like A Butterfly when I was a kid.
Do you think they'll replace him?

Amy squints at the tiny circular photo next to the comment—it's a middle-aged woman holding up a coffee cup. Replace him? Fuck you, Isabella Harris. How dare you.

"I'm going upstairs," Amy tells Max. She pulls the blinds close and crawls into bed in her clothes. She stares at the ceiling and tries not to think about what she's going to say at the funeral, about what she's going to wear, about what Alice should wear. She tries not to think about the comments piling up on Facebook. She tries not to think about Fran, curled up in the guest bedroom.

Amy ignores the texts from Julie, from Emily. She deletes Facebook from her phone and watches a video of a cat lip-synching "Total Eclipse of the Heart." Max knocks on the door with whiny and whimpering Alice on his hip.

"Sorry," he says. "I think she's hungry."

"I fed her an hour ago. She probably needs a new diaper. Can you just—can you just please deal with her?"

He closes the door, turning the handle so it doesn't click, and Amy sobs into her pillow—raging at the grief that's taking over, the grief everyone wants a piece of. She thinks about Fran in her empty house, the house where every corner, every cupboard, every wall is filled with Jim. The thought of Fran's grief is too much, a burning element she cannot touch.

Amy flicks through Instagram, but she's tagged in too many tribute posts, so she logs on to whatever Twitter is called now. Her mentions are blowing up—*Miss you, pal*, Jim Cuddy wrote. *Rest in power, Jimbo*, the Grateful Dead account posted. *Forever in our hearts*, the prime minister tweeted out, or at least his social media manager did. There are so many photos of them, the three of them, smiling, and singing. There are photos from Jim's Mariposa days in fringed leather vests. He's trending. #RIPJimPowell is trending. Amy takes a screenshot, and almost sends it to Ben, but she doesn't. Jim would fucking hate it. He loathed social media.

Amy turns her phone over and tries to put together a highlight reel—but all she can remember is Jim's baby-bald head, the slack skin on his neck. She's terrified that the only Jim she's going to remember is sick Jim, the one with the oxygen tube in his nose, his skin like tissue paper, his mouth gaping, asleep, his eyes sunken back into his skull, no eyebrows, no eyelashes, no beard. God, his beard—

She doesn't mean to, but, somehow, she sleeps and wakes up disoriented. She doesn't know what day it is, or what time it is. It takes a moment to remember she's at home. It's Friday. And then it hits her, again. Jim is gone.

She can hear Alice babbling downstairs. Amy wants her body on hers, her warm weight against her. She wants to scoop her up and bring her back up here, to this dark room, to this tangle of sheets, but she's afraid of contaminating her with her grief, so she makes herself go downstairs.

"How's my sweet girl?" Amy asks Alice in the living room.

Alice is on all fours, rocking back and forth, on the cusp of crawling. "Dadadadadadadam," she babbles.

"My perfect little girl." Amy picks her up and kisses her cheeks. Alice kicks to be put back down. "I'll eat something and then put her to bed," Amy tells Max.

"I can put her down."

"I'll do it."

"There's pasta in the fridge," Max says.

The Fun Times Brigade

Amy pours herself a bowl of cereal. She knows she shouldn't, but she opens Twitter again and checks the hashtag.

The first music my kids ever loved was the Fun Times Brigade. Love and condolences to his family. RIP Jim. #RIPjimpowell

Your spirit will live forever in the hearts of children everywhere. #RIPJimPowell

Check out this tie-dye! #RIPJimPowell

Read Ken Cullman's tribute to Jim Powell and his mark on children's music in the post-#SharonLoisandBram era: https://bit.ly/2VG01O9 #RIPJimPowell

Amy looks up from her phone. Max is holding Alice on his hip in the door frame of the kitchen. "I know you're sad."

Amy flips her phone face down on the table, relieved to have a reason not to look at it. "I'm not sad. I'm fucking devastated. There's a difference."

Max doesn't say anything.

Amy leaves her cereal bowl on the counter and takes Alice. "Time for a snooze, baby girl," she says, carrying her upstairs. Amy sits in the glider in the corner of Alice's room and reads *Brown Bear, Brown Bear, What Do You See?* and *Madeline*, then turns on the sound machine and lowers the lights. She can't bear to sing "The Crayon Song," so she sings "Baby Beluga" and pats Alice's back. Alice goes from still, to heavy, to asleep, and Amy settles back into the glider.

"You okay?" Max whispers from the doorway.

"Yeah."

"Want me to put her in the crib?" he asks.

"We're fine." Amy knows he's worried she's undoing all the sleep training, but she needs Alice's sleeping weight on her.

Max backs out of the dark room, and Amy feels a pang of guilt. She shouldn't be so short with him. It's not his fault Jim isn't here anymore. She feels a sob rising up her throat. She swallows hard. She presses her lips to Alice's head. Her tiny rib cage expands and contracts.

Once, when the Brigade was on tour out west, they stopped in a tiny town in Saskatchewan where their tour manager had grown up. Cora's parents had a bunch of houses on their farm, houses where her aunts and uncles used to live, her grandparents, too, before they died. They each stayed in their own house that night. Amy's hadn't been touched since the early seventies and had goldenrod wallpaper in the kitchen, and a turquoise shag rug in the wood-panelled living room.

They had dinner at the main house, and then Cora's dad lit a huge bonfire, and they sat under the millions of stars while Jim played old folk tunes on the tenor guitar he had found at the house he and Fran were staying in.

Amy was up early and walked over to the garden. Cora always talked about her dad's garden and Amy understood why—there were rows and rows of tomatoes, and beans twirling up stakes, peppers and eggplants, hills for the zucchini, their flowers so yellow in the early morning light.

"You can take the farm away from the farmer, but you can't take the farmer out of the farm," Cora's dad said from next to the wheelbarrow. He laughed, even though it sounded sad to Amy. "See if there are any beans," he said, pointing her down the last row.

She walked with the corn on one side almost as tall as her and the beans on the other side twirling up their pyramid stakes. She'd only picked a handful when Cora's dad called her over to the compost heap. He had a shovel and was filling the wheelbarrow. "Come look at this."

There was something white and pink and moving. Maggots, Amy thought at first, staring at the mass of wriggling.

"Mice," he said. "Baby mice. Brand new, too. Maybe an hour old. Maybe not even."

The Fun Times Brigade

Their skin was translucent. Their rib cages were, too, and she could see their impossibly small hearts, red and beating, beating. So fragile, so delicate, so persistent.

Jim went out after breakfast to try to see them, but they were gone, and he asked Amy to tell him what they looked like again, those baby mice hearts, beating so close to the surface, so close to the skin. She wants him to ask her to tell him again about those tiny flickers, those unflagging heartbeats.

42

"POWELL FUNERAL," A FUNERAL DIRECTOR MURMURS, nodding toward the open door. Amy looks past his cheap black suit to the security guards by the doors—to keep any media cameras away, she remembers Sina saying. Inside, everything is beige—the furniture, the wainscotting, the carpet, everything except a tall vase of slightly open poppies. As they walk past, Amy realizes they're fake and it makes everything feel like a sham.

Sina waves them to the front. "Here," she says, pointing to a row with RESERVED signs taped to the back. Amy is relieved that she can sit with her back to everyone. Here, she can fuss over Alice and stare at the photos of Jim blown up—his long beard and fringe-vest folk days, his and Fran's wedding photos. They're blurry, but you can still see the flowers woven into her hair, the rice on his shoulders. There's a picture of Amy, with Jim and Fran, from their second tour. It was taken in Ottawa, she thinks, and they're onstage at the NAC, beaming. The Bay

The Fun Times Brigade

of Fundy picture is in the middle, bright and blue, but her favourite is from Salt Spring Island where Jim is sitting in a Muskoka chair, holding a beer, looking off to the side, laughing.

Emily and Julie squeeze in next to them, and Emily keeps Alice entertained with silly faces. Max offers to take Alice, but Amy wants her on her lap, even if she's fussy and wriggly.

Levi waves from across the aisle, and Arlo comes over and kisses Amy's cheek. "I'm so glad you're here," he says in a tight voice.

"Of course," Amy says. "How is she?"

He shrugs, and he puts on a big smile and waves to someone a few rows back.

There's a spot for Fran next to Levi and Sina, but she doesn't come out until right before Arlo climbs up to the podium and checks the mic. She looks like a shell of herself. Her long skirt dwarfs her and silver bracelets climb up her narrow wrists. Amy tries to catch her eye, but Fran sits down and stares at the podium.

Arlo stands next to the Bay of Fundy photo and welcomes everyone and thanks them all for coming. He tells stories about being on the road with Jim when he was small, the puppets Jim used to make out of socks, how much Jim loved Fran, how much he loved Levi. It sounds like he's reading off cue cards, which, Amy supposes, he is.

Max puts his arm around Amy, and it's comforting until it's suffocating. She shifts and he removes it, but when it's gone, she wants it back.

Levi goes up next. "I love Papa," he says into the microphone. "And cancer is a bully and I hate bullies and I hate cancer and I don't know why he has to be dead."

Fran slumps forward and Amy wipes her cheeks, grateful for the Kleenex Max hands her. Amy bounces Alice on her knee and untangles her tiny fingers from her hair while Ben takes the podium. He tells the best stories about Jim—about how he insisted on making a folk album for kids, pestering him for years to get the big guns up—Stephen Stills and Garth Hudson and Mickey Hart. "He tried to get Joni, but not even Jim could convince her to travel," Ben says, and everyone laughs. He talks about his incredible artistry and musicianship, about how much joy he brought to everything he did, about his unrelenting quest for the best burger in Canada. He is bright and loud and everyone beams and laughs, and Jim feels so close it feels impossible that he's really gone.

And then it's Amy's turn. Max squeezes her hand, and she leaves Alice reluctantly, thinking for a split second that she should carry her up with her. She blinks hard and puts her papers on the podium. She doesn't know how to stand, or where to put her hands. The room is silent, except for the shifting of formal fabric on hard benches, the rustle of restless thighs.

Rows of people stand at the back, and the doors are open, and people have filled in the lobby area. Mom is sitting halfway back with Bill. And Cora, their tour manager, is sitting with the sound engineer from their last studio album. Robin and Sandra and Nathan are sitting in a row together. A CBC exec sits next to Stephen Stills, who must've flown up from Florida. Bruce Cockburn is standing at the back by the door. They're both wearing sunglasses.

"I'm Amy," she says, her voice strangled. She stares at the piece of paper, her handwriting as nonsensical as Max's math on the other side. The words shimmer off the page—*Jim was, we were, he was*. But she can't talk about him in the past tense. She can't do it. Blood pools in her feet. She feels like she's going to faint. She opens her mouth, but she can't say these words. If she says any of these words, he'll be even more gone than he already is.

"Tight and small, a perfect curl," Amy sings. Her voice is shaky but she keeps on. "Your wings, so bright, begin to unfurl."

The Fun Times Brigade

There's a tremour in the audience—a laugh, a whimper.

"Your wings stretch out against the sky," she continues. "Your wings like the petals you pass by."

People start joining in at the first chorus—Julie and Max, clapping Alice's hands in time. Then Arlo and Levi and Sina. Even Fran looks up. "And you fly, fly like a butterfly, fly, fly like a butterfly."

Tears stream down Amy's cheeks.

"Your world becomes bigger, greener, brighter. And you fly, fly like a butterfly, fly, fly like a butterfly."

And then it's done. The song is done and Amy wants to start again, but she can't. It's over. She grabs her papers, wishing there were a curtain she could duck into, a green room she could hide out in. Amy stumbles back to her pew. Max squeezes her hand, tears shining in his eyes. Arlo helps Fran up to the podium, and Alice starts fussing. She's on her way to a full scream, so Max takes the diaper bag and half runs her down the aisle while Arlo adjusts the mic for Fran. Julie moves closer and puts her arm around Amy.

Amy watches Fran's mouth moving. She's pulled down her reading glasses and is reading off a piece of paper, half into the microphone, half not, and it's impossible to hear what she's saying. Her words fade in and out of the speakers—"He grew up in the Ottawa Valley," she says, and says something about the camper van they had when Arlo was little. "He lived his life as he spent his days—" And then she stops.

The room stops with her. It is quiet, so quiet. And Fran stands there, bewildered, her eyes unfocused. She looks so small, and Amy wants to run up and put her arm around her, to take her away from this room, this crowd, these words they're supposed to say that mean nothing without Jim here.

Fran stands in front of the microphone and the silence bellies and bulges, and finally Arlo stands and guides her away from the podium and through the side door, an Exit sign blaring in red. Ben takes over at the podium.

Amy stands as soon as Ben is finished. She needs to find Fran. She needs to know if she's okay, but she's stuck behind the crowd of people shuffling down the aisle. When she finally gets out to the foyer, Fran isn't there, and Max is standing next to the plastic poppies with Alice asleep in the carrier.

"You were awesome," Max says, squeezing her shoulder.

"I'll wear her," Amy says.

"She's already asleep," he says.

Amy insists. She needs Alice on her. Of course, she wakes up and Amy has to bounce her back to sleep.

There are tables of tea sandwiches and tables of squares—lemon squares, Nanaimo bars, brownies, and butter tarts. There are urns of coffee, and Styrofoam cups that Jim would despise.

Amy's mom comes up to them. "Do you think Fran's okay?" she asks and reaches to put her hand on Alice's head.

Amy takes a half step back. "She's sleeping," she whispers.

"And the grandson?" Mom continues. "What a darling. Wasn't that so touching?"

Touching, who says that? Amy nods and breathes through her nose.

"And did you see? Bruce Cockburn was here!" Mom hisses. "Bill stood next to him in the bathroom!"

"They were friends, Mom." Amy notices her mom's wearing papier-mâché guitar earrings.

"Wait, isn't that the guy from the CBC morning show?" Mom asks, pointing across the room.

"Mom! He's not here as a journalist."

"It is him, isn't it? You know, I'd like to talk to him. I'm going to be hanging a show at a coffee shop right near the CBC."

The Fun Times Brigade

"Jesus, Mom." But Amy doesn't have it in her to stop her.

The trombone player from the Brigade's *Big Band* album whose name Amy can't remember comes over with his boyfriend. The Brigade publicist, Denise, comes over, and Cora, and Stephen Stills with his huge grey beard, and the couple who bought the bookstore from Fran and Jim, and the artistic director of the Royal City Folk Fest, and Nathan and Robin and Sandra. They all look at Amy's chin and murmur things softly, things like *sorry* and *loss* and *devastating*. Their words are soft, like the egg salad sandwiches Max brings her. Jim would've rolled his eyes at the fussy, crustless sandwiches, but Amy puts a napkin on top of Alice's head and eats one.

Someone hands Amy a scotch and someone else raises their Styrofoam cup and toasts Jim. Amy raises her glass and drinks, feeling the warm burn down her throat. She needs to pee, but she's afraid she'll wake Alice if she tries to sit down, so she keeps swaying. The room is hot, too hot, and the Nanaimo bars have softened to the consistency of baby food by the time Fran enters the reception room. She looks sedated and Amy wonders what Arlo gave her. She slumps in a chair in the corner.

Amy makes her way toward her.

"Amy," Fran says.

Amy tries to find something to say that might be a balm, something, anything. She's watched others do this all week, their mouths moving like goldfish, the words with too many vowels, unhelpful, amorphous words that of course aren't a comfort.

"I'm sorry I sang 'Fly Like a Butterfly,'" she ends up saying.

"It's okay." Fran's voice is flat and sounds like it's coming from underwater.

"I don't know what I was thinking," Amy says.

Alice starts crying.

"She's probably hungry," Amy apologizes.

"Little munch," Fran says, her hand on Alice's head.

Someone Amy's never met reaches out for Fran's arm.

"Sorry," Amy says, in the way. She moves and walks a now-shrieking Alice to the back of the room.

"You okay?" Max whispers.

Someone's brought a guitar and sings Cat Stevens next to the coffee urn.

"Let's go," Amy says.

Amy hugs Levi, who is eating a brownie in the corner, but leaves without saying goodbye to Arlo or Sina or Fran.

Max goes back to work, and Monday stretches out long and impossible in front of Amy. She drinks the coffee Max made while Alice smushes banana into her hair, and tries not to think about Fran's bewildered eyes behind the podium. She logs on to Facebook, but someone's tagged her in a photo from the funeral where she's singing at the podium, Jim's smiling face behind her. What the fuck? Who takes photos at funerals? And who would tag her?

It was the trombone player. Amy unfriends him and closes Facebook. Jesus Christ.

Samantha's sent her a text apologizing for missing the funeral. *Sandra said it was beautiful*, she's written. Amy turns her phone over.

She makes a piece of toast, but can only manage a few bites, and, as she dumps it into the compost bin, she realizes she hasn't spoken yet this morning, not even to Alice.

"How's your morning, baby girl?" she asks, but as soon as she opens her mouth, she feels tears filling her eyes. She blinks hard. "How's that banana?"

Amy gives Alice a bath in the sink and dries her off with tea towels. She glances at her phone, the messages piling up. She ignores them and lies on the couch with Alice on top of her.

The Fun Times Brigade

Alice pulls at Amy's ears and nose and gives her slobbery open-mouth kisses. Alice gnaws on Amy's knuckle and Amy looks up at her and Jim and Fran smiling down from the wall, their three Brigade posters beaming. She can't bear to see his face, his guitar, his suspenders. She can't bear to see her and Fran happy beside him.

Amy takes the posters down during Alice's first nap, but there are sun stains where the frames have hung for years. Is it worse to have the reminders of the posters, or leave them up? She puts them back up and reheats her coffee in the microwave.

Max texts, wondering how she's doing, reminding her that there's lunch in the fridge. Amy doesn't want to write back. Her phone feels like a brick in her hand, but she knows he'll start to worry, so she sends him back the thumbs-up emoji.

I'll be home by 5, he writes. *Spaghetti?*

Amy's phone bings again. But it's not Max. It's Fiona.

There's something on your porch, she's written.

It's a taped-up diaper box. Amy looks to see if Fiona's pushing the stroller down the sidewalk, but she's not there. Amy doesn't see her car, either.

I read about Jim, the note inside says. *I'm so sorry for your loss. I know it's not going to fix things, but here are a few things for you and Alice. I'm around if you ever want to chat (or not chat!)*

There is a box of rice puffs for Alice, a pine-scented candle, three chocolate bars tied with a ribbon, a yogourt container full of peach muffins—*no sugar, Alice-friendly*, it says on the lid. Amy tries to send a thank-you, but she stares at her phone and wonders if Jim had been alive when she walked down the hall to nurse Alice. Was he alive when she picked Alice up out of her crib, sleep-warm and hungry? Was he alive when she sat in the glider, staring into the dark at Alice's bookshelf? Was he alive when she put Alice back in her crib? And what did

Fran do when she found out? Did she sit with him? Did she call Arlo right away? Could she bear to leave Jim? Could she bear to stay with him? Did it still feel like him, like Jim? When did he become a body, and not Jim?

Amy finds the scotch Jim sent over when Alice was born and pours out a finger, two fingers. She swallows and lets the burn spread, thick and warm in her chest.

She didn't ever drink scotch before their first tour. Jim couldn't believe that she had only ever had Jameson, and took her down to the hotel bar and ordered five different scotches, lining them up from peatiest to cleanest. Jim liked the smoky, peaty ones the best.

Fran hated scotch. "It tastes like I'm licking an ashtray," she'd say.

Amy didn't love the peaty ones at first, but she'd drink them with Jim. It was their thing, on tour after Fran went to bed, a single ice cube from the hotel ice machine, or a tiny splash of water, "just to open it up."

How is it possible that she will never again drink scotch with Jim? She stares at the brown liquid, then pours it down the drain and eats a peach muffin over the sink.

43

DECEMBER BEGINS WITH ERRANT SNOWFLAKES that melt before they hit the ground, and breath that puffs out in small white clouds. Alice turns eight months, and Amy takes a photo of her on the bed. She usually takes fifty to make sure there's a good one, but she leaves it at two, and doesn't bother posting them. It's Henry's eight-month birthday too, and Amy thinks for a moment about sending a note to Fiona, but she didn't ever say thank you for the package so she doesn't send anything.

Mum has some stuff for you, Arlo texts later that morning.

Amy stares at her phone. She hasn't spoken to Fran since the funeral a week and a half ago. She's tried. She's called and hung up when Fran didn't answer. She's called and left messages. She's texted. She even walked Alice over, but she stood on the sidewalk and couldn't bring herself to ring the doorbell.

Hey, Amy starts typing to Fran, but can't figure out what to say. She stares at the blinking cursor and eventually types, *Arlo mentioned you have something for me?*

The Fun Times Brigade

You can come over, Fran texts Amy back.

Sure, Amy writes. *Of course. When works for you?*

Tomorrow sometime? Fran writes back.

The next morning, Amy texts Fran the minute Alice wakes up. *On our way in 10,* she writes, even though it ends up being another twenty-five before they get out the door. Max carpooled to work so she could have the car—she has no idea what Fran has for her, and there's only so much room under the stroller.

Alice fusses and yanks off her mittens.

"Look, baby girl," Amy says, picking up her mittens, forcing her voice to be light and upbeat. "We're at your Grandma Fran's house."

Walking in feels intrusive so she loosens Alice's car-seat straps and rings the doorbell.

"Amy. Alice." Fran opens the door and hugs Amy. She's gaunt, her cheekbones sharp, her eyes hollow.

Amy hauls the car seat into the house. It smells different, like lemon cleaning supplies and Windex, and suddenly she can't remember what it used to smell like.

"Thanks for coming," Fran says. Her voice has a strange, formal thread woven into it.

"Of course."

"Sorry the house is a bit of a mess," she apologizes.

But it's not. It's neater than Amy's ever seen it. There are garbage bags in the front hall, and it takes Amy a moment to realize they're filled with clothes. Jim's clothes.

"The Diabetes Association is coming to pick it all up tomorrow," Fran says.

Amy unbuckles Alice and unzips her fleece suit. She tries not to look at the garbage bags.

"I've got coffee on," Fran says.

"Great," Amy says, even though the last thing she needs is more coffee.

Fran disappears into the kitchen, and Amy sits on the couch, trying to distract Alice with the strap of the diaper bag. The coffee table is back where the hospital bed used to be. Fran comes out with a mug she bought when they were on tour out east.

"Thanks," Amy says. It has the right amount of sugar and milk, and she can't help but think about Jim calling it "coffee candy" and trying to convince her to drink it black. She digs around in her diaper bag for something for Alice to play with. "Here you go," Amy says, shaking the David Bowie rattle Emily sent when she was born.

"Look at her go," Fran says, admiring Alice's army-crawling.

"How are you?" Amy asks, blowing across her mug.

"Some days are easier than others."

She nods, waiting for Fran to elaborate.

"And you?" Fran asks.

"Okay," Amy lies. Her eyes start to fill.

"Don't start." Fran lifts her hand. "Don't."

Amy swallows hard and stares at Alice, who looks up at her with a wide smile. Amy wants to talk about how Jim taught her to drive stick in the middle of the prairies, about how he had way too many opinions about barbeque sauce, about how they used to order in room service and shoot the shit until the wee hours, but Fran says nothing, so Amy says nothing, and they slip into a pocket of silence that Amy doesn't know how to get out of. Eventually, Amy scoops Alice up and onto her lap. She protests and wriggles back to the ground.

Amy glances to the mantle, to the bookshelves, to see if Jim's ashes are anywhere, an urn, a box, but there's nothing that she can see. She's relieved. She's not sure she could handle sitting here with Jim propped up on the shelf. But all the photos are gone, too—the photos of Levi's first birthday, and Fran's fiftieth, and their trip to Italy, and when the Brigade met the prime minister. They're all gone.

The Fun Times Brigade

Amy feels pressure mounting behind her eyes, tears threatening. "Can you watch Alice for a sec so I can pee?" she asks.

"Of course. We can hang out, can't we?" Fran says to Alice.

Amy runs up the stairs. *You're okay, you're okay,* she tells herself.

Even in the bathroom, there are no traces of Jim. All of his medications and vitamins are gone. His razor. His toothbrush. Amy sits on the edge of the bathtub and presses her hands into her eyes, but she can hear Alice starting to cry in the living room, so she splashes water on her face and dries her eyes with the hand towel.

"She missed her mama," Fran says, holding Alice and bouncing.

Amy reaches for her and Alice hiccup-gulps into her shoulder. "You're okay, you're okay," she tells her. Amy manages to get Alice nursing.

"I don't know if Arlo mentioned, but we went through Jim's will," Fran says. "Well, Arlo did. There wasn't very much in it, everything's mine until I go, but Jim said before he"—she waves her hand—"he wanted you to have this."

Amy holds her breath. His Gibson? No. Couldn't be. His harmonica? Or mandolin maybe?

Fran pulls a bag from under the coffee table and hands Amy the ukulele she gave him for his birthday, the one with the Grateful Dead quote laser-etched onto the back.

"Oh," Amy manages. "It was a gift for him." She hands it back.

"He wanted you to have it," Fran says, passing it back to Amy. "He said it could be for Alice. I should probably go through the instruments in the basement, and all those pedals and, you know, if there's anything else you want, just say."

She does. She wants one of his mandolins, or one of his guitars, his pedal steel, something that was really his—anything other than this posthumous regift.

Alice pops off, and Amy tries to get her to relatch, but she won't.

"Too much to see and do, right little munch?" Fran says.

Amy puts her back on the ground and Alice takes off.

"So, Christmas!" Amy says as brightly as she can. She and Max have been coming here for Christmas Eve for years. "We could host. Alice goes down by sevenish, and we can eat after that? Eight, maybe?"

Fran looks away. "Arlo didn't tell you?" she says, and something spins slowly in the centre of Amy's chest. "We're going to Florida."

"Florida?"

"I thought you knew. I think Arlo told Max. Levi wants to go to Disney World."

"Oh," Amy says.

Fran shrugs. "It's just a week. We'll be home for New Year's," she says. "We could do something on New Year's Eve instead."

But New Year's Eve isn't the same as Christmas Eve. It's not the same at all.

Alice smashes her Bowie rattle against the hardwood.

"I should probably get her home for lunch," Amy says, trying to keep her voice steady. "Between naps and feeding her food-food, there's no time for anything anymore."

"Are you sure you can't stay? Ben brought by some sandwiches the other day. He's worried about you, by the way. Says he hasn't been able to get a hold of you."

Amy stuffs Alice's rattle back into the diaper bag. "I should really get her home." She carries Alice to the front hall and puts her in her fleece suit. Alice bucks and kicks as Amy buckles her into her car seat and Amy has to yank the straps to hold her in. Fran takes their mugs to the kitchen, and Amy reaches into the closest garbage bag and shoves the first thing she can grab into her pocket.

The Fun Times Brigade

"Don't forget the uke," Fran says, handing Amy the gift bag.

Amy rushes Alice out to the car and shoves the ukulele under the seat. She slams the door shut and rests her forehead on the driver's side window. She pulls out the piece of clothing she shoved into her pocket. It's a sock. A purple sock.

"Fuck!" she yells. She whips the sock into the passenger seat and grief yawns open, an empty pit from her throat to her belly.

You knew about Florida? she texts Max after she turns on the ignition.

He calls immediately.

"How could you not tell me?" Amy says.

"It didn't sound like it was confirmed. They probably need to mix things up—change of scenery, you know?"

She does know, but she needs Fran here. Amy leans her head against the top of the steering wheel.

"We can do something just the three of us," Max says. "Start a new tradition for Alice's first Christmas."

But Amy doesn't want a new tradition. She wants to wear a Christmas cracker crown and eat goose, or duck, or venison, or whatever elaborate meal Jim cooked, and sip the world's smokiest scotch and listen to the Boney M Christmas album and dance with Fran in the kitchen.

Alice screeches from the back seat. Amy really needs to get her home. She needs to get her lunch and get her down for her nap, but she can't bear the thought of being back at home, not yet. Instead, she drives to the grocery store and has to fight to thread Alice's legs into the grocery cart seat. "Come on, you usually love this," she says.

Alice sits eventually, and Amy pushes the cart through the perfect pyramids of oranges and orderly lemons. "Look! Strawberries!" she tells Alice in a cheery voice, pointing to the clamshells of anemic berries. Alice blows a bubble with her spit.

"What do we need, baby girl?" Amy asks her. "Bananas. How about some bananas? We can make you pancakes. And sweet potato. Let's get you a few of those."

She wheels the cart to the potato section—Yukon gold, baking potatoes, fingerling potatoes, purple potatoes. When they reach the sweet potatoes, Amy hears her name.

She spins around. It's Fiona. Henry is sitting in the cart, chewing on an empty box of raisins.

"Hi!" Amy says, startled.

Fiona hugs her, and Amy feels a sob rising up in her throat. She swallows hard.

"I thought it was you!" Fiona says. "Look at you, so big," she says to Alice, who puts her fingers in her mouth.

"How are you?" she asks Fiona, keeping her voice bright.

"Good," Fiona says. "Well, Henry's getting another tooth, so no one's slept this week, and I've been pumping him full of Advil. Probably too much, but it's the only thing that works, you know? And how are you?"

"Good," she says. "Alice is great. Not teething at the moment, thank god."

"I'm so sorry about your bandmate," Fiona says. "I read a beautiful tribute about him in the *Globe*."

Amy tries to keep the smile on her face, but her eyes start filling. "Thanks," she says, trying to find something, anything to say, but there are tears streaming down her cheeks, and before she can stop herself, Fran and the ukulele and Christmas Eve come spilling out. "Fucking Disney World. And his clothes, his clothes were all in garbage bags as if they're garbage. And I took something, so that I could have something that was actually his, not a ukulele he didn't even play, but it was a sock. A fucking purple sock. When did he ever wear purple socks?"

"Oh, Amy. That is so hard. It's so hard." Fiona hugs her and Amy sobs into her neck. "I lost my grandpa when I was pregnant with Henry, and it was devastating. And I knew a lot of people were like, well, he was old, he lived a good long life and all that, and it's true. He was ninety-four, but it still undid me," Fiona says. "I hate that Henry will never get to meet him."

But Jim wasn't ninety-four. Jim wasn't even old, and they had shows to do, and albums to put out. They had songs to write. Amy forces a smile. "I'm sorry." She wipes her cheeks with the backs of her hands. She takes a deep breath.

Alice bangs the push bar of the cart with her drool-covered hands.

"It's almost nap time," Amy says, desperate to get out of there—the produce aisle, the grocery store, this conversation. "We just came for sweet potatoes and bananas," she says, gesturing toward the cart.

"We've still got a full shop to get through," Fiona says. "We should hang out, though. We're going to Sudbury for the holidays, but we'll be back on the second."

"That would be great," Amy says, but while Alice shrieks from the cart and Amy fumbles with her debit card, she realizes she didn't thank Fiona for the package, for the note and the chocolate and the muffins for Alice. Amy grabs the receipt and pushes Alice to the parking lot.

"Fucking hell," she says to Alice, even though she shouldn't swear in front of her.

४४

AMY DEBATES CANCELLING CHRISTMAS. ALICE IS so little that she wouldn't know the difference, and she knows Max doesn't care either way. She's not sure she can do it without Fran and Jim, but her mom drops off a box of ornaments she made as a kid—felt reindeer, and clothespin Santas, and a snowman she made in Grade 1 out of glue and toilet paper—and she decides to go all in.

She sets the radio to the all-Christmas station and during naps makes Alice a stocking out of felt. She makes matching ones for her and Max, cutting out scalloped holly leaves, and decorating the first letter of their names with silver glitter glue. She even convinces Max that they should get a real tree for the living room, so they go to the 7-Eleven parking lot and pick one out, and Amy makes mulled cider while Max jams it into the plastic stand. When they cut away the plastic netting, it takes over an entire corner of the living room.

She buys way too much for their stockings—bath toys and board books and a mermaid stuffie and bamboo spoons and a dinosaur sippy cup, and new crib sheets Alice doesn't need, and an Alice Cooper onesie. She buys hot sauce and expensive mustard for Max and fancy soap for herself, because she doesn't want to have an empty stocking on Christmas morning and doesn't know if Max will think to fill it.

Even though they miss the first few days of Hanukkah, Max finds his menorah in the basement and drives up to Bathurst and Eglinton to find candles. They haven't celebrated Hanukkah since Max's parents moved to Florida, but Max decides if Alice is going to do Christmas, she's going to do Hanukkah, too.

Christmas Eve falls on the last night of Hanukkah, and Max makes latkes, and reads the prayers off his phone while he lights the candles. Amy takes pictures of Max and Alice with the menorah in the foreground and sends them to his mom, who sends back a row of heart-eye emojis. His dad calls and they say the prayer together again over FaceTime, and his dad laughs when Alice starts chewing on a plush dreidel.

"Look at our little *mamaleh*," Max's dad says into the screen.

Max is still talking to his dad when Alice starts getting cranky, and eventually Amy takes her up to bed. When she comes back downstairs, Max is sitting on the couch with a smile on his face.

"What?" Amy asks.

"Close your eyes," he says.

"What is it?"

"Just do it."

So Amy sits and closes her eyes. She hears him walk to the kitchen and back.

"Okay, open," he says.

He's got a mug of mulled wine, and a Toblerone bar the size of his forearm. "And," he says, "your choice—*Elf* or *National Lampoon's Christmas Vacation*."

"But you hate Chevy Chase. And you can't stand *Elf*."

"Which one first?"

"Seriously?"

He nods.

They watch *Elf* first, and drink mulled wine. Amy fills their stockings while Chevy Chase chases the squirrel around the house, and it's not till the credits start rolling that she starts thinking how Jim and Max would usually be smoking cigars on the porch around now and she and Fran would be harmonizing in the kitchen while they washed dishes and picked at the rest of the bacon-wrapped water chestnuts.

"You okay?" Max asks.

Amy shakes her head. The missing opens up like a cavern in the centre of her chest. "I just can't believe Alice will never know him," she sobs into his shoulder.

"She will," he murmurs. "We'll tell her stories and play his music. She'll know him."

But she won't know them—her and Fran and Jim—together.

"I just wish—I just—"

Max rubs her back until Amy has no tears left.

"Do you want some scotch?" Max asks. "We could have a toast?"

Amy shakes her head. She finds the Valdy record she found on the curb, the one she was going to take over the day Jim died, and puts it on the record player. It's crackly and scratched but the keys and guitar fill the living room. Valdy sings about Memphis and Winnipeg. It's way more seventies easy rock than the political folk Amy expected.

The record starts skipping.

Amy tries to move the needle, but the record is in such bad shape it skitters and skips through songs. She yanks the record off the turntable.

"You choose something," she tells Max.

He puts on Sharon Jones's Christmas album, and Amy stares at the tree. The lights burn the backs of her eyelids and the missing swells against her sternum.

45

WHEN FRAN IS BACK FROM FLORIDA, AMY TAKES her soup, and they sit in the living room, but neither of them says anything and it's like they don't know how to be without Jim. Amy is desperate to talk about him, to collect stories about him like lucky pennies. She wants to talk about being on the road, and hear about when they opened the bookstore, and what it was like during their folk music days. She tries to remember how Jim would smile in the middle of a song, the specific tone of his "Fuck yeah," after a good show, but he's disappearing. She can already feel him slipping away.

Fran stares at the wall, and it feels like Amy's lost both of them.

"I can't believe I wasted that year," Amy says, sobbing into Max's shoulder that night after Alice is down. She remembers the confused look on Fran's face when she said she was staying at the Yorkton Music Festival, how she had revelled in her confusion. She remembers the look on Fran's face after Ben had confronted Amy about recording with the New Pornographers, the tone of Jim's voice when he told her things weren't working. "I can't believe I was so shitty. I was so shitty," she says.

"You can't shame-spiral," Max reminds her. "That's what Debbie would say."

She knows he's right. She knows it's not serving her, but she has no idea how to save Fran from this chasm she's fallen into. She and Jim brought Amy back, but Amy can't figure out how to do that for Fran.

The next time Amy visits, she brings Alice, thinking she might make things easier. Alice crawls and pulls up to standing on the couch, and plops down on her diaper-covered bum, and Fran asks how she's sleeping, and what she's eating, but Fran's eyes still have an impossible faraway look to them.

On Saturday, when Max is with Alice, Amy takes her guitar over to Fran's, even though it's been months since she's played. She hands Fran the guitar that's hanging on the living room wall. "Jim said that music fixes everything," she says.

She tunes the D string and waits for Fran to do the same. But Fran looks bewildered, like she has no idea what a guitar even is. Amy strums a G chord, but Fran looks so agitated, Amy puts her guitar down and berates herself for thinking this could work.

After that, Amy starts bringing crossword puzzles over, and she and Fran do them sitting on the couch in almost silence. It's better than nothing, she tells herself, even though she feels like her heart is breaking every time they fill out a small square with a pencilled-in letter.

Have you heard from Fran? Ben texts one morning while Amy's putting Alice down for her morning nap.

. *I was over a few days ago, but haven't heard from her since,* Amy writes back.

Ben calls Amy as she's scraping Alice's half-eaten pancakes into the compost.

"I just got off the phone with Arlo," he says.

"Arlo?"

"I'm working on details for the July show and was going to book us in for a meeting, but I couldn't reach Fran."

"I was over on the weekend," Amy says, thinking about the blank look Fran had sitting on the couch.

"She's in Spain."

"Who?"

"Fran."

"Fran?"

"Yup."

"Fran's in Spain?"

"Apparently she found a flight last minute and took off."

Amy can't picture Fran alone on a plane. She can't picture her taking off anywhere without Jim. "That doesn't sound like Fran."

"I know."

Spain. She didn't tell Amy she was going. She didn't even tell her she was thinking about travelling.

"But we have to release the album, right?" Ben asks. "Otherwise, we say goodbye to the twenty thousand copies we're having printed."

Amy leans her forehead against the sliding glass door. The snow has been melting and freezing all week and is now grey and slick.

"Jim would want us to put it out," Ben says. "He'd hate it, if all that time and energy went into it and it just sat there."

Amy can't bear to invoke Jim right now. "I don't know, Ben."

"But if she doesn't come back before the release date?"

"It's still early," Amy says, the bridge of her nose burning. "Did you ask Arlo about her return flight?"

"He doesn't know. And you're still on the books to headline the Children's Festival in Ottawa," Ben says.

"It's February. She won't be gone till July," Amy says, though she really doesn't know.

"But what if she's not home by then? And even if she is, she might not want to play," Ben says.

"I'm pretty sure the festival organizers would understand."

"Would you be okay playing solo?"

Amy pictures herself in front of the Parliament Buildings onstage by herself. "Fuck, I don't know."

"You could pull it off. We could get you a backing band."

The prospect of being on that huge stage alone when she hasn't performed in over a year makes her want to vomit. "I really want to talk to Fran first."

"I'm just trying to make things easier."

"This is definitely not easier."

"He would want the album out," Ben says. "She knows that."

Amy glances at the monitor. Alice is still asleep.

"We'll get it out. It'll be good." Ben's voice is solid and resolute.

"Do you know where she is in Spain?" Amy asks.

"Arlo said she flew into Barcelona, then took the train to Seville."

"Why Seville?" she asks.

"No idea."

"Where's she staying?"

"An Airbnb, apparently. Arlo said she's not even really on email, but I'll send her a note. Let me know if you hear from her."

They hang up, and Amy looks up Seville. It's famous for flamenco dancing and a cathedral that used to be a mosque. Amy wonders what Fran's doing there—drinking sangria and, and what? She doesn't know. She doesn't know at all.

46

AMY GOES THROUGH THE MOTIONS OF BEING A mom—picking Alice up out of her crib and carrying her on her hip to say goodbye to Max, cutting up scrambled eggs, showing Alice how to stack Fisher-Price stacking rings. She puts on CBC Radio in the kitchen so the house isn't so quiet, and naps whenever Alice naps because she can't bear to be awake for any more minutes than she has to be.

There are days when Alice and Amy stay inside all day, avoiding the unshovelled sidewalks, and Amy tries to imagine what Fran is doing in Seville.

There are days when the sun shines bright against the melting snowbanks and Alice sits in her puffy purple snowsuit and licks her mittens and giggles. These are the good days, the days when Alice makes Amy laugh and they flip the flaps on the *Spot* books and stick their finger through the holes in *The Very Hungry Caterpillar*. Amy feels guilty for the good days.

The Fun Times Brigade

Alice turns eleven months, and there are no longer snowbanks blocking the stroller from the sidewalk, and Amy can wear Alice in the carrier without worrying about slipping on ice. The house is quiet, except for the melting snow drip-drip-dripping from the eavestrough like a metronome, and CBC calling out the news at the top of every hour. Alice is sleepy and warm after her second nap, and Amy nurses her in the glider, the early March light streaming through the window. When she's done, Amy changes her diaper.

"One leg! Two legs!" Amy says, pulling Alice's pants off. She's pulling the sticky tabs to the centre of the diaper when she hears BIKES in the kitchen—an instrumental song from their first album.

She needs to turn it off. "Just a sec, baby girl," Amy says, putting Alice back in her crib with her onesie undone. "I'll be right back."

Alice whimpers, and Amy runs down the stairs, but the CBC host is already talking with Christophe and the director of the Manitoulin Opera Company about his libretto. "Fuck off," Amy says, shutting off the radio.

Fucking Christophe and his stupid libretto. Amy wishes she had told Jim that his name was really Christopher, and that he changed it after living in Montreal for four months. She wishes she could've laughed with him about that.

Alice starts crying from her crib.

"I'm coming. I'm coming, baby girl," Amy calls up.

Amy leaves the radio off, but can't bear the silence, so she downloads a bunch of albums—Dire Straits, Bruce Springsteen, U2—music that is so unlike any of the music she's ever played, or even ever listened to. She doesn't know if Jim liked Bono, or the Boss. She has no idea. She wishes she could text Fran and ask her.

Springsteen's "Dancing in the Dark" quickly becomes Amy's new favourite song, and she plays it on a loop all morning, while Alice bounces in her Jolly Jumper hooked over the kitchen door frame. Amy does a Google image search during one of Alice's naps—Bruce with his electric guitar and cut-off T-shirts, his bad-boy ripped jeans. *I think I have a crush*, she texts Julie and sends her a photo. She hasn't texted her in weeks, and Amy knows she's worried about her.

The Boss?!? Julie texts back right away. *You know he's old, right?! Like old-old.*

But he has nineteen albums for Amy to get through, not including all the live ones, and she cranks "Waitin' on a Sunny Day" and drowns out any tears that might eclipse the rest of the morning.

Bruce is singing about the streets of Philadelphia when Amy's phone bings. *Albums are en route*, Ben has texted. He sent Amy something a few weeks back about the songs being mastered, but she hadn't responded. She didn't realize the album was already done. The box arrives after Alice's morning nap, and she texts Ben to tell them it's there.

Let me know what you think! Ben writes back.

She and Fran and Jim always listened to their albums for the first time together. They'd gather in Fran and Jim's living room, and Fran would insist on champagne, and they'd sit and sip and listen straight through.

Amy cuts open the tape and tries not to cry. Alice grabs at the box flap and Amy pulls out a CD. On the cover is a photo of the three of them onstage at Massey Hall—Fran has a tambourine; Jim is playing the guitar, with a harmonica sticking out of his pocket; and Amy's playing the ukulele. They're all smiling. Tears prickle at the backs of her eyes. This was before they knew

Jim had cancer, though maybe it was there, lurking, and insidious. This was before she was pregnant, when she thought she'd never be able to be pregnant, when she spent hours sobbing over single-lined pregnancy tests.

"Mamamama," Alice says, grabbing the CD and smashing the case against the carpet.

"That's right, baby girl. That's Mama."

"Mamamamamamama."

"Easy, easy." Amy takes off the plastic wrap. "Here," she says, giving Alice the liner notes. "Gentle. See Fran? You know Fran. And that's Grandpa Jim," she says, trying to keep her voice from breaking.

"Should we listen, baby girl?" Amy asks. It feels wrong, listening to it without Fran, but what else can she do?

The album opens with "The Crayon Song"—the three of them singing together, their voices braiding into one another's like they had since their first jam at the Royal City Folk Fest's Rainbow Stage. The kids cheer and cheer and they go straight into "Puddle Jumping."

"Plonk went the rain, and plink went the rain," Amy sings on the recording.

"And our umbrellas started spinning," Amy sings, harmonizing with Fran.

Alice pulls all the books off the bottom shelf while Amy listens to herself tell a knock-knock joke before "The Bright Blue Sky." Alice starts screaming when she can't reach a bunch of Max's biographies. Amy wants to finish listening to "The Vaccine Waltz," but Alice is too upset, and Amy has to press pause.

It's a really beautiful album, she texts Ben while Alice eats lunch.

47

BEN KEEPS ASKING AMY IF SHE'LL PLAY THE OTTAWA gig solo, and eventually she agrees. "But don't publicize it yet. And if Fran comes back and wants to play, then we'll play together," she insists.

To distract herself from missing Fran, and the terrifying reality of playing a Brigade show on her own, Amy goes overboard for Alice's birthday and gets her a wagon, a Little Tikes car for the backyard, rainbow nesting blocks, beeswax crayons, and a doll. "I think we should get her something, I don't know, important, something to commemorate the year," Amy says to Max.

She remembers Jim saying that music fixes everything, so she decides to record a song for Alice. She googles Long & McQuade during Alice's nap to see how much it would cost to rent a few microphones and a small interface to plug into her laptop. She picks them up the next day, along with a pair of mic stands, loading it all into the trunk while Alice babbles from her car seat.

The Fun Times Brigade

Amy waits until Alice is down for her nap to unload the car, then threads the cables to the interface in the basement and sets up the mic stands. She checks the baby monitor—Alice is still sleeping and she has forty minutes, maybe. She tunes her guitar and strums a few chords, her fingers burning under the strings. She plugs in her keyboard, but after she plays two scales, Alice is awake.

The next morning, after Amy gets Alice down, she props up the baby monitor on the box of new Brigade CDs she made Max bring down to the basement and keeps an eye on the green lights at the top. They'll blink red if Alice starts crying. She adjusts the mic stand and angles the guitar mic so it's close to the strings. She presses her lips against the cross-hatched metal. "Check check. Check one two three four monkeys running out the door." She's missed this, even if she's just sound-checking for a mountain of outgrown baby clothes.

She tunes her guitar again and starts playing around.

"Alice, Alice, you're one year old."

Amy tries out something about her laugh, her eight teeth, her learning to climb the stairs. She switches up the chords, hoping something will click. Still nothing. She starts picking something, but then realizes it's the intro to "Reggie the Friendly Raccoon."

Amy checks the monitor. Alice is still asleep.

She plays a G chord, then G6, a G chord, G6, her pinky lifting off the top string. Her uncalloused fingers hurt, but she presses on. She waits for the lyrics to come, but nothing. Nothing. Until on a whim she starts singing "Dancing in the Dark."

G, G6, G, G6.

Her voice sounds nothing like Bruce Springsteen's, but it feels good to have words and a melody ballooning in her throat.

G, G6, G, G6.

She does the chorus twice in a row, and then the monitor starts flashing red. She turns on the video screen, and Alice is sitting up, bashing Bun Bun against the rungs of her crib. Amy flicks off all the equipment and leaves her guitar on the stand.

She keeps working on a song for Alice, but nothing comes, so she turns three Springsteen songs—"Dancing in the Dark," "Waitin' on a Sunny Day," and "Born to Run"—into lullabies. She sings into the microphone, the weight of her guitar around her neck comforting. She wonders if Jim would like them, what Fran would think, and has to blink away the tears that threaten to take over the afternoon.

Alice's birthday party is a disaster. It feels wrong celebrating anything without Jim and Fran, Amy drinks too much, and Alice cries when everyone sings "Happy Birthday" and refuses to even try the smash cake Julie made. After Max drives his parents back to their hotel, Amy spends the rest of the day in bed.

When she wakes up on Alice's actual birthday, the crocuses have bloomed—tiny purple secrets dotting the front lawn, and she promises herself that it's going to be a good day.

"You're one!" she tells Alice, picking her up out of her crib. She's heavy now, a solid eighteen and a half pounds. Alice gives Amy a toothy smile, and Amy carries her back into bed to nurse her.

It seems unfathomable that exactly a year ago her water broke. It seems unfathomable that Alice—their fierce, determined little Alice—hasn't always been here. It seems impossible that last year at this time she was still curled up inside Amy, waiting, both of them waiting. A year ago, Jim was alive. A year ago, Fran was still here. The missing is unbearable, and Amy tries to distract herself by looking through photos from the day Alice was born—the puddle on the bed when her water broke, the hospital room, and then Alice, hundreds of photos of Alice all red and wrinkled. It seems impossible that this person who can stand now—not for long, but still, she stands and beams, showing off her eight teeth until her knees give out—used to sleep on Amy's chest, legs still folded up as they were in utero.

The barista at the coffee shop gives Alice a croissant and won't let Amy pay for her latte. A huge bouquet of flowers from Julie is waiting on the porch when they get home, and Emily has sent over a box of board books, and Amy's mom calls while Alice is eating avocado and prunes spread on pancakes.

All day Amy hopes she'll hear from Fran, but gives up when Max gets home from work. Fran is grieving, she reminds herself. There's no way she'll remember Alice's birthday. Max orders in sushi, and Alice opens her pile of presents. She doesn't care about any of them, of course, and instead plays with the box the rainbow blocks came in.

"I've got one more thing," Amy says while Alice puts the box on her head.

"Something else?" Max asks.

"I made something," she says, suddenly feeling nervous. She connects her phone to the speakers in the living room and puts on the three songs she recorded.

Max looks at Amy during the first verse of "Dancing in the Dark." "This is you?"

She nods.

"Oh my god, Ames," Max says, pulling Amy into him. "This is so amazing." He leans over to Alice and scoops her up. "You hear this? This is your mama. This is your mama singing."

Alice screeches and kicks to be put back down. "Waitin' on a Sunny Day" starts playing.

"I tried to write something about her, for her, but I just—Well, this is what came out."

"These are really beautiful, Ames," Max says. "This will mean so much to her."

Alice throws the wrapping paper against the floor.

"I mean, maybe not today," he says.

Amy laughs and Alice screeches.

"But it will," he says.

48

AS THE WEATHER GETS WARMER, AMY TAKES ALICE to the park, but she yanks away toys from other kids, tosses handfuls of sand, and screams when there is another kid close to her. Amy apologizes to the moms hovering at the edges, embarrassed by her rage-filled kid who doesn't know how to be around others. Amy picks her up, and Alice protests, kicking and flailing. She feels like such a failure while Alice screams and fights the straps of her stroller. She hurries out of the park and pulls out her phone and finds the last message from Fiona. *Do you want to meet up in a park one of these days?* she texts.

Amy doesn't hear back from her and feels like an idiot for thinking she could just send her a note as if things were normal. She deserves this silence.

Sorry I just got this! Fiona writes back a few days later. *We're in B.C. visiting Lisa's family. We're here for the next few months. Park hang when we're back?*

Sure, Amy writes back, reminding herself she has no grounds to be disappointed. *Sounds great.*

Alice is waking up from a nap when Amy gets a text from Nathan. It takes her a moment to remember Nathan. BIKES Nathan, the trumpet player.

Jill Barber is recording an album and is looking for a backup singer, he's written. *You interested?*

Amy saw Jill Barber open for the Indigo Girls years ago. She stares at her phone until Alice starts wailing from her crib.

"Hey, baby girl," Amy says, lifting Alice out of her crib. There's a small puddle of drool on her crib sheet, and she's still warm with sleep. "Should Mommy sing with Jill Barber?" she asks into her soft, wispy hair.

Amy doesn't sleep that night. Instead, she pulls up Nathan's text. She still hasn't responded, and she's not sure what she wants to do. She digs up old photos from the road—their bathing suits dangling from their bunks in the tour bus, a hundred photos of them kneeling next to fans, the three of them onstage somewhere in the prairies on their last summer tour. Max half wakes and tells Amy her phone is too bright, so she slips downstairs, and before she can stop herself, she types *BIKES* into a Google search. *Pitchfork* has included them in their top hundred bands of the decade, though there's no mention of their last album. It's like it doesn't exist.

In the morning, Amy straps Alice into the running stroller she found at a garage sale. It's been years since she's gone for a run, but she needs to move, she needs her blood pumping hard in her ears. *Jill Barber, Jill Barber*—her cadence the whole way down to the lake. It feels like a betrayal, even considering playing with anyone but Fran, but Fran is still in Spain and no one knows when she's coming back. Amy pauses at a light, not bothering to jog on the spot. She could get an actual babysitter, so it wouldn't be like when she tried to record with Sandra.

The light changes and Amy pushes the stroller across the road.

She'll have to figure out how to stand behind a microphone without Jim on one side and Fran on the other. She'll have to figure out how to be in a recording booth without Fran's harmonies, without Jim keeping time with his hand on his thigh and driving the engineers crazy.

Amy reaches the lake where boats are docked, their sails bound to their masts. There are a bunch of Canada geese paddling around. She goes to pick Alice up and show her the water, but she's asleep. "Fuck," Amy says to no one.

She turns the stroller around and realizes it's uphill the whole way home.

Can I come by? Fran texts in early May.

Amy stares at her phone. Alice smashes her hands into her high chair, demanding another pumpkin muffin. Amy passes her one and stares at the screen again.

Of course! Whenever! Amy types fast and presses send. *We're around all day!*

Alice squishes the muffin in her fist. She lifts her hands, and before Amy can stop her, she smears it into her hair.

Fran knocks instead of ringing the doorbell, and Amy opens the door with Alice on her hip.

"Hi," Fran says, giving Amy a sideways hug. She runs a finger on Alice's cheek. "And look at you! You're getting so big!"

"Hey," Amy says. "Come in."

Fran looks small and frail, all bone.

"Coffee?" Amy asks as Fran sits on the couch.

"Maybe tea if you have any?" she asks.

Amy puts Alice on the ground, but she whines until she picks her back up.

"I've only got Earl Grey. That okay?" Amy calls from the kitchen.

"Sure," Fran says.

Amy puts Alice down to carry their mugs to the living room, and she crawls to the coffee table.

"Look at her go," Fran says.

"She's getting speedy," Amy says.

She waits for Fran to say something about Spain. She waits for Fran to tell her about Levi, or something, anything, but she doesn't say anything.

Amy sips her tea. It's too hot and burns her tongue. The quiet is unnerving.

"So how's our little Alice?" Fran asks, eventually.

"Good," Amy says.

Alice pulls herself up to stand.

"Would you look at that," Fran says.

"She's started cruising," Amy says, and waits for Fran to tell her a story about Arlo learning to walk, but Fran watches Alice fall on her bum, and blinks. "They really do grow up so fast," she says.

Amy holds on to her mug with both hands. "How was Spain?" she asks.

"Good. Well, not good. I don't know why I just say 'good' like that, like a reflex," she says. "It was lonely. God, it was so lonely. I cried most of the time."

"That's so sad," Amy says, feeling the back of her eyes burning.

"It was. But it was good to be away, mostly from Arlo and Sina hovering and asking me a thousand times a day how I'm doing. Good to sit in the quiet. I climbed the bell tower almost every day. It has a great view of the city, though, really, I'd just stand up there and cry and scare all the tourists."

Amy laughs.

"And I ate a lot of oranges. They were so good, but then I'd think about Jim never being able to try one, that I couldn't even tell him about them, and then I'd be back to crying."

Amy's eyes start filling. "It's so hard."

"It's truly impossible," she says, and puts her hand on top of Amy's.

"I didn't know you were going," Amy says, wishing her voice didn't sound so hurt.

"*I* didn't even really know I was going," Fran says. "I woke up one morning and I couldn't bear to be in the house anymore."

Alice whimpers, and Amy pulls her up on her lap. "I'm sorry," Amy says. "I know this isn't about me."

"You don't have to apologize," Fran says with a short laugh. "I should've told you."

"I probably would've gotten the fuck out of here too if I didn't have…" Amy waves her arm at the toy-strewn living room.

Fran squeezes Amy's hand. "I'm sorry I missed Alice's birthday. Did you have a party?"

Amy nods. "It was a shit show," she says. "Alice cried and wouldn't eat the cake, and I got drunk, and my mom was in a passive-aggressive competition with Max's mom, and offered to babysit every week, though I don't know if she meant it or not. She did make Alice a paper-mâché '1' sculpture, but Max thought it was a pinata and my mom was not pleased."

Alice wriggles out of Amy's lap and grabs a block.

"Look at you, all grown up," Fran says.

Alice smashes a block into the top of the couch cushions. She throws it and then starts whining.

"Well then don't throw it, you goose," Amy says, and hands it back to her.

She throws it again.

"What have you been up to?" Fran asks Amy.

"Not much," she says. "I found a running stroller, so I've been taking Alice out."

"Running! Good for you," Fran says. "Have you been playing at all?"

Amy shakes her head. "Not really," she says, not wanting to tell her about the Springsteen covers, or the text from Nathan.

Fran looks at Amy. "If I said I wanted to play, would you?"

"Pardon?"

"Jim always said, 'Music fixes everything,' so I'm starting to think playing might be my way out of this," she says. "Our way out, if you want it to be."

Amy doesn't say anything. This was the last thing she was expecting. She had been preparing herself to play the Ottawa show alone.

"Do you want to?" Fran asks.

Amy nods.

"Okay," Fran says.

"Okay what?"

"Then we'll play," she says. "Ben's sent me a thousand emails about the Ottawa show, so we can start there. If you want."

"Yes," Amy says, her heart hammering in her chest. "Are you sure?"

"No," Fran laughs, "but I know Jim would want us to, and if you want to, I say we do it. We can start with Ottawa and go from there."

49

BEN IS ECSTATIC AND BOOKS THEM MORE SHOWS at Harbourfront, and at Royal City Folk Fest, and the Kensington Pedestrian Festival.

Is it too much? Amy texts Fran. *We can get Ben to scale back.*

It's fine. Don't worry about me, she writes.

Amy finally texts Nathan back. *Sorry it's taken me so long. Thanks for thinking of me, but I'm working on a Brigade launch.*

Cool, he texts back. *My sister's kids love you guys. Lemme know when the new album drops.*

Amy laughs, startling Alice, and sends back a thumbs-up emoji.

Amy's phone buzzes throughout the day—emails from Ben and his assistant.

The Fun Times Brigade

Denise is hiring another PR person to manage all of the interviews, Ben texts Amy and Fran. *There's going to be a lot of interest.*

Before Amy can respond, her phone rings.

"I can't do press," Fran says, her voice cracking.

"No problem," Amy says quickly. "I'll do it. I'll tell Ben."

"You sure that's okay?"

"Positive," Amy says, even though she's never done press on her own.

"We're still good to rehearse tomorrow?" Fran asks.

They'd only ever rehearsed at Fran and Jim's—in the basement, usually, and sometimes their living room—but Fran has been staying in Arlo's guest room since she's been back, going home only to water plants and bring in the mail, so Ben found them rehearsal space in the west end.

"Yup," Amy says. "See you then."

Even though there's a chance she'll bail, Amy asks her mom to watch Alice. Amy insists that she can't be late, and she's not, thank god. Amy walks her mom through Alice's nap routine—the sleep sack, the pile of books, the blackout blinds, the Sleep Sheep on the rain setting, the night light, and tucking her in with Bun Bun. Amy's pretty sure she's not going to do any of it, but at least she's said it all.

"Call me if there's an emergency," Amy says.

Her mom waves her off, her cheetah earrings swinging. "We're great, right, boogitybub?" She sits with Alice building block towers in the living room. Alice giggles every time the blocks crash to the floor. Amy kisses Alice goodbye twice and then grabs her keys and rushes herself out the door. She waits outside for a moment, straining to hear something, anything, but Alice doesn't cry, not even a whimper.

Text if you need me, Amy writes to her mom.

We're fine, she writes back by the time Amy gets to the streetcar stop.

The walls of the studio on Ossington are padded with dampeners, and cables are coiled on the wall. Old carpets are layered on the floor, and there are a bunch of amps near the drum kit. If Jim were here, he'd be playing around on the drums, or picking out a melody on the baby grand in the corner.

"What is this place?" Amy asks Fran.

"It was abandoned for a long time, but they've turned it into artist spaces," Fran says and plays a C chord, the sound ringing in the space.

Amy takes her guitar out and pulls the strap over her head.

"Ben said we're supposed to open with the national anthem," Fran says.

"Right. And the kids' choir will join us for it."

Fran nods.

"And I think Ben said they've also been working on a few other songs, so we could do 'Puddle Jumping' next, so we don't have to get them off and back up," Amy says.

"Sure." Fran fusses with her A string. "Guitars, or not, for the anthem?" she asks.

"Maybe just vocals?"

"Okay, let's try it, then. You want stage left or stage right?"

Amy was always stage left, Fran was always stage right, and Jim was in the middle. But there is no middle anymore. There's only stage right and stage left.

"Left is good."

Fran nods. "All right. Kids file onstage. Introduction—can you do it?"

"Sure," Amy says.

"And then 'O Canada,'" Fran says. "I'll do harmonies?"
"Great."
"And maybe the second verse in French?"
Amy nods.
They sing it. It's fine, but not great. They sing it again and again, and Amy tries not to think about all the places it needs Jim's tenor.
"We need a set list," Fran says.
"I'll write it on my phone and email it to you," Amy says.
"Maybe we should do 'The Crayon Song' after 'O Canada' instead of 'Puddle Jumping'?" Fran asks.
"Or maybe we should close with 'Crayons'?" Amy asks.
"So 'O Canada' and then 'Puddle Jumping,' and then..." Fran trails off.
"Then 'Bright Blue Sky' or 'The Dinosaur Stomp'?" Amy asks.
"Either one," Fran says.
They come up with a list of sixteen songs, and Amy types them into her phone, ending with "The Crayon Song."
"Should we do a run-through?" Fran asks.
"Yeah," Amy says, but they both busy themselves tuning their guitars.
"This is weird," Amy starts. "I just, I miss—"
Fran stops her. "I can't right now, Ames. I can't go there if we're going to play, okay? I just can't."
Amy nods. "Okay, okay. Got it." She blinks hard.
Amy props up her phone between them, and they start from the top. She misses Jim's steady voice, his foot keeping time, his noodling around at the end of every song until Fran told him to quit it. They sing "The Vaccine Waltz," but there is a huge gaping hole that their two voices can't fill.
Amy stops midway through "Ants Go Marching." "Sorry," she says, setting her guitar down. "I need to pee."

She tries not to run, but she wants out—out of this artsy warehouse, out of this missing. The bathroom smells like pee and fluorescent-pink hand soap. She holds on to the sink, stares at her reflection, and breathes deeply. Jim would want her to figure it out. To keep rehearsing. To get it right. She splashes water on her face and washes her hands with the pink soap.

"Sorry," she says, back in the studio. "Do you want to pick up at 'Ants Go Marching,' or rewind to 'The Rainbow March'?"

"'Ants,'" Fran says, and they start again.

"Maybe the kids' choir could come back and do two more songs near the end?" Amy suggests when they've done another run-through.

"Good idea," Fran says.

They sing the national anthem a few more times and work out the harmonies on "I Spy with My Little Eye." The next time Amy looks at her phone, it's already four thirty. "I'm so sorry," she says. "I have to get going. My mom can only stay till five." She puts her guitar away and calls a cab.

"I think this is going to be okay," Fran says, but it sounds more like a question.

"It's going to be good," Amy says, more confidently than she feels.

"It's hard without him," Fran says, her face falling.

Amy hugs her and Fran collapses into her.

"He'd be so proud of you today," Fran says, wiping her eyes.

"He'd be proud of *us*," Amy says.

Amy gets a text that her cab is there, so she picks up her guitar, then puts it down to hug Fran again.

"Talk soon," Fran says, but Amy hates thinking of Fran getting into a cab by herself, so she invites her over for dinner.

"Sure," Fran says. "Well, as long as it's not tofu. That is all Sina and Arlo eat these days."

"No tofu," Amy promises, and they walk out to the cab together.

After Fran leaves and Alice is down, Amy rereads the set list, but there's no way there should be two marches in a row. And the final chord of "The Dinosaur Stomp" sounds weird followed by the opening of "Bright Blue Sky." She hasn't made a set list in years, but she moves "Bright Blue Sky" after "Puddle Jumping," and switches "Mr. Sun" and "Ants Go Marching," so "Mr. Sun" is after "The Rainbow March," which is a way better fit. She makes sure all of the action songs aren't lumped together in the middle, then does the same with the call-and-response songs. She takes out "Battle of the Snowsuit," even though it's on the live album, because they're going to be playing in July, and replaces it with "Reggie the Friendly Raccoon." She puts "There Was an Old Lady Who Swallowed a Fly" before "Where's My Hat?" and makes sure "Sittin' on the Potty" and "Wash, Wash, Wash Your Hands" are paired up.

In the morning, she writes down a few knock-knock jokes while Alice eats halved blueberries. Ben confirms that the choir can sing "Ride Your Bike" and "The Crayon Song" at the end of the set, so Amy makes a note and then sends the new set list to him and Fran.

It's perfect, Fran writes back. *Love the transitions.*

Amy glances over at the posters of Jim beaming in the living room. He'd like this set list. She knows he would.

50

AMY DOES A FULL MONTH OF RADIO, TV, MAGAZINE, and newspaper interviews.

"And Jim," every interviewer says, in a sad, sombre voice.

"We miss him," Amy says, fighting tears. "We miss him so much." It's like tearing the Band-Aid off every single time, and she's so glad Fran opted out of doing press.

She's sitting on the *Breakfast Television* couch when the host asks her for her favourite memory of Jim. Amy freezes and her brain spins through a Rolodex of Jim moments—jamming in the back of the tour bus, jumping into a quarry in Manitoba, fiddling with his earpiece during a sound check, swearing like a sailor before going onstage. She pastes a smile on her face and tries to think of something TV-friendly. "When we recorded our folk legends album," she says. "Seeing him play with such iconic musicians—Garth Hudson, Stephen Stills, Mickey Hart—his friends," she adds. "He was so in his element."

The Fun Times Brigade

Amy can tell there's a producer talking into the host's ear.

"Yes, your *To Every Season* album," she says.

Amy nods.

"Now, tell me about your baby," the host says.

"Alice," Amy says, still thinking about Jim and Stephen Stills jamming. She tries to stay focused and not let grief capsize her on live TV. "She turned one in April."

"Well, isn't that lovely. A new Brigade fan. And do you have any solo projects on the go?" The host looks at Amy intently.

"Between the Brigade and Alice, there's not really time these days," Amy says and forces a laugh.

"And you were a member of the Dovercourt Bicycle Collective," the host says.

"Yes," Amy manages. She can see Jim standing over the craft services table telling her how sloppy they were, how big bands like that use people like her. *You were right*, she wants to tell him. Of course he was right.

The host looks at the camera. "Tune in Thursday for BIKES frontmen Jason Evans and Christophe Williamson talking about their new album," she says.

A new BIKES album? Amy fixes a smile on her face.

"Amy Scholl from the Fun Times Brigade," the host says, opening her hand toward her. "Thank you for coming in today. The iconic children's band is launching their most recent live album and performing throughout the summer."

Amy keeps the smile on her face as the show cuts to the traffic camera and the sound guy unthreads her mic. She keeps smiling into the green room where she gets her purse, and in the elevator, and out on the sidewalk, where she signs a kid's backpack and takes a photo with a little girl who tells Amy her favourite song is "Sittin' on the Potty." Amy keeps smiling until she gets into a cab, then googles *BIKES* as soon as the door shuts behind her. They're rerecording their original instrumental album. *Back to Basics*, they're calling it—Christophe, Jason, Daniel, and Joseph. Seeing his name makes Amy's stomach flip. She takes a screenshot and sends it to Emily.

The cab pauses at a red light and Amy's phone rings. It's Emily.

"Oh my god!" Emily yells. "And did you see they've started a blog? I mean who even reads blogs anymore?"

"What? I just heard about this new album bullshit when I was doing an interview on live TV," Amy says.

"Okay, check your phone," Emily says.

Amy puts her headphones in and clicks on the link she's sent. "What is this?" Amy asks squinting at her screen. There's a quote from Camus in scripted font across the top. "What the fuck is this?"

"Christophe is blogging about the process."

"And he's calling it *Back to Back to Basics*?" Amy asks. "Is this for real? Like, it's not ironic?"

"I don't think so," Emily says. "Honest to god, what a dinkus."

Amy laughs. "No one says dinkus."

"Yeah, but if you look it up in the dictionary, there's a picture of Christophe and his ridiculous mustache," she laughs. "Also, I wasn't going to send you this, because you don't need to be wasting your time thinking about Captain Dinkus, but his libretto got destroyed by the media."

"I love you," Amy says. "Thank you for telling me."

"They're dicks with egos and microphones."

Amy laughs. "It's true." And she wonders if Joseph is still cheating on his wife on every tour but reminds herself what Debbie said about not letting herself fall into a shame spiral.

"So, how's the album promo going?" Emily asks.

"Okay," Amy says. "I'm fine on camera but then I come home and lose it."

The Fun Times Brigade

"Fair," she says. "I can't imagine how hard it would be."

Amy's phone buzzes. A text from Ben.

Nice work on the BT interview, he writes. *Can you do a CBC radio thing this aft?*

"I'm so sorry, but I've got to go," Amy tells Emily. "Thanks for telling me about Dinkus McGee."

She laughs. "I love you. Give Alice a kiss for me."

Yup, Amy writes back to Ben, grateful that her mom followed up on her babysitting offer and has been taking care of Alice while she does press. *Send me the details.*

Amy opens Instagram and doesn't let herself look up BIKES. She starts scrolling, and stops at one of Sandra's recent photos. It's a selfie of her and Jill Barber sharing a microphone. She must've taken the backup gig. Amy waits for the jealousy to creep in, but it doesn't. She adds a heart emoji to the comments and posts a photo of the coil of cords from her last rehearsal with Fran. *Gearing up for the Ottawa Children's Festival*, she writes as the caption. *Can't wait to be back onstage.*

51

AMY WAKES UP BEFORE BOTH MAX AND ALICE AND figures out how to work the hotel room coffee maker in the dark. She's so excited to be playing again that she doesn't even care that Alice was up three times last night. She makes a second pot after Alice and Max are up, but her hands start shaking, and she regrets it a few sips in.

Alice holds on to Bun Bun and toddles the length of the room with her unsteady drunken-sailor gait. Amy tries to keep her from falling into the corners of the bed, the desk chair, the coffee table.

"Cah!" Alice says, pointing to the cover of one of the hotel's complimentary magazines on the coffee table.

"That's right, kiddo," Amy says. "Car."

After breakfast, Max goes down to the hotel gym, and Amy pulls the curtains closed and blasts the sound machine, hoping

Alice will go down early. But Alice is dropping her morning nap and refuses to sleep, and Amy pulls her out of her Pack 'n Play just as Max comes back in.

"I should get down to Fran's room," Amy says.

"You nervous?" he asks, kissing Amy's cheek. He's sweaty and damp, and Amy wishes Alice were sleeping so they could have pre-show sex like they used to before Toronto shows.

"A little bit," Amy says. "But mostly excited."

"You're going to be amazing. Isn't your mama going to be amazing?" he asks Alice.

"Mamama."

"That's right, baby girl," Max says, picking her up and flying her over to the bed.

"Don't forget her sun hat," Amy says, kissing them both goodbye. "And sunscreen. Lots of sunscreen."

Amy walks down the hall with her makeup bag and takes the elevator to Fran's room.

"Help yourself," Fran says, gesturing to the room service tray she's barely touched.

It's been almost seventeen months since Amy's put on stage makeup and she's out of practice. Her eyeliner is wobbly, and it takes three tries before it looks half decent. She stares hard at her eyelashes in the mirror, brushing the mascara up, up, up. She has to stay focused. She bends down and laces up her red Converse. She's been looking forward to this day since she first saw the plus sign on the pregnancy test.

Fran's doing her lipstick, but her hands are shaking.

"You okay?" Amy asks her in the mirror.

Fran looks at her like she doesn't know where she is.

"Are you all right?"

"I can't do this," Fran says.

"I can do it. Here," Amy says, holding out her hand for her lipstick.

"No, *this*. I can't do this."

"Wait, what?"

"The show," Fran says, her eyes frantic. "I can't do it without him."

"You're okay," Amy tells her. "We've been rehearsing. We'll be okay."

"I can't, Amy."

Amy's heart starts pounding. "But music fixes everything, remember? You said it was what you needed. This is what Jim would have wanted."

"I know, I know," Fran says, her voice cracking. She puts her face in her hands. "But I can't."

They're supposed to be sound-checking in less than an hour. And they have Royal City booked, and Harbourfront, and Kensington.

Amy takes Fran's hands. "You're going to be okay. We're going to be okay. Let's take a deep breath."

They breathe together, and Amy's mind races.

"How about one show?" Amy says. "Just this one. Let's just do this one."

Fran takes another deep breath and holds on to Amy's hands.

"We'll go one song at a time," Amy says. "And this can be our final show, our send-off." Amy can't believe she's saying this.

Fran nods slowly, then hugs her. "Our send-off," she says into Amy's shoulder.

"Okay, I'll finish your makeup. Can't let the stage lights wash you out." Amy tries to make her voice jokey, but she can't keep the tears from falling. She wipes a balled-up Kleenex under her eyes to keep the mascara from running.

Their phones start buzzing.

"It's Ben," Amy says. "Car's waiting for us."

Amy finishes Fran's makeup and redoes her eyeliner. She holds Fran's hand as they walk to the elevator in a daze.

When they get to the venue, Amy wants to tell Ben that this will be their last show, but the stage manager is running a tight ship and they're already five minutes late for sound check. Fran and Amy switch into Brigade mode, shaking the choir director's hand, introducing themselves to the kids, taking a few selfies for Denise to post on their social feeds.

The national anthem sounds great with the choir, and "Puddle Jumping" is even better with it behind them. The kids end the song by jumping around onstage. There's no time to go back to the hotel after the stage manager ushers them offstage, so Amy calls Max from the corner of the talent tent.

"She's finally asleep," he whispers, his voice echoing against the bathroom tile. "I'll get her up around one thirty and head down."

"One," Amy says. "One at the latest. The crowds are already starting. You won't be able to see the stage if you don't leave the hotel by one thirty."

"Okay," Max says.

Amy glances across the tent. She wants to tell him that this is their last show, but she can't say anything without the possibility of someone overhearing. "Don't be late. You can't be late."

"I won't."

"Promise," she says. She realizes she's swaying, the way she used to when Alice was little and she was trying to get her to sleep in the carrier.

Ben brings Fran and Amy burritos, but Amy's too nervous to eat.

"You have to eat something," Ben says. "Remember Vancouver?"

They played the Olympic Opening Ceremonies, and Amy was so nervous that she couldn't eat beforehand and then got so light-headed that she almost passed out onstage.

"Okay, okay," Amy says, taking a bite of the burrito. She hasn't eaten since the continental breakfast this morning, and she realizes a few bites in that she's starving.

Ben shows Amy the press clippings Denise sent over. "You done good," he says. "And our streaming numbers are through the roof."

Amy feels a knot of tears gathering in her throat and distracts herself by scrolling through #FunTimesBrigade. There are photos of kids holding up their new CD, and photos from their sound check. They look good up there—the stage full with the choir.

"It's time," Ben says.

Amy redoes her lipstick and checks her phone. *We're close*, Max has texted with a photo of Alice strapped in the carrier. She wishes she could call him and hear his steady, even voice telling her it's all going to be okay, but Ben puts his hand out and Amy passes him her phone. Fran and Amy and Ben follow security over to the stage, and Fran squeezes Amy's hand before they step out.

"Let's do this, fuckers," Amy whispers, and they step onstage to huge applause.

There is a sea of parents and kids spread out on picnic blankets and folding chairs in front of the stage. Julie and her kids are in the front row. She waves, and Amy smiles, and scans the crowd for Max and Alice.

"Welcome, friends!" Amy says into the mic, her voice as cheery as she can make it. "We are so thrilled to be opening the Ottawa Children's Festival. Please stand for the national anthem."

After "O Canada," Amy still can't find Max and Alice. She gets the nod from the choir director and makes eye contact with Fran, and they launch into "Puddle Jumping." "Plonk went the rain, and plink went the rain and our rain boots started

The Fun Times Brigade

dancing." It hits Amy after the second verse that this is the last time they'll ever sing "Puddle Jumping." She smiles hard at the audience and blinks fast.

The choir marches offstage while Fran and Amy sing "Bright Blue Sky," and Amy looks for Max and Alice, and when she still can't see them, she starts feeling panicky. They have to be here. This is their last show. This is the only time Alice will ever be able to see the Brigade onstage.

Amy stumbles in the chorus of "Where's My Hat?" and Fran looks over, eyebrows raised in a "you okay?" look. Amy nods and picks it up at the next verse.

"Knock-knock," Amy says to the crowd after the song is over.

"Who's there?" the audience yells back.

"Woo."

"Woo who?"

"Woohoo, I'm excited, too!"

Amy makes her smile even brighter, slapping her knee and fake-laughing while the kids laugh and laugh.

Still no Max and Alice.

Amy goes on autopilot through "The Vaccine Waltz" and "Ants Go Marching." Halfway through "The More We Get Together," Amy finally sees Max's curly hair and Alice's big blue ear protectors on the far side of the stage, a third of the way back. She's so relieved she could cry.

Fran and Amy play "The Sleeping Song" next—Jim's favourite from their lullaby album. Fran's taken over the picking intro Jim used to play.

"Crawl under the sheets, read one more book. No monsters here, but we'll take a look," Amy sings, letting her voice ground Fran's harmony. "It's time to sleep, it's time to dream, of rainbows, sunshine, and ice cream."

This is it. This is the end. The biggest and most significant chapter of her life, done. She has no idea what she's going to do now.

"It's time to sleep," Amy whisper-sings into the mic. "It's time to dream of rainbows, sunshine, and ice cream."

Her eyes shine with tears, and she watches Max sway with Alice in the crowd.

EPILOGUE

WHEN FRAN GOT THE CALL THAT SHE AND JIM were being awarded a Lifetime Achievement Award at the JUNOs, she insisted Amy be onstage with her.

"It's not a Brigade award," Amy pushed back, but Fran insisted. "It's the only way I'll do it," she said.

And so they're waiting to go onstage at a hockey stadium in Edmonton. They've come to the JUNOs for years. They've received eight of them, but the kids' music awards are given out in a hotel ballroom the day before the televised portion, not in an arena with twenty-five thousand people. It's a way bigger deal than Amy anticipated.

A woman with a headset and a clipboard leans over. "You're on in thirty seconds."

Dan Levy is hosting in a sequined tuxedo. He cracks a joke about falling in love with Jim Cuddy's baby blues, then segues into the Canadian Music Hall of Fame. He talks about Jim and Fran's first album, about them playing with Joni Mitchell and

The Fun Times Brigade

Gordon Lightfoot. He talks about their reinvention with the Fun Times Brigade, about the TV show, and how much his friends' kids love it. He talks about Jim having cancer—Fran refused to let the writer put in "battle with cancer." He talks about the tributes for Jim that happened across the country. Photos are projected on the screens at the back of the stage—the cover from their first folk album, a photo of them with their camper van and Arlo as a tiny baby in Jim's arms. There are photos of the three of them singing the national anthem at a baseball game, and standing in front of Lake Louise, and playing on the chemo ward at the children's hospital.

"And you're on in ten, nine—" the clipboard woman says.

"Let's do this, fuckers," Fran and Amy whisper in unison. Dan Levy opens his hands to the wings. Amy follows Fran to the centre of the stage. The audience is a black swath interrupted by the light of the teleprompter and its rolling script. They walk over to their microphones.

After the Ottawa show, Fran had insisted Amy keep playing. "*You* be the Fun Times Brigade," she said over coffee on her porch.

"I can't," Amy said.

"Why not?"

"Why not? Because a brigade can't be one person. Because our songs need more than one voice, and one guitar would sound ridiculous. And who would come to see just me? I'm not the one with the legendary folk career. And who would I write new songs with? And who would write the set lists? And do all the press? And the photos are of the three of us—"

"Photos? That's what, a couple hours, done. And no one's coming to see an old folk geezer anymore," Fran insisted. "Maybe for our first tour, but not since. You did the set list, if you remember, for the Ottawa gig, and all the press, and it was amazing. And how many songs did you write on our last studio album? At least half if not more. This is your baton, Ames. This is all yours."

"But—"

"Look, before he died, Jim insisted how important it was that you keep playing, even if I didn't. He thought you were so talented. You *are* so talented. And I've already talked to Ben. Any new songs can be yours, one hundred per cent royalties. Albums, too. Whatever gigs you want. We'll draw up an agreement so you can play all the songs, have the name, whatever you want. It's yours."

"What else do I have?" Amy asked Max that night.

"You shouldn't do it because you have nothing else. You should do it because you want to do it."

But Amy didn't know what she wanted to do, so she spent the summer meeting Fiona and Henry at wading pools. She got a kid seat installed on her bike and biked Alice around the neighbourhood with a basket full of snacks and sunscreen. Amy ignored the invites to Sandra's album launch. She didn't touch her guitar. She didn't look at the agreement Ben sent over.

Alice got into a home daycare, and Amy's days stretched long and empty in front of her. She caught up on doctor and dentist appointments and got massages and a pedicure and baked her way through the *BraveTart* cookbook. Nathan sent her a text about the Decemberists looking for a backup singer for their Toronto gig, but she couldn't stop thinking about standing on that stage in Ottawa, singing "Puddle Jumping" with the choir. Eventually, Amy called Ben and set up a meeting. It was strange, going from four, to three, to just two of them sitting at a huge boardroom table.

The Fun Times Brigade

"What if you had a backing band?" he asked. "I mean, if you're worried about filling the stage."

"Maybe. And maybe we—I," Amy corrected herself, "could partner with kids' choirs. I loved playing with them in Ottawa."

"Sure. I mean, there's at least one in every city, and I'm sure most of the kids know the songs."

Ben sent over the names of a bassist Amy used to see on the summer festival circuit, and a drummer, and a guitarist. He sent a pianist, a banjo player, and a mandolin player who lived around the corner from her. It took a while to find the right people, real musicians who still wanted to play "Sittin' on the Potty" and "The Battle of the Snowsuit." Amy asked Robin and Nathan if they might be interested in joining and was surprised when they both said yes.

They had some awkward, bumpy practices in the rehearsal space on Ossington, but eventually Amy formed a backing band with a guitarist, a banjo player, Nathan on trumpet, and Robin on keys. They didn't yet have the ease Amy'd had with Fran and Jim, but it was good to be playing again and figuring out how the songs worked in this new configuration.

They became the Fun Times Brigade and Friends and started playing a few shows—in the city, and cities within a few hours of Toronto, nothing too far away—it was too hard to be away from Alice overnight. But sometimes Ben would get them a weekend gig in Winnipeg, or Halifax, and Alice and Max would come with them, and Alice would nap in the green room, or refuse to nap and then tantrum in the lobby of the auditorium with Max while Amy played onstage.

They have to rehearse more than Fran, Jim, and Amy ever did, but it's okay—they're filling auditoriums and selling merch. They're going to record their first album later this year.

Fran accepts the award from Dan Levy and reads off the teleprompter. Her voice is steady, with only the smallest waver. She thanks Ben, Arlo, Sina and Levi, and Max and Alice, who are all sitting together in a box somewhere above the stage. She thanks the JUNOs, and everyone for buying records "and then tapes, and then CDs, and now," she waves her hands, "whatever it is now." She laughs and the audience laughs with her. She thanks music teachers across the country. She thanks Jim for being her one and only. "He would be so honoured. This would mean everything to him."

Amy blinks hard, grateful that the makeup person used waterproof mascara.

The Edmonton Children's Choir files in and Dan Levy exits stage left. Fran glances over at Amy. Amy nods, and they sing "Fly Like a Butterfly" with the choir. Three of the youngest kids wear butterfly wings and skip across the stage, jumping over mic cables.

"Your wings stretch out against the sky. Your wings like the petals you pass by. And you fly, fly like a butterfly, fly, fly like a butterfly."

Fran plays Jim's part after the first chorus, and Amy plays Fran's part. Next, they play "The Crayon Song."

"Red met Yellow and they gave a high-five and they did a little dance and they did a little jive—" Amy's fingers go on autopilot, and she makes sure she has a smile on her face.

The audience joins and Fran and Amy do-si-do around their mic stands after the chorus.

"Crayons, crayons! Dancing, twirling, skating, swirling, all the colours are unfurling—"

After they play the final chord, the choir heads into the wings and Amy catches a glimpse of the live video of her and Fran blown up a storey tall on the screens behind them.

The Fun Times Brigade

"For our last song, we were going to sing 'Turn! Turn! Turn!,'" Fran says ignoring the teleprompter. "It was one of Jim's favourites, but we couldn't get through rehearsing it without crying. And then we tried 'Ripple,' but we had the same problem."

"I still might cry," Amy says into the microphone, pulling a Kleenex out of her sleeve. Fran pulls one out of hers, too, and the audience laughs.

"We might need your help then," Fran says to the black swath in front of the stage. "This one is for our Jim."

"Oh, we ain't got a barrel of money," she starts.

"Maybe we're ragged and funny," Amy joins in, letting the tears roll down her cheeks.

"But we'll travel along, singing a song, side by side."

ACKNOWLEDGEMENTS

I'M GRATEFUL FOR FINANCIAL SUPPORT FROM THE Canada Council for the Arts, the Ontario Arts Council, the Ontario Government and the publishers who recommended my work through the Recommender Grants for Writers program, and the Toronto Arts Council.

My heartfelt thanks:

To Jay and Hazel Millar for believing in my writing, and championing Amy and the Brigade.

To Meg Storey, who always knows exactly how to get to the heart of a story.

To everyone at Book*hug Press: Stacey May Fowles, Britt Landry, Reid Millar, Michel Vrana, Shannon Whibbs (because every copy edit should have band-sighting anecdotes in the margins!), and Laurie Siblock. I am so lucky to have you in my corner.

To Dani Kind, Heidi Reimer, Carrie Snyder, and Jennifer Whiteford for your generous, kind words and support.

The Fun Times Brigade

To Joshua Van Tassel for the invaluable interviews about the ins and outs of the music industry, tours of your studio, and answering all my millions of music questions.

To Fred Penner for the generous conversation about writing kids' music, the children's music scene in the seventies and eighties, writing music, creating kids' TV shows, and the importance of creating high quality art for kids.

To Sharon and Bram for sharing stories about your years as children's performers, and Evan Munday for setting up the interview.

To therapists Tricia Lee and Jen Towndrow for your insight and conversations about couples' therapy.

To Jessica Romero and Dr. Chris Nielsen for the endless cups of tea, and all the university job and tenure talk. And Vera Romero Nielsen for the idea about a song about a groundhog who eats cheese.

To Dr. Kate Poirier and Dr. Jason Bell for being generous math consultants, disclosing all the chalk drama, and for sharing that there are not one, but three pi days to celebrate each year. Any mistakes are very much my own, with apologies to topologists everywhere.

To Peggy Baker Dance Projects' *who we are in the dark* for inspiring Emily's dance show.

To Sharon, Lois & Bram, Raffi, Fred Penner, Eric Nagler, and Ken Whiteley for making wonderful, inspiring music I listened to for all of my childhood (and then again with my children).

To the Hillside Festival for being the highlight of every summer, and to all of the brilliant people I went with over the years.

To music teachers, Syl Lebar for bringing piano to life for me, and Faria MacDonald, for reviving my love of playing.

To Joni Mitchell for decades of inspiring music, and a truly transcendental show at the Hollywood Bowl.

To Bruce Springsteen for being the best company during the early days of lockdown, and for playing "Waitin' on a Sunny Day" at your Toronto show in 2024.

To Jeni Besworth and Mike Bickerton for the TV insider help.

To Sarah Campbell, for being a crucial early reader, and a generous cheerleader; and Adrienne Kerr for your incisive and formative early edits.

To midwives Savannah, and Jenn, and CJ, Hava, and Corinne from Kensington Midwives for your extraordinary work, for bringing my babies into the world, and especially for the postnatal care. And a special thank you to midwife CJ Blennerhassett for your postpartum insight.

To Carey Toane and Karri Ojanen for the pool where I did all my narrative problem solving.

To the 2020–23 Raptors for keeping me company and reminding me about perseverance, especially Kyle Lowry, OG Anunoby, and Pascal Siakam. And to Scottie Barnes for all the unbridled joy and enthusiasm (and being so kind to my kid).

To Kelly Jack, for being our fairy godmother (and for the tickets to see the Boss!)

To Joe Nowak and Michael McKinnon for bringing so much music into my kids' lives (even if this house is VERY loud as a result!)

To the 2024 9U Annette A's families, thank you for the delightful distraction when I was deep into the final stretch of this novel, and for always supporting my kid even when I wasn't there. Who wants seven? We want seven!

To Patrice and Jamie and Rags for that hike in Gatineau so many Novembers ago when we made our joke kids' band—a long ago seed for all of this.

To my beloved Hens, Samantha Garner, Teri Vlassopoulos, and Julia Zarankin for always having my back and navigating the wilds of the publishing world together. I couldn't do this without you. And to Teri for dreaming up hipster band names, and discussing TS tunes in the early mornings.

To Rhya Tamasauskas for pre- and post-kid friendship, and articulating that motherhood is like lightning over newborn tulips and chips.

To Kate Holden for trading off childcare so I could write, for endless conversations about how to be a mom and an artist, and for being a most inspiring artist mom.

To Adele Phillips for showing me newly born mice in Nebraska all those years ago.

To Kathryn Esaw, my one and only mat-leave friend!

To Dr. Suzanne Watters for the insight into cancer treatments, and years of friendship.

To Stacey May Fowles for being an anchor in these bewildering parenting and publishing days.

To my beloved friends Esther de Bruijn, Katherine Boyes, Chris Jancelewicz, and Laura Wills.

To my brilliant book witches: Jacqueline Whyte Appleby, Carey Toane, Michelle Arbuckle, Hazel Millar, and Vikki VanSickle.

To my school mom crew, for the always-too-short school drop off/pick up conversations, burn nights, and neighbourhood walks. And a special thank you to Talia Regan for the always-insightful readings.

To Emily Arvay for the years of letters.

To my incredible family—Katie, Mike, Finn, Rhys, Mom, Robin, Dad, and all of the Berards. A special thank you to Katie—there's no one I'd rather do this parenting thing with.

To my mom, Sharon Zier-Vogel, for filling my childhood with books and music, and for taking me to countless Raffi and Sharon, Lois & Bram concerts as a kid.

To my dad, Ted Zier-Vogel, for sharing your deep love of reading.

To Jack and Clare—my extraordinary children—this book would not exist without you. Jack, your deep love of music is so inspiring, even if you do need to turn the volume down. And Clare, your imagination inspires me every single day. Our "Stingsteen" dance parties will forever be a highlight of my life.

And to Adam Hess, whose love of music knows no bounds. Thank you for making up ridiculous songs from 1997 until now, for falling in love with me at a Hawksley Workman concert, for bringing so much music into my life, and for introducing me to the Grateful Dead. What a joy it is to spend my days with you.

PHILLIPA CROFT

LINDSAY ZIER-VOGEL is a Toronto-based author and the creator of the internationally beloved Love Lettering Project. After studying contemporary dance, Zier-Vogel received her MA in Creative Writing from the University of Toronto. She is the author of the acclaimed novel *Letters to Amelia*, and her first picture book, *Dear Street*, was a Junior Library Guild pick, a Canadian Children's Book Centre book of the year, and was nominated for a Forest of Reading Blue Spruce Award in 2024. *The Fun Times Brigade* is her second novel.

Colophon

Manufactured as the first edition of
The Fun Times Brigade
in the spring of 2025 by Book*hug Press

Edited for the press by Meg Storey
Copy edited by Shannon Whibbs
Proofread by Laurie Siblock
Type + design by Michel Vrana

Printed in Canada
bookhugpress.ca